WEST TO NORTH

BY THE SAME AUTHOR

WEST TO NORTH

By

COMPTON MACKENZIE

THE BOOK CLUB
121 CHARING CROSS ROAD
LONDON, W.C.2

THIS EDITION 1942

NOTE

IN view of the fact that many politicians and public men are mentioned by their own names in this volume it may be as well to insist that the Attorney-General who represents the Crown in the trial at the Old Bailey in January 1922 is an imaginary lawyer and as different as I could make him from either of the two distinguished lawyers who did hold the post of Attorney-General in 1922.

PRINTED IN GREAT BRITAIN

TO
ROSAMOND LEHMANN

My dear Rosamond,

Just over four months ago I dedicated to you 'The West Wind of Love'. I explained that the economic strain of war had made it necessary to cut the book in half and publish it in two parts. Luckily the construction I had planned allowed me to make this break almost exactly in the middle and to present 'The West Wind of Love' and 'West to North' as long books complete in themselves.

In calling the continuation of 'The West Wind of Love' 'West to North' the publishers and I have been actuated by a desire to avoid confusion for booksellers and readers; but I am anxious to insist that 'West to North' is as much an integral part of the original 'West Wind of Love', nearly three-quarters of which had been written before I made the break, as every volume in this series is an integral part of 'The Four Winds of Love'.

Several very kind critics have found John Ogilvie too much of a Cassandra about the future and to that extent unreal. I have tried to discover in him these uncanny powers of divination, but in this matter I can judge him and his friends only by myself and my friends, and there are no qualms about the future recorded in these pages which were not expressed by us on innumerable occasions from 1917 onwards. If my final volume of memories of the last war called 'Aegean Memories' is allowed to appear— it has been held up since last September—more uncannily accurate prophecies will be found in letters written by me at the time than any I have allowed to John Oglivie or his friends. Moreover, throughout 'The Windsor Tapestry' I made it clear that I believed the conduct of certain politicians to whom we had lazily entrusted the guidance of our country during the last twenty years would involve us in catastrophe.

I have tried to recapture in these latest two volumes of 'The Four Winds of Love' the mood of the lustrum 1918–22, and I do not believe I have allowed myself to be unduly influenced by the contemporary tragedy. Yet, as I reached the final pages and was wondering whether I had written too harshly of politicians once upon a time, the stupendous events of May and June 1940 have justified a greater harshness than any I could have contrived.

Our soldiers and our airmen have been betrayed. The politicians and permanent officials who failed them may not be driven with appropriate ignominy from the public life they have abused nor debarred with appropriate severity from holding office again; but the exaltation and gratitude with which heroic youth has filled our minds need not beget a weak mood of generosity toward those who have sacrificed that youth to their own complacency. Such complacency can never be forgiven. I know how passionately you will agree with this denunciation.

Yours affectionately,

Compton Mackenzie

June 8th, 1940

West to North

ATHENE AND JOHN STAYED FOR A WEEK OR TWO IN HAMPSTEAD
when they left Cornwall, but later took a service flat in St
James's for two months. Their plan was to go out to Citrano at
the end of June.

London in that spring and summer of 1920 was in a fever of
squandermania. The tendency had been apparent to John the
previous year, but he was astonished by the rise of temperature in
a few months. The prices of many commodities had trebled and
the very necessities of life had risen by over 150 per cent above
the level of July 1914. The insolence of the shop-assistants in the
West End was fed by the *nouveaux riches*, who swarmed to buy the
luxury articles that could not be manufactured fast enough.

John wanted a new pair of hair-brushes and went into a Bond
Street shop he had dealt with in former days. He exclaimed at
the price demanded, and a languid assistant suggested that he was
mistaking Bond Street for what he implied was John's better
acquaintance with the suburbs or the provinces.

"Fetch the manager," John ordered.

"Eh?"

"Fetch the manager."

"Aim afraid the maynager is too busy to attend to aynybody,"
the assistant drawled.

John noticed a hungry-looking man with a shiny red face and
a scrubby black moustache hovering round.

"Are you the manager?" John demanded.

"I happen to be the manager, yes."

John complained of the assistant's insolence, but the manager
hardly listened and cut John short by saying that they had many
customers who did not appreciate the costliness of really first-class
goods. The only satisfactory reply to the manager and the shop-
assistant would have been to knock their heads together; such an
action being liable to misunderstanding, John walked out of the
shop.

The squandermania of the public was reflected in the shame-
lessness of the new Ministries brought into existence by the
emergency of war. The country was infested with K.B.E.'s and

peers with scenic titles, who grew richer than before from the prizes that fell to them from the disposal of the mass of surplus material accumulated by the new Ministries for the prosecution of the war. A serious scandal was once or twice imminent, but the thieves of politics and big business, nervous of the discontent beneath the surface, by not falling out defeated the efforts of honest men to expose them. The merchant service might have lost men from enemy action, but the shipping industry had thriven on it, and there was hardly a magnate who had not waxed fat as a lobster on corpses. To the banks and the insurance companies, which worked loyally with big business, the greater part of the country and even of the Empire was now in safe pawn. At almost every by-election the uneasiness created by the Coalition Government was noticeable in Labour victories or tumbling Coalition majorities; but the deepening corruption of public life was not fully apprehended in the glitter of superficial prosperity. Louder than the boom of the guns was the boom of business, as it set about creating the new world which the politicians had promised but found themselves without the imagination, the energy, or even the common sense to direct. It seemed a sign of progress to hear that Devonshire House had been bought for a million pounds and was to be pulled down to erect business premises in its place. It seemed a sign of progress to hear that the Oxford Convocation had framed a proposal to abolish compulsory Greek in the examination called Responsions.

"They've been trying for twenty years and more, and now they've done it," John said bitterly. "Good-bye to what was Oxford. Presently they'll give degrees to women." And a few weeks later such a statute was framed.

"But why do you object to degrees for women?" Athene asked him.

"I don't object to degrees for women. I object to Oxford degrees for women. They should have a university of their own. Cambridge won't give them degrees."

Sugar went up to one and twopence a pound. Bread went to a shilling a quartern loaf. Butter was three shillings a pound. The bank rate was raised to seven per cent. Wages rose, but not fast enough to keep pace with the rise in the cost of living. Household coal went up fourteen shillings a ton, industrial coal only four shillings. Letters cost twopence. Dame Nellie Melba sang at Chelmsford into the wireless telephone and was heard over much of Europe. It was all progress of one kind or another. Two or three gentlemen refunded anonymously some of the profits they had made out of the war, and this was regarded as a sign of moral progress, though the motives of anonymity are not always easy to dissect. The Prince of Wales was sent to impress on the West Indies, Australia, and New Zealand the determination of Britain to develop the British Empire, but his personal success was considered to relieve big business from any further interest in the development of the British Empire while there was so much more money to be made out of financing a distracted Europe.

The French were beginning to contemplate seriously the possibility of having to go to war with Britain over Britain's unwillingness to be severe enough with Germany, and started a heavy submarine-building programme. Having been granted the mandate for Syria they proceeded to improve it by shooting up Damascus. Britain received a mandate for Mesopotamia and Palestine which was exploited in the interests of oil, though the National Home for Jews was proceeded with. British Israelites, who were found in some quantity among the generals and admirals that had fought in the war, were more firmly convinced than ever that the Anglo-Saxon race was the representative of the Ten Lost Tribes deported by King Sargon of Assyria in 721 B.C. The Anglo-Japanese Alliance was to come to an end in 1921 because it did not fit in with the Covenant of the League of Nations, and Japan embarked on a huge programme of martial expenditure by sea and land. Armenia was blotted out by the Turks and the Bolsheviks. India was full of discontent, and in April General Dyer suppressed rioting in Amritsar by firing into an unarmed mob and killing 379 of them. The British in India said the General's prompt action had averted another Mutiny; but Mahatma Gandhi established himself as the leader of Indian national aspirations.

Yet if Asia was disturbed, Europe was distracted. The French elected a President on the verge of a nervous breakdown who walked about always in black kid gloves and fell out of a train before the year was done. D'Annunzio and his Legionaries still maintained themselves in Fiume and were prepared to declare war even on Italy. The Poles were attacking the Bolsheviks and making an effort to recover the territory lost after the First Partition of 1772. Sweden and Finland were on the verge of war over the Aaland Islands. Portugal was the prey of internal disorder. Germany had to deal with Spartacist risings in the Ruhr and was forbidden by France to send troops to quell them. Austria was still starving. Hungary was in despair. Jugoslavia was inclined to go to war with Italy. Mustapha Kemal Pasha was gathering an army to resist the terms imposed by the treaty of peace. Holland refused to surrender the Kaiser for trial. The United States would have nothing to do with the League of Nations their own President had invented.

In fact it looked as if the new post-war world was tumbling to pieces a good deal faster than it was being built.

Meanwhile, in order to set an example to the rest of Europe of justice, equality, toleration, and respect for national aspirations, the British Government intensified their methods for compelling Ireland to remain quietly conquered and discouraging her from supposing that her case bore the slightest resemblance to that of Poland or Finland or Bohemia or Moravia or Slovakia or Estonia or Lithuania or Latvia. Besides fresh troops added to those already in Ireland a new force was invented that spring to supplement the Royal Irish Constabulary, some of whom were suspected by now of being too kind to their rebel fellow-countrymen. This force was dressed in khaki coats with black trousers and caps. The men were paid ten shillings a day and were nicknamed 'Black and Tans'. They were largely recruited from desperate characters that seemed likely to prove too much for their own police. At the same time an even more sinister force was recruited to serve in Ireland as auxiliary cadets to the R.I.C. These men were all ex-officers in the army. They were paid a pound a day. Their deaths were not to be a charge on the British Government for pensions to their dependents. They were exempt from military discipline, but they could not be tried for their actions by a civil court. These 'Auxies', as they were called, were responsible for many of the brutal murders and acts of violence attributed to the Black and Tans. Simultaneously with the mustering of these ruffians, a Canadian became Chief Secretary for Ireland, and a Lowland Scot was appointed joint Under-Secretary to Lord French, the Lord Lieutenant. The descent and kindly folk of England were poisoned by successful propaganda, and the country, unaware, in the words of a great Liberal weekly, that "the government which refuses to give peace to Ireland may find, sooner or later, that it has broken the peace of the world," was prepared to welcome any enormity as reasonable treatment for what were believed to be a band of assassins.

"Those whom the gods wish to destroy they first drive mad," John declared to his father. "The reputation of England will not recover abroad from this Irish business for a century."

"But something must be done to put an end to violence in the country," said the Judge, "though I confess I am not enamoured of the particular method chosen by the Government."

"Either we have accepted the principle of self-determination," said John, "or we have not. If we have not, why did we devote six months at Versailles to applying self-determination in such a way as will lead the world to suppose that it was applied entirely with the intention of ringing Germany and Russia round with hostility? Can't you see the madness of creating conditions favourable to war in the future unless we are inspired by sincere belief in the rightness of what we are doing? I rejoice that Poland is herself again, because I believe that a free and independent Poland can become a bulwark of civilization. I rejoice equally in a free and independent Finland. But I would not rejoice in either if I thought the intention behind them was strategic. How can we justify to Germany in the future what we have done when we behave like this to Ireland? I'm not saying that the kind of war that Ireland is waging is a pretty war; but small minorities have never been able to fight pretty wars. Fifteen thousand armed men cannot fight prettily with fifty thousand troops, a force of constabulary, these Black and Tan brutes, and those vile Auxiliaries."

"Have you heard from your friend Fitzgerald lately?" the Judge asked.

"Not for a long time. I suppose he's what they call 'on his keeping' by now."

"Which means?"

"That he's an outlaw fed and sheltered when possible by the people for whom he is fighting."

"The world's in a very disturbed condition everywhere," the Judge observed.

John shook his head at his father.

"I disapprove of using platitudes as pillows on which to turn over and sleep," he said. "Meanwhile, in spite of the condition of the world, big business is booming and so God must be in His heaven. I'm glad to say my own particular boomster, Turner Rigden, is doing so well out of the theatre and his paper that he is not mixed up in any of these disreputable transactions between the various new Ministries and eager buyers of surplus material at bargain prices. Queer thing, I notice that most of the names which crop up in awkward questions asked by the Opposition held posts in those Ministries during the war. Did you read the question and answers about the Slough Dump we so much admired from the train a couple of years ago?"

"Yes, and they weren't very reassuring to the taxpayer, I'm afraid," the Judge agreed. "Still, we must expect business men to seize their opportunities after a war like this."

"Oh, I know that when big business men can make enough money they earn the respect even of His Majesty's Judges. However, so long as politicians are allowed to issue prospectuses on the eve of a General Election that would earn them seven years for fraud if they did it in a private capacity, I suppose you can't expect a high standard of morality from the business men they call in to help them through a mess like the last war. We should get a much better parliament if it were chosen by lot and if the second chamber were elected to represent occupations and interests. Why do we presume that a successful parliamentarian should make a successful administrator? In practice of course we don't, and we leave administration to the Civil Service, which in practice means that we are ruled by permanent officials."

"There is also something called the Common Law," the Judge reminded his son.

"No, we mustn't forget that," John admitted. "And it's such a complicated business that half the legislature consists of lawyers put there to see that no statute shall be passed the interpretation of which will not make lawyers more than ever essential to the carrying on of the State."

"Well, in spite of the lawyers we remain the greatest nation in the world," Sir Alexander declared.

"And so long as capitalism lasts we shall remain so," John agreed. "But how long is capitalism going to last? That's the question."

"You're not going in for communism, are you?"

"Not the Russian variety. Nevertheless, you can't educate a country run on the methods of the Board of Education and expect the grand swindle to last indefinitely without being found out by too many people all at once. And I doubt if you can expect the British Empire to last by making kids wave Union Jacks on Empire Day."

"I see the Prince of Wales has had another enthusiastic reception, at Wellington this time. He's a remarkable young man that."

"He will be a remarkable young man if, when he comes home again, he manages to persuade his father's subjects here to keep out of European entanglements and look across the Atlantic instead of the North Sea and the English Channel. Not that I'm prejudiced one way or the other. But if we intend to pull our weight in Europe, oughtn't we to make a Channel Tunnel and become continental? We can't indefinitely treat Europe as a place with which we interfere only when somebody like Napoleon or the Kaiser comes along with big ideas. The only way to have a satisfactory Europe again is to break it up rigorously into small states, and in that case we must set an example by breaking up the British Isles into four component parts, and perhaps dividing the Crown Colonies among Ireland, Scotland, and Wales, or if Ireland prefers to get out of the concern altogether, among Scotland and Wales. The English have shown themselves incompetent either to administer or develop most of the Crown Colonies."

"Well, to descend to the practical matters of everyday life," said Sir Alexander, "how are the rehearsals of the new play going?"

"Capitally since I managed to persuade my leading lady that I knew better than she what I wanted the part to convey," John replied.

The morning after this talk with his father John came downstairs into the entrance hall of his club to find the portress trying to rid the sacred spot of an intruder with an open suitcase full of coloured feathers.

"I'm sorry, but I really must ask you to take your bag away, please," she was saying, overcome by embarrassment that a member should have witnessed a scene so shocking to the decencies of club life.

The intruder, a thin worried-looking man somewhere in the forties, closed the suitcase reluctantly.

"You're sure you wouldn't take that plume you rather liked, miss? I could let you have it very cheap."

"No, thank you."

By this time the portress had steered the intruder to the swing-doors. Just before he went out he turned and said to John:

"I must ask you to excuse my apparent persistence, sir."

With this he passed through the doors, walked down the steps, and was lost to sight on the Piccadilly pavement.

"I'm sure I'm very sorry, Mr Ogilvie," said the portress, "but we get so many of these ex-officers trying to sell things, and I hate to be rude. I mean to say, you can't help feeling sorry for them."

"Nothing to apologize for," John assured her. "I'm sorry I came on the scene before you'd bought anything from the poor chap."

"Oh, I wasn't really going to buy the plume," she said quickly. "Well, they're not being worn now."

John noticed a printed card on the ledge of the portress's box. He picked it up and read:

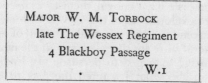

MAJOR W. M. TORBOCK
late The Wessex Regiment
4 Blackboy Passage
                    W.1

The face of the man apologizing for his persistency haunted John all through the rehearsal that morning, and when he left the theatre he walked to the address on the card..

It was a typical eighteenth-century Soho house, flat-faced, thin and tall, in a street barred as a thoroughfare to wheeled traffic by a row of inebriated posts at one end. A perpendicular line of chipped and tarnished bell-pushes beside the door, which not even the blistered paint and marks of children's games could deprive of its solid dignity, showed that the house was let in floors. John rang the bell beside which the name Torbock was inked on a piece of cardboard. Presently a window on the third storey was thrown up and a feminine voice called down that Major Torbock was not in. John suspected that he was being handled as a dun, and asked the harassed woman with untidy hair if he might not speak to her a minute.

"I have not come on unpleasant business," he told her.

Whether his face or his voice was reassuring, she came down to the front door.

"I happened to see Major Torbock's card in my club this morning and I felt rather guilty because I was afraid I'd interrupted his business. . . ."

She smiled wearily.

"Business," she murmured on a sigh.

"I'm speaking to Mrs Torbock?"

"Yes, I'm Mrs Torbock."

"I don't want to intrude, but I was wondering if I could help in any way. It struck me, to be quite frank with you, that selling old plumes and feathers was rather a precarious business."

Mrs Torbock looked at him keenly.

"You'd better come up and speak to the Major yourself."

John followed her up the steep flight of stairs which smelt of the dust and dirt of a century of accumulated neglect and gradual decay. The sitting-room he entered was furnished with flimsy summer bungalow stuff which did not suit the faded Victorian wallpaper and the sombre Georgian hob-grate.

"I must apologize for intruding on you, Major," John said to the thin worried-looking man who rose from a deck-chair at his entrance, "but we spoke to one another this morning and I realized after you'd gone out that I'd spoilt a deal."

"Oh, don't mention it. Sit down, sir, won't you? I'm afraid I can't offer you a drink. We're—er—not really settled in here yet. I don't think you've had time to replenish our cellar yet, Sophie?" he asked, turning to his wife.

"I'm afraid not, Walter."

"Quite, quite. Well, as our late Allies used to say, à la guerre comme à la guerre, what? I expect you're an ex-Service man and used to roughing it? It's very kind of you to look in on me. I've rather lost touch with people during the last year."

John pulled out his case and offered the Major a cigarette.

"Mrs Torbock won't mind our smoking?"

"Not at all, she smokes herself. But look here, I *can* give you a cigarette." He plunged hastily into his coat for a packet of some popular brand. It was empty. "By Jove, dash it, I've let myself run out of cigarettes. I say, I'm ashamed to give you such a welcome. So kind of you to call too."

Mrs Torbock had accepted a cigarette from John's case, and the Major, after protesting again that he was really ashamed of his own carelessness, took one also.

Gradually the course of events which had brought him and his wife to this third-floor in Soho was related. Before the war he had been in partnership with his brother in the manufacture and sale of a patent pipe that his brother had invented. At the outbreak of war he had been a captain in one of the London Territorial regiments and had reached the Front by October 1914. He had then been transferred to The Wessex Regiment, with which he had served right through in Flanders and France without a scratch,

being promoted to the rank of Major early in 1918. He had
decided to invest his war gratuity in the family business, but his
brother, who had died just before he was demobilized, had allowed
the business to go to pieces.

"Not that it was entirely his fault, poor old chap," the Major
explained. "Pipes have been very badly hit by cigarettes, and
the big firms have stolen all the patents anyway, so that there's
nothing left for the small business any longer. We had to close
down last summer and with what was left I started chicken-farming
in Essex. Well, that was no good. We managed to save a few
odds and ends of furniture from our bungalow and I got this
floor fairly cheap. But I couldn't get a job anywhere, and I'd
amused myself for a while colouring feathers and I thought I
might manage to make enough to pay the rent and our keep
while I was looking for a job. However, it looks as if I won't
even be able to do that," he went on, with a wry smile. "And
of course it is a deuced unpleasant way of earning money. I mean
to say, you meet a good deal of unpleasantness. Oh, I don't
blame people. I should get annoyed myself if a shabby fellow
came in with a suitcase and started trying to sell me old plumes
and coloured feathers."

John had been wondering during the tale what future there was
for this weak diffident man in the new world rising from the ashes
of the war, the ruthless new world with no room for small family
businesses.

"I mustn't complain, though," said the Major. "I really had
a splendid war. Enjoyed every moment of it. You know, one
had no responsibility, except of course to do one's own job of work
as well as one could. And we had an awful nice bunch of fellows
in the Wessex. My battalion's out in Palestine now. Only wish
I were still with 'em."

"I can't promise you a job," John began.

"No, no, quite, quite, old man. Jobs are jolly difficult these
days. Look here, I'm ashamed to go on smoking your cigarettes."

"But I'm going to speak to a friend of mine," John continued.
"And I feel hopeful of his finding you something. I don't suppose
it'll be anything very grand, but it'll be better than feathers. And
now I'm afraid I've got to be a little embarrassing, but I hope you
won't embarrass me by refusing me something. I want to buy
those feathers."

The Major smiled and shook his head.

"Why don't you offer to give me a pound right away?" he asked.

"Now you see, you *are* embarrassing me," John said reproachfully. He turned to the Major's wife.

"Mrs Torbock, you're a woman, and therefore you must be more realistic than your husband. Would you mind telling him not to be an ass and embarrass me by his stupid pride? If he pulls off this job he can repay me the loan I was going to suggest as he won't sell me the feathers, but I have eyes, and I can't help seeing that you've touched bedrock and I've a notion there are various things that might be got out of pawn. . . . Oh, now for goodness' sake give me the pleasure of feeling useful."

The Major's wife again gave him that keen glance. Vaguely her face was familiar to him.

"Walter won't mind accepting a loan from you," she said.

"Oh, but look here, my dear . . ." the Major protested.

"You're John Ogilvie, aren't you?" she asked.

"How on earth did you know that?"

"I was an understudy in your play *Annette* in 1912."

"That's why your face is familiar," John exclaimed. "What was your stage name?"

"Sophie Morell."

"I remember the name well."

She smiled.

"I don't think," she murmured.

"Well, as you know my wife, I feel that perhaps I can accept a loan from you," said the Major. "But I'd rather have waited till I found myself in a job."

"Yes, I'm sure you would, but you see, Mrs Torbock comes into it now. I expect she's been haunting the agents and hoping for an engagement, and when you're right up against it your confidence goes. Now as you insist on a loan and as I want that loan to be enough to—well, to have something in hand, I must insist that you pay it back only as you can spare it in small amounts. My idea was fifty pounds."

"I couldn't dream of accepting that," the Major declared at once. "Even a fiver is a bigger responsibility than I care to undertake."

"There you are, you see," John remonstrated. "If you're going to pull off this job you must believe in yourself. Now please oblige me over this. I'm forcing something on you. You've not asked anything of me. But do burn those damned feathers. I can't stand the thought of them in that suitcase. And perhaps Mrs Torbock might like to see my play at the Sheridan."

"I'd love to," she put in.

"So I'll send you a couple of stalls. I have a new play coming out at the Muses at the beginning of June, but I shall have another play with May Lavender sometime in the autumn and it will be easy to give Mrs Torbock a part. Well, that's not quite what I meant to say. I know that there is a part in that play which will suit her, so that even if you don't get this job, Major, your wife can definitely count on an engagement. Now I must be going along. No, don't you come down with me, Major. Mrs Torbock will put me on my way."

Out in the frowsty passage John asked if her husband still had a bank account.

"They won't honour any more cheques."

"How much is he overdrawn?"

"Just over twenty pounds."

"He can pay in the cheque I send him and reopen his account. But look here, I know, so don't argue, that there isn't sixpence in the house. Here's three or four pounds. Buy some cigarettes, and you go and get your hair set, and both of you go and have a decent dinner to-night. This is a retaining fee for your services in the play after this one. I'm sure I'll pull off this job for your husband."

"Poor old boy," she sighed. "He'll keep the job if it depends on good manners, but . . ."

"Oh, for god's sake now don't you shake his confidence," John begged.

"But, Mr Ogilvie, this is more than three or four pounds," she said, looking at the notes John had pushed into her hand.

"I tell you it's a retaining fee," he said, and hurried down the dark steep smelly stairs.

An hour later he was telling the story to Athene.

"It's the kind of crazy notion Wacey might have had, to go around selling coloured feathers," she commented.

"Darling, don't be ridiculous."

"Yes, I know Wacey had his father to help him, but without that he might have taken to feathers. Oh, John, I'm beginning to fuss over Arthur. You'll call me crazy, but this story of yours about the feathers has just scared me. I think we'll go and fetch him as soon as *The Guinea Pig* has had its first night. You won't mind, honey?"

"I'll book our passages right away for the second week in June."

John took the first opportunity of tackling Turner Rigden on the subject of a job for the Major, though he withheld the story of the feathers for fear Rigden should scorn so profoundly such a fantastic way of trying to earn a living that he would be for ever prejudiced against Torbock.

"All these ex-officers who want jobs are a problem, you know," he told John. "He'll be no good on the *Journal*."

"I don't suppose he would," John agreed, for he fancied journalism was much too competitive a profession for a diffident creature like the Major. "But I think he'd make a capital business secretary for one of your innumerable subsidiary enterprises. A post where tact and a pleasant manner are wanted."

So Turner Rigden found a post for the Major in the Luminole Company, which had been successfully launched, and exacted from John a promise in return that he and Athene would come up and spend some time with him at his new place in Scotland.

"My girls tell me it's the last word in the way of being god-damned out of the world. Pity this chap Torbock isn't Mac-Torbock. I'd have put him in a kilt and left him to look after the place."

John asked where the place was.

"Achna something or other. It sounds like three sneezes and a yawn."

"But what county?"

"Sutherland. 'Damn it,' I told 'em, 'I thought we were going up to the north.' But they gave me a map and I find Sutherland's as far north as you can get. Cock-eyed name to give a county on the top floor of this island."

"I have an ancestral connection with Sutherland," said John. "All right, Turner, when you've found out the name of your domain we'll come and stay with you."

"It's a 36-head forest, and there are two good salmon rivers. Wait a minute"—he dug for a pocket-book—"Achnalochlannach, Assynt. Madge and Dolly are up there now, getting the house in order."

John wondered how far Achnalochlannach was from Ardvore. Rigden's invitation had given him a thrill. It was like the opening of Beethoven's Fifth Symphony.

The first night of *The Guinea Pig* was not such a marked success as the first night of *All Or Nothing*. John had mixed a certain

amount of satire on the present condition of the country which
might have been more warmly received from a dramatist who
was known to be a satirist and from whom cynicism was expected;
but John was admired as an entertainer, and it was not considered
his province to make anybody feel uncomfortably that some line
applied a little too directly to himself. However, the reception
of the new piece was warm enough to flush Athene's cheeks with
pride, and John, looking at her in the St James's flat when they
returned to it after a supper which Turner Rigden had insisted on
giving at the Savoy, although he had had nothing whatever to
do with the production, thought it would be worth writing plays
merely to see the happiness in her eyes.

"And now, precious one, there is something to tell you," she
said softly. "I've thought so for two weeks or more, but I'm
sure now. We're going to have a child."

"When, Athene?"

He felt as insignificant as a small boy asking some tremendous
question of a being far removed from himself by the wisdom of
the ages.

"About the fourteenth of January."

"Do you want it to be a son or a daughter?"

"I believe I'd like it to be a girl, John."

"So would I," he declared. "I'm so glad we both want that.
Shall we call her Corinna?"

"We'll call her whatever name you choose."

Two days after this there came a letter from Henry Pendarves:

> *Dear John,*
>   *Just a line to let you know that I shall get at least one
> pod of ripened seed from Saffron Maid. So now in April 1926
> or 27 we shall hope for a beauty.*
>   *I hear that Edmund Corfe is lying very ill in Paris, and not
> likely to recover. If Nanphant comes into the market as is most
> likely you would probably get the place very reasonably, and
> we all wish you'd make up your mind to do so. The family
> send love to you and Athene.*
>
>   *Yours ever,*
>   *Henry Pendarves*

John showed Athene the envelope addressed to *J. Pendarves
Ogilvie.*

"Henry is the only person who writes to me like that," he said. "May I tell him about our hopes?"

"Why, I think he deserves to know, John, but isn't it a little premature?"

"I'll tell him as a secret. Henry loves to keep something from the rest of the world."

A week later, after the packing up for the voyage to America was nearly finished, it looked as if Athene's doubt about prematurity might unhappily be justified; and although the misfortune was averted the doctor insisted that she should stay quietly in England and not risk the fatigue of a voyage.

"Darling, I dread the notion of leaving you, but you'll fret if Arthur does not come over as we had planned?" John asked.

"It's no use pretending I won't."

"Then I think I'd better go and fetch him. We can be back by the middle of July if I leave in the ship in which we intended to travel. You could stay with my people in Church Row. Elise will be enchanted to have you, and my father will become famous as the most merciful judge who ever sat on the bench."

And thus it was settled.

When John reached New York at the beginning of that July of 1920 he found it as much changed as anybody does find New York who visits it after a lapse of eight years, but the violent contrast between America and Europe which had overwhelmed the imagination the first time it was seen was less impressive now, because in these eight years America had become so much nearer to Europe and exercised over European taste such a steadily increasing domination.

"It's clear that within another twenty years the United States must be the leader of the so-called Anglo-Saxon world," John declared to Julius in the big room of the Sterns' apartment looking over Central Park. "It seems to me idiotic of us to demand votes from our Dominions or the League of Nations and expect the United States to be content with one vote. And more than ever idiotic when we are denying the status to Ireland that would give Ireland a vote. What will happen at the Presidential election this autumn?"

"The Republicans are certain to win," Julius asserted. "Wilson like many another politician has given up to party what was meant for mankind."

"You'll soon have to ask me these grave questions, John," Leonora put in, her bright eyes twinkling. "We expect women to have the suffrage pretty soon now. And now, as you hope to be a father yourself at the beginning of the New Year, you've got to come and admire my angelic daughter."

This was Monica, who had been born on the 4th of May.

"And Emil and Astrid are expecting an infant in the autumn," John said. "We're certainly doing our best to populate the wonderful new world which is to be built out of the debris of war."

"I do hope I won't be quite so dumb when I'm called upon to show off my own infant," he added, after staring with due respect at the small sallow lump of womanhood called Monica. "What can one say about a baby at an age when they all look exactly alike? Now I might have been able to comment on Sebastian if you hadn't dispatched him to Vermont."

"It's too bad, John. But Marian Carpenter adores to have him with her, and we're going right along up there now. We just stayed to see you. It's too bad you couldn't persuade Miriam to come over with you."

"You won't lure Miriam across the Atlantic easily. She expects you and the family to come over to England next year."

"What a queer time it must be for grandfolks," Leonora said. "Seeing the whole business begin all over again and feeling no direct responsibility. I guess I'll enjoy being a grandma."

"Grandparents are rather a painful subject for me at the moment," John told her. "I have to face two lots presently, when I go to fetch Athene's boy from Georgia."

"Oh, you'll adore Atlanta, John," she promised him. "And now listen. We've invited a friend of your far-off childhood to dinner to-night. Bob Redroad, the Hollywood director. He's terribly anxious to meet you again."

John's memory raced back to a little house in Brook Green and the wizard Redroad who had allowed small boys to help with the lighting of his toy theatre and wait in awed readiness behind a curtain to hand him the minute cardboard figures of his characters as he called for them, and even sometimes, greatest thrill of all, to pull away a section of the stage and create the abyss into which Demon King or Barber would descend.

"Steady now, blast you, young Ogilvie, you're going too fast with that trap," Redroad would threaten in a hoarse aside. "Now light the red fire. Hurry up, you little duffer."

Great occasions, from which Redroad had vanished over the Atlantic, announcing that he was going to see Charlie Mitchell fight Jim Corbett.

Bob Redroad was a great breezy fellow with a resonant voice and a handclasp like a couple of millstones.

"Say, it's pretty near thirty years since we met," he told John, beaming at him. "There's not much left of either of us to recognize in the other. But, gosh, I'll say I'll take some of the credit for your success, John Ogilvie. I taught you stagecraft before you were out of sailor-suits. And listen, I'm coming over to Italy either next year or the year after on location with Janet Meriday to make three pictures for Vitofilms, the company I'm tied up with now, and I want your advice."

"Are you going to offer him a contract to write a scenario or a script?" Julius asked.

"Yeah, you would try to make a business proposition out of an old friendship," Redroad bellowed. "Give me a great musician and I know I've gotta watch where the dollars are going. No, but seriously, boys, we'll get together over in Europe one day and maybe we'll hit on a big picture. What makes me so mad with fellows like you is the way you turn up your darned noses at the pictures. I tell you the pictures are only beginning. In another ten years we'll have pictures that do their own talking and make their own music. The future of the drama and the future of music lies with the despised movies, and the sooner you get wise to that the more money you'll make."

"Not from you sharks," said Julius. "The meanest bunch of crooks I ever came up against! And that's saying some after the business side of the musical world both here and over in Europe."

They talked of the future of the films until the enthusiasm of Bob Redroad, coupled with the excellent wine as yet untouched by the prohibition amendment, inspired John to improvise a tremendous picture of the Odyssey made on the very places in the Mediterranean where the legends had been born.

"Yumph, it sounds fine the way you tell it, Ogilvie, but the picture public doesn't want this Greek and Latin stuff," Redroad objected.

"Then what the deuce is the good of jeering at people like me and Julius because we won't take the films seriously?" John challenged. "The moment we try to see something big in them you tell us our ideas won't meet the approval of the nursemaids and shopgirls you film people believe are the only audience that matters. The art of the future you say, and it turns out to be spending thousands of dollars on servant-girls' novelettes or twopenny bloods."

"Give us time, Ogilvie, give us time," Redroad begged. "Gee, we only really started about the beginning of the war. I'll admit we've gotta go up all the time, but it's not a hell of a bit of good us going up unless you darned highbrows come down a step or two to meet us. I wish I could persuade you to come right along back with me to Hollywood next week."

"I've no time for that this trip," John said.

"No, of course you haven't. You never *will* have. Because you don't believe there is a future for the pictures. You can only see what they are now, and even now they're something much bigger than you suppose. However, we'll talk it out when I come to Italy with Janet Meriday."

"Strange fellows these film directors," Julius observed to John when Redroad had left them at the end of the evening. "To hear them talk you'd think they were minor prophets. But pin them down to the fulfilment of their prophecies and they become as frightened as a curate who's taken the town hall for a parish entertainment and is wondering if the church workers will sell enough tickets to pay expenses. Mind you, I think he's right. I believe the natural art form of the future will be the film, but I doubt whether the people who now run it as an industry will ever carry it much beyond where they've reached already. It's too much in the hands of my race. Jews like listening to dreams. It gives them a warm feeling. But they wake up a bit faster than other people. A Jew knows he can always go to sleep and dream without spending a penny. To spend money on other people's dreams strikes him as silly. Give Redroad the money and he'll spend it on his own dreams and other people's, but Redroad never will have the money. He'll always be on a salary, and so long as he knows when his employers are awake the salary will be a large one."

"Do you believe there's any likelihood of his prophecy about speaking films and recorded music coming true?" John asked.

"I should imagine so. This wireless telephone must lead to developments all round. I hear talk of successful experiments already with phonograph recording by electricity. I don't think one can set any limit to what may happen in that way during the next ten years. The war held up developments in one direction, but in another way it has speeded them up, and we shall get the advantage or the disadvantage of them, whichever you like to call it, presently. Music itself is in a queer state. I think we're all of us wondering where we are. All this Relativity business seems to have shaken people. Einstein had a triumph over that eclipse last year."

"I don't see why Relativity should upset people," John said. "It's only the old argument whether the monkey goes round the pole or the pole goes round the monkey."

"I agree with you. Actually it reinforces theology and strikes a blow at the mechanistic universe, but why because the human conception of time and a bit of Newtonian physics have been jarred the thinking world should be so much disturbed I fail to see. The Christian idea of God has always recognized that His time and human time were not reconcilable. Blake's infinity in the palm of a hand and eternity in an hour said in two lines of verse all that Einstein has discovered. The trouble is that in spite of all the fuss about Galileo man has remained geocentric, and for my part I cannot see why Relativity should not confirm his geo-centricity. I do not believe that the particular combinations of life which God created on this planet to fulfil His purpose are to be found elsewhere in the universe. Merely by analogy from the countless variations of the life we know here I cannot believe that this planet can be repeated. Once accept God as an objective Being and the logical consequence of such an acceptation must be the relevation of Himself to man in a comprehensible form. Christianity provides that. Deny the objective reality of God and the universe becomes a madhouse. Man refuses to love God or his neighbour, and then yowls because his world is in a muddle. You see, I don't believe that Christ gave a lot of sentimental advice. I believe He gave practical advice. I don't believe in a just war, because I don't believe that any individual or any nation can be entirely right. I don't believe in this League of Nations, because it has started off wrong by passing a moral judgment on Germany. The Germans may have been ninety per cent to blame, but if their opponents are even a half of a half per cent to blame the moral judgment cannot be passed. Poor old Emil is outraged by the contemplation of life's inequity, and in order to put it right he loves his neighbour hard but forgets to love God. The result is that if his theories could be put into practice we should only have one inequity substituted for another. It's damned hard to love one's neighbour if he is a rich man, but some-how we have to love the rich just as much as the poor, and having the authority of Christ that a camel can go through the eye of a needle more easily than a rich man can enter the Kingdom of God we can feel that the rich man requires all the love we can give him. . . .

"But I was talking about music. Something has gone wrong with it, and what has gone wrong is that Beethoven said as much in music as man is capable of saying until he has passed on into another stage of his earthly development. We can't go back now and write pre-Beethoven music any more than we can paint pre-Raphaelite pictures. Sibelius, who is the only securely immortal contemporary composer, has not attempted to go beyond Beet-hoven, but he has expressed the spirit of a small nation and made that spirit comprehensible to the rest of the world in terms of Beethoven. Superficially Sibelius is much nearer to Wagner than Beethoven, and I think growing nearer as his work develops; but whereas he is expressing the regeneration of a small nation whose very language was almost dead a century ago, Wagner, as I think, entered on a blind alley of music when he set out to express a primitive Germany, the finest flower of whose spirit had *already* been expressed by greater composers than himself. If Germany accepts Wagner as its supreme composer it renounces by so doing its European heritage. As a Jew I should enjoy a great advantage because although my race has produced more great executants than any other it has not produced one genuinely creative musician. But I suspect that Jewry cannot produce a genuinely creative musician yet because the race chosen by God to show the world the best and worst of humanity has not fulfilled its destiny. I shall achieve something in music because I have accepted Christ, and such a surrender by a Jew is a creative act, but the time is not ripe for a Jewish Sibelius and far less ripe for a Jewish Beethoven."

"And atonality?" John asked.

"It will continue—perhaps for a long while. But it is an unnatural expression of music because it denies to music form and order, and inasmuch as it is the function of music to give form and order at the end of an epoch to the whole of that epoch's artistic expression the present tendency of music condemns itself. It is abortive. It is a hideous foetus pretending to be a developed infant. It does not know how to give form and order because it is trying too soon, and the best of its endeavours are nothing better than empirical improvisations. No, I'm not optimistic about great music in our time. What I am optimistic about is the possibility of bringing the great music we already have to a vast number of people who have heard no great music. That's why I'm watching with such excitement the developments of the phonograph and the wireless telephone. I believe music stands a chance at last of becoming a common language, and if this is achieved we needn't worry about the comparatively minor contribution of this period to creative music. It's a bad time all round for creative, artists, John, and we must face up to it. Nature did not evolve her masterpieces in eras of volcanic activity and change. I see no prospect of tranquillity for the rest of this century. We have an illusion now that there was a period of comfortable calm at the end of the nineteenth century, but you and I know that was just exhaustion, a breather for material progress before it started off again. Goethe saw what was happening. It all started while he was still alive. The speed of material progress by the first quarter of the nineteenth century had gathered such momentum that it was bound soon to move at a pace beyond man's ability to guide it. If I were a materialist I should indeed take a gloomy view of humanity's future. Last summer a Welsh Capuchin friar said to me as casually as one makes a remark about the prospect of to-morrow's weather that he thought the end of the world would occur in perhaps another fifty or sixty years. And thinking over it since I'm inclined to agree with his forecast."

John was able to bring good news of Athene when he reached the Gilmers in Atlanta. He had expected to like Lawton Gilmer, but in fact he liked him even better than he had expected.

"This is just about as difficult for you as it is for me," his host and father-in-law said when they shook hands in the cool spacious hall. "And our womenfolk have let us down. My wife was called away a couple of days ago to visit a sick sister in Charleston, but she hopes to be home by to-morrow. One of my daughters is away in California, another is in New Orleans, and the absence of the third I don't have to explain to you. Well, come along, and we'll have a mint julep on the verandah. I expect you're finding it pretty warm."

The white-gloved coloured butler brought the drinks, and they sat looking out at a garden full of fine trees round a wide lawn.

One of them must be the magnolia of which Athene had told him. John wondered which it was.

"Forgive my staring, sir, but I was looking for bits of Athene in you," John said.

Lawton Gilmer tugged at his white upcurving moustaches.

"Well, what's the verdict?"

"I can see quite a bit," John told him.

"They all insist that her boy takes after me—especially about the chin. And that's strange, because Athene's chin is more like her mother's. Well, well, these are mysteries, and mysteries they'll remain in spite of these scientific fellows." He was silent for a moment or two. "By the way my girl writes you've made her a happy woman," he went on. "I'm grateful to you for that. Parents oughtn't to have favourites, but as we're by ourselves I don't mind telling you, John, that Athene was always my favourite daughter. It was a disappointment she couldn't make the crossing, but of course it wouldn't have done to risk it. No, sir."

They talked on for a while about the externals of existence, and then Lawton Gilmer said abruptly:

"This business over the boy will be difficult for you. The old Langridges are going to take it very hardly. I could wish that Athene had given up the notion of fetching Arthur back to Europe. But there it is, I understand her point of view. The boy's nine now, and naturally she wants to have him with her for the next few years. It's right she should feel like that about it. All the same the Langridges are going to take it very hardly, and though I've no time for either of them, I can't help being a little sorry for the old people. The boy's with them now, but my wife has arranged he's to come here. I think Mrs Langridge will want to meet you, but the old man probably won't from what I hear. Well, I don't believe anybody alive or dead has made me come nearer to losing my temper than Langridge, but his son's death broke him up. I never cared a bit for Wacey. I daresay Athene has told you I did my damnedest to stop the marriage. Why, I knew Athene had too much of me in her character to be patient for ever with the future tense. Perhaps I would have been wiser if I had given the engagement my blessing from the start. She might have found out for herself then instead of blinding herself by having to justify her choice to me. May I ask you a question I've no right to ask?"

"I'll try to answer it," John said.

"Suppose Wacey hadn't died in Paris the year before last, would you and Athene still have aimed to get married?"

John gave his father-in-law a perfectly frank account of the story.

"I'm obliged to you, John. I'm very much obliged. I may have old-fashioned notions, but I hadn't altogether liked the idea that Athene had . . . well, carried on a long intrigue with another man and then because her husband happened to die found it convenient to get married. But your account takes a weight from my mind."

John spent an extremely agreeable forty-eight hours with his father-in-law before Mrs Gilmer returned. He had caught glimpses of Athene in Lawton Gilmer, but in her mother he saw Athene twenty-five years hence. She was as tall as her daughter, and she had kept much of the grace of what once must have been as beautiful a figure as hers. She had the same long legs, the same dark brown eyes which with her grey hair looked even more brilliant than Athene's. Her complexion was still high, and her neck for a woman of her age was well preserved. Shyness made her voice ridiculously like her daughter's as John had so often heard it in the past, when Athene was overcome by an attack of party manners.

"I feel so terribly ashamed of myself not to have been here to welcome you when you arrived. I don't believe Athene will ever forgive me when she hears about it. I do hope Lawton looked after you properly."

It was after dinner next day that she and John had their talk sitting out on the verandah, when the head of the house was attending some civic function.

"You know, I just can't tell you, John, what it means to have my beloved Athene so utterly happy. Lawton told me last night what you so very very frankly told him. I suppose women aren't quite so romantic as men about these matters, and I'll say right away that it wasn't worrying me at all. I knew Athene had made a mistake and whatever way out of it she found I'd have welcomed. Still, Lawton has a great idea of *noblesse oblige* and you've cheered him up. I don't have to tell you that Athene was just turning to stone inside, and it broke my heart to think of the way life was going against her. Marriage is a lovely arrangement when one marries the right man, but it's plain hell the other way around. And now you and she are going to have a child, which will be lovely for both of you, and I know I did right to insist all I knew how that Athene should go to you by herself first of all, though don't let me suggest Athene didn't agree right away with what I said. Still, it's good to have firm support from others in making up one's mind. It's been a disappointment she couldn't make the crossing now, but I think it was fine of you to come over by yourself like this. I said to Lawton when I heard you were coming, 'Lawton, that man's the right man for Athene.' "

"Tell me, Mrs Gilmer, why did you give Athene her name? Was it anything to do with Athens, Georgia?"

"Why, just because I liked the name, John. No other reason at all except a young mother's foolish fancy. It had stuck in my mind ever since I was a little girl reading *Tanglewood Tales* and a governess we had used to give me the Greek names for the gods and goddesses because old Nathaniel Hawthorne always used the Latin ones. And I liked Athene better than Minerva because we had a Miss Minerva Wilkes in my home town who was the terror of the place. And Athene tells me it was your mother's name. Isn't that lovely for you both? And now we've got to manage this taking Arthur away from the poor old Langridges," she sighed.

"You won't think me churlish if I say I want to go back as soon as possible?" John asked.

"My dear man, you certainly do. You want to be back with Athene just as soon as ever you can."

"I thought I would leave Arthur alone with her for two or three weeks, and then that will really have to be the last of being separated for a long time."

"Sure. You'll find Arthur very much grown. You haven't seen him since . . . how long?"

"Since September, 1918, and I don't suppose he'll remember me, though we were good friends then."

"Well, you know, he's crazy about the pony his grandfather gave him. So, you'll want to promise him another pony in England. I expect you'll be thinking of school for him?"

"I shall leave that to Athene," John replied. "I hated school so much that it would be very hard for me to sentence any boy to school. But if he did go to school in England I'd suggest his going to an American university. Perhaps I'm looking a long way ahead, but I like to make plans about education, and not improvise it. Arthur is a bit of a responsibility for me."

"Indeed, and don't I realize that! And now there's the question of the old Langridges. I understand that Mr Langridge has gone away but that Mrs Langridge wants to meet you. She's a sweet

woman. Just a little too sweet for my taste, but that's because
like to face up to realities. Now when actually are you planning
o sail?"

"I booked berths in the *Gigantic*, which sails on July 18th."

"Then we'll leave Arthur with Mrs Langridge till the 15th.
That's next Wednesday."

John did not look forward to the prospect of meeting Mrs
Langridge, and when he found himself with the tall old woman
n her cape of grey silk and her bonnet with a streamer of grey
ilk that gave her the look of an austere nurse he wished himself
a thousand miles from Atlanta.

"I wanted to meet you for so many reasons, Mr Ogilvie," she
said in her gentle voice. "I wanted to meet the man our dear
Athene has married and I wanted to make my husband's excuses.
I know you'll understand just how he feels. He's over seventy
now and not so easily able to adapt himself as once upon a time.
And I wanted to meet the man who will have to be a second father
to our beloved grandson. And . . ." she paused and fixed John
with those large grey eyes . . . "I wanted so much to meet my
dead son's friend."

"He was a very good friend to me," said John.

"I know you were great friends. He used to write us lots
of news about you and your beautiful Torre Saracena."

"Wacey put it in order for me while I was away at the war."

"I know, I know. And then Wacey went to the war."

There was a silence.

"Mrs Langridge, I guess what you're wondering," John said.
"You need not wonder about that. As soon as I found I was
in love with Athene I left Citrano. I left within twenty-four
hours. When poor Wacey died I wrote a month later and asked
Athene to marry me. You must not wonder any more. I knew
nothing of any disagreement with Wacey. And nobody except
you and Mr Langridge and Mr and Mrs Gilmer will ever know
anything about that disagreement."

"Wacey loved Athene with his whole heart. He loved her
from the time she was a little girl," the old woman declared
passionately.

"I know. He has told me so himself."

"And Athene loved him."

This was the challenge.

"I'm sure she did, Mrs Langridge. The war broke up their
marriage as it broke up many a marriage."

"You didn't break it up?" she asked, searching for his heart with those grey eyes.

"No, I did not," John averred. "I cannot convince you of this. I have told you what happened to me and what I did. *I* do not know even now what caused the disagreement between Athene and Wacey. And I shall never ask."

"*I* know, Mr Ogilvie. And Athene misjudged Wacey. But my poor boy died before he could prove to her that she had misjudged him. That was my poor boy's tragedy. But I believe I have misjudged you, and I am sorry."

"It is good of you to say that, Mrs Langridge."

"And I wish you happiness."

The old lady rose and put her hands on John's shoulders.

"Yes, I wish you happiness," she repeated. "I don't have to ask you to be kind to Arthur. I know that you will be kind to him. And I hope we shall see him sometimes. We have nothing left, you know."

"I shall tell Athene what you have told me. She will appreciate your generosity."

"Nothing left, nothing left," she whispered to herself, and then she turned and in what seemed a voice of perfectly controlled sweetness she called softly:

"Oh, Arthur! Arthur dear, come and say good-bye to Grandma."

On the first day out homeward bound the ship's wireless news announced the death of the Empress Eugénie in Madrid. Her body was to be brought to England to lie beside her husband and her son in the mausoleum at Farnborough. John was sitting on the after-deck of the *Gigantic* in the deepening afternoon of the bright July day, thinking about that very old woman whose life had flickered out in the palace of the Duke of Alba. The ninety-four years seemed to tumble away into the past as the long wake of the great liner faded into the gold-washed ocean. The lovely little daughter of a grandee of Spain and granddaughter of an American Scot . . . sent from Madrid to Paris to escape revolution and cholera when Queen Victoria was still a little girl . . . revolution again in '48 . . . young Louis Napoleon the Prince President falling in love with her at the balls in the Elysée . . . the lovely young

Spaniard encouraging Louis Napoleon's political ambitions . . .
the lovely young Spaniard invited to Fontainebleau and riding
with such grace and spirit and skill at the hunts . . . the mad jealousy
of this upstart Mademoiselle de Montijo . . . the Prince President
proclaimed Emperor of the French in '52 . . . the fêtes at
Compiègne . . . the Tuileries ball on New Year's Eve . . . the
insults by officialdom to the lovely Spaniard . . . the complaint to
the Emperor . . . *je vous vengerai* . . . and three days later the formal
proposal for her hand . . . officialdom's rage . . . *mésalliance* . . .
the speech from the throne . . . 'I have preferred a woman whom
I love and respect to a woman unknown to me, with whom an
alliance would have had advantages mixed with sacrifices' . . . the
marriage at Notre Dame . . . the Crimea . . . the war to free Italy
from Austria . . . Magenta . . . the war with Prussia . . . Sedan . . .
the Republic proclaimed in Paris, but the Empress remains at her
post as Regent . . . deserted by all except a few loyal ones . . . at
last persuaded to escape to England . . . Chislehurst where the
broken Emperor joins her . . . she has seen the doom coming . . .
it is a judgment of God for his treatment of the Papacy . . . yet
she cherishes him for the two wretched years of agonizing illness
left to him . . . and then all that she kept of her hopes set on the
young Prince Imperial . . . and then '79 and the Zulu War, and
her only son killed . . . the great mausoleum at Farnborough built
in '87 . . . and for thirty-three more years alone she spends every
summer near the bodies of her husband and her son . . . the friend
of Queen Victoria, whom she will outlive by twenty years . . .
alone . . . and a mere twenty of such lives would reach to the foot
of Calvary . . . the years tumbling back like the white wake astern
on this golden July afternoon.

John let fall the volume he had taken out of the ship's library in
which he had been reading about Eugénie. And now his thoughts
streamed back along the wake to Atlanta. He was glad he had
seen Athene's background and could picture her in childhood.
He pulled out a photograph of three little girls, standing beside
the verandah in floppy sun-hats and white frocks. The oldest of
them, aged eight, was standing just as Athene often stood now,
seeming to be smoothing down her skirt above her hips with
long-fingered hands. 'That was taken in 1897,' Mrs Gilmer had
told him when she gave it to him. 'But I'm so mad with myself
now that I never had the children painted. Their colouring was
just exquisite.' Yes, he must have Athene painted next year, he
decided as he put the photograph back in his pocket. There would

B

probably be a painter at Citrano. It would be jolly to have her painted on the Punta beyond Cantone. She could be looking at the chipped terra-cotta head of Minerva . . . Miss Minerva Wilkes . . . when Mrs Langridge had told him about her he had pictured a fierce spinster like Tom Sawyer's aunt. . . .

John sat up and looked round to see if Arthur were in sight. In the way of small boys on board liners he had already struck up an intimacy with the steward and was at present enjoying some adventure of exploration below in his company. John's thoughts went tumbling astern again with the liner's wake. He wondered if Athene would prefer to live in America. He must find that out. There was so much to tempt one in American life. It was so comfortable. And the people, even defiant conservatives like Lawton Gilmer, were so much quicker to respond to the variety of life and the novelty of ideas than they were in England. There was a great deal in what Bob Redroad had said. In a year or two it might be a good move to settle in the United States. If England were going to be gradually Americanized it would be much more agreeable to enjoy the culture undiluted. Julius had no desire to return to Europe except as a visitor, and he had as keen a sense of life's values as anybody. Yes, if Athene showed the slightest inclination to abandon Europe she should have no opposition from himself.

At this moment Arthur presented himself before John. His cheeks, always high-coloured, were more deeply flushed than usual with excitement. His dark eyes were glittering.

"Hullo, my lad, have you been steering the ship?"

"No, but I saw the laundry with Roker," Arthur proclaimed. "I saw about a million towels, I guess. Or perhaps two million, and they smelt burnt. Gee, I never saw so many towels. When we crossed in the *Mafalda* last year I didn't see the laundry, but I guess there are more towels in the *Gigantic*."

He curled himself up in the deck-chair beside John.

"What have you been doing, John?"

"I've been thinking."

This was a dull answer, and Arthur picked up the book John had dropped.

"Who's this old dame?" he enquired.

"The Empress Eugénie. She has just died, the wireless news says. She was ninety-four."

"Ninety-four? Say, that's pretty old, isn't it?"

"Very old."

"Grandma Langridge is sixty-six and she's pretty old. And Grandma Gilmer is fifty-five. I was expecting they might die any old time. Gee, I'd like to ride my pony to a funeral. Say, John, do you think my pony's feeling discouraged because I've gone away?"

"I should think he was missing you a lot."

"Poor old Cawffee," Arthur murmured sentimentally. "I wouldn't like him to die before I saw him again. I've got a yen for that old pony. Roker said there was nothing to stop him coming across with us," he added with a hint of reproach.

"It would have been a tricky job to get Coffee from Atlanta to New York, and ponies get pretty sea-sick."

"They do? Gosh, I never thought ponies were ever sea-sick," the boy exclaimed.

"You ask Roker." Roker? Roker? Of course! That had been the name of Rose Medlicott's great-aunt.

"I sure will," Arthur declared, thrusting forward that aggressive chin he had inherited from Grandfather Gilmer.

"And if you have an English pony you'll keep up your riding and when we go back to America Coffee will get a jolly surprise. . . ."

"I don't believe I'll find a pony in England as good as Cawffee. I don't believe there's a pony as good as Cawffee anywhere in the whole world. Poor old Cawffee! I guess he's wondering what can have happened to me."

A day or two later Arthur suffered a heavy blow from the news that *Shamrock IV* had beaten *Resolute* off Long Island in the first race for the America Cup.

"Gosh, that's terrible," he muttered. "Well, George Washington licked the British anyway," he added courageously. "Yessir, George Washington licked the British, and yet he didn't win quite every battle he fought."

A little later he came back to John, smiling in triumph.

"Say, John, I've been talking to Roker and he says *Resolute* broke something or other. I knew *Shamrock* couldn't have beaten *Resolute* fairly. I guess the British won't take that old cup away so easy as they think."

"Arthur, I don't think I care very much for all this patriotic rejoicing," Athene told her son in Hampstead at the end of that

July when Sir Thomas Lipton's yacht lost the fifth race to *Resolute* and thus failed to bring back the cup. "I'm afraid Lady Ogilvie will think little American boys are extremely boastful."

"Well, Mother, I said we'd win sure enough, didn't I."

"Look here, Arthur, I'll make you a sporting offer," John intervened. "We'll go to a shop I know of where they sell model yachts, and you shall choose one and I'll choose one—same size and rig of course—and we'll have a race for the America Cup on the pond upon the Heath."

"Say, wouldn't that be bully? Gosh, John, I never heard anything so bully since Grandpa Gilmer gave me Cawffee. Say, Prudence, will you bet on my yacht?"

"No, I'm going to back John's."

"Aw, come on, Prudence, be a good sport. You're going to bet on my yacht, Mother?"

"No, I'm going to back John's too."

"Aw, gee, isn't anybody going to bet on my yacht?"

And in spite of the out-thrust chin there was a moisture in Arthur's dark eyes.

"I shall bet on you," Elise Ogilvie told him.

"Oh, that's bully, Lady Ogilvie. And we will win. You see!"

"What are you calling your yacht?" the backer asked.

"*George Washington*," Arthur proclaimed defiantly.

There was a general laugh, at which the young patriot flushed.

"Arthur," his mother threatened, "if you say what's on the tip of your tongue, there'll be no race for the America Cup in Hampstead."

A struggle went on within Arthur's breast, but deciding at last that his country could be better served by winning the America Cup he refrained from proclaiming that George Washington had licked the British. He would have chanced it even with Grandma Gilmer, but he had no hope of his mother's going back on her word.

While Arthur was tidying himself for the expedition to the model-yacht shop Athene protested that John was spoiling him.

"No, I'm not, Athene. He's got to grow into this new life."

"I'm just horrified by the effect of these last ten months," she declared. "I feel so ashamed of him, Elise. Of course I know perfectly well from whom he gets all this bragging. It's old Mr Langridge. And my own father's very silly with him too. So please, John, I don't want you to start spoiling him."

"John won't really spoil him," Prudence put in eagerly. "He can be frightfully severe sometimes."

"Yes, yes, he was always so very severe with you," her mother observed sarcastically.

On the evening of that day when the *George Washington* had won three races out of five against the *Lion Rampant* and Arthur was sailing through sleep attended by Nereids and Oceanides, Athene told John that she thought the sooner she had her son to herself for two or three weeks the better.

"I can't bear the idea of your going away from me again so soon, John, especially now, but really I must have you away while I pull Arthur together. I daresay I'm more irritable than I ought to be just now, but that's intelligible, and I don't want to be irritated. Where shall he and I go? Down to the sea somewhere, I think."

"The answer to that is easy," John replied, handing her a letter from Henry Pendarves.

"John, we have Nanphant as our very own! Isn't that divine?"

"We got it wonderfully cheap too," he commented. "Sixteen hundred pounds, furniture and all. Henry has done well."

"Wait, I must put that into dollars before I know whether it's cheap. Eight thousand dollars? Why, that's terribly cheap! John, I can't tell you how thrilled I am. And Arthur and I can just go down right away. And you'll go up to Scotland to stay with the Rigdens."

"I thought of getting an invitation for David. He'll enjoy having a go at the stags, and his first experience of stalking will give him something to brag about at Balliol next term. That will please Elise too."

"I think it's a splendid plan."

"The Rigdens will be depressed that you can't come," John said.

"Darling, I couldn't have gone away just now."

"There's nothing visible."

"I daresay not, but I'm going to be quiet. I have had one bad alarm. I know what this means to you, but, honey sweet, it means just as much to me."

"I'm glad you're happy about Nanphant. I was thinking on the way coming back from New York, that perhaps in a year or two you'd like to go and live in America. If you would, promise me that you will say so frankly. I mean, don't think that *I* wouldn't want to go and live there. I really did enjoy myself, you know, staying with your people."

She looked at him, and then shook her head.

"No, John, your background is Europe."

"But you would like to go back?" he pressed.

"On visits, yes. But we have Nanphant now. And we have the tower. Poor tower, so deserted."

"If all goes well we'll go there next summer. But Noel writes that Citrano is more crowded than ever this year. Oh well, what plans can we make till after January?

> *"So when or you or I are made*
> *A fable, song, or fleeting shade,*
> *All love, all liking, all delight*
> *Lies drowned with us in endless night.*
> *Then while time serves, and we are but decaying,*
> *Come, my Corinna, come, let's go a-maying."*

John saw Athene settled in at Nanphant before he went North.

"You don't want another pony called Coffee," he told Arthur the day before he left. "So I've got you one called Tea. Don't throw it into the sea like your Boston friends."

Arthur found this an exquisite joke.

"I wish audiences were made up of Arthurs," said John. "*The Guinea Pig* would have had a longer run. No matter, Rigden is putting *The Balloon* on at the beginning of October."

"Gosh, that's some pony," Arthur declared when he saw the neat dun his stepfather had secured for him. "I can't promise I'll like him better than Cawffee, but I guess I'll like him an awful lot. But, John, he isn't the colour of tea the same way Cawffee is the colour of coffee."

"He's exactly the colour of most of the tea I saw under the Star-Spangled Banner. I don't wonder your Boston friends threw it into the harbour."

And again Arthur responded with boisterous laughter.

John had been greatly disturbed by the news from Poland since he returned from America. Thanks to the shilly-shally of the British Government and the refusal of the Danzig dockers to unload a cargo of 150,000 rifles sent by the Allies for the Polish Army the situation was becoming critical for Poland. By the end of July the Russians had crossed the eastern boundary laid down by the Supreme Council. Bolshevik papers were demanding an indemnity of live-stock, salt, machinery, and seventy per cent of Polish rolling-stock. Poland was to be occupied for twelve months under a Soviet régime, at the end of which time she was to be allowed to determine her own form of government, but the military occupation by Russia was to last another five years. Meanwhile the Polish troops were being driven back all along the line. General Weygand was authorized by the French Government to act as military adviser, but forbidden to take the command. Pilsudski was organizing the defence of Lemberg. Warsaw itself was in peril. So grave was the situation that Polish officers were empowered to treat for an armistice. These delegates had been dismissed by the Russians, who had realized that they themselves were love's young dream to British Liberalism and Labour, on the excuse that they had been empowered to treat only for an armistice instead of for peace.

By the 3rd of August the Bolsheviks were in Brest-Litovsk and had imposed a Soviet régime on the conquered territory under a renegade communist Pole. This puppet Government called upon the working classes of Poland to rise against Pilsudski.

The heads of the British and French Government conferred, and it was finally agreed to send war material to Poland but not to help her with men. Even this feeble compromise was too much for the British Labour Party, which began to mutter threats of a general strike if any kind of naval or military intervention were allowed to interfere with the obviously pure intentions of the Bolsheviks, who would prove to the world the completeness of their idealism as soon as the Polish delegates walked into the parlour at Minsk to treat for peace.

On the August day that John travelled up from Cornwall to London, the day on which railway fares were increased a further twenty-five per cent on the fifty per cent they had already gone up since August 1914, the Polish Government had issued an appeal to the world.

"The armistice proposed by Poland to Soviet Russia has been rejected. The Soviet Government acted throughout with deceit, freely altering messages, refusing to allow the Polish delegates to communicate with their Government, and delaying negotiations so as to make them fruitless. . . . The Soviets want to gain time: they want to take Warsaw and dictate their terms of peace to a defeated Poland. . . . The people of Poland, peasants and workmen, are rallying to the flag . . . and will permit the invader to enter the city only over their bodies. . . . Poland is being accused of imperialism, but from the moment the world recognized her independence, Poland was continuously forced to fight for her life. The Armistice was not yet signed at Spa in 1918 when Lemberg had to fight against an enemy led by an Austrian archduke. At the same time the Soviet armies took Lithuania and threatened to march on Warsaw. . . . Trotsky announced that the Cossacks of the Red Army would water their horses in the Rhine. All these attacks have been repulsed. Lemberg was saved actually by children. . . . In this critical hour of her decisive struggle Poland turns to the nations of the world to tell them that Poland fights for her life under the standard of freedom and progress, and that her fall would be due not only to overbearing might, but also to the indifference of a world which calls itself democratic and freedom-loving, a world of principles of liberty for individuals and nations. . . . At this most tragic hour, in view of the crime to be committed on the Vistula, we are making the conscience of the nations of the world responsible. Your indifference can, as in 1772, 1795, 1831, and 1863, allow these troops of the East to destroy the beginnings of a freedom which, founded on the ruins of the Caesarism of Nicholas and Wilhelm, may now disappear beneath Bolshevik imperialism. . . . If Polish freedom dies, to-morrow yours will be threatened. . . . A Bolshevik victory on the Vistula threatens all the West. . . . Wake up, nations of the world. Humanity, justice, and truth call you. You hesitate? Are you afraid of war? It will come to you as it came to us. When it is on your threshold, it will be too late to save yourselves. Not only our future, but your future too, is at stake to-day on the Vistula."

In response to this appeal the British and French Prime Ministers talked away at Hythe, and in Parliament the British Prime Minister told the Labour M.P.'s, who could read the noble intentions of Russia as easily as they had read their own Sunday School prizes when young, that the Allies had agreed that if Poland accepted the terms of the Soviet Government they would not intervene to upset any arrangement that was reached.

The British Government may have felt embarrassed by Poland's invitation to save the West, for at that moment a Bill was being rapidly passed through Parliament to make it easier to overthrow the West by empowering the military authorities to incarcerate any Irish man or woman for an indefinite period without charge or trial, to try any Irish man or woman by secret court-martial and only in cases liable to the death penalty to provide the accused with a lawyer nominated by the Crown, and to arrest any Irish man or woman whom they believed capable of informing against a prisoner and require him or her to testify, on pain of six months' imprisonment or a fine of £100. The Lord Lieutenant was empowered to withhold grants to local councils and suppress coroners' inquests. This Bill, Royal Assent and all, was rushed through in under a week. Its Canadian sponsor called it The Restoration of Order in Ireland Bill. The Labour Party, though agreeable to handing over Poland to Russia, were not quite sure about handing over Ireland to the military, and they opposed the Bill, perhaps because the House of Lords was apparently under the impression that the defenders of the West were on the salary-list of Moscow.

John had twenty-four hours to spend in town before David joined him for the journey up to Sutherland, and finding that Emil was in London by himself, Astrid having gone away with his mother to some watering-place on the East Coast, he asked him to dine at Bélanger's, for he wanted to hear what defence Emil was prepared to offer of Soviet falsity and imperialism.

"Soviet imperialism!" he scoffed. "Russia is only trying to recover a Russian population stolen from her by the Poles when she was trying to defend herself against those infernal counter-revolutionaries."

"Poor maltreated mammoth," John jeered.

"Finland is managing to come to terms with Russia," Emil went on. "Why should not Poland? You have the same sentimental idea about the Poles that you have about the Irish. They're both mediaeval nations and must come into line with to-day or perish."

"But I thought your friends the Bolsheviks were financing Sinn Féin."

Emil uttered an ejaculation of contempt.

"They would be as likely to finance a miraculous madonna! But I'll tell you one thing, John: if this Government tries to use military or naval force against the Soviets there'll be a small revolution in this country."

"Yes, so long as the weather keeps dry," John jeered again. "But it usually rains in August."

"I don't think you'll find British troops willing to fight to put Poland back on the map," Emil murmured.

John looked at him sharply. There was something in his tone which suggested more than a general impression of opinion.

"I hope you're not monkeying about with propaganda among

the armed forces," he said. "It'll get you into trouble. You can depend upon it that the War Office people have plenty of informers and *agents provocateurs* among the troops. They're bound to get you."

"That's really my own business, isn't it, John?"

"Absolutely," John agreed.

"And I happen to know a little myself about the working of Military Intelligence," Emil continued coldly.

"All right, all right, let my unrequired advice be as if unsaid," John told him. "But I was hoping to have your picture of Russia as an ill-treated mammoth. You and the chubby little pinks of the Labour Party are as much concerned about her as once upon a time animal-lovers about the cruelty to dancing bears. Do you seriously believe that a communism applied to Western Europe from the East could be a practicable communism?"

"There's no difference between Russian communism and any other kind."

"Oh, don't be ridiculous, Emil."

"The communism that Russia has adopted came from the industrialized West. All this talk about the East is part of your sentimentality over anachronisms like Ireland. I don't love English conservatism . . ."

"Not when it can breed oily-locked premiers like Disraeli?" John put in.

"I disregard Disraeli," said Emil lightly.

"You're lucky. I wish to heaven I could. I regard him as one of the major disasters Britain has had to suffer. If we get another he'll finish the country off."

"He understood how to deal with Ireland," Emil commented. "But as I was saying, I don't love English conservatism, but at least it grasps what an impossible nation the Irish are. The most superstitious, primitive, petty-minded, reactionary race in Europe!"

"It's a pity you gave up bureaucracy. You might have become a peer in time and then you might have convinced a few moth-eaten dukes that the last country on which Moscow was going to waste its gold was Ireland. Yes, you'll find the solemn abolition of God by partially washed commissars and entirely unwashed peasants and workers difficult to put across in Ireland. I'm still open to be converted to communism as a solution of the economic difficulties caused by machinery, but I don't see why God has to be abolished . . . now, don't say religion is a narcotic, because I shall only retort that no religion is an even more potent narcotic.

The cold fact remains that you want to let loose on the West the Tartar hordes in order to enforce your economic theory, and that the only civilized nation standing in the way at present is Poland. You feel sure of Germany if Poland is defeated, and with Germany bolshevized you feel sure of the rest of Europe. Thanks to the imbecility and greed of our plutocratic politicians we've established a German Republic instead of breaking up Germany into its component parts and making Vienna the capital of the federation."

"You are just as imbecile as the politicians you deride," Emil answered. "You are still thinking in the terms of an age that has gone by. You want to go on playing chess with half the pieces missing on a board whose squares are half obliterated. You were always the same, always looking back into the irremediable past to find a remedy for the present and a panacea for the future. You're Gothic, John, your Gothic. Your mind sprawls. You feel, you don't think. You aspire; you cannot plan. You're living in a lumber-room. I become impatient with you now that your closing in on forty. When you were seventeen you could carry off your romantic individualism. I had my own romantic dreams about you. I used to feel like Rebecca the Jewess with Ivanhoe. At that age your Jacobitism and Chopinism and Byronism added to your charm, but now at thirty-seven you're going to a fancy-dress ball in an unsuitable costume. This tenderness about Poland, for instance. What was the first thing that civilized country did when it won back by luck its independence? There was a pogrom. All that a century and a half of lost independence had brought it was to revenge itself on the unfortunate Jews. There's your bulwark of the West."

"But in the condition of the country, in the uncertainty of being able to hold what had cost so much to win back . . ."

"Yes, you'll make excuses for Poland, but you'll make none for the Bolsheviks. Their efforts to quell the counter-revolution show them to be nothing better than a lot of bloodthirsty savages. Most nations revert to savagery when they're frightened. The English are frightened of what may happen in Ireland. Hence your Black and Tan outrages. Irregular warfare must lead to more savagery on both sides. Poland is a perpetual menace to the October Revolution. The Soviets must protect themselves. As for Poland, it can only retain in alliance either with Germany or Russia the independence it has won back. And to my thinking it would be wiser to take the opportunity now of making friends with Russia. The Poles under Russia were better off than those

under Germany. Or let us say that the Germans treated them
as the English treated the Irish in the eighteenth century and that
the Russians treated them as the English treated the Irish in the
nineteenth century."

"And the Austrians?"

"Oh, the Austrians treated them as the Liberals wanted to treat
the Irish before they were outmanœuvred by the Unionists."

"But it's a different matter now that Russia is communist and
officially atheist," John argued. "You can't expect a Catholic
nation to shake hands with Satan."

"A Catholic nation has managed to do so in France, and for
that matter in Italy," Emil pointed out. "It's only when Satan
starts putting his hand into the pocket of Catholicism that Catholic
nations refuse to shake hands with him. But once again, John,
I tell you that all this talk about Catholic nations is romantic
fiddlesticks. Christianity has had nearly two thousand years to
make a success of the world, and it has failed. The time has
come to sweep it from the earth when as in Poland it becomes
militant and stands in the way of humanity's advance."

"Humanity's advance behind a horde of semi-Asiatic barbarians
commanded by city clerks, Jewish malcontents, and village
atheists," John expostulated.

"These stale jibes!"

"We grow apart, Emil. You're too romantic for me and I'm
too romantic for you."

"I romantic?" Emil echoed in disgust.

"When you talk about humanity's advance you're not inviting
me to consider you a realist, are you? Still, I prefer your romantic
red to the sentimental pink of those who think that Russia is an
innocent Teddy bear being prodded by the wicked Poles. Don't
let's grow too far apart, Emil," he added gently.

The news from Poland was still bad when John and David
reached Euston the following evening; but by now it was clear
that if Poland was to be saved she would be saved by her own
exertions, and John allowed himself to be distracted from the
menace of the Russian advance by the bustle of Euston a few days
before the Twelfth of August. Young women with eyes alert for
friends or relations they were meeting and dressed in very tweedy

tweed coats and skirts were being dragged up and down the platform by spaniels and retrievers which, skilful enough at retrieving
grouse, were less adept at retrieving friends or relations. Young
men in very tweedy tweeds were dragging spaniels and retrievers
to the vans or telling porters not to let cases of guns fall off overcrowded barrows. Older women with chaffinch-egg complexions
and less tweedy tweeds were waving to daughters or sons or
husbands lost in the press of travellers. Older sportsmen, one or
two actually wearing the deerstalkers seen in back volumes of
Punch, were bellowing to daughters or sons or wives that their
compartment was over there. Fishermen in tweed caps covered
with flies that stupid fish would lack the entomology to know did
not exist outside shops were making their way placidly along the
platform unmoved by the damage they were doing with their rods.
Ladies' maids, footmen, valets, butlers, porters, sleeping-car attend-
ants, newspaper-boys, pillow-hirers, chocolate-sellers, ticket-inspec-
tors, and people who had paid a penny to come on the platform
added to the crowd and confusion.

The clock marked twenty minutes past seven. The guard's
whistle was heard. The train for Inverness started. In the dining-
car John looked mournfully at the menu, and David, whose tweeds
were almost the tweediest of any in sight, looked critically at the
wine list.

"I'll stand you a bottle of fizz, John," he said at last.

"I was going to drink Bass, but I expect you want to live up
to those natty Glen Urquhart checks, so I won't refuse."

"They are rather bright," David zgreed. "But the Ogilvie
tartan is brighter."

"You've bought a kilt, have you?"

"Well, I thought I'd better."

"Thick or clear soup, please?"

"Clear," they called with one voice, and two plates of faintly
turbid liquid rocking to and fro over a fragment of carrot were
set before them.

"Fish, please?"

A minute portion of brill rolled up like a rug beside a drop of
greenish paste was set before them.

"Chicken or roast beef, please?"

"Chicken, please," they voted.

"Sorry, sir, there's only one portion of chicken left," said the
steward.

"You have the chicken, David."

"No, rather not. You have the chicken, John."

"It doesn't matter. They both taste exactly alike, and neither tastes either of chicken or beef," John said.

And so the weary British railway meal took its course, to wind safe at last to a glass of Benedictine.

"St Benedict saved learning in the dark ages," observed John, "and now thirteen hundred years later he saves a British railway dinner from disaster. I think we'll repeat the dose. I want to get the taste of that coffee out of my mouth. Damn!"

"What's the matter?"

"I forgot to put a case of cigars in my pocket. Oh dear, now we must have a railway cigar, which will be rather like smoking a torpid slowworm. The same consistency, and I should imagine the same flavour."

"It's not so bad," David pronounced.

"It's the perfume of that old boy's Harris tweed you're getting, not the smell of your cigar," John assured him. "Now, look here, I don't ask much of you, David; I don't think I ever have asked much. But this I demand! You will cultivate a taste for cigars, because when you're a prosperous . . . by the way, what are you going to prosper at?"

"I think I shall go to the Inner Temple."

"Well, when you're a prosperous junior I want to be able to dine with you and know that you will give me a good cigar. I trained myself on Sir Alexander's from fifteen onwards, but of course I had more opportunity than you at a day-school. And believe you me, Sir Alexander knows a cigar."

Turner Rigden had sent the new Sunbeam to meet his guests at Inverness and spare them the crawling railway journey to Lairg. John found to his relief that he and David were the only arrivals. A commentary from others upon the passing scene, were they enthusiastic or foolish, was not what they wanted on this return to the land in which he had greeted the first moment of the twentieth century and which he had not revisited until all but a few months of twenty years had gone by.

It was a relief also to escape from the self-conscious swarm of tweedy people in the station-square of Inverness, all so earnestly excited at the prospect of killing stags and salmon and grouse before they went south again to kill pheasants and partridges and foxes. It was like the sudden peace which descends when the doors of the parrot-house in the Zoo are closed behind one to sit back in the Sunbeam beside the Beauly Firth, the shores of the Black Isle gliding by across the quiet silver water.

It was about noon when they entered Strath Oykell, and John began to stare ahead for the first glimpse of Suilven's huge grape-dark hand westward miles away beyond the rolling moorland. The solitary shape of stone rose at last; but upon that sunny August morning it was neither grape-dark nor blue-grey as John had first and last beheld it from the old horse-coach between Lairg and Lochinver. It melted into the haze like a ship upon a summer horizon. It was there, and it was gone. Perhaps it was not Suilven at all but a wandering cloud. Before John could make up his mind about this the car turned off to the right along a narrow road which after crossing the level green of the strath went winding beside a stream between gradually narrowing steep braes. The chauffeur announced that Mr Rigden's lodge was another twelve miles up the glen.

"Properly what you might call the back end of nowhere," observed the chauffeur, who was a Cockney called Banny. "Still, it was me and Miss Madge and Miss Dolly who found the place. So I didn't ought to grumble. And in fact I like it. I wouldn't say I'd like to spend all the rest of my life here. But you know. After London and what not it's a change. This is what they call Glen Grean, though I don't see where the green comes into it. Over there to the right about five miles up the only turning is Grean Lodge. That belongs to Mr. Gilkes."

"Who's he?"

"I don't really know, sir. I think he came up during the war, as you might say. They say he's very wealthy."

The braes ran more steeply. Escarps showed a grim face of rock from time to time. Ahead of them to the left the great bulks of Conival and Ben More Assynt gathered clouds round their summits.

"It's wild right enough," said Banny with relish. "I think Mr Rigden wondered where I was bringing him the first time I drove him up."

"Well, David, do you feel yourself stirring to this fierce country?" John asked his brother. "Our great-grandmother came from Assynt. Isabel Macleod was her name. She married Patrick Ogilvie, who was an Edinburgh lawyer."

"It is marvellous country," David said. "I wonder where Rigden's forest begins."

"This is all Mr Rigden's, sir," Banny informed them.

Achnalochlannach Lodge was a conventional shooting-lodge built in what is called the baronial style, which meant that it looked like a much swollen suburban vicarage. Two or three oblongs of overcrowded pines tried to spoil the grandeur of the surroundings, but that was impossible.

"A couple of months in the year is all I'll be able to stand of it," the new owner prophesied. "And I'm not sure yet I'll be able to stand even that. It makes Canada look like Piccadilly Circus. Anyway I must be back in town by the end of the month if we're going to put *The Balloon* on by the first week of October. In fact I think I ought to go back in a fortnight!"

"How does Dorothy like it?" John asked.

"Dorothy likes it better than Wickets! But she's got a queer streak in her. And Madge and Dolly are going to stay on through November. Through November! Yes, hind-shooting. My god, John, fancy this place in November! *Macbeth* would be a farce compared with this place in November. I'm glad May didn't come up. Before I knew where I was she'd be wanting to play Lady Macbeth at the Sheridan. Forty miles from a railway station! Forty! In this country!"

"Your driver likes it."

"Banny? He's got a queer streak too. His father was an undertaker. Well, I'm glad you've brought this young brother of yours along. He'll be able to knock these stags about, I hope. It's not my sport, John. I oughtn't to have listened to the girls. I ought to have bought a grouse moor. However, I told my head stalker to shoot me a couple of dozen of these stags, and I'll have the heads put up at Wickets."

"I think you've found a wonderful place, Turner."

"It would be all right if we could fill it up. But it's too far away. And the name frightens people. I asked the Gilders, but they've gone to Le Touquet, and T. T. and Muriel Vawdry have gone to the Riviera. I tell you, old man, you're in for a dull time. We don't get the papers till the evening of the next day."

At dinner that night David appeared in his kilt, which became him well. He had already made friends with Nicolson the head stalker and was looking forward to the possibility of getting his first stag next day. He had been delighted by the absence of other guests to criticize his novitiate. Madge and Dolly Rigden, pleasant unaffected young women, were prepared to thimk him marvellous and to listen eagerly to the minutest details of his prowess. Next year he planned to secure invitations for a couple of his Balliol friends and enjoy the pleasure of being an old hand at stalking.

Dorothy Rigden told John how glad she was to be living the simple life in Achnalochlannach.

"With two chauffeurs, half a dozen maids, a butler and a footman," John commented, with a smile.

"It seems simple after Wickets, but poor old Turner hates it. I'm quite happy sitting in the garden and looking at that lovely hill reflected in the lake—oh, I mustn't say lake, must I?—in the loch. And it's good for Turner to have nothing to do for two or three weeks. I do wish we had had a boy, John. He would have so loved being here. Do you want to play Mah Jong, Turner?" she called across the room to her husband, who was laying out the board.

"Gee, we've got to do something," he declared. "I'm going to have a billiard-room built for next year. That's the worst of these Scotch shooting-lodges. The rooms are all so damned small."

John took an early opportunity of going over to Sandwater. He invited David to come with him, but with two stags already to his credit David's interest in ancestral origins was cool. So John went with Banny, who was delighted at the prospect. They drove in an open two-seater.

"Well, I reckon this is the grandest country anyone could want," the chauffeur declared.

The car was running along the side of Loch Assynt under the furrowed precipices of the mighty Cuinneag. The melancholy ruin of Ardvreck Castle, the dark contorted pines on the islets, the sombre steeps of Ben Garbh with the cloud-capped Canisp looming beyond, and the ancient churchyard of Inchnadamph composed a scene of classic austerity. They hooted to warn a figure in the middle of the road who was apparently lost in contemplation. The figure turned and to John's surprise revealed a Japanese. He raised his hat and bowed ceremoniously. John told Banny to pull up and apologized for disturbing him.

"Please, it is my fault," said the Japanese. "But I admire so much."

"You are touring in Scotland?" John asked.

"I make a tour—yes."

"And what have you admired most?"

"Assynt," the Japanese replied.

John drove on, elated.

"It gives me a good deal of pleasure, Banny, that a Londoner and a Japanese traveller should both agree with me in thinking that Assynt provides the grandest landscapes of Scotland."

"Oh, it's a knock-out all right, sir," Banny asserted. "No mi s take about that. Fancy a Jap coming all the way up here. He must feel a bit further than just round the corner from where he hangs out at home."

The sea was breaking quietly in Sandwater Bay, and John looked out for the little thatched house where the road began to wind up the opposite brae to Ardvore. It had vanished, but where it stood twenty years ago now stood the typical small Highland house of to-day, with a square stone porch and a couple of dormer-windows out of proportion to the roof, covered mercifully this one with black Highland slate instead of red asbestos lozenges.

John decided to enquire after old Mrs Roderick Macleod. She had been dead five years. He asked if anybody was living at Ardvore and was told that a Mr Wilson was there for the shooting. Had the Miss Macleods given up the house? Miss Una was dead, but Miss Maeve and Miss Bride were still living somewhere near London. They had neither of them been to Ardvore for several years.

Mr Wilson had a long lease of the place. A very nice gentleman from Edinburgh. Was Norman MacIver the tailor still in Melvaig? Oh yes, indeed he was. He would be found in his shop.

And sure enough, at the end of the diminutive cluster of shops at the top of the brae that formed the 'village street' of Ardvore and served three or four crofting townships in the neighbourhood, John found the hunchbacked tailor sitting crosslegged on a platform that resembled a wooden bedstead and surrounded by odd bits of homespun and half-made garments. He was stitching away at a pair of trousers, and but that twenty years had passed and that the tailor's black hair was now white it might have been the same pair of trousers on which he was at work when John just eighteen years old bade him farewell.

"You don't remember me," he said when Norman MacIver looked up without a greeting for what he was supposing was an unwelcome customer.

"No, I don't remember you at all," the tailor replied, and bent morosely over the pair of trousers. "But if you were not standing in the doorway I would be seeing better what I am doing," he added.

John moved further inside the dim little shop with the drouthy odour of cloth and wool and brown paper.

"We saw in this century together," he said.

"Then we saw the worst sight since Adam and Eve 'all the Eastern side beheld of Paradise, so late their happy seat.' "

"Was the nineteenth century such a Paradise?" John asked. "I shall go to Milton too, and call it a Paradise of Fools."

"Maybe you're right. Ay, maybe you're right," the tailor nodded. "Ay, the comparison might have been better chosen. I remember you now. You would always be blethering to me about politics and suchlike. So here you are again. Well, well."

The tailor dropped the pair of trousers at which he was stitching and held out his hand. John shook it, thinking how soft it was, how soft and dry.

"And what have you made of the world?" the tailor asked.

"I've been lucky. I've made a success of writing plays."

"Is that so? Well, I don't know much about plays except the plays of William Shakespeare and some Gaelic comicalities I write myself to scandalize the Reverend Alexander MacAulay, the Free Presbyterian minister, and annoy the Reverend Hector Mackenzie, the United Free minister, and frighten the Reverend Murdo Maclennan, the Church of Scotland minister. Yes, in my small comicalities I try to bring back some of the spirit that is gone; but I am preaching to the dying. There will be nobody left in Assynt to see in the twenty-first century. Perhaps a few gillies and stalkers and shepherds among the deer and the sheep and the rabbits and the bracken. A land fit for heroes to live in we were promised by the man who has betrayed our race. I read somewhere that somebody said it would take a hero to live in it. That wass very good, I'm thinking. Very good that wass. And now in the Long Island where there is still a spark of life they will be putting in prison men who sailed among the submarines and mines all through the war to bring food to the glorious United Kingdom of Great Britain and Ireland. Och, but the estates must not suffer because men wish to grow corn for themselves and their families and good pasturage for stirks and sheep. It is abominable whatever. It does not matter that such estates drove men and women and children from their crofts into the emigrant ships and left them to starve in Canada. Property must be respected. The holy name of Mammon must not be blasphemed. Let the trawlers take the fish so that the banks can be paid their interest! Let the long lines of the inshore fishermen be destroyed! What right

have the fishermen of the West to put out long lines when the
trawlers must feed the cities with fried fish and chips and pay
dividends for the big companies that own them? Property is
sacred in the eyes of the Lord God. Let them have all the fish
they can catch outside or inside the miserable three-mile limit,
all the fish they can catch except salmon. The salmon must be
protected because it is property's pet fish when property wants a
little sport and recreation. And let the deer be protected for the
same reason. The crofters are a nuisance, always grumbling
because the fences are not kept up and the deer eat their patches
of thin corn. Fifteen thousand families the Duke of Sutherland
evicted in the last century, and made a desert from which the few
that were left will soon be gone, the young people to the cities,
the old people to the grave. And when a spark of life flames up
and land is raided, then to prison with such blackguard heroes . . ."
the tailor broke off abruptly. "I don't know for why I'm blethering like this. I haven't tasted a dram since the New Year."

"You used to say that the West Highlands and Islands should
join Ireland," John reminded him.

"Ay, that was Michael Davitt's idea. It was a grand idea, sure
enough. And Ireland is showing them something now. Mr
Lloyd George will not be finding it so easy to manage the Irish
as he found it to manage the bodachs and cailleachs up here with
his old-age pensions. There is still life in Ireland. He will be
beaten. Och, yes, indeed, he'll be beaten sure enough. It's a
big disgrace though for the Welsh. Man, I'm sorry for them the
way they must be feeling now. It is usually a Scot who does the
dirty work for England. That was a terrible disgrace for us when
Jamie Macpherson took the job of Secretary for Ireland. Terrible,
terrible! A Gaelic speaker too. Old Cluny must have turned
in his grave at the devil's work a Cattanach was doing. Well,
well, poor Seumas Iain, it's himself that's after being glad he
handed over his job to Sir Hamer Greenwood. 'Under the merry
greenwood tree, who loves to lie with me?' " the hunch-backed
tailor chuckled to himself.

"I wonder if it is too late to rouse the same spirit in Scotland
as there is in Ireland," John asked.

Norman MacIver shook his head.

"Too late, too late," he muttered. "Och, yes, it is too late.
It may be too late in Ireland to recover what has already been lost.
My own idea of England is taken mostly from William Shakespeare
and a fellow called Cobbett who wrote a book called *Rural Rides*.

Och, man, it's grand stuff sure enough. Well, by what I can see of it England itself is finished by any standards of decent living. And if the English countryside cannot hold out against the cities how will our Highlands and Islands hold out? We are entering upon a new world. That's all there is to it. We shall die in Scotland first, because a tree dies from the top. But the depopulation and ruin of the Highlands is only a warning to the country folk of England which they will never heed. And as I was saying, perhaps it is too late even in Ireland. There will be coming there a new generation which will not understand what Ireland has suffered for her freedom, and they will see the way the world is going and will want to keep in step."

"I was inclined to fear that," said John. "But I cannot believe that a nation will suffer what Ireland is suffering now and forget it in a few years."

"We forget more easily nowadays," the tailor answered. "We have more to remember and we read so many newspapers. But if you are still interested in the question of independence for Scotland you should like to meet Mr Maclean Sanders. He's a very interesting fellow. He has a lot of queer ideas. He's always hunting for the fairies, and och, there's a lot of nonsense in him, but he's a good Gaelic scholar when he doesn't try to speak it. That's terrible when he tries to speak it. And he has political ideas which are good, very very good. I wish I wass thirty years younger. I might be tempted to join his society."

"What's it called?"

"Scottish Life."

"It sounds like a newspaper or an insurance company," John commented.

"Ay, it is a foolish name right enough, and I'm sure half the members are daft, but there is a beautiful idea behind it. You ought to meet him. He's in Lochinver now. Are you staying in the neighbourhood? At Achnalochlannach? Is that so? Och, then you're in the heart of one of the most populous parts of Sutherland. Yes, yes, among the deer," he added with a bitter chuckle. "Achnalochlannach. The field of the Norwegians. It will have had that name for many hundred years. This was their Southland once upon a time. But you ought to meet Mr Maclean Sanders. He's full of tales and fancies."

"Suppose I come over next Saturday? Will you introduce me to him?"

"Yes, I'll gladly do so. Come along here early after dinner.

I'll be seeing Mr Maclean Sanders between now and then. He comes up for a ceilidh almost every other day."

"You were right about Ardvore," John said.

The tailor looked a question.

"You told me he wouldn't see out the first year of the century."

"Ay, the old man went the way of his forefathers." Norman MacIver nodded. "We quarrelled a good deal, he and I. He considered me a disturbing element, but we understood each other. Well, he was the last of them."

"What's the present tenant like?"

"Wilson? Och, he's not so bad. He's just a little Edinburgh fellow. Maclean Sanders, who, mind you, is an Edinburgh fellow himself, has no use at all for him. No use at all. But he has good intentions. He gives a treat to the children every Christmas and subscribes two guineas to the Ardvore Mutual Improvement Association, and his wife is a strong power in the W.R.I."

"What's that?"

"The Women's Rural Institute. You've travelled far from the land of your forefathers if you don't know what that is. Man, it's the foundation of cultural life in the Highlands," he said, grinning. "Och, yes, Mr and Mrs Wilson. Nice kind people with no more comprehension of the people round them than a pair of missionaries among the savages. Well, well, good afternoon; we'll be seeing you then on Saturday."

During these days the news from Poland was worse all the time. By August 14th it looked from the papers as if the Bolsheviks would be in Warsaw before Monday. The various accredited Ministers had all left with the staffs of the Legations. It was not mentioned that the Papal Nuncio, Monsignor Achille Ratti, had refused to leave with the rest, asserting his belief that the city would not fall. People in Warsaw supposed him to be awaiting a miracle, and indeed the miracle was granted. Afterwards people in the world without said it was not a miracle, but only the treacherous jealousy of one of Lenin's protegés, a Georgian called Stalin, who deliberately countermanded an order by a rival which would have saved the Soviet army from the humiliating and complete defeat it suffered on Sunday, August 15th, being the feast of the

Assumption of the Blessed Virgin Mary.

"You don't seem to worry, Turner, about this Russian advance," John exclaimed to his host.

"What the hell's the use of worrying? We can't do anything about it. We can't get supplies through to them because of these Danzig fellows, and if we send military reinforcements it may mean a general election."

"Then have an election," John said angrily. "Good God, it would be better to have another election than let the Bolsheviks overrun Poland."

"But the Coalition might lose a general election now. The bye-elections have shown a very sharp turn over in public opinion. We lost South Norfolk last week and we've only just held Wood-bridge by under two hundred votes. I tell you, we're all a bit worried. It's a nuisance the Prime Minister has to keep rushing about all over Europe to these conferences. He gets out of touch with the feeling at home. Europe is a nuisance anyway. What we've got to do is to concentrate on the Empire. Look at the Prince of Wales. That boy's doing great work on this last tour. We're boosting the Empire in the *Sunday Journal*. Keep out of Europe and let's put our own house in order. That's the line I'm going out on. Oh, and that reminds me, John, I'm thinking of agitating for peace in Ireland. We might build up a big cir-culation for the *Journal* in Ireland. You wouldn't like to take a run over and write me three real scorching articles? You can go for the Government as hard as you like. You might begin with Belfast. If we're going to have an Empire Policy in the *Sunday Journal* we can't stand for this muddle in Ireland. Did you see about that Archbishop chap?"

"Mannix?"

"Fancy arresting an Australian Archbishop on board ship and bringing him in a destroyer to Penzance, and what's more, for-bidding him to go to Liverpool, Manchester, and Glasgow, let alone to Ireland. I call that sort of thing plum lunacy."

"It beats me how you can remain in Parliament on the Coalition ticket," John said.

"But that's the whole point of a coalition. It's . . . what's the word? . . . it's inclusive, yes, a coalition is so damned inclusive. Besides, I'm not looking for office, old man. I'm building up the *Sunday Journal*. Well, will you go to Ireland for me?"

"Perhaps I will."

"I want to get started on this Empire Consolidation stunt. I can see the first leader: 'For weeks now the *Sunday Journal* has been advocating strengthening the ties of Empire . . .' "

"Have you?"

"No, but what's that matter? People don't keep last Sunday's newspapers. And then I want to give the Prince of Wales a big boost. But I must shake people up over these Black and Tans first."

"I suppose your newspaper stunts, Turner, are the equivalent of poetic phrenzy?"

"Poetic how much?"

"Inspiration, if you don't like the word 'phrenzy'. The cynic would suppose you thought of Empire consolidation merely in terms of a larger circulation and a higher advertisement revenue, but actually it's Dionysaic."

"You swallowed the dictionary this morning, didn't you?"

"Or Orphic."

"Oi! Step off the gas, John."

"And of course it's nothing new. The Delphic Oracle of 500 B.C. and the popular press of to-day are merely different aspects of rigging opinion. I suppose you haven't got any of your money in Mesopotamian oil?"

"Not a bean. That's a scandalous waste of public money."

"And no shares in the Suez Canal?"

"Certainly not."

"And no mineral interests in Spain or Sardinia, or cotton investments in Egypt?"

"What are you getting at?"

"There's a great deal to be said for clearing out of the Mediterranean."

"Of course there is."

"It only involves us in the complications of Europe. If we built up the old trade route round the Cape, air transport would give us all that's wanted in the way of rapid communication."

"Sure!"

"We could restore Gibraltar to Spain, hand over Malta to Italy, and present Cyprus to Greece. I suppose a too intensive development of the Empire would land us in trouble with the United States at last. And yet, I don't know; surely there's room enough for both to prosper, and between us we could keep Japan in order. A real imperial parliament moving from capital to capital of the dominions overseas. London to be constituted a District of Britannia as Washington is of Columbia. Federal independence for Scotland, Ireland, Northumbria, Mercia, Anglia, and Wessex. York the capital of Northumbria, with Liverpool and Newcastle for its ports. Oxford the capital of Mercia, with Bristol for its port. Winchester the capital of Wessex, with Plymouth and Southampton for ports. Norwich the capital of Anglia, with the port of London. I believe Scandinavia might enter such a federation. And Holland. And Portugal. It would be the greatest thalassocracy the world has known."

"Oh, for god's sake," Rigden protested, "don't empty the whole bloody alphabet over my head!"

"Thalassocracy is sea power. And aerocracy must go with it," John declared with fervour. "Britannia must rule the air as well as the sea."

"I'm with you there," Rigden agreed, lighting up an immense cigar. "The *Journal* has taken a strong line on air supremacy since I bought it."

"And if we are going to develop the Empire we must have free transport. Speed is no use unless everybody can take advantage of it. Once people can move round the world freely the problem of ill-adjusted population will solve itself. Transport is the life-blood of sea-rule and it must belong to the people. Freights must be calculated by weight and room, but not by distance. The system of the post-office must be applied throughout the British Empire. Every argument that will be used against such a proposal was used against Rowland Hill's penny post. The reform must start at home. We must nationalize transport, shipping and railways alike, and we must nationalize mines. And no compensation. Those living on the incomes of investments in railways may receive five per cent on the invested capital until death and then the capital must revert to the Commonwealth. Banks and insurance companies must be nationalized too, and of course armaments."

"I thought you were afraid of the Bolsheviks, John. But you're a Bolshie yourself."

"Oh no, subject to the basic industries belonging to the Commonwealth, individual enterprise will be encouraged. The crime of Bolshevism against nature is collectivism in agriculture, which is merely a device to enslave the peasants in the interest of the megalopolitan tendencies of the age."

"If you'd keep to words of four syllables . . ."

"We are sacrificing humanity to big cities, or rather humanity is sacrificing itself. Whenever that has happened in the past humanity has destroyed itself. There is only one way to counter this mad instinct to congregate. Freedom of movement and cheapness of transport. That's what will consolidate the Empire, Turner."

"Colonial preference is pretty important."

"That's a palliative, not a cure," John replied. "And if you succeed in closing the British Empire to the rest of the world, you're inviting the rest of the world to have a shot at kicking the door in. By the way, how's Torbock getting along in Luminole?"

"I'm afraid he's not much use, but I've put him in charge of the front of the house at the Sheridan."

"That's good, and his wife has a small part in the show. I hope *The Balloon* won't burst too soon."

"*The Balloon's* all right, John. I'll be disappointed if it doesn't run through to next summer."

John reached Melvaig about three o'clock on the afternoon of this conversation. Norman MacIver and a dark hatchet-faced man in a faded kilt of Hunting Maclean tartan were sitting in the sun outside the porch of his house. They were gazing over a row of sparse sweet-peas and a wind-dwarfed bush of veronica at the spread of earth and sea and sky. Southward below a stretch of tussocky land gilded and scented by drifts of bog-asphodel the sea ran silkily into Sandwater Bay, and far beyond the dark and jagged peaks of the Coigeach gashed the faint cerulean. Eastward, behind a country of granite outcrops and lochans choked with water-lily leaves, the great isolated bens towered, Suilven from here a titanic sugar-loaf. Westward the Minch gleamed placidly to the long dim line of Lewis forty miles away, but deepened northward to a cold slaty-blue along a sharp horizon that hinted of the Polar seas.

John did not remember having seen the tailor in the sun before and he was struck by the pallor of his countenance, which matched the whiteness of his hands.

"There you are," he said, slipping down from his chair to the shell-strewn path and coming forward to greet John. He was wearing a conical knitted cap of blue worsted which gave him more than ever the look of a troll.

"And this is Mr Maclean Sanders."

"Cia mar tha sibh?" Mr Sanders enquired in a strong Edinburgh accent.

"Tha mi gu math, tapadh leibh," John replied in an equally strong English accent.

"And that's about as far as both of you will get," the tailor chuckled. "So I think we'd better return to the English."

"These fellows will discourage anybody who tries to speak Gaelic," Mr Sanders complained. "They groan at the way the language is dying out, but when one tries to talk it they do nothing but laugh at one."

"Not at all, Mr Maclean Sanders, not at all," the tailor contradicted. "I respect the great battle you have made with the Gaelic, and that last letter you wrote me was beautiful. Och, it was nobly expressed. You were using words never written since Macmaighstir Alasdair was after writing them."

Maclean Sanders smiled.

"Norman always pulls my leg about my Gaelic," he explained to John. "Well, I'm glad to meet you, Mr Ogilvie. Norman tells me you and he have been discussing the future of our country. We're trying, some of us, to revive the national spirit. I wish you'd give us a visit in Edinburgh on your way south."

"I will, if I don't go over to Ireland," John promised.

"To Ireland, eh? What a shocking state of affairs over there! I'm not a great friend of the Irish myself. They're overrunning us in Scotland, you know. Oh yes, Glasgow will be an Irish city at this rate in another generation. Still, that's no excuse for the way the Government are behaving."

"It's a pity there's so little of the spirit of Ireland left in Scotland," said the tailor sharply. "There wass a time. There wass a time. We had that spirit in the 'eighties when they had to send the soldiers to Lewis and a gunboat to Skye. Och, I was mad to be off and have a smack at them myself."

"The crofters in the Long Island are putting up a fight now," said Maclean Sanders.

"Ay, they're putting up a fight, but they're not receiving the support. It is no use to be sporadic." The tailor was pleased with this word and rolled it over his tongue again. "Sporadic! That's all it is, sporadic!"

"But when a fire is going to burn up it begins with a flicker here and a flicker there," John reminded him.

"Ay, and when it's going out it finishes with a flicker here and a flicker there," said the tailor.

"Well, we're making an effort down in Edinburgh, Norman," Maclean Sanders declared. "And all over the country I see signs of uneasiness about our future as a nation. The movement will grow."

"If it isn't talked out," Norman MacIver observed.

"Ah, you old cynic, you'd discourage Bruce himself," Maclean Sanders remonstrated. "But we shall prove you wrong. How about taking a stroll to the cliff's edge? It'll do you good, Norman. You spend so much of your time stitching away on that platform of yours that you let your thoughts grow in on you."

So they wandered along over the rough cliff-top where the bog-asphodel threaded the tussocks with copper and gold, until they came to the edge, where they sat down under the spell of the wide view. On the southward horizon small island shapes floated.

"Are those the Summer Isles?" Maclean Sanders asked.

"Not at all. Not all. You cannot see them from where we are at all. They are hidden by the Coigeach. Those are the Shiel Isles," the tailor informed him.

"The peaceful isles," Maclean Sanders murmured, "or perhaps the enchanted isles. The names must have something to do with *sith*. *Sith* is the Gaelic for 'peace', and for 'fairy'," he explained to John.

"Och, now he's away in pursuit of the fairies," MacIver chuckled. "Now we've finished with reasonable conversation for the rest of the afternoon. Did I ever tell you, Mr Maclean Sanders, the strange thing that happened to Hugh Mackay on this very cliff?"

"Never that I remember."

"Hugh is dead now these thirty years, but he wass telling me the story himself. When Hugh wass a boy it wass the custom to gather birds to fill the beds with feathers. We buy the beds from Glasgow now. We do not collect the feathers any more. And one day Hugh Mackay came with his friend Donald MacAulay for the feathers. And it wass Hugh's turn to go down the cliff and it wass Donald's turn to hold the rope fast at the top. It wass a beautiful morning in the month of Chune, and Hugh wass after filling his sack with birds and began to climb up again, and when he wass near the top of the cliff he came to a difficult part and shouted for Donald to pull hard with the rope, but what did poor Hugh feel like when he found that he wass pulling the rope down towards himself? And he knew that Donald would have fallen asleep in the sun and let go of the rope. Poor Hugh felt he had come to the end of his days, for although he wass clinging fast to the cliff he could not cling fast for ever, but must let go and fall three hundred feet down into the sea at the foot. He called 'Donald' as loud as he could, but Donald wass fast asleep in the sun and there wass no answer. And just when poor Hugh wass thinking there wass nothing for him but he must let go and take the plunge, hundreds and hundreds of birds came fluttering round him and he felt himself lifted up from below, and in a moment he wass on the grass beside Donald, who wass still fast asleep. And Hugh remembered that when he wass thinking he must surely fall he had called out, 'A shluaigh!' and he wass always saying that without a doubt the slaugh had heard him and come to his rescue."

"Sluagh?" John echoed.

"The fairy hosts of the invisible world," Maclean Sanders cried, evincing such excitement that he was nearly going over the edge of the cliff himself. "You never told me that story before, Norman. That's a splendid story!"

"It wass not at all so splendid for poor Hugh Mackay afterwards," said the tailor, "because from that moment poor Hugh had no peace from the slaugh, no peace at all, at all. He would be sitting quietly in the corner at a ceilidh in somebody's house and all of a sudden he would call out that they were coming for him, and there would be a kind of whistling sound at the door and Hugh would get up to go to the door and open it, and he would be finding himself taken now to the Lews, now to Achiltibuie, now to Tongue, now, oh, there wass no saying where the slaugh would be carrying him. Once the people tried to hold him back, but he could not stay, and though it was a quiet clear night of frost the door came in as with a great wind and nobody could close it until Hugh wass gone. And I'm thinking that wass the time the slaugh took him to Eilean a' Chille, which is one of the Shiel Islands, and he wass found there by the lobster fishermen, who brought him to Gairloch. Och, he had a terrible life, poor Hugh. It wass well known what a terrible life he had with the slaugh. He never knew at all when they would be coming for him."

"Most interesting, most interesting," Maclean Sanders bubbled. "Were you ever on the Shiel Islands, Norman?"

"No, I wass never there. They say they are beautiful islands. Plenty fish, plenty birds, and very good grazing for sheep."

"In this light they might be St Brendan's Isle," Maclean Sanders murmured, gazing southward.

"Or the lost Brasil," John added.

"Or Antilia or St Atanagio or Avalon," said Maclean Sanders.

"Royllo, Tanmar, or Asmaide," John capped.

"You're interested in Atlantis, eh?" Maclean Sanders asked.

John expounded his theory of Celticism.

"You may be right, you know. It would account for a great deal which is not easily accounted for," Maclean Sanders allowed. "It would account for our friend Norman."

"Och, it takes a second deluge to account for me, does it?" the tailor chuckled. "My old mother used to be saying it wass whisky not water which wass accounting for me whatever. I'd like to have a crack with the Reverend Hector Mackenzie about the lost Atlantis. He's very strong on the deluge is the Reverend Hector. A sermon by the Reverend Hector on the deluge is better than a visit to the Zoological Gardens in Edinburgh."

"On the other hand, if, as the Atlantis believers aver, the remains of the population were to be found among the Basques or the guanches of the Canary Islands, how shall we establish a kinship between them and our Iberians?" Maclean Sanders queried.

"Obviously we can't," John replied. "Plato puts the destruction of Atlantis nine thousand years ago in his time. And I should imagine that much of the Atlantis legend was confused with Minoan legends. Oh, of course the theory must remain the vaguest speculation, but what I want to insist on is that the habit of mind we call Celtic is not Celtic at all but Iberian, and that even the smallest trace of that strain is likely to assert itself in any individual above all the rest of his origins. We recognize it at once in Norman here."

"I'll be the wild man of Borneo before you have finished with me to-day," the tailor chuckled.

"You and I, Sanders, believe we can detect the influence in ourselves, you through your Maclean grandmother, I through my Macleod great-grandmother and probably in my case more strongly still through my Cornish mother. But you and I may both be kidding ourselves. We may be seeking an escape from contemporary existence through ancestor-worship. That's got to be considered. It may be a form of infantilism. We may be racial Peter Pans disliking the notion of being grown up in this machine age. Oh, look at the Shiel Isles now!" John exclaimed.

The sun's rays had caught the islands at an angle which gave them a clouded blue tralucency and they seemed raised above the horizon by a steely band. For a minute they floated between sky and sea. Then the sun westered further and the islands dissolved into the southerly haze.

"They have stolen my fancy away, those islands," John murmured. "I wonder who owns them."

"They belong to the sluagh," said the hunchbacked tailor. "You can be asking them to give you their islands."

The spiritual elation which uplifted John when the news came from Poland that the Bolshevik armies had been driven back in confusion almost from the very gates of Warsaw, was followed hardly a week later by the most profound spiritual abasement of his life, when in response to Turner Rigden's insistence he left David with the deer and reached Belfast in the middle of an organized attempt by the Orange faction to drive the Nationalist minority out of north-east Ulster. The mob was led by armed Ulster Volunteers of whom the Government was proposing to form a Special Constabulary. Five thousand Catholic workmen were driven out of the shipyards, and now methodically, district by district, the mob, directed and encouraged by authority, was destroying their homes. Refugees from Lisburne and Bangor were pouring into Belfast, only to find a greater horror of human ruthlessness there. Houses were being burned to the ground, women were being murdered, and even children were being flung into the street, with chairs and tables and bedding.

Dear Turner, John wrote,
I cannot do these articles you want. The facts are too bad. The Turks may have behaved with a greater brutality in Armenia, but nothing the Germans did in Belgium to the civil population was any worse than what is happening now in north-east Ulster. If I had the faintest hope that anything I said would do good I would write for you. But to tell the truth and find it disregarded would turn my blood to rennet. I dare not expose myself to a rancour which would ruin my sense of proportion for the rest of my life. Send a junior reporter from the 'Journal' and print his narrative unedited. You will be suspected of trying to blackmail the Government into giving you one of their 'honours', but I do not believe you can impress the ignorant bulk of English opinion, which has been fed for too long now with Sinn Féin outrages. Unless you can convince the English people that there is a war between them and the Irish people, and that these murders by Sinn Féin are courageous acts

*of war and not cowardly assassinations, you cannot do any good.
The moral sense of the average Englishman has been shocked
by the behaviour of Sinn Féin because that behaviour has been
most skilfully presented to him with that precise intention. Tell the
average Englishman that a lorryful of drunken Auxiliary Cadets
wantonly shot a woman and her baby sitting in a garden as they
drove by, and he just won't believe it. Tell him that British
officers in uniform have authorized the torture of prisoners to
extract information, and he won't believe it, he can't believe it.
Tell him that MacCurtain the late Lord Mayor of Cork was
deliberately murdered by British agents, and he won't believe it.
Tell him that the District Inspector who was shot three days
ago in Lisburne was named by a Coroner's jury as one of
three responsible for the murder of the Lord Mayor of Cork and
whose death resulted in the whole Catholic population of Lisburne
being driven out except a few nuns whose convent was protected
against the mob by some generous Protestants, and he won't
believe it. Tell him that most of the individual murders by Sinn
Féin are the executions of Government spies, and he won't believe
it. Tell him that thousands of pounds' worth of damage is being
done every day by irregulars deliberately employed by the Government to avoid responsibility for acts which might even lead to
the United States breaking off diplomatic relations with this
country, and he won't believe it. Tell him that throughout the
civilized world the name of England is beginning to stink because
of what his Government is doing in Ireland, and he won't believe
it. Tell him that Russian behaviour in Finland, Prussian behaviour in Poland, Austrian behaviour in Italy, Turkish behaviour
in Greece, or German behaviour in Belgium are not considered by
the rest of the world any more cowardly, barbarous, and irrational
than British behaviour in Ireland, and he won't believe it.*

*If I thought any words I wrote would change the heart and
clear the mind of the average Englishman at this moment I
would write them with my own blood, but I do not want to hate
the average Englishman, and hate him I should if I told him the
truth and he paid no heed. What is to come out of the shame
and horror of the Coalition's handling of Ireland I cannot imagine,
but until this bestial folly ceases I must withdraw from any
kind of public life in England. I shall not attend either the
rehearsals or any performance in this country of my new play
until the Coalition Government is either kicked into the cesspool
of past history or repents and makes atonement for what are its*

> *crimes not merely against Ireland but equally against England herself. It is because I know the generosity of the average Englishman that I resent his deception. I know that I cannot undeceive him in his present mood, and therefore I prefer the despairing alternative of not trying to do so.*
>
> *I am going down to Cornwall now. I wish 'The Balloon' success for your sake and for the sake of the cast, but its success or failure will leave me personally indifferent.*

John wrote this letter in the Caledonian Hotel, Edinburgh, where he had gone on his return from Belfast to pick up David on his way south. When he met the train from the North he ran into Maclean Sanders, who pressed him to stay three days until the first meeting of the season of the Scottish Life Society. So he and David hired a car and drove round Angus to explore the Ogilvy country.

"It's a bit tame after Sutherland," David commented.

"You prefer Assynt to Thrums? You think the deer forest a nobler work of man than the kailyard?" John asked his brother.

"I thought Achnalochlannach marvellous. Rigden told me I was to bring up a couple of men with me next autumn, and I shall bring Noll Erpingham and Tom Price-Harley. We're going into digs together next year. We shall get some good heads."

There being no stags to secure in Edinburgh, John persuaded David to accompany him to the meeting of Scottish Life in Maclean Sanders's flat at the top of a grey house in George Street, where he sat in a corner staring at the company with an expression of courteous bewilderment.

"I'm afraid we won't have a very large gathering to-night," said the convener. ". . . So many of our members are still away on their holidays. Still, I think you'll get the atmosphere. We're having potatoes and salt herring half-way through the evening," he added hopefully. "And I brought back a sack of peats with me from Assynt."

Maclean Sanders himself had donned a red Dress Maclean kilt for the occasion.

Indeed, it was not a very large gathering. To be exact, including the convener himself, there were but seven patriots present to hear Mr Robert Nimmo read a paper to the Society on the injustice done to the Picts in not recognizing more fully the major contribution they had made to Scottish culture. In the course of his remarks Mr Nimmo, the thin sandy-haired agent of a suburban branch of the British Linen Bank, was so severe upon the Gaels as Irish invaders that Mrs MacCorquodale, a stout fresh-complex-ioned woman of middle-age with her roots as deep as bonny Mary's in Argyll, swelled throughout the speaker's remarks and had to fan herself with a handkerchief of inadequate size to avert what looked like an impending apoplexy. From time to time she would gasp in a high indignant squeak 'Question!' and every time she registered such a protest Mr Nimmo would look up over his type-written sheets, adjust his prince-nez, and observe in a high-pitched dry cracked voice:

"I will be very happy, very happy indeed, to answer any ques-tions the member desires to put to me when I have finished my observations. Mr Convener, I would be extremely obliged if in the meanwhile you would call the member to order."

At last after three-quarters of an hour of a somewhat reckless overdraft on pre-history Mr Nimmo sat down and, with a glance at the picture of William Wallace over the mantelpiece, coughed his challenge to Mrs MacCorquodale to oppose if she dare the charge of the Picts through the stereotyped tale of Scottish origins.

"The meeting is open to members for any observations they may wish to make," the convener declared. "But first I think we'll draw the curtains." He turned to John, and in a voice darkened by mystery murmured that he had reason to suppose that the English Secret Service had been taking an interest in the proceedings of the Scottish Life Society lately. "And we don't want to make it too easy for them," he added.

At that moment a young man, wearing a kilt of bright light Saxony cloth, beneath which a pair of white knees gleamed above thick stockings turned over twice, and a doublet of brown tweed so heavy as almost to have defied the efforts of the tailor to give it shape, still more to give it cut, appeared among the company. He looked so nervous that John thought he must have been dodging the Secret Service; but what he had really been dodging was Edinburgh street-opinion, which at this date regarded with disgust and amazement, even in the gloaming, the wearer of a kilt who was not on his way to a dance.

"I'm glad Mr MacInnes has joined us," Mrs MacCorquodale panted. "I will leave him to deal with the slanders of Mr Nimmo."

But as Mr Angus MacInnes had not heard Mr Nimmo's display of Pictish chauvinism he begged to be excused and retired to the window-seat, where the draught twitched as wantonly at his kilt as a satyr at the draperies of a nymph.

"Captain MacQueen," Mrs MacCorquodale appealed, and an old gentleman of seventy with a heavy white moustache rose to his feet. The Captain, who had been in a rage with the ingratitude of England ever since his services had been declined for the late war, was in no mood to bother about the Picts. What he wanted to know was when the Scottish Life Society proposed to give up worrying about the past and form itself into a militant society to deal with the present.

"Give me the men," he barked at Mr Nimmo, "and I'm prepared to seize the Castle and hold it. That's what's wanted to-day."

"Hear, hear," cried a pretty rosy-faced young woman from the back of the room. "Captain MacQueen is right. We're just wasting our time, is that not so, Helen Gow?"

"I agree with Jean Cumming," declared a tall dark woman with sombre fanatical eyes. "If you can't get the men, Captain MacQueen," she went on with a contemptuous look at Dr Malcolm Fletcher, Mr James Baird, Mr Robert Nimmo, and the kilt-encumbered Mr Angus MacInnes, "you'll get the women."

"This is very rash and foolish talk," declared Dr Fletcher, who had a good practice in Corstorphine and did not want the reputation of a dangerous rebel.

"It's worse than rash and foolish," said Mr Baird, a dried-up lawyer, "it's unpractical."

"Without going to the lengths advocated by Miss Gow and Miss Cumming," said Mrs MacCorquodale, "I feel it my duty to say that Scottish Life will never survive so long as we hear Scots like Mr Nimmo who are prepared to sneer at our glorious Gaelic heritage. Would Mr Nimmo tell us if the Picts built the Cathedral of Iona, and if it was the Picts who broke the English knights at Bannockburn, and if it was the Picts who routed the Nimmos and the Bairds and the Fletchers at Prestonpans?" Her voice died in a faint squeak of indignation.

"Order! Order!" the convener demanded. "Nobody sympathizes more than I do with Mrs MacCorquodale's Gaelic fervour, but she must not introduce a spirit of faction into Scottish Life. Our beloved country has suffered too much from faction in the unhappy past. The only hope of impressing on the Westminster Government Scotland's desire for independence within the framework of the Empire,—for mark you, we are not going to let go of the Empire we have done more to build up than the English themselves . . ."

"Hear, hear," muttered Dr Fletcher, Mr Baird, and Mr Nimmo,

with the discreet enthusiasm of professional men.

"To hell with the Empire!" cried Jean Cumming passionately. "If we can't save Scotland without bothering about the British Empire . . ."

"Intolerable!" Mr Baird ejaculated through thin lips. "We don't want this kind of Sinn Féin madness in Scottish Life."

"Sinn Féin has fought the English in Ireland," cried Helen Gow, "and Sein Féin is fighting them now."

"We are not Irish," observed Mr Nimmo, tartly. "And I think I may venture to assert that I have demonstrated this evening how little, how comparatively very little we owe to the Dalriadic incursion."

The Maclean in the convener urged him to fling this assertion into the teeth of Mr Robert Nimmo, but the Sanders warned him not to reawaken the memory of old unhappy far-off things and battles long ago. He decided to calm the storm by inviting the guest to address the Society.

David threw an apprehensive look at his brother. He did not think a member of his family ought to be involved in this eccentric dog-fight. John, oblivious of any indiscretion, rose to his feet:

"I have recently had the pleasure of discussing the future of Scotland with your convener, Mr Maclean Sanders, and I need not assure you what an added pleasure it is to meet this evening some of those who have been stirred by a common doubt about the future of our country in the complicated tangle that the European —indeed the world scene presents to the speculative mind.

"There may be superficial disagreement among you at present. Such disagreement is inevitable when people inspired by discontent with what is and with dismay over what the future may bring first get together and try to put their ideas in order. What seems to me more important than the superficial disagreement is the fundamental agreement that must exist to bring you together at all in a society like this. I am not enough of an archaeologist to argue with the author of that most interesting paper we heard whether the Picts played as important a part as he maintains. Mr Nimmo must forgive me if I say that it seems to me an academic rather than a practical question. What cannot be denied is that the fusion of various races has produced a nation marked by an unmistakeable, an almost aggressive personality of its own. And what I want to know, and what the rest of the world will want to know, is whether that personality has enough confidence in itself to stand alone in the future or whether it will be satisfied with the provincial status into which it is declining.

"I believe I am right in assuming that Captain MacQueen and Miss Cumming and Miss Gow on the one side would agree with Mr Nimmo, Mr Baird, and Dr Fletcher on the other that such a provincial decline is not merely imminent but has already been in process for a number of years."

This statement was received with murmurs of approbation from every part of the room.

"I am not, I am ashamed to confess, sufficiently intimate with the Scottish life of to-day which your Society expresses in its name to know what chance of success such a determined line of action as that advocated by Captain MacQueen would have in rousing the country in general to a consciousness of its gradual Anglicization."

"None whatever," Mr Baird interposed sharply.

"Well, I am not going to argue about that, but I cannot refrain from pointing out the effect of the Easter Rising in Ireland, though at the same time I will admit without qualification that it was only the stupidity of the military authorities which by a series of executions roused the great mass of the Irish people to approve what those young patriots did. At the risk of being considered timorous by Miss Cumming and Miss Gow I shall venture to express my opinion that any violent action at present would almost certainly be premature in Scotland and, though God knows there seems no limit to the stupidity of the official and governmental mind, I cannot believe that it would extend so far as to take too seriously an attempt to seize Edinburgh Castle. What I fear is that such an attempt might be killed by ridicule—at present. What might be the success of such an attempt a few years hence or even a few months hence when the national idea has had time to make itself known as a potentially active force is another matter. And here let me say at once that I should set no bounds to the independence which Scotland has the right, and indeed, if Scotland is to live, the duty to claim. And to such an independence as I am imagining I fancy that the serious opposition will come not so much from England as from Scotland itself.

"The lesson of the war to me has been that rival imperialisms must end by destroying one another and that the future happiness and peace of the world depends on the break up of those imperialisms, be they British or German or French or American. We shall most of us agree that a United States of Europe is a desirable Utopia of the future, but I can only envisage the possibility of such an Utopia when what are called Great Powers have ceased to exist.

You had a good example of power politics the other day when the British Empire claimed five times as many votes in the League of Nations as the United States of America. There can be no domination of an association like the League of Nations if such an association is to function naturally and not artificially.

"I think that a commonwealth of British nations might set the rest of the world a great example provided that as such independence were secured by Scotland, Ireland, and Wales within that commonwealth as has been secured by Australia and Canada, and if at the same time such a commonwealth turned its back on Europe. When Mr Maclean Sanders demands independence for Scotland within the framework of the Empire he seems to me to be introducing what he must forgive my calling a pusillanimous qualification. The only logical demand I can see is absolute independence. Whether such an independence will elect to remain within the Empire should be the choice of a sovereign nation and will presumably depend on how far the framework of the Empire fits in with Scottish aspirations. Scotland might prefer to join a Scandinavian federation, and there should be no question of a conditional independence subject to a previous pledge to remain within the Empire.

"As I see the impulse which has led to a recreated Poland and a reconstructed Czechoslovakia, it is due to the feeling of smaller nations that they were being submerged under imperialisms. It is basically the assertion of the individual's right to freedom, and his refusal to yield to the tendency of this age which demands the sacrifice of the parts to the attempted perfection of the whole. I believe myself that we are in the throes of a great evolutionary movement, and that we are in danger of denying our birthright as human beings. I don't want to go to the emmet! I don't want human society to emulate the ant and the bee and the termite. But I'm under no delusion about the strength of the movement in that direction. I readily recognize that nations like Ireland or individuals like myself may be in the fullest sense of the word reactionary, and that we may be overwhelmed by the forces moving in the contrary direction. It seems to me that the trend towards cities and city life which is universally apparent is a sign of humanity's surrender to the advantage of the swarm, and should Ireland gain her freedom it will be interesting to see how successful she will be in withstanding urbanization. When we talk of the Anglicization of Scotland we do not mean that. We mean the Londification of Scotland. Every complaint you hear in Scotland could be matched by similar complaints in Yorkshire or Devon-shire. It is the city of London which is sapping the life-blood of this island, north and south, east and west. Naturally, if the trend is toward cities, then the greatest city in the world will grow greater out of such a trend. It is even doubtful whether if Scotland regained her independence she could support two large cities like Edinburgh and Glasgow within fifty miles of one another. Their existence may prove an inseparable ban to a prosperous indepen-dence. I do not myself think the political independence of any small country is worth achievement unless such a country be willing to endure the sacrifices necessary to make itself economically inde-pendent as well. I do not see at present any signs of such willing-ness in Scotland. There is discontent at industry's inclination to move southward, but that is not enough to save a nation's soul.

"The Irish are not enduring their present misery because Dublin manufacturers have moved to London. They are animated by an idea. They are determined, whatever the cost, to lead their own life. Is that determination evident in the Scotland of to-day? You can answer that question better than I, and I believe you will have to answer it at present with a negative. If I may say so, the argument we heard earlier this evening about the Picts was a sign of uncertainty and hesitation. I cannot believe that so much fervour would be spent on an academic question if the practical question were urgently insistent upon an answer.

"Prophecy may be dangerous, but I feel no danger in prophesy-ing a growth of industrial discontent in Scotland right through this decade, and indeed right through England except at the centre. London will always prosper. Now, any unemployed man is a menace to the security of what is, because he has so much time on his hands in which to speculate whether what is is quite so good as what might be. I see no prospect of ending unemployment under the system of London First, but I do see a possibility of grappling with the problem if we can escape from the domination of the whole country by London. And I believe that if Scotland showed the way many parts of England would follow the example. I think it is a waste of fervour to talk so much about Anglicization. In fact the east of Scotland is much nearer in point of view and temperament to the north-east of England than it is to the west of Scotland. We have made a mistake in stressing the polarity of the north and south in this island. The true opposition is between west and east. Why, you can even see it in the opposition between Lancashire and Yorkshire. In the south of England they look upon it as a local rivalry, but the difference between Manchester and Leeds is almost as sharp as between Glasgow and Edinburgh. And the problem for an independent Scotland will be whether Glasgow or Edinburgh is to be the spiritual capital. One or the other must take the lead. I would make Perth the technical capital and solve the rivalry that way. You may say I'm anticipating, but there is no use working for the independence of Scotland unless you have a clear notion of what you aim to effect with such independence. Mr Nimmo's indignation about the neglect of the Pictish influence was, if he will let me call it so, a romanticization of the East's grievance against the West. It was another version of Martha's complaint against Mary. I am an Ogilvie and East on one side, a Macleod and West on another; but I am also half Cornish and therefore the West dominates my temperament. I offer this explanation because I am going to make an assertion which Mr Nimmo will challenge. I am going to assert that the major disaster of Scottish history was when the Lord of the Isles and the western clans were defeated at Harlaw. When the power of the Lord of the Isles was broken the natural links between Ireland and at least half of Scotland were broken. The internal history of Scotland ever afterwards was the desperate struggle of the West to preserve itself against the influence of the East.

"It is customary to refer slightingly nowadays to Jacobitism as a form of sentimentality. The inspiration of Jacobitism was not personal devotion to the Stuarts, but the longing for a way of thought and action which had been destroyed and to recover which the Stuarts afforded the only chance. The Stuarts were the expression of an idea, and at this moment young men in Ireland are going about in battered Trilby hats and stained Burberrys shooting earnest British officials in trams and through windows. Tell any of them that he is inspired by Jacobitism, and I believe he'd waste a precious bullet on the man that so insulted his sense of the fact. Nevertheless, the spiritual kin of these young Irishmen of to-day are the men who fought at Prestonpans and Falkirk and Culloden.

"I'll be frank and confess that I cannot feel passionately anxious to restore the independence of Scotland in the interests of some industry threatened by English competition. I have no confidence in the ability of the Scottish character to resist the greed and avarice which are believed to be dignified by calling them thrifty. I have seen too much of the ways of Scottish Big Business men and Scottish bureaucrats during the war to have the faintest desire to entrust such men with the direction of a country. I have no ambition to help in the re-creation of a Scotland which will preserve all that was worst in what I believe to have been the disastrous nineteenth century. I want to see an independent Scotland which will lead a social revolution and show the way of salvation to England. However, I am not proposing to inflict on you to-night an exposition of plans for the future which are not yet fully shaped.

"Last week I was in Belfast. It was a terrifying experience. I do not mean terrifying in the physical sense. I was far too much terrified spiritually to worry in the least whether some Orange fanatic was going to hit me on the head with a paving-stone. The horror I felt was the revelation of the extremes to which vested interests would go in defence of those interests, for this hideous mob had been deliberately incited by the acknowledged leaders of Northern Ireland. You have to face a similar state of affairs in Scotland if vested interests here should feel themselves seriously threatened. And they will not hesitate to stir up the dark foul depths of human nature if they believe it suits their purpose. The same material exists both in Glasgow and in Edinburgh. Therefore, if I may make a suggestion, a Society like this which gathers together people who are perplexed and perturbed over the future of their country should continuously stress the agreement not the differences of Scottish life.

"I had not meant to talk at such length, but you must forgive me and attribute it to the exciting effect of finding myself in this room among a few people who, though they be prepared to come to blows over those elusive fellows the Picts, are united at heart by that divine discontent which is the foundation of all the greatest edifices of the human mind."

"Well, David, what did you think of the evening?" John asked his brother as they made their way back along Princes Street toward the Caledonian Hotel.

"I thought they were rather a queer lot of birds. Almost mad, some of them."

"You didn't feel any response to that divine discontent I mentioned?"

"I'm rather bored with politics. We have an awful lot of political jabbering at Oxford. All these fellows who were in the war and came up later. One feels rather out of it with a man who went through the war and is five or six years older than one-self, although he may be the same year. I didn't realize *you* were particularly interested in politics till I heard you spouting away to those birds this evening."

"There's a pretty muddled world in front of us all," John reminded his brother. "I doubt if any of us can afford to take no interest in politics."

"But it's always the same old ramp, isn't it? Promising a lot of things you don't believe there's the slightest chance of giving, and then doing it all over again at the next election."

"You're thinking that is a proof of what I say. If you've come to regard politics and politicians in that way, it's about time we thought seriously of making them something better than a ramp, something more than a game."

David gave a vague assent to this proposition, but it was clear to his elder brother that he was unimpressed by the necessity, and John asked him when he intended to start keeping his terms at the Inner Temple.

"I'm going to start eating my dinners next vac."

"Are you really keen on the Bar?"

"Not frightfully, but it seems the obvious thing for me to do."

"Why not be a stalker—I mean a professional gamekeeper?" John asked.

David stopped under a lamp-post in Princes Street and looked anxiously at his brother.

"I'm serious, David. You are keen on stalking?"

"Of course I am."

"Well, then, why not become a professional? It seems to me a much better way of spending one's life than going to the Bar merely because it seems the obvious thing to do."

"You really are a weird bird, John. How on earth could I seriously announce to Mr Justice Ogilvie that I was going to take up stalking as a profession? He'd think I was mad. And in fact I would be if I did seriously propose doing that."

"I should think you sane."

"You'd be the only person who did."

"Isn't the real thing that's the matter with modern life the way most of us treat it as a mskeshift?"

"I'm afraid I don't get you," said David; and John noticed the same courteous bewilderment in his expression that he had noticed on it when he saw the members of the Scottish Life Society.

"Well, I'm one of the lucky ones," John explained. "I wanted to write plays and I had success before I was thirty. Indeed, I had too easy a success, and I'm running the risk now of following the easiest way of success. It is true I might write plays of another kind, but once you've tasted success as a popular playwright it is very difficult to write another kind of play which you know can't be popular, won't even be produced perhaps."

"But what's the point of writing another kind of play?" David asked as they reached the hotel and walked along to the smoking-room for a drink.

"The point is that in such a play one would try to express oneself, or at any rate one's ideas."

"Not the sort of ideas you were spouting about tonight?" David asked a little anxiously.

"Possibly."

"I don't think you'd get a theatre audience to be interested in that sort of talk," David said. "I expect it was very interesting for those queer birds we saw . . . what a frightful kilt that fellow was wearing, and, my god, his stockings rolled over and over as if he was wrapped in bandages!"

"All right, we'll agree a theatre audience would be bored. That's the point. Therefore I say find another kind of audience. I want something difficult to do."

"Just looking for trouble," David grinned, as he picked up his whisky.

"Yes, if you like, but the point is I'll still be doing something I definitely want to do. What I don't understand is going to the Bar not because you particularly want to go to the Bar, but because it's the obvious thing to do. How are you going to get the full flavour of life from that?"

"I'm not going to be in chambers all the time. One great advantage of the Bar is that you get a reasonable amount of vacation. I shall go up to Scotland every autumn for my stalking."

"Which means that you'll give the best of yourself to your sport instead of to your work," John observed.

"What of it? Isn't that what most people do?"

"But suppose you had no vacations? Suppose you had to spend the whole of your time in your chambers or in the courts?"

"Well, of course that would be pretty bloody."

"The vast majority of human beings have to spend all their time working at work which doesn't interest them," John pointed out. "And this means that the vast majority of human beings pass through this life dissatisfied. Perhaps in time, when man has learnt to make machinery his slave instead of surrendering to it as his master and handing it over to the elemental powers of evil, that will change. But what depresses me is to find somebody like yourself with the opportunity to choose work that he wants to do, choosing the line of least resistance as meekly as some poor devil of a scholar who has to take a job as an usher because the economic struggle compels him to assure himself and his dependents a livelihood."

"Well, what is one to do?" David asked.

John shook his head gloomily. Now that the war was over and it was no longer the duty of every young man to regard his life as a brief prelude to death, young men did not know what to do with their lives. Probably it was symptomatic of the lowered vitality caused by spending the critical years of adolescence in a period of unnatural strain. No doubt a younger generation would recover that vitality. Nevertheless, it was a grim look-out for the next decade.

"I'm sorry, David. I'm afraid you've had rather a tiresome evening."

"No, I haven't. I was thinking most of the time about Achnalochlannach and about going up next year with Noll Erpingham and Tom Harley."

"I jolly well know that if I felt like that about stalking I'd devote my life to it."

"Ah, but then one might get bored with it," David pointed out, with the wisdom of one who has experienced the pitfalls of pleasure.

"Perhaps you'll find when you start that you are just as keen on your profession as Sir Alexander or your mother's father. He was a wonderful old boy. I learnt a good deal from him."

"Noll Erpingham thinks of taking his duties as a hereditary legislator seriously," David said encouragingly, as if thereby he would reassure his brother that the younger generation was not entirely flippant. "And Tom Harley's going into banking. He's a bit bored by that. But of course it's a family duty. Well, I've had a marvellous time, John, up in Assynt. It was awfully good of you to think of taking me up."

"What are you doing for the rest of the vac?"

"I hope to do some execution with Noll Erpingham's partridges

in Norfolk next month, and then in the first week of October he
and I are going to the Harleys in Somerset for one good bang at
the pheasants before term."

The full moon of harvest was clear of the autumnal mists in
which she had been seen like a ripe golden fruit of earth. Through
the uncurtained window of Athene's room the silver air streamed
in, and with it the sharp scent of the geranium leaves. It was
hardly ten o'clock yet. John was sitting on the edge of the bed,
talking to her before he went back to the wood-fire and the lamp-
light of the sitting-room to wrestle with Spengler's *Untergang des
Abendlandes*, which Ostápov had pressed upon his attention in
Citrano last year as the most significant recent exposition of the
German mind.

With his return to Nanphant and the recovery of the deep
intimate peace of married life with Athene, John had found that
the harsher force of the west wind had quickly died down again
to a zephyr.

"Athene, I'm in danger of becoming uxorious," he declared
abruptly, after he had been contemplating in silence for a minute
or two the glow of her warmth amid the cold moonshine. "I'm
too happy with you."

"I'm glad you're happy," she murmured, her hand seeking his.

"And I'm not going to leave you again before January. I told
Rigden they must get *The Balloon* produced without my spectral
presence among the dust-wrappings of the stalls."

"But don't you think you ought to go, darling?"

"No need at all. Lucas is a good producer. I went through
everything with him. If it's a success we'll go and see it together
after the great event. Two years ago in September! And the
pair of us wondering how long it would be before we were together.
And next month we'll have been married a year. I think Arthur's
enjoying himself in Cornwall, don't you?"

"My dear, he's having a perfectly wonderful time."

"There's this business of school. You're still set on that?"

"Oh yes, John. Your notion of teaching him is all very fine,
but I think Arthur was meant for school."

"All right, then, in another ten days I'll take him along to

Hampden House. Poor lad, he'll probably loathe his first term at an English prep-school. However . . ."

"It won't hurt him at all to loathe it," Athene declared firmly.

"And David's housemaster will have him in September, 1924. It's good for him, because there's a terrific run on Eton now. I'm afraid we're giving Arthur some difficult times. Of course he'll be quite happy at Eton after four years at Hampden House, but then four or five years later he'll have to face Harvard with an English education. Another ordeal."

"Ordeals are good for people," she insisted. "And if the time ahead for young people is going to be as difficult as you expect, the more ordeals with which Arthur is provided in preparation for it the better."

"And I used to think you so unduly agitated over Arthur," John said.

"That was because I expected to have to battle for him. The responsibility is entirely my own now. You don't know what it means to have as the only link with somebody you don't love a child you love and who is half that somebody you don't love."

"But he is still Wacey's son."

"Yes, but I can no longer hurt Wacey by being severe with Arthur for what Wacey used to think were signs of himself in Arthur. That's what used to make me seem agitated. I was leading an artificial life with Wacey, and I dreaded lest the effect of it should be an equally artificial life with Arthur. He seemed in a way so much more my responsibility because I did not love his father, and yet I could never assert that responsibility without exposing myself to an emotional appeal from Wacey, who seemed to spend all his time watching for such opportunities. You see, John, I'd made a mistake, but it was made, and for the sake of Arthur chiefly the pretence that I had not made a mistake had to be kept up. It was not until something Wacey did relieved me from pretending any more, that I could see a clear way through life."

"You've never told me yet what that something was."

"Darling, I so hate to think about it. It was so utterly humiliating." She hesitated a moment. Then she told him about her discovery on the night he had come back from Greece three years ago. "But don't let's talk about it ever again," she begged.

"What a critical year 1917 was in our two lives," John said. "I begin to grow apprehensive of such happiness, my Athene. It has an almost narcotic quality. Sitting here with you in this moonshiny room I feel withdrawn from the restless world and begin to fear some wakening shock. I hope everything will be all right in January."

"Foolish one, why shouldn't it be? It is not even my first child."

He bent over to kiss her, seeking reassurance from the warmth of her breast, and the perfume of her tossing rich brown hair.

"When I was at that queer gathering in Edinburgh I was vaguely disquieted by the thought that it was my duty to fling myself into the middle of that political movement instead of surrendering so completely to the contentment of my life with you, with no responsibility except to provide entertainment for the public at a highly remunerative figure. I suppose the fatigue of one's excessive action is beginning to pass. I thought of Edward Fitzgerald, who could be happy with his wife and his boy as a country doctor, willing to give his life for a passionate cause. I thought of Emil Stern, who has a charming wife and who expects a child this autumn, risking not his life but his career and perhaps his liberty for another passionate cause. It is true I can claim that what I did in Greece has borne fruit and that it was not entirely sterile action. Nevertheless, I began to think it was not enough for a time in which the world is as it were deciding which way it will turn for the fulfilment of its evolution. And now back with you I feel no more interest in that queer group of people than my younger brother David. That's why I exclaimed just now I was in danger of growing uxorious."

"John darling, you're not trying to tell me that our life together is standing in your way? I wouldn't have that happen for anything I can think of."

"No, no," he assured her, "what I am trying to tell you is that if I were to decide to involve myself actively in politics it would not mean that I was tiring of our life together but that I was being driven by what I'll have to call an impulse of duty. I hope I won't be. I am only forewarning you in case it happens."

"My dear, I hope I'm too sensible to torment myself by looking for wrong reasons. Don't forget I had a difficult year in which I learnt something about you in separation. And don't forget, above all, that I love you not as a possession but as a part of yourself."

"You always understand," he murmured. "And now I'll go back to Spengler's turgid German and leave you to sleep. Shall I pull the curtains?"

"No, leave me the moonshine and the sweet garden scents, precious one."

In the third week of September John left Arthur at Hampden House, an agreeable private school in the Gloucestershire high land. The boy's chin was jutting out suspiciously, when the moment of farewell came.

"I'll see that Tea gets plenty of exercise," John promised.

"That's what Grandpa Gilmer promised when I went to say good-bye to Cawffee," Arthur muttered gloomily. "I guess I'll soon have ponies left with other people all over the world."

"I know. It's rotten for you," said John, and tore himself away. These first disillusionments of boyhood!

In October came the news from Greece that the young King had died from blood-poisoning after being bitten by a pet monkey. John knew the effect such an uncanny death would have upon the Greek people. When Prince Paul refused the throne he expected that the Liberals would be defeated at the General Election, but he was not prepared for the completeness of that defeat, and the news of it took from him the faint hope he had cherished that those months in Greece had contributed something toward a valuable political achievement.

The fact that *The Balloon* looked like being as great a success as *All Or Nothing* and that it was to be produced in America almost immediately seemed utterly unimportant beside the news of the Greek fiasco. Venizelos would no doubt retire with dignity from the country he had built up in the teeth of jealousy, malice, and obstinacy; but whither would folly lead the Greeks? They had undertaken to hold Turkey to the obligations of the treaty and they had large commitments now which only a political genius like Venizelos was capable of leading them to fulfil successfully.

John's thoughts turned from the louring scene in the Eastern Mediterranean to the horrors which not even the most careful editing of the news from Ireland could hide. He had had no word from Fitz for several months, and he had feared to embarrass the house beside Caragh by writing for news of him. He wished now that he had gone southward from Belfast instead of allowing himself to be deterred by the degradation he had felt in himself at the bestiality of the Orange mobs. Yet he might have done more harm than good by trying to find his friend. And as for writing anything in the press, it was useless. The propaganda of the Government had been so successful in convincing the people of Britain that the war for Irish independence was in effect a campaign by the forces of law and order to punish a number of cold-hearted murderers that reason had deserted all except a few humanitarians, who signed joint letters of protest to the press against the Government's methods and were derided as sentimentalists by the majority.

Early in November John had to go up to London to see Gosnell about the American production of *The Balloon* and left his club in disgust at the approval most of the members awarded to a speech by Lloyd George at the Lord Mayor's banquet, in which, after giving his opinion that Bolshevism was a passing phase of thought that called for sympathetic treatment from ourselves to save Russia from anarchy, he boasted that the Government had murder by the throat in Ireland.

"I think these speeches Asquith is making are preposterous," one member grumbled. "Of course, he's had a grudge against Lloyd George ever since December 1916. It's just encouraging these Irish blackguards."

"Why should the advice of a sane statesman be considered preposterous?" John asked.

"Sane?" scoffed another member. "You think it's sane to talk of surrendering to these criminals?"

"And at a moment when, as Lloyd George said last night at the Mansion House, there is every prospect of suppressing these murderers for good," commented another.

"By the way," said the member who had spoken first, "I was surprised by the verdict in that poison case in Wales. However, the jury found him not guilty."

"Moreover," said John, "Harold Greenwood—I must be careful to distinguish him from Hamar Greenwood—had a fair trial. Harold Greenwood was not tortured by these filthy Black and Tans to extract his evidence."

"These wild assertions," protested one of the members.

John looked at his fellow members who were taking part in this conversation. Two of them were distinguished Civil Servants. Another was a successful barrister. A fourth was a fashionable surgeon. The fifth was a banker. It was a completely representative expression of London opinion. They were cultivated and charming men of the world such as are to be found in a higher

proportion at a good London club than perhaps anywhere on earth.
Individually John admired and liked every one of them, but at
this moment he found the conglomeration of their idiotic opinions
unbearable, and walked out of the club where he had intended to
dine.   He decided to go instead to Belanger's Soho restaurant,
wishing suddenly that James Yarrow was in London that they
might rail together over a bottle of good claret at the Coalition
Government.   However, James Yarrow was still wandering about
Asia.

As John was passing the Monico he saw coming along the
pavement towards him with a drunken gait a figure in a khaki
coat and dark breeches wearing a limp Balmoral bonnet.   Each
of its hands was on a holster, though once it raised one of them to
sweep a woman out of its path.   The face of this figure had the
dank pallor of the drunken man who does not know how long he
will hold his vomit.   The mouth was squirming like a turned-up
worm.   The glazed beady eyes were trying to fix the passers-by
with a fiery glare.   Was it a Black and Tan, or was it an Auxiliary
Cadet, one of those ex-officers chosen for gallantry on the field
to earn a pound a day for terrorism?

"Who the —— hell are you staring at, you —— bastard?"
the figure demanded and, with a sweep of the hand from the hostler
it guarded, pushed John into the gutter.   He stepped back and
hit the figure, by luck, for he was no boxer, hard under the chin.
It collapsed on the pavement.   A crowd gathered.   A policeman
stepped up.

"You saw that swine push me off the pavement?" John
challenged.

"That's all right, sir.   I'll take your name and address, though."

He took out his pocket-book, saying in a low voice as he did
so, "I wouldn't worry myself about this.   I don't think you'll
hear any more about it.   We've had trouble before with these
fellows on leave from Ireland.   You'd better move along, sir.   I'll
see to him."

John slipped his hand into his pocket and walked on down
Shaftesbury Avenue.

"Have you got any peroxide, Bélanger?   I've just hit something
pretty foul," he said to the restaurant-keeper.

After the peroxide Bélanger brought John a bottle of Château
Léoville which he insisted was upon the house to commemorate
the fact that John had dined with him on Armistice Day.

"Yes, yes, of course to-morrow is the second anniversary.   And the body of the Unknown Warrior is waiting at Victoria Station for its funeral to-morrow," John said. "Admirals of the Fleet and Field-Marshals for its pall-bearers and the King for its chief mourner."

"It was a very fine idea," said the patron. "I think we shall do the same in France. It is very poetic, you know."

"*Si, si molto molto commovente*," the waiter agreed, "*son sicuro che noi altri Italiani faremo tale quale.*"

Just over a week ago the body of Terence MacSwiney, the Lord Mayor of Cork who had died in Brixton Jail on the seventy-fourth day of his hunger strike, had been taken to Euston from the Roman Catholic Cathedral in Southwark. Irish Volunteers wearing the proscribed uniform had formed a Guard of Honour. The coffin was draped with the Republican tricolour. The people of London, the decent kindly magnanimous people of London, had watched the procession with reverence and compassion, and then all the value of that gesture from the people of London was destroyed by the action of the Government, which refused to allow the coffin to be carried through Dublin but shipped it direct to Cork, and what was worse, ordered that the brothers and sisters of the dead patriot should be removed from the train by force and led aboard after the coffin like criminals. And on the day following the funeral of Terence MacSwiney the Government had hanged Kevin Barry, a university student of eighteen who had been captured from an ambush in which a British soldier had been shot. There was no evidence that Kevin Barry had fired the shot, but he was the only prisoner taken. J. H. Thomas had tried to save his life, reading to the House of Commons an affidavit of the boy taken after his sentence of death had been confirmed, of his torture by the two officers and three sergeants while one of the Dublin Castle bureaucrats asked him the names of his companions in the ambush with the promise that if he answered his sentence should be repealed. He had not answered, and had been hanged at dawn, in Mountjoy Jail. And during the week that followed ex-officers decorated for valour on the field like that besotted scavenger outside the Monico had killed a couple of women and a baby in arms and a little girl. The adjournment of the House of Commons had been moved to call attention to the policy of frightfulness being pursued in Ireland, but the motion had been rejected. There was no general desire for self-enlightenment among those who were running the country. They had murder by the throat. The Prime Minister and the common hangman were enjoying the popularity of a double-turn on the vaudeville stage.

"You do not like the Léoville?" Bélanger came up to enquire anxiously.

"It's a grand wine, but I have the *cafard* with me to-night," John replied.

"Your hand hurts you, yes?"

"I wish it hurt more. It would mean I had hit harder."

Bélanger filled John's glass solicitously.

"*C'est dommage que Monsieur Yarrow n'est pas ici ce soir.* He would know how he could make you feel gay."

When dinner was over John had an inspiration. He would call on the Hanshaws. He had not seen them for a long time now. Maudie and Ethel were both married. There would be only the old people at home, and perhaps Charlie. He called a taxi and drove to Willow Crescent, Camberwell. The door was opened by the tombstone-maker himself.

"Why, it's Mr Ogilvie! Come in, come in. The missus is snoozing by the fire. Charlie's out at the pictures. So we're all alone. I miss those girls of mine. They made a lot of noise, but it kept the place lively. After Maudie, Ethel's going to make me a grandfather now."

"Their husbands are still in good jobs?"

"Yes, Bert and Maudie have a nice little house in Balham, and Syd and Ethel have rooms in Brixton, but they're hoping to get a house soon. She's coming here to have the baby."

They had entered the snug little sitting-room by now, where Mrs Hanshaw was asleep in an armchair.

"Wake up, Ma. Here's Mr Ogilvie come to pay you a visit."

"If you aren't the limit, Fred," his wife protested in the confusion of the suddenly awakened slumberer. "Fancy letting callers come in and catch me like this."

"You go and draw a jug of ale," Fred told her. "That'll give her a chance to titivate," he muttered to John, with a wink.

John asked how business was, as they made themselves comfortable by the fireside.

"Well, it's been better than what I expected," the tombstone-maker admitted. "Whether it is that people like to be able to bury them they've lost at home after losing so many in the war, or whether it's the boom, or whether a lot of old folk have gone quicker from the strain of the war I don't know, but there's no denying business has been better than what I expected. Will the boom last, though? I doubt it. Doubt it very much I do."

"It depends on the banks," John said.

"On the banks?"

"And of course high finance all round. I hear they're out to stop what they call squandermania. It would not suit high finance if this country became self-supporting. From what I hear, the banks, which have taken advantage of the war to form large amalgamations and thus deprive the smaller banks of an independent policy that might run counter to general policy, are determined to make money difficult to get hold of for the small man. To put it shortly: they are proposing to bleed the country into a state of submission. Yes, I'm afraid your doubts about the boom's lasting are well founded, Mr Hanshaw."

"Ah, I thought it was too good to last."

"You lamented to me once the way the small business was already being put out of action by big combines. That suppression of the small business will be quickened up. The small business is a nuisance, Mr Hanshaw. It makes prices difficult to regulate. It fosters a spirit of independence which is not desired. It holds up national progress. Worst of all, it encourages good workmanship, and that is bad for trade. It is better for trade to build houses that will soon fall down, make clothes that will wear out in a year, put cars on the road that will come to pieces in two or three years. Change, change, change. In another twenty years, perhaps in much less time, it will spoil custom to tell a prospective purchaser that an article will last him a lifetime."

"I believe you're right, Mr Ogilvie. That's the way of it already. And it'll grow worse. Look at my boy Charlie. He's already on at me because he says my methods are old-fashioned. 'People like something a bit more showy and up-to-date even on a tombstone, Dad,' he'll say to me. And of course I'm not equipped to compete with that sort of thing. Ah well, I suppose it'll end in me selling the business to a bigger business, and Charlie'll get a job on the staff, and I'll take to playing bowls in Kennington Park of a summer evening."

Mrs Hanshaw had set down the tray with a jug of ale and glasses.

"And even beer isn't what it was," the tombstone-maker continued. "This is as good a draught ale as you'll get nowadays, but lumme, if my old father had have been offered a glass of this he'd have thought . . ."

"Fred," his wife interrupted sharply, "don't you go getting coarse now."

Mr Hanshaw grinned. There was evidently a familiar comparison for what his father would have thought wrong with the ale.

"He'd have thought it had been watered," he declared, with a tremendous wink at John.

"What terrible things have been happening lately," Mrs Hanshaw said. "That poor fellow who wouldn't eat in the Prison at Brixton. I didn't see his coffin pass myself, but where our Ethel lives she saw it all. They felt quite upset about it round Brixton."

"Bad job. A very bad job," Mr Hanshaw averred, knocking out his pipe on the top bar of the grate to emphasize his opinion. "By my way of looking at it he'd shown himself very sincere in what he was doing and I reckon the Government made a big mistake when they let him die. And in fact I reckon the whole of this Irish business is a big mistake. I pay a lot of attention to what Mr Asquith says. They laughed at him of course and called him 'Old Wait and See', but I reckon the present Government could do with a bit of wait and see."

"I'm afraid I can't quite agree with you there," John said. "Think we've trusted too much to 'wait and see.' Indeed I think if Mr Asquith had taken a bolder line over Home Rule just before the war we might have been spared the present disgraceful state of affairs in Ireland. I daresay you may think the Irish are entirely in the wrong, but you see, the papers over here suppress almost all the outrages the Government forces commit."

"Oh, I'd made up my mind to that long ago," Mr Hanshaw nodded. "The way I look at it is this. If you tell the Irish to elect members of Parliament, and they elect a lot of people who made it clear beforehand that they didn't intend to take their seats at Westminster, you're in duty bound to pay a bit of attention. The Irish may be right or they may be wrong in wanting to cut loose from us, but if they want to, I can't see what right we've got to try and stop 'em by force."

"I wish the members of my club had as logical a conception of democracy as you, Mr Hanshaw," John said.

"Democracy! That's another word we've heard a lot of talk about the last few years. That means the will of the people must prevail, don't it? Well, I daresay if it did come to a proper barny the will of the people would prevail after a lot of heads had been broken in the prevailing. But as I see it now, the way things are worked, the will of the people only prevails as far as the polling-booth and it doesn't prevail again till the next General Election. That blooming war gave the Government a lot of power because they made it out the more power they had the more patriotic the people were. And once a Government get power they don't let it go so easily. Take this Defence of the Realm Act—this Dora as they call it. She hasn't shed all her petticoats yet, has she? I think people have lost their taste for freedom, I do. I think they like being ordered about and managed. I do really. It becomes a habit. I remember once I was in hospital for an operation and, do you know, I was really sorry to come out. It's a shocking thing to say, but it's true. Yes, I enjoyed being bossed around by nurses and having to be washed and dressed like a blooming kid and go to bed when I was told and eat what I was given on the dot. Ma here'll tell you that when I came out I used to get quite huffy with her if she expected me to do anything for myself. And that's the way they swing it over on our democracy. They get 'em in the habit of being waited on. Oh, I'm not going to argue there isn't a lot of things much better nowadays, and I expect man for man, outside the unemployed, the country's more comfortable than what it used to be. But there's two sides to comfort, and if comfort means we've got to see three million poor devils unemployed to keep us comfortable, well, I don't give much for all this so-called progress. Besides, a lot of it's on the surface. It's like the lettering my boy Charlie would like to use on our headstones. Plenty of cheap gilt and flourishes, but cut shallow. Oh yes, they've pushed the slums out of sight, but they're still there if you go and look for them. Well, we'll see what the future holds. But I'm glad it isn't my job to straighten things up."

"Getting old, aren't you, Fred?" his wife chuckled. Then turning to John she added, "It's a new one to hear Fred think he can't straighten things up."

"Likes to get one in at me, Ma does," Fred remarked, with a benevolent wink.

"Next thing we'll be hearing is that you're not fond of the sound of your own voice," Ma countered. "It's a pity Mr Ogilvie can't give you a job at his theatre."

"I believe I *was* opening my mouth a bit wide," Fred agreed, and lapsed into a meditative silence, puffing away at an old bulldog-pipe which looked like the charred stump of a tree.

John was silent too, his gaze fixed on the glowing scene of caves and forest in the heart of the fire. On the mantelpiece with its tasselled valence a black marble clock ticked comfortably. This was flanked by two vases, both inscribed *A Present from Margate*, both with the same view of the Hoy, and both filled with bunches of honesty in seed. On the wall above hung a large framed photo

graph displaying an extensive view of Kensal Green Cemetery.
On either side were portraits of Mr and Mrs Hanshaw at Margate
just after they were married in 1893, he with a waxed moustache,
she with a headdress of tight curls and both staring with that
expression or lack of it produced by clamping the head in a photo-
grapher's rest to keep it rigid. The mahogany table in the middle
of the room was covered with a thick cloth of crimson serge and
the windows hung with curtains of a darker shade in plush. The
patterns of the carpet and wallpaper were equally florid. A
gaselier of three jets, one of them with an incandescent mantle,
the other two with white porcelain globes, hung from the middle
of an efflorescence of plaster. By all the standards of modern
taste the living-room at 12 Willow Crescent was sombre, stuffy,
and overcrowded with heavy furniture; but it had homeliness and
tranquillity. The people next door were not audible through
grimcrack partitions. Such little traffic as there was outside was
muted by the solid windows. A cat could purr in this room with
that sense of proprietorship and permanence in which a cat delights
and of which the big tabby was at this moment taking full advantage
on the hearth-rug. It was a room intended to make the thought
of home desirable as an abode of peace and shed a balm upon the
busy restless day. To the owners of such a room the notion of
using it as a corridor between the day's work and an evening of
pleasure abroad was an inexplicable perversity of the new age. To
leave it dark and empty for half a dozen evenings in the year when
the pantomime at Drury Lane was visited and the pantomime at the
Metropolitan Theatre, Camberwell, with two or three melodramas
at the Elephant and Castle or the Brixton Theatre, was the utmost
extent of desertion that could be tolerated, except of course for
the annual fortnight at Margate or Ramsgate or Clacton-on-Sea,
when the room was covered with dust-sheets and suffered the
equivalent of a fortnight's death, and the big tabby spent the time
with Mrs Jarvis at Number Sixteen. It was one of thousands of
rooms still left in London in which the spirit of the great city chose
to dwell and diffuse its authentic essence. How long that spirit
would find such rooms to enshrine it was another matter, for
London itself was gradually ceasing to be London in order to become
an immense hotchpotch of sprawling citydom.

"Are you going to see the Unknown Soldier taken to the
Cenotaph to-morrow, Mr Hanshaw?" John asked, pulling himself
out of his reverie.

"I didn't think of it. But you know, Mr Ogilvie, I don't much care for this Cenotaph. It's not my idea of a memorial. But there you are," the tombstone-maker went on. "That only goes to show I'm what my boy Charlie calls me, old-fashioned."

"It's difficult to see what better design could have been used, once they'd made up their minds to use that particular spot for the commemoration of those killed in the war."

Mr Hanshaw looked dubious.

"I don't know," he muttered. "I think I'd have liked an urn on top of a column. It would have seemed more familiar somehow."

"You and your urns!" Mrs Hanshaw exclaimed severely. "If Fred had his way he'd like to fill the cemeteries with urns. I don't like them myself. Senseless things I call them. Give me a nice cross of pink granite."

"There's a lot to be said for a good urn," her husband urged. "Specially if you get the lid a bit on one side and the grave clothes coming out and draping themselves in a nice easy flow round the pediment. But people have turned against urns of late years. I think it's these crematoriums. They've done a lot of damage to the tombstone business. I know one woman who travelled everywhere with her husband's ashes in a black handbag. Kept it on the mantelpiece she did and never went out, not even for a morning's shopping, without this bag. However, they're not going to bury the Unknown Soldier at the Cenotaph. He's to be buried in Westminster Abbey. I wonder who he was."

"And you will have to go on wondering till the Last Day," said Mrs Hanshaw. "Well, we've got to thank the dear Lord we didn't lose our Charlie. There's many a poor soul will be thinking to-morrow it's the funeral of her husband or her son. I think we ought to go, Fred. I think it would show a proper spirit."

"Yes, well, I suppose that's right," her husband agreed.

John went back to his club that night refreshed by his contact with Frederick Hanshaw as by a glass of English ale brewed in the days of its quality. The one or two members left of those who had exasperated him by their assumption that there was no case to be stated for Ireland appeared suddenly effete and ridiculous after that visit to Willow Crescent, Camberwell. It was with something resembling compassion that he said to one of them:

"It has an odd effect to visit the club as I do at long intervals and find everybody saying the same things and ordering the same drinks and reading the papers with the same expression. It's like going to a waxwork show."

"We can't all be successful dramatists and move about the world as we like," snapped the member thus addressed.

"But your minds could move," John commented.

"What an extremely offensive observation, Ogilvie!"

"Was it? Yes, I suppose it was. I apologize. Have a drink."

"No, thanks. I've just ordered myself one," said the member curtly.

"I must keep away from London till this Irish trouble is over," John declared.

"You won't have to keep away very long," said the member. "We intend to make a quick end of it."

"And damn what the rest of the world think, eh?" John asked.

"Why should we bother what the rest of the world thinks about a purely domestic matter?"

"Well, you never know when you want to be good boys again and defend another small nation like Belgium. Still, I expect you'll be safe from disinterested interference in Europe until this Irish business is sufficiently remote to be forgotten."

Next day John went back to Cornwall. The weather was soft, the sky cloudless. The garden of Nanphant was red with Kaffir lilies. Then came a booming sou'wester, veering to the west with driving squalls, and at last blowing icily for two days from the north-west. Then more blue days and the first fat Czarina violets.

"But all weather is equally delicious with you," John told Athene.

In the heart of the mountains above Caragh five men were sitting round the turf fire in a small stone bothy indistinguishable at a short distance from the wild crags among which it was set. The time was near the shutting in of a drear November day, during the whole of which the south-west wind had been driving the rain in dark tattered masses across the waste of rock and bog. Four of the five men were dressed in stained Burberrys and nondescript weather-worn suits. The fifth man was in khaki with the three stars of a captain and the badge of the Duke of Cambridge's Light Infantry.

"I hope to hell it's good news we'll be having," said Edward Fitzgerald. "Go, take a look, Larry, and see if anyone's coming."

Larry Keenan, a sandy-haired boy of eighteen with thin features and a strained expression in his light-blue eyes, rose and went out crouching through the low doorway.

"Devil a sign of anybody," he came back to say.

Fitz bit his nails. His fingers were embrowned by cigarettes as deep as dung. So too were the fingers of his companions.

"I hope for your sakes as well as for my own that it will be good news," said Captain Guy Marlow. "I know just how you poor chaps are feeling."

He spoke in the unemotional tones of a regular officer of the British Army, a neatly-made fair man with a tooth-brush moustache. On his breast was the faded purple and white ribbon of the Military Cross and the brighter ribbons of the three war medals; but his fingers were not less restless than those of the four Irishmen.

"Begod, it's you that's right, Marlow," said Fitz bitterly.

A silence fell upon the company. The dim interior grew duskier. Larry Keenan kicked the turf fire; but it burned sullenly, and presently he lit candles and stuck them on the projections of the rough stone walls.

"For the love of Jesus not three of them," Fitz cried in the frayed tones of utter exasperation.

Larry blew one out, crossing himself.

"You can't avert a bloody omen like that," he was told.

"All right, I'm not superstitious," said Marlow.

"I won't believe they've hanged Peter Shanahan this morning," Fitz burst out. "They were given fair warning at the Castle."

"The Castle may be overruled from London," said Marlow. "And of course one must see their point of view. It would be considered weakness to surrender to the threat of a reprisal. And indeed, let's face up to it: it would be weakness."

"If it were an Auxie or a Tan we held!" Fitz groaned.

"I don't think you'd care for the job of shooting even an Auxiliary in cold blood," Marlow insisted.

"It wouldn't be so bad as this. This is the worst thing I've faced in all my life," Fitz affirmed despairingly. "Still, I don't believe they've hanged Peter Shanahan. I think we'd have heard by now if they had."

Silence fell on the company again, and under the low roof of the bothy, by the light of the two candles flickering in the draughts that pierced the crevices, they felt so close to one another in the wilderness of the mountain-side and the booming wind.

At nine o'clock, after they had eaten a rough meal and drunk some toddy listlessly brewed by Fitz, there came a sharp knock at the door. The four men in Burberrys sprang to their feet, pistols levelled.

"Who's there?"

"Joe Taylor from Brigade Headquarters."

"It's Joe's voice all right," said Larry Keenan.

"Put up the bar," Fitz ordered; but he kept his pistol levelled.

The door opened, and a fair round-faced young fellow came in. He was drenched.

"It's a terrible night, boys," he said, blinking in the candlelight. "And it's terrible news I'm after bringing. They've hanged Peter Shanahan."

From the four Irishmen in the bothy a simultaneous moan rose above the noise of the storm.

"So that's that," said Captain Marlow.

"But you've brought no orders from Brigade Headquarters?" Fitz asked of the newcomer, with a painful eagerness.

"I have that," replied Joe Taylor, digging into the recesses of his clothing, and with a quick look, half anxious, half uneasy, at the English officer he gave Fitzgerald an envelope.

"You'd better have some of this excellent toddy," Marlow suggested to Taylor. "You look as if you'd had a pretty rough journey. Your teeth are chattering, man." He offered a glass.

"God forgive me, Captain. I'd sooner take it from another hand," said Taylor, drawing back.

A big man, Michael Shea, who had returned to his place in the corner and was scowling at the fire, moved along the bench to give Joe Taylor room, and as he did so took the glass from Marlow and gave it to the unwelcome arrival.

Fitz by now had read the fatal order.

"Well, Fitzgerald?" Marlow asked.

"To-morrow morning," he answered, choking.

"Then I think I'll turn in," said Marlow.

"I'll sit up," Fitz decided. "The rest of you get to your beds."

"I think poor Taylor ought to have a chance of drying himself first, Fitzgerald," said Marlow. "And because I'm going to lie down there's no reason to spoil your evening."

"Spoil our evening, Captain?" Larry Keenan called in his high voice. "This is no evening at all for any of us."

And one by one they betook themselves to their beds of dried fern and heather—except Joe who sat over the fire, his clothes steaming, and Fitz who brooded with his head in his hands.

Half an hour later Taylor went to his bed, and Fitz, after blowing out the candles, went back to his brooding. There were no sounds of sleep in the bothy, but the faint crackle of the heather as sleepless men turned over and over persisted long after midnight.

The wind dropped around four o'clock, and by then heavy breathing filled the bothy.

Fitz heard his name called in a low voice, and by the flicker of the blue flames round a fresh piece of turf he saw that Marlow had raised himself upon his elbow.

"It will be best for you all if what you have to do is done before it grows light," said Marlow. "I know how you feel. You will find it easier before it is light. Six o'clock, I think, would be the best time. That gives you another two hours."

Fitz groaned to himself.

"I was never even wounded in France or Mespot," Marlow went on dreamily. "It's queer to come to an end of everything like this. Will you light a candle? I want to write a few words to my wife."

Fitz stifled a blasphemy.

"You fellows have been very decent. I want to make that clear," Marlow said. "And that poor chap who was hanged this morning was innocent, you say?"

"He did not shoot that spy—that Intelligence officer," Fitz replied.

"Still, rightly or wrongly, we've taken on this job of squashing you fellows, and that being so, we have to face up to everything that may happen. All the same, it's a queer kind of end to everything. Not the kind of end one could have dreamed of at Sandhurst in 1910. Well, they won't give a medal for this war," he added, and sitting up among the fern and heather he began to write his last letter.

Through Fitzgerald's mind the phantoms raced. The guns and munitions he had smuggled over when he took the furniture from Trelawny Road before the war . . . it had seemed such a lark in those days . . . just a grand score over those playboys of Ulster . . . Ulster will fight and Ulster will be right . . . and the drilling with the Volunteers . . . carrying camans instead of rifles . . . and then the folly of the British Government which held up the Home Rule Bill at the outbreak of war and gave the Republic a chance . . . and the Easter Rising . . . and the shootings . . . and the jails . . . and the country coming to life . . . and then the refusal of the British to recognize that the country had come to life . . . the beginning of violence to prove it . . . violence in return . . . the Auxies and the Tans . . . the murder of MacCurtain . . . the self-starvation of his successor . . . the murders arranged by British Intelligence officers at the Castle . . . the torture and hanging of Kevin Barry . . . the determination to break the murder-plot of the British Government by which it thought it had murder by the throat . . . last Sunday week in Dublin . . . fourteen Intelligence officers pulled from their beds and shot, one or two of them in front of their wives . . . and that same afternoon the Auxies shooting up the crowd at Croke Park and killing twelve men and women . . . and that night the shooting of Dick McKee and Peader Clancy and Conor Clune by Auxies in the guard-room of the Castle . . . and Father Griffin's body found last week in a Galway bog . . . all because the British Government had gone mad . . . and now the hanging of Peter Shanahan on no more evidence than was found against Kevin Barry . . . and because they had captured a British officer in an ambush and the Government had been warned that if Shanahan was hanged Captain Guy Marlow would be shot as a reprisal . . . and it was for him, Edward Fitzgerald, to give the order . . . well, there was only one justification for such a deed and that was the willingness of those who shot him to give their own lives rather than surrender to the British . . . no compromise . . . if after this the country accepted a half-loaf let it be choked in the eating of it. . . .

Marlow was sealing up the envelope.

"I'd be obliged, Fitzgerald, if you'd send this to my Colonel. I have written to him and asked him to see that my wife receives her letter. I've just mentioned how well I've been treated. I don't want to be the subject of sensational stories. I only wish my death could end this miserable business."

"More will die yet," said Fitz somberly. "I've a notion I . . . will die myself."

"I don't think those presentiments are to be trusted," Marlow answered, with a smile that to the Irishman was almost unbearably gentle. "I noticed that during the war. It's depression usually."

"I had the notion years ago," Fitz went on. "I had a sight of my death long before the troubles ever started. So maybe we'll meet again soon, Marlow."

"I wish I could believe one met like that after death," the hostage murmured. "But to me it's just a fairy tale."

He sighed and looked at his watch.

"Let the Commandant know I'll be along at Headquarters this evening," Fitz told Michael Shea. "You can report what happened up there. I'm going to spend the day at home."

He left his companions by a rough mountain road and kept on toward Caragh.

It was a placid day after the gale. The fern was ruddy, and a myriad streams were burbling down the mountain side. After two hours of hard walking Fitz reached the wooded road beside Caragh, half of which was as blue as the lake itself with water from the hillside streams and torrents the leaf-choked ditches could not carry away fast enough. He passed an empty cottage on the walls of which some enthusiast had painted in green capitals, 'DOWN WITH VICTORIA'S TANS AND BLACKS.' The conservatism of hate which held Queen Victoria responsible for the present terror! How bitterly endured the memory of one who had spent in Ireland six weeks out of her reign of sixty years!

Presently he arrived at the gate of Tinoran, to see that one of the posts had been broken and that the gravel of the short drive was ploughed up by some heavy vehicle. The stucco front of the house was pitted with bullet-marks and several of the window-panes were smashed. He hurried to the door, fear at his heart.

The hall was in confusion. The hat-stand had been thrown down. Two or three flower-pots had been broken. The pictures were grotesquely askew.

"Nora! Nora! Joe! Bridget! Mother!"

There was no answer. He called loudly again and was on the point of going round to the back of the house when at the head of the stairs appeared the black form of Father Doherty, the parish priest.

"It's yourself, Doctor!" he exclaimed. Then coming quickly down the stairs he seized Fitzgerald's arm. "Keep a grip of yourself, man. Keep a grip. I have bad news to give you."

"Bad news? I suppose the Tans have looted the place."

"Worse news than that. Keep a grip of yourself," the priest

repeated, fixing Fitzgerald with eyes at once stern and compassionate.

"They've killed somebody? They killed Padraig?"

"No, the boy is safe. He's down the road with his grandmother and Bridget at Mrs O'Malley's. And Joe MacCarthy is away to report the unhappy business at the nearest police station.

"And Nora?" Fitz breathed.

"Your wife. Almighty God be good to her and comfort you, my dear man . . . your wife . . ."

"She's dead!"

"She is dead. I was watching by the body when I heard your voice. She is lying upstairs."

They went upstairs. Nora's body was lying on the big double-bed from which how often Fitz had wakened her to come to the window and look down with him at the beauty of the lake in the morning, and now she could never be wakened again. The waxen face upon the pillow seemed asleep, but Fitz pushed back the coverlet to see the dark bloodstain over the heart.

"She died almost at once," he muttered, "almost at once after an instant's agony."

"Pray, my son, pray," Father Doherty urged.

And he knelt beside the bed where they had always knelt to say their evening prayers and morning prayers together.

"I will stay here," said the priest. "Do you go along to Mrs O'Malley's and speak to your mother."

It was the story of too many a woman's, of too many a child's death in those days. A lorryful of Auxies or Black and Tans had driven up about two o'clock in the morning. The door had been broken down and the party had set about searching the house for the owner and failing to find him had ransacked the place for arms and papers. The terrified women had dressed themselves as much as they were able during the demoniac search, and at last after about half an hour of destruction and noise the raiding party had re-entered the lorry. The women with young Padraig were gathered in the sitting-room. Perhaps it was the branch of a tree which snapped in the wind, but suddenly the party were seized with a panic as one cried "Look out, boys, it's an ambush." There was a mad rain of bullets, one of which found Nora's heart. The lorry had surged away. It must have been then that the driver hit the gate-post in his anxiety to escape from phantom Shinners conjured by the wind.

"Let this be the end of it for you, avic," old Mrs Fitzgerald.

begged of her son. "Almighty God has shown you that He requires no more violence from you."

"The end, mother?" Fitz cried. "For me this is the beginning."

"Ah no, son, don't be talking like that, my poor boy. Let our sweet Nora's death bring peace to your heart," the old lady implored.

"Her death will not bring peace to Ireland," said Fitz in a voice of ice. "There are no coroner's inquests allowed to find that she was murdered. The Court of Inquiry will find that her death was caused by a precautionary measure of military necessity. They shall have military necessity. They shall have it, they shall have it," he vowed.

And two or three weeks later Fitz watched a lorryful of Black and Tans go up in limbs and fragments of flesh when a road mine exploded beneath them.

Brutality bred brutality, ruthlessness bred ruthlessness, violence bred violence, murder bred murder.

"You know, I think these reprisals by irregulars are giving the Government a bad name," a distinguished general—himself an Ulsterman—told the three statesmen—a Welshman, a Scotsman, and a Canadian—on whom rested the responsibility for the introduction of the Auxiliary Cadets and the Black and Tans.

"If these men ought to be murdered, then the Government ought to murder them," he elaborated.

"No government could possibly take the responsibility," one of the statesmen declared, dancing with indignation at such a preposterous notion.

So the murders went on.

"When is this going to end?" asked a great Liberal weekly. "The Government still cling to the belief that they can crush the Irish spirit, destroying some of the bravest and most promising of Ireland's young men, and win by these means an outward victory. They are wrong. . . . Men of noble spirit and unfaltering courage are dying, but their race does not perish. . . . A week ago a deputation from the American Relief Committee waited upon General Macready and Sir John Anderson to explain that America proposed to raise thirty million dollars for repairing the havoc caused by the armed forces of the British Empire in Ireland: there have been prouder moments in our history. We can spread death: that we are doing. We can do to Ireland just as much as Austria did to Italy or Germany to Belgium or Russia to Poland. But the end is as certain in their case as in those."

And an Irish General who before the war had been supposed to cherish intentions of leading a mutiny at the Curragh if the troops under his command were ordered to march against the Ulster Volunteers, a mutiny fostered by that same distinguished Ulster General who had just been giving advice to those three statesmen, wrote:

"Law and order have given place to a bloody and brutal anarchy, in which the armed agents of the Crown violate every law in aimless and vindictive and insolent savagery.　England has departed farther from her own standards, and farther from the standards even of any nation in the world, not excepting the Turk and Zulu, than has ever been known in history before."

It was under this General that Captain Guy Marlow had fought night and day during those terrible March days in 1918 when the Germans broke through the Fifth Army, and two and a half years later his life was not considered worth that of a young rebel who was to be hanged on the evidence of paid spies.　So two patriots died—an Englishman and an Irishman.　And the whirligig of time would bring in for both his revenges.

Emil and his mother came down the steps of a Marylebone nursing-home into a dense November fog, through which they walked cautiously eastwards.

"And what are you going to call him?" Miriam Stern asked.

"Jan Frederick, but it will be spelt Y–A–N.　The initial is more distinctive and it will ensure a more approximately correct pronunciation," her son replied.

"You are calling him after his uncle," she challenged.

"Yes."

"I wish you wouldn't, Emil dear.　It was such a brief unfortunate life."

"It was a life given for a cause," he answered.

She thought of that brother for ever holding forth about the ways of the poor and downtrodden and of the way she used to listen to him as a girl more than forty years ago, when he had required from her the ceaseless tribute of sympathetic attention. And she thought of his arrest that night in Warsaw, of his attempted escape from Siberia, of his death from starvation and exposure.

"But so brief and so unfortunate a life," she repeated.

"That's being superstitious," Emil said severely.

"Isn't it being equally superstitious to call your baby son after him?" she asked.

"I do not consider it superstitious to commemorate one of the hundreds of the unknown and forgotten comrades whose bones lie in Siberia," he replied. "He will be called Yan."

She knew it was useless to argue further, and they walked on slowly through the disintegrated city of fog.

"I doubt if you'll get a taxi to take you up to Hampstead," Emil said presently. "You'd better come back with me to Brunswick Square. You can go home later if it clears, or if not you can spend the night in the flat. I can sleep in the sitting-room. Do you mind if we call in at the shop on our way? We might get a bus down Oxford Street."

Even in an omnibus the progress was painfully slow, and being separated from one another each was occupied with thoughts. Miriam tried to shake off the morbid fancies which were conjured by this mournful fog and the hearselike progress of the omnibus through the dim lights of Oxford Street. She forced herself to concentrate on the picture of Astrid lying in the bed at the nursing-home with the tiny bundle beside her. She had looked as slim and as fair as a wisp of barley lying there. And that tiny bundle already dedicated to revolution by the pair who had brought it into the world. Boy or girl, it would have made no difference. A safer future lay before her other grandchildren, Sebastian and Monica. Or did it? The forces seething up from the depths of centuries were as likely to overwhelm them as their young cousin on the other side of the Atlantic. More likely indeed, for this infant would be brought up from the beginning to expect and welcome tremendous change.

The grandmother, so unlike the conventional figure which the word still evoked, so much one of those youthful-seeming grandmothers of the ageing world of to-day which clings so desperately to what youth is left to itself, failed to keep her thoughts in the present. She was back in her girlhood on such a night of fog as this when the air was creeping like a hooded death into that half-furnished Notting Hill house. She was mounting at her mother's bidding the uncarpeted stairs to light the gas for her father in the studio. She was seeing the windows like blind eyes, and beyond them the dim fulvous oblongs of gaslight in the backs of the houses opposite, across which the shadows of human beings, incredibly alive, made phantom gestures. She was singing to the exile old folk-songs of Central Europe. She was fancying when he gathered her to him that this singing was a sure consolation. She was remembering that foggy November twilight when she came upstairs to minister to his gloom and found the canvas on which he was working slashed to ribbons and beneath the dust-sheet with which he was wont to cover it the dead body of the painter, his throat slashed too. That was in the November of 1880, and now in just such another November of 1920 she was filled with presentiment for her son's future. Yet it should have been so joyous a moment, coming away as they were from the nursing-home in which the woman who had so obviously brought so much emotional and intellectual help to the dedicated purpose of his life had given him a son. She looked across the omnibus to where Emil was sitting so straight and pale and clearly cut among the listless workers returning home from the dull day's work that seemed to have deprived them of shape, dragging them down to its own shapelessness of uninspired effort to enrich people who were themselves incapable of enriching the world. Oh, there was enough to kindle in anybody's heart the resolve to destroy the present constitution of human society; but those who led destruction were always themselves destroyed. The pioneers always fell, either slain by the enemy or trampled on by their own victorious forces as they collapsed exhausted beside the path they had hewn.

"But this is mere maternal fondness and folly," she said to herself as the omnibus stopped at Tottenham Court Road and Emil rose to lead the way out.

"My dear, wouldn't it be better for me to take the tube to Hampstead?" she suggested. "I'll easily find my way down Fitzjohn's Avenue however thick the fog."

"No, you'd better come back and have something to eat at the flat. We can ring up Anna and tell her you may not get home to-night."

She divined that he was anxious for her company, and it was so rare for Emil to show the faintest sign of being anxious for any-body's company that she assented at once to his suggestion.

The little shop in New Oxford Street occupied the ground floor of a narrow old house which with two or three on either side had so far escaped the indiscriminate lust for rebuilding in the main thoroughfares of London which was to lend an air of vulgar progress to the decade after the war. The two top stories were occupied by the offices of the Liberty Press which represented Emil's newly started publishing enterprise.

"I must go upstairs and sign a few letters," he told his mother. "I shan't be very long. Will you come up or stay here in the shop?"

She elected to stay in the shop, where Mr Edenburg, the manager, brought her a chair.

The two or three customers engaged in turning over the pages of books looked up, and stared. They were evidently disapproving of such attention's being paid to this distinguished and well-dressed woman in the Liberty Bookshop, which already was a recognized haunt of reformers to whom distinguished well-dressed women were a displeasing manifestation of what they called bourgeois mentality.

Miriam enquired after the prosperity of the new venture.

"Oh, we can't complain, Mrs Stern," Mr Edenburg replied, rubbing his hands and beaming at her through the thick lenses of a pair of black horn-rimmed spectacles. "We're gradually getting known." He lowered his voice, and added, "But I wish more of our customers were purchasers instead of lookers. Still, as I say, we mustn't complain. Business improves slowly all the time. And I think one or two of the books we shall be publishing in the spring will create a small sensation. Nothing like defeat for stimulating artistic expression."

Miriam looked puzzled.

"I was thinking of Germany. We have translations of some really remarkable books already."

"Defeat stimulates artistic expression," Miriam repeated. "I had not thought of that before. But yes, that was true of France after the war of 1870."

Mr Edenburg's hands were in a ghostly lather by now and his eyes beamed more brightly than ever.

"Precisely, Mrs Stern."

Two of the customers put back the books they had been reading and moved toward the door.

"Good-night, Mr Romford. Good-night, Miss Jenden." Mr Romford in a saxe-blue jumper and dark-green corduroy trousers and Miss Jenden in a sort of Norfolk jacket of velveteen with a scarlet silk handkerchief muttered curt good-nights. The manager's subservient attention to that ghastly bourgeois had disgusted their conception of liberty.

"Claude Romford is a student at the London School of Economics," Mr Edenburg elucidated. "He was a conscientious objector. Had a very tough time in 1918, I believe. But he has brains."

"And so perhaps will learn manners in time," Miriam observed. "And the young woman?"

"She works at a Birth Control advisory bureau. As a matter of fact, Mrs Stern, we sell far more books on—er—sexology than politics or economics," said Mr Edenburg. "It's really remarkable what a great interest the war seems to have stirred up in sexology."

"Yes, I daresay," Miriam observed distastefully.

Later when she and Emil were walking slowly down Museum Street through the fog on the way to Brunswick Square she asked him if he did not find some of the titles displayed in his shop a little undignified.

"Why?" he asked in evident surprise.

"Well, it seems to suggest these horrid furtive little shops one passes on the way to Charing Cross."

"But, my dear mother, a shop like ours deals a mortal blow at such shops. It is just that furtive atmosphere which has surrounded sex like this foul fog which we are helping to dispel with the Liberty Bookshop."

"I wonder," she murmured pensively.

"We want to bring sex into the open. We want to make it as natural a topic as any other. The minds of these people groping toward a richer mental existence have been poisoned by repressions. It's useless to expect them to have a clear political vision so long as their mental processes are clogged by sexual taboos and riddles. They must all be cleaned out of their systems."

"Then you don't consider it an unhealthy sign that you should do the bulk of your bookselling in what Mr Edenburg calls sexology?"

"On the contrary," Emil replied, "I consider it an intensely healthy sign."

"I wonder if you realize, you who have faced up to the facts of sex with so much cold detachment ever since you were a small prodigy of worldly knowledge, that most of the people who dip into the books on your shelves are searching not for knowledge but for sensation, and that when a purchase is made you must not count it as a victory for knowledge, but a triumph of . . . of, oh let's call it, anticipated sensation."

"I don't agree with you at all," he replied with a touch of irritation.

"In that case you are allowing clouds to pass across your own mind. Indeed, you are a prey to the sentimental thinking you so much despise."

"My dear mother, I must ask *you* to face up to facts now," he expostulated. "I will admit, if you like, that the beginning of sexual knowledge for these people may be more sensational than intellectual. But that phase soon passes. You forget that in a world from which the idea of God has been banished sex becomes relatively more important."

"So that all man has achieved through the faith of our race, Emil, is to be flung away for him to revert from his religion to the fertility-worship of savages?"

"I did not say that with the elimination of the idea of God we were to worship sex," Emil argued. "What I meant was that this central fact, which is the one universal link for all mankind, should not be degraded by ignorance and superstitious taboos and the falsification of values by religion. Rightly regarded, sex is the foundation of a brotherhood of man."

"I'm not convinced. To me the atmosphere of the Liberty Bookshop was all wrong."

"That's old-fashioned fastidiousness, which is only another word for intellectual cowardice," he scoffed.

"I don't accept them as the same thing," Miriam asserted. "But we won't argue any more. I don't like to be reminded that between me and one of my children the years have dug a chasm which prevents either of us from understanding the other at certain points."

They walked on in silence through the fog which turned the garden of Russell Square to the confines of a mysterious forest and the hideous façade of the Russell Hotel to a precipice.

At the door of the house in Brunswick Square a figure emerged from the swirling circle of dim light shed by a lamp-post.

"Ah, is that you, Minchin?" Emil exclaimed. "You're early."

"Yes, Mr Stern, I am a bit early," a high-pitched Cockney voice agreed.

"You'd better come right up."

"Yes, Mr Stern," said the visitor. Then he hesitated with a glance at Emil's companion.

"That's all right, Minchin. This is my mother."

"Oh, pleased to meet you, I'm sure," and Miriam found herself shaking a plump soft cold hand which made her shudder as when in gathering flowers one touches a slug unaware.

"Pity we can't always have a nice foggy evening like this, isn't it, Mr Stern? It'ud save me a lot of walking round the houses. That's why I was so early. I came direct this evening."

"Yes, well, would you mind not babbling all the way upstairs," Emil said coldly.

"My mistake," Minchin replied, with a grin at Miriam.

His face was plump and soft, like his hands, pale and round as a puff-ball.

When they entered the flat at the top of the house Emil took the little Cockney into a small room he used for work and left his mother in the sitting-room.

"Well?" he asked sharply, and one who had watched Emil working in Icaros to obtain military information about the enemy would have known at once that Minchin had not come to see him about publishing.

"To rights," the little pale round-faced man announced cheerfully. "Couldn't be going better. I've got a rare good feller working Portsmouth and building up a nice little cell. I've heard of two more good fellers for Aldershot, and I'm in touch with a proper knockout in the first battalion of the Westmorland Fusiliers. Bit by bit I reckon we'll have comrades in every blooming regiment in the country. And it won't be too long before we get things going in the Navy. This feller at Portsmouth does a lot of joring in bars, and he's willing to pass leaflets where he thinks they'll create interest. It's a pity they don't close down on this Irish business. Troops actively employed are rotten for propaganda. These Irish keep 'em too blooming busy. Still, as I say, we're moving along nicely all the time, and it don't do to hurry things along *too* fast."

They discussed at some length items of the propaganda that was to be circulated among the forces.

"But the main point to keep in mind every time and all the time is refusal to do the work of the police in the event of a general strike. For our purposes nothing else really matters," Emil insisted.

"Quite so. I fully appreciate that, Mr Stern."

"I don't want a lot of gasbags such as you can hear in Hyde Park," Emil said. "I want the men to grasp the practical immediate issue at stake."

"Quite so, Mr Stern. I know just what you want. And what about the leaflets?"

"I'm not so fond of leaflets."

"Oh, I don't know; a nice rousing little leaflet goes down well," Minchin argued. "They get handed around, and a feller can read over a leaflet to himself, and not let on what he's thinking. Fellers are a bit shy of speaking up in mixed company. You never know whether there might be a Government spy sitting in a corner and drinking of it all in. But nobody can say anything to a feller for reading a leaflet he's picked up in a public bar."

"Very well, I'll consider the leaflet question, but I repeat that the main point is refusal to fire on the workers. All right, you'd better get along."

"Yes, Mr Stern. And . . .?" The round-faced little man hesitated.

"Here are twenty pounds."

"Thank you, Mr Stern."

"Which must last till the new year," Emil added.

"Quite so. I'll place it as required."

"And, Minchin!" said Emil sharply.

"Yes, Mr Stern?"

"If you accost me again like that in the street it's the last time you will ever speak to me."

"I thought a foggy evening like to-night . . ."

"Don't think. Do what I tell you."

"Yes, Mr Stern."

"You'll get a message when and where I wish to see you again. And don't think because it's a foggy evening you can't be shadowed."

"Eh?"

"You heard what I said. Get along now."

Minchin sniggered uneasily.

"Give me quite a turn, you did. Do you mean the cops . . ."

"I didn't say anything about cops," Emil interrupted. "I said 'don't think because it's a foggy evening you can't be shadowed'."

"No, Mr Stern, I won't, Mr Stern. Good-night, Mr Stern."

The pale round-faced man went down the quiet stairs of the house in Brunswick Square, pondering his employer's warning. Who was going to shadow him?

Minchin closed the heavy door behind him and peered to right and left into the fog, which was thicker than ever. The light of the lamp-post in the swirling circle shed by which he had recognized and greeted Emil Stern was now a murky orange stain upon the darkness. He shivered and turning up his overcoat walked down the steps. On the pavement he stood listening. Not a footstep sounded, not so much as the whisper of a dead leaf.   The traffic by King's Cross murmured faintly like a distant beach.   He turned to the left and walked slowly along for fifty yards.   Then he turned sharply on his tracks and walked as fast as the fog would let him in the opposite direction until he was fifty yards on the other side of Emil's house.   Then he crossed the road and moved quietly back along the railings of the garden.   He met nobody, and finally turning round again he set off in the direction of Holborn. Here he picked up an omnibus crawling towards Oxford Street, but after taking his seat he rose immediately and muttering to the conductor that he was blooming well going in the wrong direction he jumped off and picked up a taxi, telling the driver to go to the Marble Arch.   Here he alighted and walked a short way down Edgware Road, turning off to the right until he came to a house not far from Bryanston Square.   At this house he pressed the bell once and then twice.   The door opened at once.

"Mr Bacon?" he asked of the man that opened it, a man who resembled those figures like a cross between a footman and a reception-clerk that open the doors of medical hives in Harley Street.

Minchin was shown into a small waiting-room at the end of the hall, and a few minutes later he was shown up to Mr Bacon's room.

A narrow-headed dark man with an aquiline nose, seated at a large desk, indicated with his hand a chair opposite.   The lamp on the desk shone upon Minchin's face.   Mr Bacon leaned back into the shadow.

"Well?" he asked.

And Minchin gave an account of his interview with Emil Stern.

"All right, get on with the directions he gives you and report again next month," said Mr Bacon.   "You were careful about coming here?"

"Yes, Mr Bacon . . . yes, sir.   I was extra careful after what Mr Stern said to me.   And . . ."   The round-faced little man hesitated.

"I suppose you want some money?" Mr Bacon asked.

"Well, sir, I've had a good deal of expense of late.   I took a taxi to-night part of the way.   I thought it better after what Stern said about shadowing."

"Here are ten pounds.   Sign that receipt.   Not your own name!"   Mr Bacon tore up the piece of paper, and gave Minchin another.   "I thought you knew better than that by now."

"Yes, sir, but I was a bit flustered by what Stern said.   Give me quite a turn, it did."

He wrote 'Number Fifteen', and handed back the receipt.

Mr Bacon pressed a bell on his desk and a moment or two later Minchin followed the doorkeeper downstairs. Mr Bacon walked along the passage and entered another room.

"I think we shall get this bird Stern all right, Brinsley," he said to Major Brinsley Rossiter of the Princess of Wales's Flintshire Regiment.

"Oh, good," said Major Rossiter. "By the way, Porker, a queer thing: that bloody man Ogilvie who was with the Spicer lot is apparently a friend of this Stern blighter as well as of that damned Irishman Edward Fitzgerald."

"You'd better enter him up on your list, Brinsley," said Mr Bacon, or rather, to give him his real name, Major Alured Hogge of the King's Own Birmingham Regiment.

"Don't worry, Porker, I've *got* him on the list." And tapping his teeth with a pen he whistled through them the air from *The Mikado*.

"Pity you're not in Ireland," said Major Hogge, with a grin.

"Why?"

"Such a lot of blighters on the list who never would be missed there."

"Thanks, Porker, but I'm not sorry to be back in London. I might not have been missed myself in rather an unpleasant way."

It had been the intention of John and Athene that their child should be born at Nanphant. Nurse Widehose had been engaged. Arthur was to spend his holidays at 57 Church Row. Then in the middle of December Arthur's letter from school, on hearing of the plan prepared for him, had sounded a little woebegone at the prospect of seeing neither his mother nor his pony. By the next post came the news that Nurse Widehose was laid up with pneumonia and so unable to keep her engagement.

"Perhaps it will be wiser for you to go into a nursing-home in London," John said to his wife.

"But, dearest, you were so anxious it should happen here," she demurred. "And I was so anxious too," she added quickly.

"I don't think it's quite fair on Arthur. After all, it is his first Christmas holidays, and I know what that kind of disappointment means."

"But I'll be away from him anyway in a nursing-home," Athene argued.

"Yes, but I'll be at hand, and . . . oh, I think it's better. And you'd feel happier, now, wouldn't you?"

The dark eyes melted to that look which could set John's heart beating as fast as when first he saw it.

"You wouldn't be too terribly disappointed?" she pressed.

"No, no," he insisted. "I already feel a kind of guilt in my happiness, when I think of that ghastly news from my poor Fitz, and have no patience left for romantic whims."

"Dearest, you had ghastly news for yourself three and a half years ago when your lovely little Zoe was lost," she said, her woman's love unwilling to cede even a superiority of grief to another man.

"We can't make comparisons about our sorrows, but I know that the happiness I have in you still makes me feel guilty for the excess of it."

"And shouldn't I feel equally guilty?" she asked, in her voice that low vibrancy which for him outplayed all music.

"How close and close we grow to one another," he whispered.

"And always closer, my heart, closer . . . closer," she whispered in response.

"That one day you will speak to me for the last time, or I to you . . ." His voice came back from the future it had been traversing, as he brushed away the shadow of mortality in a kind of dazed gesture. "Athene, there is something I want to ask you. Would you mind if, whether it be Corinna or whether it be Alasdair, we have our child baptized into the Catholic Church? I think she or he will be happier in such security the way world is going."

"Why, no, John, but—mightn't it create a barrier between us and our child one day?"

"Well, you see, could I but find positive faith I should become a Catholic myself, and that would never create a barrier between you and me."

"I wonder," she murmured.

"It did not create a barrier between Julius and Leonora. True, she has become a Catholic herself since, but not until she was convinced of the truth. However, I am still without that conviction, and so the question does not arise between you and me. If you feel any doubt about baptizing our child as a Catholic, shall we leave it to fate? If it be Corinna, let her be baptized into the somewhat vague but highly respectable religion to which both of us superficially, but very superficially, adhere."

"No," Athene said, after a pause, "let us decide, whether it be Corinna or Alasdair, to do what you suggest. I suppose my prejudiced Southern ideas suddenly stuck themselves up. But as I think about your suggestion, it begins to seem wise. It means a code, a rigorous code, and that is good for people. Besides, if you were to become a Catholic yourself it would be unfair to a child to let it think that it had been wrongly taught. It might do harm at a critical age. I suppose everybody will think us very odd to do what we intend to do, but that doesn't matter to me any longer. Once upon a time because I was untrue to myself I lived in the opinions of other people, as if by their conventional approval I could restore myself to myself. Oh dear, I'm afraid that all sounds very muddled."

"I perfectly understand," he smiled.

"You understand almost too much," she said, shaking her head. "You spoil me with understanding."

John went over to St Pedoc next day to let Ethel Pendarves know about the change of plans. She applauded the change, but Henry Pendarves was depressed that Cornwall was to be slighted.

"These new-fangled nursing-homes," he grumbled. "Lot of nonsense. Children managed to get born in the Duchy before now."

"It's not Cornwall, Henry. The real reason is Athene's small son. We don't want to spoil his holidays more than we can help."

"Very fussy," Henry grumbled. "Did you notice the Scilly Whites are in flower already?"

"I did. We might be in Italy."

When John reached the gates of the drive to Pendarves House Jennifer and Christabel, grown lanky now, stopped the jingle.

"We'll drive a bit of the way with you," they announced.

"Enchanted, fair cozes."

There was a certain amount of prodding and whispering by the two girls until at last Jennifer, her freckled cheeks in a blush, demanded that what he was going to be asked should remain for ever an inviolable secret. The promise was given.

"John, is Athene going to have a baby in London?"

"She is."

"Well, we knew it a long time ago," Christabel declared, relief in her tones. "But mother *is* so stupid. She will treat us like two kids in the nursery. I do think parents are foul."

"I'm sorry to hear that," said John, "at this critical moment in my career."

"Well, perhaps you won't be so narrow-minded," Christabel allowed.

"I wonder if it'll be a boy or a girl," Jennifer said. "John, which would you like it to be?"

"That question I won't answer."

"Well, what will you call the baby if it's a girl?" Christabel asked.

"Corinna."

"Gosh!" she ejaculated. "I thought my name was pretty affected."

"You've survived it."

"We must go back now," Jennifer announced. "Swear you won't tell mother what we asked you."

"I swear."

"And thanks awfully for telling us," Christabel said. 'Corinna', she repeated to herself. "It's rather a nice name when you get over the first shock. And when do you think we'll see Corinna?"

"About Valentine Day, I hope. But it may be Alasdair."

"The names you think of!" Jennifer exclaimed.

"That's just the Gaelic name for Alexander, my father's name."

"Well, good-bye, John dear," Christabel said. "We'll rag you like anything when you're a father."

"Rather," Jennifer declared. "Like anything we'll rag you. Good-bye, John dear."

The January morning on which Corinna Ogilvie was born was clear and blue at Hampstead, with a light wind blowing from the north, and even in Marylebone the mica in the paving-stones glittered like gold in the low winter sun.

As John came down the steps of the nursing-home for the second time that day, he said to Arthur, "Well, my lad, you have a sister," and then suddenly reflected how many millions of fathers must have made that remark to small boys.

"She's pretty ugly," Arthur commented. Even in the space of a term at Hampden House with childhood's facile mimicry he had almost lost the American accent he had picked up during his months in Atlanta.

"All babies are pretty ugly," John observed.

"I never looked at one close before. I don't know why folks make such a terrible fuss about babies."

The following day after revisiting his daughter John took Arthur to the Zoo. When they left the monkey-house Arthur walked along in pensive silence, and John asked him what he was thinking about.

"I was thinking Corinna's terribly like a monkey. Only she hasn't got fur and that makes her a bit more ugly."

"I wouldn't tell your mother that."

"Poor mother, I guess she's feeling pretty sad Corinna's so darned ugly. Do you think those wrinkles will ever come out?"

"Oh yes, they'll come out in a very short while."

"I hope they will. Say, John, those giraffes are grand, aren't they? Some necks, eh?"

Toward the end of January Arthur went back to school, cheered by the prospect of seeing his pony Tea again in the Easter holidays. Athene and the baby came up to Hampstead for a while before going back to Nanphant. A nurse was engaged, a pleasant impersonal elderly woman, who was to take charge of the baby until the right Gaelic-speaking young nurse was found from the Catholic West of Scotland. John wanted to have Corinna baptized by the priest to whom more than twenty years ago he had entrusted the erection of a stone cross on the grave of Cissie Oliver in Kensal Green cemetery. He could not remember the name of the priest, but he thought he could find the little church in Somers Town. He did do, but the name of the priest was Dixon and this had certainly not been the name of the priest he had met. However, he called on Father Dixon and told him the story.

"That would have been Father Burke," said Father Dixon, a dried-up anxious-looking little man.

"Yes, that's the name," John exclaimed eagerly.

"I'm afraid Father Burke—God rest his soul—has been dead five years now. He left Somers Town for a parish in Acton six years before the war. I succeeded him here."

John explained the object of his visit, by which Father Dixon was evidently much puzzled.

"I never remember such a request being made before," he said. "You say you have no intention at present of making your submission yourself? It seems a little strange."

"I'm sure it does, Father Dixon," John agreed cheerfully. "But there is nothing to forbid such a baptism?"

"No, no. It's merely most unusual. Of course the infant will have a Catholic godmother who will be responsible for her spiritual future?"

"The godmother of the infant is in America.   But I understand a proxy may act," John said.

"Oh yes, certainly.   Yes, that is possible," the priest assented. "But in the circumstances I do not like the idea of a proxy."

John and Athene had decided that Leonora was the obvious godmother for Corinna, but it flashed across his mind now, since a second godmother on the spot was essential, that Ellen Fitzgerald should be asked to accept what in this case might be a greater responsibility than godmothers were accustomed to bearing.

"You are quite right, Father Dixon.   I will ask a Catholic friend of mine of over twenty years to be godmother."

"That would be much more satisfactory," the priest agreed.

"Then can we arrange a time and day?" John asked.

It was impossible even yet to wring an enthusiastic response from Father Dixon, but at last he named a time and a day, and so Corinna Mary Ellen Ogilvie was baptized after Candlemas in the little church among the mean streets of Somers Town, whose parish priest twenty years ago had advised her father that if ever by God's grace he made up his mind to be received into the Church he should not seek out some intellectual Jesuit father for instruction, but go to a simple parish priest.

"John, you and Athene have made me so proud and important," said Ellen Fitzgerald.   "Corinna Mary Ellen is my first godchild. Edward didn't think me a good enough patriot to ask me to be Padraig's godmother.   John, you've brought me such happiness. You gave me my chance in a London theatre and now you've trusted me with Corinna."   She blinked away the tears.   "And won't my mother be glad?   And it's she that needs all the gladness one can give her in these days."

"Who'd have thought that evening in Trelawny Road when you were rehearsing *As You Like It* with Connie Fenwick that you'd be my daughter's godmother?   How life unfolds, how it unfolds . . . unfolds . . ."

John's voice died away on a murmur.

Corinna was in Nanphant by St Valentine's Day, where she thrived as well as the daffodils of Henry Pendarves.   Jennifer and

Christabel declared that their cousin was a lovely baby.

"It's very kind of you to say so," John told them, "but, if I may express an opinion, she looks to me exactly like every other baby. And I'm sure your father, in spite of his eye for the minutest difference in the cup of a daffodil, would agree with me."

"Father!" Christabel scoffed. "What *does* Father know about babies?"

"Damn it, he produced four of them."

"Mother did. He didn't," Christabel contradicted, and then on an afterthought she added, "I was considered a lovely baby."

"A jolly look-out for Corinna if she *is* a lovely baby," John laughed.

"Don't listen to him, Christabel dear," Athene advised.

"I don't!" Christabel declared scornfully.

Arthur came back from his holidays. Smelling strongly of the stable, he examined his sister critically and expressed an opinion that she did look a bit better now. Then he returned to the stable to murmur fonder endearments upon his pony's neck than the fondest nurse in the country to her charge.

The Truro Show was held. Henry Pendarves received an Award of Merit for a flower for which he thought he should have received a First Class Certificate, and brooded during a fortnight on the blindness of judges from up along.

"They understand form, John," he growled. "But they do *not* understand colour. They can't get the colour up along. They see an *Emperor* which they don't recognize because they've never seen an *Emperor* with such depth of yellow till they come to Cornwall, and then out of pique at their own ignorance they start giving lower marks in proportion to fine colour. That *King Midas* Ajax of mine should have had an F.C.C. I'll show it at Vincent Square next year, and you see if everybody doesn't say it ought to have had an F.C.C. But I don't know that I will show it. I've a good mind to give up daffodils."

"You'll never do that, Henry."

"Yes, I will," he vowed. "I'll carry on my work with rhododendrons, but I'll never show another daffodil."

"Oh yes, you will. You'll show *Corinna* in 1926, or will it be 1927?"

"Well, of course *Corinna* may be a real beauty. Now this year I couldn't get a single pod of seed from *Saffron Maid*. We had luck last April, John."

"We did indeed," John agreed.

May Day came, and the Helston Furry Dance. Arthur went
back to school, having chosen his future career. He would be a
jockey. May ripened. On the cliffs the wild columbines, or Blue
Men's Caps as the Cornish children called them, nodded in the
light May breeze, and John worked at a play that was just as light,
promising himself that next winter he would devote his pen to
something more serious. There was no news from Fitz, but there
was a faint glimmer of hope that the British Government was
taking stock of its own insensate behaviour. Emil wrote in depression about the failure of the Railway and Transport Unions to
support the Miners in their strike. He had evidently counted on
the rapid development of a general strike.

June came in. The weather was warmer and drier than ever.
Never was such a summer. Yet prices and wages were falling
fast all the time, which made for misery and want and unemployment. It looked as if the country which had endured so much
was now to be slowly strangled by the money-power. It looked
as if Europe was not to be allowed to recover. Tired statesmen
blundered on. The only active brains were financial, and these
were devoting all their talent to making money safe, at no matter
what cost to humanity. To this everything was subordinated.

July blazed as fiercely as June. It was weather in which to
forget the misfortunes of Europe and sit beside the pool where
the rose and crimson water-lilies were in bloom, sit there and read
and dream and talk to Athene and watch Corinna asleep in her
perambulator.

Elise Ogilvie came to Nanphant for a fortnight with David, and
when they were gone the Judge came with Prudence. The Judge
and his wife went off to Marienbad. Prudence stayed on at
Nanphant. She was critical of her first season.

"All the young men are so silly and conceited," she complained.
"Were you silly and conceited, John, when you were twenty?"

"And you were even smaller than Corinna," he added.

"Never mind about me. Were you silly and conceited?" she
pressed.

"I don't suppose he was silly, but I expect he was conceited,"
Athene put in.

"I expect I was, from a young woman's point of view," John
admitted. "But you must remember, my superior young sister,
that to the youth in his early twenties debs are apt to appear somewhat conceited and extremely silly."

"But we don't want to talk about ourselves all the time,"

Prudence protested. "And young men never want to talk about anything else. David's just as bad as the rest. Now, I ask you, is it interesting to listen to long accounts of the stag he would have shot if he had done something different from what he did, but which was more boring, if possible, than what he did do? Some girls get away with it over sporting conversation, but I loathe all sport. Of course, we never had a chance in Paris to know what young Frenchmen were like, but I'm sure they're not so foully vapid as young Englishmen."

"I fancy they're just as vapid as Englishmen with respectable *jeunes filles*," said John.

"Oh, but one or two young men did try to make love to me," Prudence insisted.

"And how did you receive it?" her brother asked.

"I laughed."

"Well, if you yawn when a young man tells you about his sporting exploits and laugh when he tries to kiss you . . ."

"Only one tried to kiss me," Prudence interrupted. "Well, as a matter of fact he did, because I thought I saw a girl I knew and I bumped right into his mouth before I knew he was trying to kiss me."

"It must have been the greatest moment since Romeo met Juliet," John declared enthusiastically.

"Now, John, you're not to tease her any more," Athene remonstrated.

Through August the perfect weather held. Goonhilly Down was on fire with the wandering Cornish heath. Never was such a summer. Prudence went off to a round of country-house parties, the prospect of which made her groan.

"Do ask me to stay with you at the Torre Saracena," she begged before leaving Nanphant.

"There's no room any longer," John told her, pointing to Corinna in her perambulator.

"You are so brutal to me, John."

"Don't worry, angel child, we'll manage somehow," Athene promised. "You shall bring Arthur out for his Christmas holidays."

"Oh, Athene, you are so adorable and John is so utterly rancid."

"You'll think me deliquescent when I make you sleep in the bath, as I shall," John vowed.

August blazed on into September. David had gone up to Assynt with his two Balliol friends; but Turner and Dorothy

Rigden's appeals that John and Athene should bring Arthur and the baby up to Achnalochlannach were rejected.

The Nanphant garden was like a sunset with the orange and scarlet and citron kniphofias raised by Henry Pendarves, and his new sulphur and salmon-pink gladioli, the largest primulinus hybrids yet seen. Arthur was galloping his pony on the sands, and his ambition to be a jockey had enlarged itself to becoming the owner of a ranch in Arizona. He would be going back to school in the third week in September, when Nanphant was to be closed for the winter and the Torre Saracena revisited.

"It's sad in a way that we could not manage to be in Citrano for the anniversary of that September night three years ago," John said to Athene.

They were sitting out late in the new verandah which had been built and looking at the starry southern sky above the invisible ocean. The heavy scent of the tobacco-flowers seemed to drive back the faint hint of autumn in the air and hold the garden safe for summer's lingering.

"Every night for all but two years has been an anniversary for me," she murmured.

"How true," he agreed fervidly. "You and I are in no need of sentimental occasions. Do you know it's past midnight? I'll sit here and smoke a last pipe." An owl hooted, and Athene jumped up. "No, that's not Corinna," he laughed. "And we no longer have to part because one of your children wakes in the night."

"You were remembering Arthur that night at the Allegra," she said. "He's perfectly happy at Hampden House. I'm glad I didn't encourage your suggestion to keep him at home."

"Yes, school seems to suit him. But he's a bit peeved to-day about the news from his friend Oliphant."

"He didn't tell me about that."

"No, it's a male affair," John went on. "It appears that Oliphant, whose father is a director of the Great Western Railway, is under the impression that he drove a train for some twenty miles last week, and Arthur is torn between the contending emotions of envy, incredulity, jealousy, and ambition. I've promised in your name that you'll give him a chance at the wheel of the car before he goes back to school next week. It's the best we can do for him, but it's a pretty poor best after Oliphant's triumph in the cab of a Great Western engine. I hope it's not going to break up the friendship. However, perhaps his holidays in Citrano will restore the balance."

Athene went into the house and John sat on for a while, smoking in the verandah.   He had finished the farce he had started writing early in the summer, and he was once more in a mood of making resolutions to tackle a subject that demanded more than the wit and invention and neat craftmanship which were now taken for granted by his public and by which, unless he took heed, he should be bound for the rest of his working life.   Yet, if like Fitz and Emil he flung himself actively into politics, that would only mean he should write no plays at all.   This was a strange period.   One could not contemplate a serious work of art without presuming that it would be coloured by politics.   What an abominable assumption that would have appeared to the aesthetics of even twenty years ago!   Then it was a dogma that a work of art could not survive the introduction of politics.   The novel or play with a purpose was condemned to death before it was written, and it was hardly possible to write a political novel or play without a purpose.   Otherwise, what would provide the passion?   There must be a missionary intention.   But anyway with the censorship the political play was not worth writing.   One could not effectively present current politics in the guise of fantasy, and that was as near as anybody could reach to the presentation of current politics on the contemporary stage.   Why, one might not even put Queen Victoria into a play.   They were wise, these politicians.   Remove the censorship, which was disguised as a moral eraser, and the dramatist might overthrow governments.   Think of an Aristophanes turned loose on Lloyd George and Bonar Law and a dozen others.   What could we put up against Aristophanes?   The operas of Gilbert and Sullivan!

John knocked out the ashes of his pipe and went indoors. Athene was in bed when he reached their room.   Usually he read for a while before sleep, but to-night he put out the lamp immediately and turned upon his pillow to pore upon her dim shape in the air glimmering through the starlit casements.

"I have been chiding myself out there in the garden with being too easily content," he told her.

"Why, dear heart?"

"I was thinking about that play I've just finished.   Life goes so easily for me, and for others it is so hard.   I fear I might slip out of the present in this drowse of happiness and wake up suddenly to find myself put contemptuously aside by those who have struggled too hard to have any more patience with a mere entertainer.   You see, I don't really enjoy just amusing people.   I feel

I ought to be stirring them up. I feel I haven't done enough to
bring before people the appalling Irish business. I read an article
in the *Morning Post* the other day by one of our reputedly intelligent generals in which he discussed the most effective way of
suppressing the Irish, and cited as examples of methods for sub-
duing nations fighting for their freedom the Turkish way with
the Greeks, the crushing of the Polish Rising in 1830, the Austrian
handling of Hungary and Italy, and our own subjugation of the
Boers! Well, I ought to have done something about it."

"What could you have done?"

"I could have gone up to London and rammed the blasted article
down his throat."

"John, how violent!"

"I know. That's what I said to myself. And of course in the
end I did nothing. Yet this country demands violent methods
for these damned survivals if the future is not to be ruined for
youth. I suppose it's becoming a father which makes me so
enraged with the way we are setting out to lose the peace. It's
not Ireland only. This Greek business is worrying me. I was
one of those who helped to create the notion that after the war
we should be grateful for what the Greeks did. But because they
have brought back their King we are treating them like naughty
children. I think they're mad to reject Venizelos, but that doesn't
justify us in refusing their support against the Turkish Nationalists
in Asia Minor. It was we who put them into Asia Minor. And
then there's Italy. The Italians are behaving outrageously in the
way of helping the Turks with arms and ammunition, but if we
did not want the Italians to intrigue in Asia Minor we should have
given our support to their ambitions in Africa. You can't expect
a nation to go through what Italy went through in the war and then
find herself swindled by her partners at the end of it. Oh, it
doesn't matter where one looks in Europe. Generosity! Generosity! Why cannot this country display practical generosity instead of collaring millions of acres more under the pretence of a
tom-fool mandate from this lopsided League of Nations? The
idea was a grand one, but from the moment the United States
refuse to have anything to do with it there is no League of Nations.
I could go on interminably. And I'm growing worried by my
own inaction."

"You're not thinking of going into politics, John?" she asked
in an apprehensive tone of voice, for to Athene as an American
going into politics still suggested a social stigma.

"No, because I could not attach myself to any of the existing parties," he replied.

"Then what could you do more than you're doing?" she pressed. "It worries me when you talk like this. It makes me think you're feeling marriage is a burden."

"Athene, it is marriage, or rather it is the responsibility of a child which is making me feel that I am not doing enough to help those who will have to take our places. So get right out of your dear head the notion that I feel hampered by marriage. What I worry about is acquiescence. Things are comfortable for me, therefore I acquiesce in the misery of others. I pay my taxes and acquiesce in the management of them by those stale careerists who have been given the leadership of the country through these critical years. I pay my royalties into the bank and acquiesce in a system of finance which must end in destroying the country. I write my plays and acquiesce in the existence of a censorship invented to protect politicians and claiming to protect morality. Acquiescence! Acquiescence! We shall go on acquiescing, and wake up one day too late to find that we have acquiesced in the ruin of the world."

She put out an arm and drew him to her breast.

"To have made one human being as happy as you have made me is something *I* can't call just acquiescence," she whispered.

The emotion of revisiting Citrano at the end of September was bound to be intense, but it was slightly saddened by seeing how many improvements had been made during the two years John had been away and the longer time still of Athene's absence. The Hotel Excelsior and Imperial was now matched by an even larger Hotel Splendide, and three new hotels of moderate size occupied what but a few months since were olive-groves or vineyards. A company from Turin with a sonorous title had acquired all five of these hotels and also Don Augusto's old Albergo delle Sirene where he had stayed seven years ago with Julius and Leonora in the spring and summer before the war. All the pensions belonged to the new company, which had also brought up most of the villas that were let furnished every year. Alas, one of these was the Villa Allegra itself. And on top of this Fofo informed them that he was seriously considering the sale of his café and shop.

"Too many strikes. Too many confusions," he declared. "I

don'ta know what will succeed in Italia soon. Always fights between the *fascisti* and the *arditi del popolo*. We can have a revolution, I think. My family marry themselves. Margarita has now one *bambino* and must have another very soon. Caterina is *fidanzata*, but she comes to be with you at the Torre Saracena for all winter because she will not marry herself yet, and Concettina who has now sixteena will come also. And when Concettina will marry herself then I am alone. It is better I sella the shop and make wine. I am too fat."

"Well, I think the idea of Fofo's without Fofo himself is just too terrible," Athene exclaimed. "You'll make me burst into tears in a minute."

Fofo's little eyes almost vanished like a pair of currants in the pudding of his smile.

"No, it is better to go now, signora, when the price is good. This morning I have seen your *bambina*. *È bellina assai.* She have smiled to me. *Come si chiama?*"

"Corinna," he was told.

"*Corrina? Bel nome! Un poco Italiano, evvero?*"

"And now I want to order a lot of things, Fofo," Athene announced.

"It is good," he said, with a tremendous wink at John. "What you want?"

John retired with a vermouth and seltzer to a corner of the café, where soon he was joined by Geoffrey Noel.

"My dear man, I heard from Francesco you'd arrived last night, and I very nearly came along with some flowers. It's really delightful to have you back. My goodness, what a sensation you gave Citrano with your marriage." Noel became incoherent at the recollection. "I need hardly say Mrs Heighington was not in the least surprised. She grows more intolerable every year. You'll enjoy the autumn here. We were packed out this summer. I never saw so many people. The Marina looked like Deauville or Cannes. And Vanessa who had arranged to come changed her mind at the last minute—m-m-m—and went off with some friend to Greece, entirely forgetting my money which she was going to straighten out when she arrived."

"Citrano is changed outwardly, but not otherwise," John smiled. "I hope everything's all right now."

"At the moment, yes. And of course this fall in the lira has helped me a lot. I only hope it won't recover. But the country's in a very critical state. You hear open talk of revolution everywhere."

"Come and dine with us to-night, Noel," John invited, "and you shall unfold the long tapestry of Citrano scandal that must have been woven in two years."

So Goeffrey Noel arrived at the Torre Saracena with a sonnet to Corinna, and after dinner the weather being still like summer they sat on the roof of the tower in the moonlight over coffee and scandal until Geoffrey Noel said it was time for him to be going home.

"By Jove, it's half-past twelve," he gasped. "You used to be the one to let me know when it was time to go," he added, turning to Athene. "But I don't have to escort you home to-night."

They watched from the roof of the tower the white-clad figure wending its way up through the rosemary.

"Oh, John, my beloved, I feel as if we were married only yesterday," Athene sighed as he held her in his arms.

On a blazing day in the middle of the hottest October ever known in England Turner Rigden was sitting by the open window of the smoking-room in his Piccadilly club, supported by a large brandy and soda. From time to time he looked up from the copy of the *Financial Times* he was reading to gaze beyond the flickering haze over Green Park into space, a frown on his genial rosy countenance. Into the room came Sir Thomas Trollope, K.B.E., mopping his brow.

"Hullo, T. T., have a drink," Rigden invited.

Sir Thomas subsided into a low armchair and accepted the offer. "I never knew such heat in October," he puffed.

"There never has been such heat recorded," said Turner Rigden.

"Damnable," Sir Thomas growled. "I wonder you came back to town from Scotland, Turner."

"Hell, I spent two months up there," Rigden protested. "Besides, Parliament meets on Tuesday. And I'm worried, T. T."

"What's worrying you, Turner?"

"This credit restriction you blasted bankers are applying."

"It was high time," Sir Thomas guffawed. "We've got to get the country back on gold."

Turner Rigden made the noise called a raspberry just as the waiter bent obsequiously to hear his requirements.

"What are you drinking, Turner? Brandy and soda? That'll suit me," said Sir Thomas.

"Two double brandies and two large sodas," Rigden ordered. "I think you'll ruin the country if you aren't careful," he went on, with a challenge to the banker's financial theory.

"You fellows don't begin to understand finance," Sir Thomas declared contemptuously.

"Hell to that," Rigden snapped. "How could business men do business if they didn't understand finance? The truth is you bankers manipulate credit the same way I manipulate public opinion in the *Journal* or the paper market or any other scheme in which I'm interested."

"Yes, but you can't manipulate any of your schemes if we restrict credit," Sir Thomas pointed out, with a mirthless grin.

"That's what I'm grousing about," said Rigden. "The other day a member of the Cabinet was reported to have said that the half-dozen men who control the Big Five Banks can make or ruin the country. Listen what the *Financial Times* has to say about him." He picked up the paper and read: "Whoever may be the indiscreet Minister who revives the money trust bogey at a moment when the Government has most need to be polite to the banks, he should be put through an elementary course of instruction in facts as well as in manners. Does he, do his colleagues realize that half a dozen men at the top of the Big Five Banks could upset the whole future of Government finance by refraining from renewing Treasury bills?"

"So they could," said Sir Thomas.

"Then, my god, they ought to face a firing squad," Rigden declared. "And I'll say so in next Sunday's *Journal.*"

"I wouldn't if I were you, Turner. You've got a lot to keep up, you know. Credit restriction might be applied rather unpleasantly." Sir Thomas drank down half his brandy and soda and exhaled a sense of refreshment in a gust of breath. "Listen to an old friend, Turner, and don't start quarrelling with the banks. The new Governor of the Bank of England is not the kind of fellow to stand for any criticism of his policy from a Sunday newspaper. Remember what Dewar said the other day. 'The banks have called a halt, and the manufacturer has been obliged to obey.' That goes for the Government too. And for newspaper proprietors. Take my advice, Turner. Don't quarrel with the banks."

"But the banks are deliberately making the country poor," Rigden asserted.

"That's Montagu Norman's plan," said Sir Thomas. "He

believes it's bad for a country to be too rich. He thinks it makes for idleness and decay. He believes the peace of Europe will be secured better by a central bank of international finance than by this League of Nations nonsense. He's a big man, Turner."

"Is he?" snarled Rigden, biting off the end of a Larrãnaga. "He sounds to me a bloody small man. In fact he doesn't sound like a man at all, but a bloody old woman."

At this moment a couple of scared-looking waiters hurried into the room and began closing the windows.

"Say, what the devil do you two boys think you're doing?" Rigden demanded in amazement.

"We've orders to put up the shutters, sir," said one of the waiters.

"Put up the shutters for a bit of sun?" Rigden exclaimed.

"It's not the sun, sir. It's the unemployed. There's been a bit of window-smashing, and the police have just telephoned through."

Sir Thomas Trollope, K.B.E., paled sufficiently to give his complexion the appearance of an unripe mulberry.

"Hurry up with those shutters," he quavered.

"There's your bloody banks," cried Turner Rigden. "A million and a half unemployed, and rising at the rate of over a hundred thousand a month, and Mother Montagu Norman thinks it's good for them. Who lays the golden eggs? Not the bloody bankers; but they sit on them and think they'll hatch out peace and prosperity for the world. I'm no Bolshie, T. T., but I hope the unemployed will wring their necks."

Turner Rigden's nursery mythology grew more and more confused as darkness enveloped the smoking-room and from along Piccadilly sounded the murmur of resentful, cheated, hungry men.

A few windows were broken with bricks. A few shops were looted. That was all, that and a decision to rebuild the Bank of England and create a fortress in the heart of the City of London at a cost of five million pounds. There was no lack of credit for that. A month later the housebreakers would begin to knock down Devonshire House. The Whig oligarchy which had controlled the democracy so long was a thing of the past; but democracy was to be more ruthlessly ruled by the sinister oligarchy that controlled the credit of the nation, that created money out of nothing, that in the words of an ex-Chancellor of the Exchequer, now Chairman of the Midland Bank, 'directed the policy of Governments, and held in the hollow of their hands the destiny of the people.'

The golden Dance of Death had begun.

Just after six o'clock on such another foggy evening as that of the day on which a year ago Yan Fredrik Stern was born the telephone rang at 21 Claremount Gardens.

"Is that you, Miriam? It is Astrid speaking to you. A terrible thing has happened. Please come to me if you can. They have taken Emil away to prison. Perhaps it is better I do not say more on the telephone, but please come to me if you can."

Miriam, her mind spinning like a polychromatic top of which disc after disc creates a new pattern, rang the nearest taxi-cab rank. There was no reply. She looked out of the window. The fog was very thick. She put on a sealskin coat which had been the birthday present of Julius and Leonora and decided to find her way up Fitzjohn's Avenue to the Hampstead tube station. She kept close to the walls and railings of front gardens, and every time she touched them their dankness and chill filled her with a fresh apprehension. She reached the station at last, where the warm gusts of air smelt more rubberoid than ever after the coppery tang of the fog. At Euston she left the tube and found a taxi which crawled with her to Brunswick Square. It was Astrid herself who came down to answer her ring.

"Oh, you have come, Miriam. Oh, I am so very pleased," her daughter-in-law exclaimed with an intensity of emotion she had never yet heard in her tone. "Let us go up to the flat."

Astrid was dressed as usual completely out of the fashion in a close-cut pale-green frock with a girdle of silver lace. She was still a Hans Andersen princess.

"He will be charged to-morrow at Bow Street they say."

"Charged with what?" Miriam asked.

"It is something like exciting to disaffection. It is because he has been working with soldiers and sailors for the cause," Astrid replied.

"How foolish, how foolish! How worse than foolish!" Miriam groaned.

"But it is not at all foolish, Miriam. He has been doing most wonderful work. You do not think it wonderful that he should do all he could to persuade the soldiers not to shoot if there is disturbance by the poor unemployed?"

"But it was bound to get him into trouble," Miriam replied "Don't you understand what a serious matter that is?"

"Surely I understand it is serious. He will be a martyr."

"And it is bound to tell against him so much that he has been a Government servant," Miriam added. "This may mean prison."

"He is now in prison."

"Yes, but a long sentence. The madness of it!"

"But you do not admire him?" Astrid asked in amazement. "At first when I rang you on the telephone I was still upset. It is so frightening for a moment when these police come. But now when I think how he is heroic I am not upset, because I am so proud of him."

"I can't be proud of folly, Astrid dear. And what he has done is just folly. And so futile! How was Emil going to stop the British Army from doing its duty?"

"Its duty? You think it is the duty of soldiers to shoot at the poor unemployed?" Astrid asked, a fleck of indignant crimson on each of those cheeks—delicate as Christmas-roses.

"It is their duty," said Miriam. "And if Emil was able to convince a handful here and there that it was not, what use would that have been?"

"Other comrades were working too."

"I daresay; but that won't make it any easier for Emil. I wonder if the magistrate will grant bail. Probably not when people are beginning to grow alarmed about those processions of unemployed. And his business! Think how that will suffer."

Astrid shook her head.

"I think it will not suffer at all. I will be altogether capable to manage the offices and the shop," she proclaimed. Miriam's thoughts went back to that father who would never hear any criticism of England. England had given him a refuge when he left Poland. The English might not appreciate his painting, but they had offered him sanctuary, and that was never to be forgotten.

"You see, it's such a pity for a Jew to do anything like this," she explained to her daughter-in-law.

"I do not find any difference for Jew or Christian or Communist who wishes to help the unhappy poor," said Astrid. "I find what Emil has done brave and noble and good, and I know that he will suffer gladly what can happen."

"Dearest child, it is right you should feel like that," Miriam assured her. "And you would not be a wife for Emil if you did

not feel like that. Besides, you have the same political belief as
Emil. I have the natural anxiety of a mother without the consolation of believing that what Emil has done was of the least practical
use to anybody."

"It is not practical to set an example?" her daughter-in-law asked.

"We mustn't argue about reasons," Miriam answered wearily.
"We must think what is best to be done."

"Emil said to me I must find Mr Samuelson the lawyer who
acts for us, and ask his advice."

"I suppose Emil will insist on having Mr Samuelson," said
Miriam, frowning. "But I confess I should have proposed another
solicitor. I wish John Ogilvie was in London. I'm sure he would
have given good advice on that matter."

Astrid's lips tightened. She evidently did not agree with her
mother-in-law.

"How is dear little Yan?" Miriam asked, divining an hostility
that was painful to her.

"He is very good. He has another tooth. You like to see him?"

They went quietly into the nursery and looked down at the
sleeping infant who gave promise of being nearly as fair as his
mother.

"Fortunately he's too young to realize any of our worries,"
Miriam sighed. "And perhaps by the time he's twenty the world
will have settled down again, and his old grandmother, if she's
still alive, will not have to worry herself about him."

"You like the world to be settled down?" Astrid asked, puzzled.
"For me that is bad . . ." she murmured to herself a word in
Swedish, ". . . stagnation," she added.

"And who looks less like a firebrand than you?" Miriam exclaimed. She suddenly felt very tired. Even when Astrid had
opened the door to her she had expected from her voice to have to
reassure her and pretend an optimism about Emil's case she did
not feel. That would have been tiring. But this placid elation
was exhausting.

"Would you like me to stay here to-night?" she asked.

"I would like you to stay please with Yan, and I can then go
to see Mr Samuelson, if I can find him," Astrid replied.

So Miriam remained with her sleeping grandson.

"Soon I shall be sixty," she thought. "And for the first time
I realize that I am old. How many grandmothers of my race
have been set like this as a matter of course to watch by the cradle
of the baby?"

Two hours passed.   Astrid was still away.   The sleeping infant stirred and uttered a faint cry.   Miriam began to croon an old lullaby of Central Europe, and he slept again.

"I have arranged it very well with Mr Samuelson," Astrid announced when she returned soon after eleven.   "But I am vexed because you had no supper.   Yan has been good, yes?"

"Very good."

"I did not tell you that when he cries I leave him to cry, because so it is better."

"What time will Emil's case begin to-morrow?" Miriam asked.

"To be at Bow Street about ten.   But nothing important can happen to-morrow.   Mr Samuelson will ask for bail, but he is afraid it will not be given.   And then Emil will be sent to Brixton for a week perhaps."

"Poor boy!"

"No, I think he will rejoice in this experience," Astrid prophesied. "And now I myself too am rejoicing for him.   I am extremely serene."

"Well, then, I think as the fog has cleared I'll ring for a taxi and go back to Claremount Gardens," Miriam said.

When she reached home she found the devoted Anna in a collapse of grief.   So she had the task of consoling her instead of her daughter-in-law.

"And there's a letter from Mr Julius," Anna said, bursting into tears again.

Miriam read that Julius and Leonora with both children were coming over to Europe in January for at least six months.   He was going to conduct his Second Symphony at Queen's Hall and play the Beethoven Violin Concerto on the same occasion.

I believe an unique double, he wrote.   *Try to find us a furnished house in Hampstead fairly near the Heath, but Leonora is writing about that.*

That night Miriam wrote to Athene:

This evening Emil was arrested on a charge of inciting to disaffection and comes before the Magistrate at Bow Street to-morrow morning.   The news of this should reach you before the news in the papers.   I think John may decide to come back to London when he reads that news, and I could not bear that such a decision might distress you by seeming to attach more importance to the affairs of a friend than to those of his family.   Therefore I beg you if you do not feel you can let John go with complete goodwill you will telegraph to me and I shall telegraph to John, asking him not to come.   I am writing at the end of this disastrous day and realize how badly I am expressing myself.   But I could not bear for John to arrive and feel that his leaving you was seeming a selfish demand by me upon his happy life.   There is no doubt that Emil will be committed for trial, and I myself doubt if he will be granted bail.   It will obviously be the policy of the Government to present his case as a serious threat to public order.   I have no hope of his escaping a sentence of imprisonment, but John will have such a much better opportunity than myself of finding out what is likely to happen that it would be an immense comfort to me if I had his advice.   Incidentally, I heard this evening from Julius that he and Leonora and the children are coming over for a long stay and that Julius is to give a concert at Queen's Hall.   Could anything be more unfortunate than the moment he has chosen?   And that worries me rather.   I feel that John will deal with Julius much better than I can.   In fact, Athene dear, I feel a helpless old woman to-night, and throw myself on your mercy.

"Honey, you've got to go to England," Athene said to John from the chair where he was reading her mail on a stormy November evening.

"Nothing the matter with Arthur?" he asked, looking up from his own post.

She passed him across Miriam's letter.

"The idiot!" he ejaculated.

"Poor Miriam sounds terribly cut up," Athene said.   "It was sweet of her to write to me, though it wasn't necessary.   You know that, don't you, John?   You know I wouldn't have tried to dissuade you from going to England at once, if you'd said you wanted to go?"

"Of course I know that," he answered.   "But once I get to London it will mean my staying till the trial is over, and that probably means to the end of January.   Still, Arthur will be arriving, and if Prudence brings him out I could meet him in Paris on his way back.   Prudence could put him in the train in Rome and come back to Citrano.   Yes?"

"I think that's a splendid arrangement.   And you'll be able to

hear Julius's concert. Darling, I hate to have you leave me for
so long, but you must go at once. Surely it can't be as serious
as poor Miriam thinks."

"It sounds pretty bad," John replied. "It will suit the Government to press the case. They're anxious to build up a bogey of
revolution to cover up their failure to implement the promises
made at that scandalous khaki election in 1918."

So two days later John left Citrano for London.

"Anyway, you'll have Corinna's teeth to keep you amused till
Arthur and Prudence arrive," he told Athene.

John had decided to stay at 57 Church Row, and before seeing
Miriam he talked over Emil's prospects with his father.

"Are you likely to try him?" he asked.

"He might easily come before me," the Judge replied, "but I
shall avoid the case in the circumstances. I should find it most
unpleasant to sentence an old friend of yours to a term of imprisonment, possibly even of penal servitude."

"Penal servitude?" John exclaimed. "You're not seriously telling me there's a danger of that?"

"I should think there was considerable danger. It depends on
how far the Crown wishes to press the case," Sir Alexander replied.

"In other words His Majesty's Judges hold themselves at the
convenience of the Government in power?" John asked. "Well,
I admit I said as much to Athene, but nevertheless you've rather
shaken me, m'lud. I thought Judge Jeffreys was as extinct as the
sabre-toothed tiger."

"I don't know *what* you're deducing from my observation,"
Sir Alexander said gravely, "but I hope you are not deducing
that a Judge can be influenced by the Government in power."

"What else is it but being influenced by the Government in
power if the sentence imposed depends for its severity on the
extent to which the Crown presses a case?" John asked.

"In deciding upon a sentence in a case like this a Judge must
bear in mind the prevailing conditions at the time. The same
would apply to a convicted burglar. It may be necessary to make
an example of Stern as a deterrent to others. There is a great
deal of social unrest. But we are assuming a little prematurely
that your friend will be found guilty."

"Would the case have been brought otherwise?" John asked,
with a sardonic smile.

The next morning he went round to Claremount Gardens.

"Dearest John, you don't know how glad I am to see you! Of

E

course you know he was granted bail yesterday after the second hearing at Bow Street."

"I didn't know that. He's at Brunswick Square then?"

"Yes."

"He must have been glad to get away from Brixton."

"He wasn't. He suspects the Crown of a trick by not opposing bail after the second hearing. In fact he's being rather difficult. I'm hoping you'll be able to persuade him to be less difficult."

John made a grimace.

"When does Julius get over?"

"Just before Christmas. I've found a house for them in Well Walk which they can have till the end of April. It's so sad that when I'm going to see Sebastian and Monica for the first time everything should be clouded by this wretched business of Emil's. What does your father think, John?"

"I think he feels the Government may wish to make an example of Emil."

Miriam made a gesture of despair.

"I know, I know," she exclaimed. "I feel that myself, and Emil glories in the challenge. He says he is utterly indifferent what they do because in the end it will turn against them. I'm afraid I have a wholesome respect for what the British Government can do."

That afternoon John saw Emil in the flat.

"So they allowed you bail," he said.

"Of course they allowed me bail. They're set on my pleading guilty. And they know all my friends and relations will assist. But I am not going to plead guilty."

"But why are they all so anxious for you to plead guilty?" John asked.

"Because the Intelligence people always like to keep out of court if they can manage it. However, they'll get no help from me," Emil declared bitterly.

John knew it was useless to argue, and asked what Emil's counsel thought.

"Bertram? Oh, of course he urges me to plead guilty. Counsel always do in a case like this. They think it earns them a good mark higher up. And Samuelson wants to brief Hazlitt. I'm not going to waste money on forensic stars. Bertram must do his best alone. I know perfectly well I shall be found guilty and that I shall go to prison. It will give me time to put my ideas in order."

After leaving Emil in this mood John got in touch with Samuelson, his solicitor.

"What can I do with him, Mr Ogilvie? What can anybody do with him?" asked the plump little man whose black hair was so finely brushed and so plentifully oiled that John looked once to see if the dusty window of the Norfolk Street office really was reflected in it. "He'll listen to no advice from me. I'm sure that if he'll let me brief Sir Walter Hazlitt, and if the Attorney-General . . ."

"That's Winstanley, isn't it?"

"Sir William Winstanley. What was I saying? Oh yes, if the Attorney-General knows that Mr Stern will plead guilty at the Old Bailey I've reason to suppose from a hint dropped to me in certain quarters that he will not press the case too heavily, and I think he'd get off with a fine. But if he insists on fighting them I wouldn't be surprised if he gets a nasty sentence—a really nasty sentence."

"Will any evidence be called for character?" John asked.

"We should certainly like to call some evidence," Mr Samuelson said. "But you know Mr Stern. The question is whether he'll agree."

"I think I could give useful evidence of his work during the war."

"That might be very useful indeed, Mr Ogilvie. I tell you what, I wish you could have a private talk with Mr Bertram."

"Is that Arnold Bertram?" John asked.

"That's right. Young, but likely to go a long way."

"I know him," John said.

So the next day he went to see Arnold Bertram at his chambers. Bertram was a year senior to himself and like himself an Exeter man. They had not been intimate at Oxford, but John could reasonably call him a friend of his.

Arnold Bertram was a handsome fellow of the type that suits a wig and a gown. As a successful dramatist and the son of a Judge, John was more cordially welcomed than he might have been merely as an Exeter contemporary.

"I didn't know Stern was a friend of yours, Ogilvie. I wish you could persuade him to listen to good advice. It makes it impossible for counsel if his client won't listen to anything. However, I mustn't say any more. Mr Samuelson says you're anxious to testify to character if it would be useful. It would be extremely useful. War service still goes down very well."

It seemed to John that he spent the next month in arguments or listening to the arguments of other people. Emil allowed himself to be persuaded at last into John's being called to testify to his war service.

"I object strongly to this exhibitionism," he declared. "But as my mother threatens a serious breakdown if I don't surrender to it, I suppose I'll have to agree. Besides, I really can't put up with any more conferences. I'm sick of the sight of the Temple, sick of the dust and greed and unreality of it all. It's intolerable that because I have occupied a certain position and know a few distinguished people I should be expected to employ an expensive leader like Hazlitt. I won't do it. Bertram must get through on his own. If he's frightened for his career then let him throw up the brief and I'll defend myself."

"Oh, my god, don't talk so damned silly, Mr Stern," the plump little solicitor expostulated.

"I'm not interested in the result of the trial," Emil insisted. "Even penal servitude doesn't alarm me as a prospect. The whole business to me is hocus-pocus. I'm anxious to expose those fellows who dug themselves into a soft job with counter-espionage during the war and now want to hold on to it on the excuse of protecting the country against communism and revolution. They're keener than ever on that now that the Irish treaty has been agreed upon and they can't find any more work for the Black and Tans or the Ulster Specials."

"What would you do with him, Mr Ogilvie?" asked the plump little solicitor, as he and John left Emil after one of those arguments. "He doesn't seem to realize that when you start fighting with the Law, the Law wins every time. And not on points either."

As if Emil's obstinacy were not enough of a problem John was worried by a letter from Fitz written in answer to one from him congratulating him on the signature of the Treaty:

Tinoran,
Caragh Lake,
Co. Kerry
December 15th, 1921.

Dear Judge,
Aren't you typical of British innocence when Britain has managed to get all it wanted! We consider that our delegates were completely outmanœuvred by the British Government representatives. There was talk of having them arrested for treason

to the Republic when they came back, but it was understood that they only signed when Lloyd George offered them the alternative of signing at once or starting the war again. They felt they couldn't risk calling his bluff, for bluff it was because the British Government would not have dared outrage the feelings of the rest of the world by going back to the methods of the last two years. However, the treaty still has to be approved and we're hoping the Dail will refuse. The debate is on now. We didn't do what we did to make a good bargain with the British Empire. We fought for the honour and freedom of Ireland. We are still willing to fight for that. We don't want prosperity if prosperity can only be recovered by dishonour. We don't care if Ireland loses the whole world if she keeps her soul. Nora died for true freedom, not the pretence of it secured by the treaty. It was to be quit of the British Empire and all its humbug that we fought. And even if the treaty be approved and later on ratified we shall still fight. Even if it means fighting against men by whose side we have fought, some of us will still fight. We'd rather have no bread than half a loaf. The British have tricked us as they've tricked every nation with whom they have fought, but they can't trick all of us. And in Belfast at this moment they're shooting Catholic children at the rate of two or three a week. You saw what the British Empire loyalists could do in Belfast. Well, they're at it again. They have men there arrested on suspicions lodged in hulks the like of those in the eighteenth century on the Thames.

No, John boy, keep your congratulations. We're bitter at the thought of what Griffiths and the others signed away in London. It may be that with the fear of war starting again the people of Ireland will approve the treaty, but that's a poor way of getting the better of a small nation which has put up a fight like ours. But approval through fear does not express the will of a people, and some of us will fight on to the end.

My mother grows very frail. Nora's death shook her terribly. That's the worst thing I have to face if the fight begins again— the thought of her and Padraig alone here. Still, even that thought won't keep me back. I've dedicated myself and the vow must hold. And I know Nora's watching to see I won't hold back. I've queer dreams now. I've a notion some strange things will happen to me in 1922. It was written long since. I told you of that vision I had of my grave twenty years ago. It was on the night of the Assumption. Well, I've a notion it will come

to pass next August, and I'll be with Nora again. Try to
understand my point of view about the treaty. You've understood me better than almost anybody. You see, we weren't
fighting for Dominion status as a colony. We're a mother
country, John. Your own west of Scotland is a colony like ours.
No, for me it's the Republic or nothing, and let the British
Empire fall to pieces in its own good time. There's one thing,
there'll always be plenty of tired old British statesmen to help
it fall to pieces a bit quicker.

Well, this is a hell of a long letter, but I've spared you the sight
of my miserable handwriting for long enough now. I did not
even answer your letter about Nora.

Your old friend

Fitz

And after all I've forgotten to say how glad I was to hear
you've made a Christian of your daughter. Ellen's a proud
godmother. And now what about yourself? What keeps you
back? Damn it, Judge, if I am killed I'll haunt you till you take
the plunge into the font. You'll need the Rock in the times
ahead. Can't you see that the whole world will go to pieces
without Christianity? And if that's so, isn't that testimony
enough to the truth of it? Ah, Judge, get some common sense
into your head and you'll find supernatural religion as obvious
as the road in front of your nose. My blessings on Corinna
Mary Ellen, and may the Mother of God hold her safe in her
arms. Give the little colleen the beads I've wrapped up for her.
It was Nora's favourite rosary.

John replied to this letter at once:

57 Church Row,
Hampstead, N.W.
Dec. 17, 1921.

My dear Fitz,

I am grieved that what had seemed to the friends of
Ireland a victory seems to you a defeat. I will not presume to
argue with one whose burning assurance shames my own Hamlet-
esque indecision due to seeing two sides to every question. Should
what you saw in that vision come to pass I promise you that I
will be received into the Catholic Church in the conviction that I
shall see again a friend lost to me in this world, though I would
rather die without faith in personal immortality than be granted
it thus.

You do not want words to thank you for the rosary, and my prayer is that the year-old child who will receive it on her first birthday will be able to thank you herself in Gaelic a year hence. I have found through Ellen what I believe will be the perfect nurse for Corinna, but of course I must get Athene's permission to engage her. She is a Catholic girl from Moidart—Mairi MacDonald. At present she is with some charming Irish people called Regan, but Colonel Regan's regiment goes to India soon and Mairi MacDonald's mother objects to her being so far away.

I am tied in London for the moment by Emil Stern's trial. He is as intransigent as you. Do you remember when you called him the Infant Samuel at school? You wouldn't sympathize with his political views, but I think you'd respect his fanaticism. It seems incredible that twenty years have passed since you and he clashed in that memorable debate at St James's.

Oh, Fitz, my dear Fitz, I wish you could have your heart's desire.

Yours ever

J. P. O.

Elise Ogilvie had been greatly amused to hear of John's search for a nurse for his daughter.

"But, Elise," he protested, "I haven't actually engaged her. Naturally I shall consult Athene."

Elise still laughed.

"I'm wondering what I should have said if Alec had calmly announced to me that he had found an excellent nurse for David," she exclaimed.

Even Miriam Stern's anxiety over Emil was lightened by a smile at John's domestic adventurousness.

"But if fortune provides exactly the girl one is looking for, why is there anything odd about my recognizing the fact?" he asked, a little piqued by the reception of his plan.

"Attaboy!" cried Leonora. "But I'm used to this kind of thing. If I'd come home to our apartment from a morning with my dressmaker and found that Julius had changed the whole staff I wouldn't have been surprised. And I guess Athene will be just as sweet as pie about it."

"If Julius hadn't married you first and if I hadn't married Athene," John declared, "I'd have spent the rest of my life regretting I hadn't married you, Leonora."

Julius and Leonora had just arrived with the children and were settled in the furnished house in Well Walk. Sebastian was now nearly seven—a striking boy with his father's smoky eyes and dark eyebrows under his mother's flaxen hair. Monica at just over eighteen months was dark as a gypsy.

"And which is my god-daughter like?" Leonora asked.

"I don't think you can tell yet," John replied. "One day she'll look a bit like Athene, and the next day a bit like me and the next day like nobody in particular."

"I'm dying to see her," Leonora declared. "We'll celebrate Monica's second birthday in Citrano. Oh dear, I do hope nothing too bad is going to happen to poor Emil."

"Well, he's made a pretty good ass of himself," Julius observed severely.

A week after this John read to Elise an extract from a letter of Athene's:

> *I'm so glad you think you've found the right nurse. She sounds just what we want, and as both her god-mothers approve I'm sure I shall approve too. If Mairi—I wonder how that's pronounced—comes out with Arthur when his Easter holidays begin that will be splendid, because our present Nannie wants to go back to England at the beginning of March and I shall adore having Corinna to myself for a week or two.*

"Well, I still think Athene is a model of wifely trust," Elise declared. "And I do hope she won't find Prudence an incubus."

Prudence and Arthur had just gone off to Citrano, the latter now as firmly convinced that he could not speak a word of Italian as four years ago he had been convinced that he could not speak any other language.

"Of course she won't be an incubus," John said. "She's very good company."

Elise sighed.

"I don't know what it is, John. I'm only ten years older than you, and yet I feel the ruins of a world are strewn between me and Prudence. Do you really like the way girls of twenty talk nowadays?"

"I think it's much more healthy than the way girls talked once upon a time."

"Do you, John? I wonder. I can't help feeling that such freedom of talk may lead soon to equal freedom of action."

"David is just as free in his talk as Prudence," John pointed out.

"Not with me," Elise replied. "But I think Prudence takes pleasure in trying to shock me."

"I don't agree."

"Oh, I know I'm not allowed to criticize my own daughter," Elise murmured. "But at any rate you will insist on her coming back to England by March at latest. Oh dear, I wish she'd find a young man to marry next season."

"A nice rich young man," John added.

Elise seemed unconscious of irony.

"Yes," she replied simply.

Emil's first emotion on entering the dock at the Central Criminal Court was the size of it. Vaguely he had always thought of the dock as a place about six feet square. As he passed through the glass-topped door a constable patted his pockets to protect the court against the menace of a concealed weapon. The door clicked behind him, and looking round he saw it was without a handle on the inside. He felt as if he were crossing the polished floor of a ballroom before he reached the railing, which he did at the same moment as Mr Justice Marsden received the bows of the court and took his seat. An official mumbled some rigmarole at the accused, which Emil was hardly aware was being addressed to him until he caught the word 'guilty'. In the ensuing pause he replied coldly and clearly 'not guilty'. He then found the Judge was telling him he could be seated and he sat down in the leather-seated chair placed for his convenience. As he did so he became aware for the first time of what was presumably an elderly warder on his right sitting in the corner of the dock at a small table on which was a quire or so of blank foolscap embossed with the royal arms. This silver-haired antique was finding it hard to keep awake. Every time Emil looked at him he was nodding like an old gentleman in a train and waking suddenly with a start. It was not so long before Emil caught himself nodding in the chair. There was something about the illumination of the court which wearied the eyes. Perhaps it was the contest between the dull January day entering through the skylights and the high windows and the ill-planned electric lamps all over the court. To add to that fatiguing illumination there was the hesitant mumbling voice of Sir William Winstanley, the Attorney-General, a plum-pudding-headed man

about whose eminence at the Bar Emil passed the time for a while
in puzzled speculation. As the case progressed he found himself
growing more and more bored, more and more sleepy.   The
reiterations and circumlocutions, the corrections and counter-
corrections, the scratching of quill pens, the paraphernalia of attaché
cases in the well of the court, the twelve members of the jury looking just that much more fatuous since women had been added to
juries, the Home Office and War Office representatives watching
the case from a front seat in the gallery like half a dozen black
fowls on a roosting-perch, the unreal figure of the Judge . . . no
wonder the silver-headed warder in the corner of the dock nodded.
To endure this boredom day after day on the chance of being asked
by the prisoner for a sheet of paper on which to scrawl a communication to his counsel would drug a younger man than him into
somnolence.

Emil's own boredom was intensified by his complete indifference
to the verdict, or for that matter to the sentence.   He had pleaded
'not guilty' solely to embarrass those six black fowls up there, and
as the case dragged on he began to fear lest they had contrived to
stop the calling of their two chief witnesses.

And then Sir William Winstanley rose portentously.

"M'lud, I am now desirous of calling—er—an officer at present
employed in—er—extremely confidential and—er—highly responsible and—er—I may add—er in short I would ask for the court
to be cleared and for the next part of the case to be taken *in camera*."

"As you desire, Mr Attorney."

Whereupon the spectators in their reservation and the press
reporters in theirs were shepherded out.

The Attorney-General looked fearfully round over his bulky
shoulders.

"M'lud, I have a further request to make."

"Well, Mr Attorney?"

"The officer I was proposing to call, m'lud, is, as I have—er—
already—er—indicated to your lordship, employed in an—er . . ."

"Yes, yes, Mr Attorney, you've told me that already," interrupted the Judge with a hint of impatience.

"With great respect, m'lud, I do not think I have—er—mentioned that this officer . . ."—Sir William lowered his voice almost
to a whisper—". . . that in fact this officer is a present member of
the Secret Service."

Everybody in court except the accused in the dock and the
silver-haired warder nodding over his virgin quires in the corner

of it was electrified by this announcement. Even the Judge looked round at the witness-box with an expression of mild interest.

"And that—er—being the case, m'lud," Sir William continued, "I venture to ask permission to give the name of the witness in writing to your lordship, but to refer to him merely as Major X."

"As you will, Mr Attorney. I do not wish to break up the Secret Service by any judicial indiscretion," said Mr Justice Marsden. "He shall be Major X even *in camera*."

Emil found himself saying over to himself with a smile one of the verses that the White Rabbit read at the trial of the Knave of Hearts:

> *Don't let him know she liked them best,*
> *For this must ever be*
> *A secret, kept from all the rest*
> *Between yourself and me.*

He had hardly finished when he saw in the witness-box the foxy head of Major Brinsley Rossiter, who, under the mask of Major X, was telling the Attorney-General of the circumstances in which his attention had been directed to the activities of the accused among His Majesty's Forces.

Emil leant over and asked the silver-headed warder for paper. The old gentleman woke up with a start and pressed upon him enough folio sheets to write a moderately long short story.

Emil wrote for his counsel:

> *Ask this Major X if he ever corresponded with me on matters relating to intelligence work during* 1918 *when I was in Sweden. If the correspondence was slightly acrimonious. If I had occasion to complain of his indiscretion in Stockholm. And if a request was made in consequence through the Legation for his immediate recall to London.*

The sheet of paper was folded and passed down over the dock to Mr Arnold Bertram.

When the Attorney-General had finished his examination Mr Arnold Bertram rose to cross-examine. After he had amused himself for a while with the evidence Major X had given, Mr Bertram enquired suavely:

"You do not feel, Major X, that you have imperilled the secrecy of the Secret Service by giving evidence to-day *in camera?*"

"No."

"You do not feel any anxiety lest under your no doubt sufficiently mysterious initial you should be recognized in this court?"

The narrow foxy head of Major X seemed to grow narrower. He sent a glance towards the funereal representatives of the Home Office and the War Office in the hen-roost.

"I do not mean by your friends, Major X," said Mr Bertram, with an encouraging smile. "Shall I repeat the question?"

The Attorney-General rose.

"M'lud, in view of the fact that the name of the witness has been communicated to your lordship I do not understand the bearing of my learned friend's question."

"I was wondering that myself, Mr Attorney," said the Judge, with a glance at Mr Bertram, who inclined his head in deference.

"As your lordship pleases. I will put the question in another way. Major X, have you had any personal acquaintance with the accused?"

"None."

"I see. But you have corresponded with the accused?"

"I believe I have."

"In fact you have?"

"Yes."

"And was it a pleasant correspondence, Major X?"

"I really don't remember."

"I see. You don't remember?"

"No."

"Do you remember going to Stockholm in the year 1918?"

The Attorney-General rose like a flustered nurse who perceives that her small charge is on the verge of laxity in a drawing-room.

"M'lud, I must beg protection for this witness. I thought I had it clear that he is still employed in a responsible position, an—er—highly responsible and confidential position, and in view of your lordship's consent to his strict anonymity being preserved I regard my learned friend's question as—er, as—er . . ."

"I do not think I can allow that question, Mr Bertram," said the Judge.

"As your lordship pleases. I will put the question in another way. Major X, is it a fact that the accused once had occasion to complain of your indiscretion in the matter of carrying out your duties?"

"Must I answer that question, my lord?" Major X barked.

"I think that is not a question which involves any risk to the discovery of your identity," the Judge replied.

Major X scowled.

"I believe that there was a slight argument about something that happened," he admitted.

"And in consequence of that slight argument," Mr Bertram said slowly, "was a request made by the Legation in . . . I beg pardon, m'lud, by a Legation in a northern capital that you should be immediately recalled to London, Major X?"

"I never heard so," said Major X.

"Which perhaps shows that diplomats are as cautious as members of the Secret Service. Thank you, Major. I have no more questions to put to this witness, m'lud."

The next witness called by the Crown was Ernest Minchin, whose evidence was given while the court was still *in camera*. The pale round-faced man with the plump white hands made heavy demands on the glass of water in the witness-box. All his saliva seemed to be exuding from his forehead, as Sir William Winstanley drew from him the account of his relations with the accused, and by the time it came for his cross-examination by Counsel for the Defence his answers were so inaudible that the large glass of water had to be refilled in order to moisten his parched tongue.

"I suppose you would describe yourself as an *agent provocateur*, Mr Minchin?" counsel asked.

The Attorney-General rose at once.

"I submit, m'lud, that my learned friend by using such a word is—er—endeavouring to prejudice the members of the jury. I submit that the use of such a word is an attempt to cast odium upon men who are engaged in the difficult task of protecting the state in the—er—difficult times and who are unable to—er—speak for themselves."

"With great respect to my learned friend, m'lud," said Mr Bertram, "I have here a copy of the *Concise Oxford Dictionary*, from which, with your lordship's permission, I will quote the definition of *agent provocateur* as an 'agent enticing one suspected of sedition, etc., to commit himself'. I submit that the examination of this witness has established that that was precisely the object of his employment by the gentlemen who are unable to—er—speak for themselves."

"I do not understand why you object to the word, Mr Attorney," said the Judge.

"As your lordship pleases," Sir William Winstanley boomed lugubriously.

"I will repeat my question, Mr Minchin," said Mr Bertram.

"If you mean I enticed the accused," the round-faced man

answered, "I say I did no such thing. It was him enticed me. He enticed me to stir up feeling among the soldiers and sailors of His Majesty's Forces."

"You did not take steps to get into touch with Mr Stern?" counsel pressed.

"Not until he'd already started in making propaganda about the workers."

"And then you reported these activities to Major X?"

"No, I didn't. I never seen—never saw Major X. I always saw another gentleman."

"M'lud," Mr Bertram complained with exquisite sauvity, "I suggest that, of course quite unintentionally, my learned friend the Attorney-General has placed me in a situation of some difficulty by not allowing me an opportunity of cross-examining the even more mysterious officer whom I hope I shall not imperil the secrecy of the Secret Service by alluding to as Major Y."

"Come, come, Mr Bertram," said the Judge, "you cannot expect to be favoured with an opportunity to cross-examine every officer employed on confidential work. I think Major X made it clear that the witness was a secret agent."

"In fact an *agent provocateur*," Mr Bertran added, with a glance at the Attorney-General. "I am obliged to m'lud."

Then he turned again to the round-faced man.

"Did you ever make any suggestions to Mr Stern about ways in which propaganda among the troops might be extended and developed?"

"I don't quite follow you."

"Really, Mr Minchin, for a secret agent you seem somewhat unduly slow. Did you or did you not propose to Mr Stern certain methods of propaganda?"

"I may have made a few suggestions, yes."

"As for instance that leaflets calling upon the troops to refuse to fire on the workers should be printed?"

"I may have done."

"Though Mr Stern himself rather disapproved of that?"

"He only disapproved because it would cost money."

"And you were already making rather heavy calls on him for your personal expenses?" Mr Bertram asked quickly, thus securing the full benefit of the titter in court which Minchin's answer to the previous question had started.

"I repeat, Mr Minchin, you were making heavy calls on one of your employers?"

"I was receiving a certain amount for expenses."

"And no doubt you were receiving a certain amount from Major X?"

"I tell you I never saw Major X."

"I beg your pardon, I mean Major Y?"

"I don't know any Major Y."

"At any rate you were taking money from both sides?"

"I was receiving my salary, yes."

"Did you have to account to your official employers for what you were screwing out of your unofficial employer?"

"No, they had every confidence in me," said Minchin surlily.

"Really? A delightful peep into the Eden of Intelligence," Mr Bertram commented. "So your official employers had every confidence in you, had they? Would you consider such confidence reflected upon their discrimination?"

"I don't get you."

"Well, to put it bluntly, Mr Minchin, does not your official employers' belief in your honesty suggest for Intelligence officers a dangerous indulgence in credulity?"

"You use a lot of big words and think you're being funny, don't you?" the round-faced man sneered. "But you don't make any impression on me."

"No, I suppose not," Mr Bertram agreed. "There's no money to be made out of me, is there? Well, I don't think I want to ask you any more questions, Mr Minchin."

Emil watched the round-faced man leave the witness-box and withdraw from the proceedings. It was no salve to his own wounded judgment that Mr Minchin was unlikely to be employed again by the War Office or the Home Office. That he, an Intelligence officer with experience of Greeks and Armenians and Persians, of Egyptians, Turks, Levantines, and of his own race with their wits ripened by the sun, should have been successfully tricked by a Minchin galled him. His own fervour of belief in the workers' cause was responsible. The work he had done at Icaros had been purely intellectual. The passion he had given to it had been inspired by a desire for efficiency. He had even been willing to risk his life for that. Minchin had given him a lesson. Whatever the result of this case, the lesson would not be needed again. He would never again trust man or woman because enthusiasm tempted him to do so.

The court had now emerged from *in camera*. The spectators and the reporters had returned to their reservations. A series of witnesses from His Majesty's Forces were testifying to the truth of the Crown's allegation that they had been incited to disaffection.

The court adjourned for lunch. Emil had insisted that neither Astrid nor his mother should be present during the hearing of the case. It was John who met him when he passed out of the dock. They made their way through the spacious atrium of the Old Bailey, past the great marble staircase that would have given it a likeness to a stately museum if the place had not been infected by an atmosphere of human unhappiness and anxiety.

"The filthy place is like a glorified urinal," John ejaculated with disgust as he and Emil passed out through the swinging doors and walked down the steps. "Do you remember Newgate?" he asked.

Emil shook his head.

"I remember it well and the playing-yard of Christ's Hospital just beyond, and catching a glimpse from the top of the bus of the boys playing football, with their blue-coats kilted above their yellow stockings."

They walked on past the Church of St Sepulchre in search of somewhere to eat.

"That's where they tolled the knell for the condemned on the way to Tyburn," said John. "And for the public hangings outside Newgate when Tyburn was abolished. The whole air here is tainted. Of course I never saw the original Old Bailey before they pulled it down and built the Central Criminal Court on the site of Newgate. It must have been a pest-house."

In the restaurant they entered John noticed Major Brinsley Rossiter sitting at a table with the funereal representatives of the Home Office and the War Office.

"Good god," he exclaimed, "there's that bloody man Rossiter!"

"Major X," Emil corrected. "He was one of the hush-hush people who gave evidence under that initial *in camera* this morning."

John, with a malicious twinkle in his eye, walked across to the table at which Major X was sitting.

"Hullo, Rossiter," he said, "I hear you were in court this morning."

"I don't know who you are, sir," Rossiter snapped, the pulses throbbing in his pinched temples.

"Oh yes, you do, sir," John grinned. "Don't you remember Dublin in 1918 when you hired one of your sleuths to steal my report? Ogilvie is my name. I hear you appeared in court this morning disguised as a letter of the alphabet. Risky to eat in public, isn't it? But then you always were a rotten Intelligence officer."

John turned on his heels and walked back to the table where Emil was sitting.

"I think I've spoilt Major Brinsley Rossiter's beefsteak and kidney pudding," said John in a satisfied voice. "Well, how do you feel, Emil?"

"I'm sure the intention is to make an example of me. Obviously the jury must convict. The only point of interest is the severity of the sentence. Bertram thinks it will be a year in the Second Division. My offence, of course, is political, but in this country the political offence is never recognized as such, and so there is no chance of the First Division. However, please don't worry about me, and do try to prevent my mother's worrying. Astrid is completely sensible about it all. She is able to carry on the business. There is a great deal to be said for the experience of prison. Indeed, I consider it a necessary experience for anybody who aspires to change the social order. We have too little time for meditation."

"I wish I believed that the particular way in which you aspire to change the social order was the right way," John sighed. "But I see more and more clearly every day that man's heart must change before any revolution can be effective for good. A readjustment of the mechanism of the social order is not enough. We won't start an argument about the Russian business, because I don't want to argue with you during this short hour, for I know that if this evening you find yourself in Wormwood Scrubbs—god, what a name!—we are likely to grow further apart during the next months."

A silence fell upon the two friends, and when it was broken they talked of trivial matters like two people on the platform of a railway station passing the time until the train departs leaving one of them behind.

When John found himself in the witness-box, nearness to the Judge did not succeed in destroying the illusion that he was playing a part in a large Punch and Judy show. The Judge in his red robes would have recalled Punch in any event, but it happened that the contours and complexion of Mr Justice Marsden's face added to the likeness. This was the first time John had ever been inside the Old Bailey. Filial piety or embarrassment had insisted he should not expose his father or himself to the ordeal. He noticed that the Judge gave him a sharp look when he entered the box, and he wondered if this was because he knew he was the son of his brother Ogilvie or if it was Mr Justice Marsden's habitual glance at a witness. As he kissed the Testament his lip curled for a moment at so solemn a mockery of God by these play-actors of the Law. And then John Pendarves Ogilvie gave his attention to the questions being put by counsel.

"Did you serve with Mr Stern in the Intelligence Service during the late war?"

"I did."

"Did you form any opinion of his work?"

"I did. His energy and ability were remarkable."

"Were you impressed by his devotion to his duty?"

"Profoundly impressed."

"What were the particular duties assigned to Mr Stern?"

At this point the burly figure of the Attorney-General towered up.

"M'lud, if my learned friend is preparing to put questions to this witness in particular reference to the duties of the accused during the late war I must respectfully put it to your lordship that the public interest would not be served by such questions in open court."

"You ask me to exclude the public?"

"Under submission, m'lud, I do."

"Very well, Mr Attorney," the Judge agreed, with a slight yawn.

Ushers once more shepherded press and public from their reservations, and when the safety of the realm had thus been secured Mr Bertram rose to renew his examination.

"I think you may now tell the court what Mr Stern's duties were."

"After war was declared on Turkey Mr Stern was appointed Vice-Consul at Icaros in order to obtain military information that might be of service to the Mediterranean Expeditionary Force. He had previously been Vice-Consul at Mileto."

"What was his reputation in Mileto?"

"Mr Stern was the last of the Allied Consuls to leave Mileto, and it was known that it was his friendship with the Vali . . ."

"The what?" interposed the Judge.

"The Turkish Governor, Rewfiz Bey, my lord. It was Mr Stern's friendship with him which enabled him to influence the members of the British colony in Mileto to leave the place before war broke out with Turkey."

"Which no doubt prevented their internment?" counsel asked.

"Certainly."

"And when Mr Stern left Mileto what did he do?"

"He went to the island of Icaros, where he built up the most efficient Intelligence organization in the Aegean."

"And then?"

"And then it was so efficient that he was transferred to Stockholm."

"And throughout your personal knowledge of Mr Stern's work in the Near East were you impressed by its great value to the Allied cause?"

"Profoundly impressed."

"Thank you, Mr Ogilvie. I do not know if my learned friend . . ."

Sir William Winstanley rose to the full height of his six feet three inches and regarded John.

"You say you were profoundly impressed by the work of the accused in the Near East. Was it not the ordinary work that would be expected of any of His Majesty's Vice-Consuls?" he enquired in his deepest voice.

"Certainly not. It was work of a highly specialized character, the result of which, to my personal knowledge, was greatly appreciated by the Staff of the Mediterranean Expeditionary Force. It was for lack of attention to the work of men like Mr Stern that the British Government lost Gallipoli."

"Yes, yes," the Judge interposed. "That is nothing to do with the question you were asked. Do not elaborate your answers."

"I apologize, my lord, but I was under the impression that Sir William was unaware of the routine of a Vice-Consul."

"But with regard to this highly specialized work," the Attorney-General continued, "it was such as might possibly lead the accused to specialize in intrigue?"

"I really do not understand that question, Sir William. Do you want me to reply that any military officer or consular official who has done Intelligence work is liable to incite His Majesty's Forces to mutiny?"

"Not at all," the Attorney-General snapped irritably. "I am putting it to you that the no doubt valuable services of the accused during the war consisted chiefly of intrigue?"

"Would you call it intrigue, Sir William, to disguise yourself as a Turk and make your way alone into Mileto? That is what Mr Stern did, at the risk of his life. In fact he repeatedly risked his life through nearly two years."

"I have no more questions to put to this witness, m'lud," said Sir William Winstanley.

So John stepped down from the box. He was the only witness

called for the defence. When the court was open again, and Mr Arnold Bertram rose to make his speech, he stressed the idealistic aspects of his client's behaviour, and much to the annoyance of that client made great play with the unlikelihood of so experienced an Intelligence officer's being deceived by a man of Minchin's type unless his motives were purely idealistic. He urged that a great deal too much importance had been ascribed to his client's actions, which he maintained were innocent of the slightest intention to impair the safety of the realm. His client might have been indiscreet, but he begged the members of the jury not to judge indiscretion too harshly. Had not some of them occasionally been carried away by their own enthusiasm, he added, gazing at the stolid countenances of the nine men and three women who composed the jury.

The Attorney-General, replying for the Crown, was not prepared to accept what his learned friend called indiscretion as anything less than a determined effort by a bigoted and misguided man to let loose upon this country the horrors and crimes of Russian Bolshevism. It was sad indeed to reflect that one who had rendered valuable service in an official capacity to his country should now take advantage of that very experience and use it against the best interests of his country. He implored the members of the jury not to allow themselves to be influenced by his learned friend's observations upon the methods employed by the authorities to counteract the spread of revolutionary propaganda. All normal men and women abhorred anything that savoured of spying, but spying was sometimes necessary and he warned them not to allow their natural repulsion for the means to overlook the value of the end. He ventured to point out that the very testimony which had been called on behalf of the accused was itself a glorification of those means on which his learned friend had seen fit to throw such scorn. Let the members of the jury dismiss from their minds all they had heard while the court was *in camera*. Had not the evidence of those soldiers and sailors been sufficient to convince them that without any shadow of doubt a former member of His Majesty's Consular Service had abused his undeniable ability with the object of creating disaffection? These were dangerous times. Not all the vigilance of the Government could prevent the growth of subversive opinions. This country, he rejoiced to affirm, had been the chosen guardian of freedom from time immemorial. But that freedom must not be abused. To attempt to maintain, as his learned friend had attempted to maintain, that this prosecution was an effort to restrict the freedom of speech of which every Englishman was rightly proud was, he ventured to say, nothing more than an ingenious evasion of the issues at stake. And he was confident that the common sense of an English jury would reject such a suggestion. He repeated with all the solemnity he could muster that these were difficult times, and that any act which made them more difficult was to be reprobated. The country was in the happy position of being able to rely implicitly on the loyalty of His Majesty's armed forces, and the thought that when they were called upon to perform their duty they might have been seduced by specious arguments to refuse that duty, however painful it might be, was sufficient to undermine public confidence in the ability of His Majesty's Government to maintain order. Let the members of the jury remember what had happened in Russia. The horrors of Bolshevism had been unloosed by the corruption of the armed forces of Russia. He did not suggest that British soldiers or sailors were capable of such a dereliction of their duty, but that only rendered it more imperative that any attempt by antisocial elements in the population to foster the spirit of mutiny should immediately be met by the most vigorous action. Such action was provided by the laws of England. The very law upon which the prosecution relied dated back to the year 1779, and he did not hesitate to assert that a law-abiding public would gratefully welcome the rigorous enforcement of such a law. He asserted that the facts in this case were plain, and that the members of the jury must not allow themselves to be deterred by any pity for misplaced idealism from declaring the accused guilty of the charges brought against him.

In his summing-up the Judge warned the members of the jury that they must base their verdict on fact, not upon motive. If they believed the witnesses called by the Crown they must find the accused guilty. If on the other hand they were not satisfied with the evidence produced by the Crown they must find the accused not guilty. The members of the jury must beware of allowing their natural dislike of anything that savoured of spying to influence their verdict. The idea of spying was detestable to any decent man or woman, but unfortunately it was sometimes necessary. The Crown, however, had not relied upon the evidence of professional agents. The Crown had called members of His Majesty's Forces whom, it was alleged, the accused had attempted to seduce from their duty. Did the members of the jury consider that those witnesses were credible, honest, and trustworthy? If they did, they must disembarrass their minds of sentiment and find the accused guilty.

The jury were only a few minutes in reaching such a verdict. In the deepening shadows of the grey January afternoon the Judge sentenced Emil to twelve months in the Second Division. The prisoner turned round to see behind him a warder who pointed to a glass-topped door on the other side of the dock. Through this he passed out, to descend by a kind of stone harbour-slip, half-way down which was an iron gate which shut behind him with a click. At the bottom of the slip was a whitewashed kitchen in which a young policeman was stamping on a cigarette he had evidently flung down in a hurry at the sound of approaching footsteps. Below the kitchen was a row of unlighted cells with glass-fronted doors into one of which Emil was put and the door closed upon him. The deepening afternoon had made the corridor outside so dusky that his cell was almost completely dark, yet not so dark but that he could read scrawled in pencil on the wall close to the door: *12/1/22. Eighteen months. O God, what will my poor wife and kids do?* That agonized question had been inscribed yesterday. No doubt it would be obliterated when it was noticed to be defying the nattiness of the Central Criminal Court. But how monstrous, he reflected, that the architect of a building not yet twenty years old should have been unable to provide better accommodation for prisoners awaiting their trial, for down here in these dark narrow cells the innocent and the guilty had to sit waiting for their hour to enter the dock. What a farce it was, this so-called English presumption that a man was innocent until he had been found guilty! To one of these dim tanks a man or woman might be brought from Brixton Jail to wait all day for trial and at the end of it be taken back to Brixton to pass another night because the court was not ready for him; yes, and perhaps yet another weary anxious day and another weary anxious night before he walked up that stone slipway and through that iron gate, and on up again and through the glass-topped door into the spacious polished dock, to be dazed by the sudden sight of people and light and an old man dressed up like Santa Claus. And oafish crime reporters would comment on the apparent indifference of some man on trial for his life to the proceedings. They did not grasp, these clods, that the wretched creature was stupefied by the whole business. Emil was so indignant about the treatment of untried prisoners that he did not think about his own future while he was waiting for his removal to what presumably would be Wandsworth or Wormwood

Scrubbs. At last the door of the cell opened. He was conducted along the corridor into a room where behind a counter an elderly policeman with a walrus moustache was entering up, on various slates hanging by string from nails, his arrangements for the prison vans out in the yard. One of his subordinates had apparently made the mistake of entering on the waybill for Wormwood Scrubbs the untried prisoners who had to be sent back to Brixton, and this old man was grumbling and licking his fingers and rubbing out names from one slate and squeakily entering names upon another slate.

"Give anyone the sick it would," he growled, "to see the way some of you young fellers act so careless. Nice thing it 'ud be if these remand prisoners got took to the Scrubbs and on'y me to blame. I don't know what the Force is coming to."

Emil and his guards passed on, and a minute or two later he was in Black Maria bound for Wormwood Scrubbs.

As soon as sentence was passed John left the Old Bailey and drove to Brunswick Square, where Miriam was waiting with Astrid for the news.

"It is prison," Astrid exclaimed when she saw John's face.

"Twelve months," he replied. "It was a foregone conclusion. The Government were clearly set on making an example, and in the circumstances it may be considered a light sentence."

"Twelve months," Miriam moaned.

"It will be less than that with remission," John reminded her. "He will be out by November."

"As if that were not a hundred years," she exclaimed.

"I do not find that, Miriam," her daughter-in-law insisted. "I find that it will pass very quickly. And Emil would have been disappointed with a very small prison, because it would have meant that his work was not important. I am sure he will be so happy in prison because he will be able to think so much. He has said that to me. And he will observe the conditions by which the bourgeois hold down the workers. Oh yes, he will be extremely reinforced."

"Yes, I suppose my old-fashioned grief is just self-indulgence," Miriam admitted. "You must forgive my weakness, Astrid dear . . . I think I should like to go home."

"I'll drive you back," John said quickly.

In the taxi she leant upon his shoulder and wept.

"Forgive me," she murmured when the taxi was passing the tawny murk of King's Cross. "I'm not crying because Emil will spend this year in prison but because I dread what he may do when he comes out. The old fear that haunts the whole of our race is clutching at me, John . . . the insecurity of three thousand years. It's in our blood. And in this safe and lovely and beloved England I cannot bear that my son should help to rouse hostility."

"I don't think the fact of his being a Jew will do that, Miriam. It's the fact of his being an ex-consul which will shock anybody who is anxious to be shocked. That's why it was so unfair of the Attorney-General to get my testimony to his service at Mileto and Icaros into *camera*."

"But you heard what Astrid said. He welcomes prison as an opportunity for thinking. And what will he be thinking of all the time? Destruction, destruction. That's what I dread."

"He may decide that what he did was rather silly," John pointed out. "He must be kicking himself for having been taken in by a cheap-skate *agent provocateur* like Minchin. I doubt if he'll do any more inciting to disaffection. In fact he may emerge from Wormwood Scrubbs with more relish for construction than destruction. After all, he is intelligent, and having gratified his fervour by a minor martyrdom he'll probably be more practical now. Anyway, there it is, I shall soon have to think of going to prison myself. Between Edward Fitzgerald and Emil I feel so unenterprising."

"No, don't come in," Miriam said when the taxi reached Claremount Gardens. "I'm going straight to bed. I must somehow get myself into a condition of comparative equanimity for Julius's concert next week. Dear boy, he's been wonderfully good about this miserable case, and Leonora has been angelic."

John drove on in the taxi to Church Row, where after dinner he talked the trial over with his father.

"Well, I can't say I regret having escaped your profession, m'lud," he observed, lighting up a cigar.

"No?"

"There's too much humbug about it. You may have observed that I have never attended a case in which you were playing a part."

"I had noticed it, yes," the Judge replied.

"And I never will," his son added. "Don't you feel a little ashamed of your costume?"

"I don't see why I should feel more ashamed of that than you felt of your naval uniform."

"But a naval uniform is serviceable.   A judge's get-up is fancy dress.   Mr Justice Marsden looked exactly like a mammoth Punch, and he appeared on the Bench with a sort of sidelong glide just like Punch in the puppet-show.   There was no Judy and no Clown, but the Attorney-General was not unlike Jim Crow to look at, though perhaps inferior to him in mental agility."

"Winstanley is a solid man," said the Judge.

"Through and through, I should imagine."

"His manner may be a trifle heavy, but he's a good lawyer, in fact a very good lawyer," the Judge went on.

"Well, you have to listen to him; I don't, thank goodness. However, I rather liked your brother Marsden.   But really, you know, m'lud, what a solemn farce it all is.   The amount of time that's wasted!"

"That's very easy and superficial criticism, isn't it?   Whatever may be said about the externals of English Law no country in the world has produced an administration that can compare with it for dignity and effectiveness.   Where are to be found judges as independent of political influence as ours?"

"I hope they'll preserve that independence," John said.   "But I've been disagreeably surprised during this case to hear several times of something that sounded uncommonly like an arrangement behind the scenes.   It was certainly suggested from a high quarter that if Stern would plead guilty the Government would not press the case too hardly and that he might even get off with a fine. That surely implies the willingness of one of His Majesty's Judges to fall in with the views of the Crown before a jury has decided whether the accused was guilty or not guilty."

"You must have misunderstood," said Sir Alexander firmly. "It was perfectly proper for the Attorney-General to indicate that *he* would not press the case too hardly if your friend pleaded guilty, and any Judge would be entitled to measure his sentence by the gravity of a semi-political offence.   He would naturally be influenced by the evidence of the gravity."

"Surely by such an admission you recognize that the judicature is inclined to be influenced by the legislature, and that seems to me dangerous for the probity of the Bench.   And then there was this *in camera* nonsense.   Do you seriously tell me that a jury is any more to be trusted than the public or the press not to talk about the Home Office and War Office methods of spying on political offenders? The court went into *camera* twice. The first time, of course, I was not present, but a Major in the Flintshires called Brinsley Rossiter was allowed by your brother Marsden to masquerade as Major X because the Crown pleaded that the efficiency of secret intelligence would be seriously impaired by the revelation òf his name even *in camera*. Yet this buffoon went off and lunched near the Central Criminal Court with some of his colleagues, and I had the pleasure of addressing him by his name. I had a passage-of-arms with him in Dublin three years ago. Then when I was going to give evidence about Stern's war service the court was cleared again at the request of the Attorney-General, so that my testimony would not be read in the papers to-morrow and Stern goes to jail without a word in his favour."

"My brother Marsden would have taken your evidence into consideration when passing sentence."

"But that doesn't help Stern with the public. However, I'm not going to make a song about what happened in to-day's case. What I do say, however, is that the device of *in camera* can be used by an unscrupulous Government with as deadly an effect on human liberty as the Star Chamber, and that the Judges should refuse to tolerate such a device."

"Matters connected with the Secret Service are always accorded privilege," said Sir Alexander.

"I don't accept that as justice," John retorted. "An *agent provocateur* deserves no privilege. He's a pest in decent society, and if the Government use such men the Government should protect them, not His Majesty's Judges, who by protecting such creatures destroy the respect in which they should be held. After all, this country may explode one day, and it's unwise to encourage the growing conviction of the belief that there is one law for the rich and another for the poor. I'm sorry to be so critical of your Central Criminal Court production, but frankly I thought it was a badly constructed, badly produced, and badly acted farce."

"How many, many years since I was at one of Julius's concerts!" Miriam Stern murmured as she took her seat by John in the front row of the circle at Queen's Hall ten days after the trial of Emil at the Central Criminal Court. "This is more agitating for me than for you," she said to Leonora, who was on the other side of John.

"It's always pretty hectic for me," Leonora replied.

The programme was to open with Richard Strauss' symphonic poem *Ein Heldenleben*.

"I wonder why that was chosen," John speculated. "I should have thought that with the Beethoven Concerto for the second item a piece of music in which the violin was less prominent would have been more suitable."

"I'll tell you a secret, John. Julius is going to play the solo violin part in the orchestra. *Des Helden Gefährtin.* *The Hero's Beloved.* That's the third part. And this is the anniversary of our wedding day."

"I suppose he'll be playing to you?" John asked, with a smile.

"He never said so, John. But I like to think so."

"I'll have to be careful what I say to Julius about *Ein Heldenleben.* I've always thought that part about *Des Helden Gefährtin* rather cheap and tawdry sentiment. In fact *A Hero's Life* represents to me all that's worst in modern Germany, with its alternating braggadocio and whining and bullying and self-pity. I am surprised that Julius likes it."

"I don't think he does, but he didn't want to conduct before he played the Concerto, and *Ein Heldenleben* was his suggestion to Sir Charles Graham. He thought he'd be less nervous if he were doing something instead of wondering how London would receive his symphony."

"Good gracious," Miriam exclaimed, putting up a pair of opera-glasses. "Yes, it is, it is Julius among the first violins."

"Achilles in Scyros," John commented. "Surrounded by women. I hate this post-war habit of half-filling an orchestra with women."

"But what is Julius doing among the first violins?" his mother asked in astonishment.

Leonora explained about the device to overcome his own nervousness, and as she finished Sir Charles Graham appeared upon the conductor's rostrum, bowing in acknowledgment of the applause that greeted him.

"*Ein Heldenleben* is not a favourite of mine," Miriam said. "It's such a self-assertive piece of music. Still, Julius gave the solo part something I would not have believed possible in the way of sincere emotion."

Julius slipped away during the applause at the end of *Ein Heldenleben*, and presently came back to play the Beethoven Violin Concerto in D major.

Mother and wife listened with her own thoughts, but John, who was holding a hand of each of them, fancied throughout the performance that he was not listening merely with his own ears but with theirs too. He was back in New York ten years ago walking with Julius down Fifth Avenue to dine with the Blakistons. Honk-honk-honk-honk! Those four D sharps on the horns came from the automobiles of Fifth Avenue. And now old Blakiston, as parched and wrinkled with money-making as a bit of popcorn, was showing Julius the Amati violin of his dead daughter Carlotta for which he had paid seven thousand dollars, and Julius had picked it up and was playing the *Perpetuum Mobile*, and Leonora Blakiston, the hard wary little blonde, was watching him spellbound, and the wariness had vanished and the hardness had somehow turned into the strength of a woman who knows what she wants and intends to get it.

"He's not playing his own cadenza. He's playing the Joachim cadenza," Leonora whispered from the present.

And in the past John was leaving the Blakistons' house with Julius and walking back to their hotel along Fifth Avenue, straight and cold and spacious under a starry October sky. Honk-honk-honk-honk! An automobile passed them, and Julius was talking of Leonora. *"There's a completeness about her. You might call her porcelain till you suddenly realize she's unbreakable. Yes, a completeness. I think I've fallen in love."*

And now the muted violins were playing the sweet and simple melody of the Larghetto from which the soloist would carry his listeners to heights ethereal like an angelic guide. Up and up until there seemed nothing left of earth except the accompaniment of pizzicato strings. And at the end a ghostly horn hinting at those four D sharps—a belated neighbour knocking on that street-door in Vienna as Beethoven first heard them, fate knocking at the door as he transformed them for the Fifth Symphony, an automobile honking as we might hear them to-day. Honk-honk-honk-honk! And beauty the vanquisher. Honk-honk-honk-honk! Expiring in the figure of a ghostly horn, slain by beauty.

"He breathed peace upon our life to-day in that Larghetto," John whispered as the second movement flowed into the gay Rondo in a brief cadenza. And while the Rondo danced upon its way John was thinking of Julius's home as a boy among the great level tracts of grass and corn beyond the Vistula. He had a sudden idea. He would suggest to Julius that he should take his mother with him to Poland. It would be useless to invite Miriam to

Citrano. She would never come while Emil was in prison. She might, however, agree to accompany Julius to Poland. Leonora and the children could come out earlier to Citrano. The more John thought about it, the more he liked the idea. Astrid's triumph over Emil's martyrdom was the last emotion to suit his mother's present mood of desolation. He would go round and talk to Leonora about his idea to-morrow. The suggestion to Julius had better come from her. Then like approval of his idea the applause thundered through Queen's Hall to greet the violinist's triumph.

"And now his symphony," Leonora said. "Oh, I do hope it will have the success in London it had in New York."

"Well?" Julius asked, when they went round to congratulate him at the end of the evening, "I wish I didn't sweat so," he ejaculated, pulling irritably at his limp collar.

"I think it is great music, dear," the composer's mother said. "I think it is great music," she repeated. "The Scherzo was particularly impressive. The oboes and cor anglais and bassoons taking that odd slithery theme from the clarinets, basset-horns, and bass clarinets and fighting back until they had transformed it and won the support first of the violins and then of the rest of the strings, and the single reeds still fighting for their theme reinforced by the French horns and presently even by the brass, but defeated in the end and the transformation accepted in that glorious *tutti* at the end of the movement. It seems an expression of outrageous maternal fondness, but I really think I must go back to Beethoven's Ninth Symphony for such an enjoyable battle for a melody."

"I didn't get the notion from Beethoven," said Julius, with a suspicion in his tone of the artist's resentment of influence. "Besides, that wasn't a battle for a theme. That was a rapid rejection of the main themes of his first three movements before he started an entirely new theme for the choral part. I transformed the theme of the single reeds by the way I handled it for the double reeds."

"Yes, Julius, I realized that perfectly," his mother replied. "I only used the Ninth Symphony as a comparison for the kind of delight it gave me."

"The notion came to me first that night in Citrano when we found the Middle-West youth playing his saxophone beside the edge of the tide," Julius explained. "And we danced afterwards on the roof of John's tower."

The following afternoon John went along to the house in Well

Walk to keep an appointment he had made with Leonora the previous evening.   The notices of the concert in the daily papers had been enthusiastic about Julius's playing in the concerto and kind to the symphony.   Naturally there was a certain amount of caution in the praise given to the latter, and all the critics left themselves loopholes for the expression of second thoughts on another hearing.

John reached the house in Well Walk some ten minutes early, and the maid told him that Mrs Stern was not yet back.   He followed her upstairs to the drawing-room whence came the sound of a piano being played.

"It's Master Sebastian," she informed the visitor.

John put a finger to his lips and whispered to let him go in by himself.   He waited till the girl had gone downstairs again.   Then he opened the door very quietly and looked in.   It was a double-room overcrowded with furniture of light woods in the style of the 'nineties when the revolt against dark and heavy mid-Victorian furniture had begun under the encouragement of Maples, Oetzmann, and Shoolbred with support from Liberty's in the way of fabrics.   Through the large window of the inner room the pale January sun was shining upon a cottage Metzler of yellow satinwood.   Seated before it on a gyratory stool twisted to the extent of its height was Sebastian, his curls seeming fused by the sunlight with the satin-wood of the instrument.   He was playing what John fancied was an early sonata of Mozart, and though the tone of the Metzler was muffled and over luscious, and the keys obviously stiff for such small fingers, the music sounded as springlike as if the young Mozart himself were playing it upon a harpsichord in Cecil Court on that first visit to London.   It was music such as the first snowdrops might ring with their white bells in this pale January sunlight.

John stood in the doorway entranced by the picture and the sound, until the young musician reached the end of the sonata and with a grunt pushed against the piano and set himself revolving rapidly on the stool.

"Hullo, Uncle John, I went around three times," he announced, gazing at his audience, satisfied achievement in his smoky eyes but determination to do better in his dark jutting brows.   "I guess I'll swing around six before long.   I never swung more than two till now."

"What were you playing?"

"Oh, just some old thing.   This is a bum piano.   Father's away down town, but Mother will be home soon. She went to buy some cookies. She asked me to go with her, but I didn't want to. Well, I was walking all morning on the Heath with Monica and Nanna, and a fellow gets tired walking around with two women under a lot of old trees."

Sebastian's mother came in at this moment, to be asked what cookies she had bought.

"Delicious cookies, and now run along, old son."

"Good-bye, Uncle John."

"Good-bye. You might play again for me some time."

Sebastian looked doubtful.

"I don't suppose I will," he said. "I like playing best to myself. Say, Mother?"

"Yes?"

"That sure is a bum piano."

With this condemnation, his hands thrust deep into the pockets of his corduroy knickerbockers, his dark eyebrows meeting above his nose he strode out of the room as manfully as almost seven-year-old boys can stride.

"What will I do with him soon?" Leonora asked.

"My dear, he was playing exquisitely," John replied. "You never told me about that development. Curious, isn't it, the way music goes on from father to son? Music and mathematics and athletics. Everything else seems to be derived through the mother. Well, how do you feel after reading the notices of last night?"

"Julius was pleased. After all, he knows England. He didn't expect raptures."

"I think he can feel more than pleased," John affirmed. "And now listen, Leonora dear. I have been thinking about Miriam. You realize how this wretched business of Emil's has upset her."

"Indeed, I do."

"Well, I was thinking last night that if Julius were to discover some urgent reason for visiting Poland . . ."

"They have asked him to play in Warsaw, but he doesn't seem inclined to go."

"I don't suppose he does, but do persuade him to go and ask his mother to go with him. We've often talked about the home he insisted on taking when he was not much more than twice as old as Sebastian. If he would express a desire to revisit that house and take Miriam with him I don't think she could refuse, and it would be the one thing I can imagine that would take her mind off Emil. I know you've got this house till April, but you could come out to Citrano right away with the children. I wired to Athene to-day to find out if the Villa Allegra was available."

"I think it's a fine idea that Julius should take Miriam to Poland, John; but I wouldn't want to go out to Citrano till he came back. You see, he's conducting his symphony at four concerts, one in April in London, and three in March in Edinburgh, Manchester, and Birmingham. He's playing too. I wouldn't so much mind missing that, but I couldn't bear to miss the symphony."

"But wouldn't you find it dull by yourself in London?"

"Don't be so foolish, John. Of course I won't find it dull."

"But you won't let Julius know that the suggestion about Poland was mine?" he pressed.

She told him not to worry.

"I'm going over to Paris to-morrow," he went on, "to meet Arthur and bring him back to school. Then I shall go at once to Citrano. I've missed Corinna's first birthday as it is."

"Well, by the time you come back from Paris I'll have done my best to push Julius and his mother off to Poland."

"Dearest Leonora, you're so sweet and amenable. I was thinking last night during the concerto about meeting you first in the October before the election of Woodrow Wilson, and yesterday was the ninth anniversary of your wedding, and next October will be the third anniversary of mine, and I'll be forty a few days later. I don't feel on the verge of forty."

"You don't look it, John."

"If we played tennis as well as we throw bouquets to one another, Leonora, what world-beaters we should be," he laughed.

While John and Leonora were making plans in Hampstead, Prudence and Arthur were in the train half-way between Naples and Rome.

"Which do you think you'd rather have done, Prudence?" he was asking. "Would you rather have driven a locomotive—I mean a railway engine for twenty miles before you were eleven like Oliphant or would you rather have travelled from Rome to Paris by yourself like what I'm going to do to-night?"

"I'd rather have done what you're going to do," she replied.

"It's a pity John's coming out to meet me at the Gare de Lyon," Arthur continued. "I think if I'd gone all the way to Boulogne

alone and all the way from Boulogne to Hampden House alone
when I was ten years and ten months old I'd have made a record,
don't you? Still, there isn't any chap at Hampden House, not even
Carstairs, the captain of football and cricket, who's been two
nights in the train by himself. *Non si sputa*," he continued, reading
meditatively the notice above either seat of the compartment. "No
spitting." He cast an eye along the floor. "Somebody's been
spitting enough in here."

The only other occupant of the compartment was a slim handsome young man wearing the black shirt of the *Fascisti*.

"I can assure you it was not I who made such spitting," said
this young man from the corner.

Prudence blushed. Her cheeks rivalled the brilliant crimson
plush of the compartment's upholstery.

"Arthur, you are loathsome," she protested.

"*No, no, signorina*," said the young Fascist, seriously, "*È scostu-
mato, schifoso*. Pardon, I lose my English when I make myself
angry. It is a very disgusting habit. It is part of all the bad
things we have now in Italy. You are right," he added to Arthur.

Arthur, obviously gratified by such recognition of his acumen,
carried on the conversation in Italian, in which a month at Citrano
had been enough to restore his fluency. On being congratulated
by the young Fascist he said:

"Well, you speak English jolly well."

"I am now missing practice. I spoke very well when I was
interpreter in 1918 with an English brigade."

"Were you in the war?" Prudence exclaimed, and then most
disconcertingly to herself again blushed fiercely.

"Yes, *signorina*. I was in the war from January 1918, but I
was demobilized in the summer of 1919."

"But you look so young," she began.

"I am very young," he agreed gravely. "I shall have . . . I shall
be twenty-three this May."

"That isn't very young," said Arthur. "That's jolly old."

Conversation flowed agreeably. The young Fascist was less
inclined to talk of his experience during the war than of what had
happened since.

"It was very bad," he explained. "In uniform we must be
everywhere insulted. And when we have banded ourselves
together to create the new Italy we are always betrayed by our
Governments. We do not want to have *bolshevismo* in Italy.
Last year it has been terrible. Strikes and bombs all the time,

F

and many *Fascisti* have been killed by the *arditi del popolo*. But since last November we are a party for the Chamber of Deputies and I think this year we will be strong. Do you read what Benito Mussolini writes every week in the *Popolo d' Italia*? He has been himself a Socialist so he understands how to lead the *Fascisti*. We believe much that is in socialism, but we do not want communism. It was terrible last year when Giolitti gave the factories to be run by the workers. It has only made more violence and the factories were ruined by bad management. Yes, I think this year will bring a new Italy. This miserable Bonomi Cabinet will soon resign, and so it will be for every Cabinet until the *Fascisti* take for themselves the government. We do not want their old men. *Sono stanchi! Sono esauriti! Sono finiti! Basta!* These tired, used, finished old men must go. It is youth who has given itself in this war. It is youth who must make a new Europe. Do you know the song of the *Fascisti*? *Pardon, signorina.*"

And in a light tenor he sang:

> "*Giovinezza, giovinezza,*
> *Primavera di bellezza,*
> *Nel Fascismo è la salvezza*
> *Della nostra libertà.*"

The ivory of his clear-cut profile was faintly flushed upon the cheek-bones by the emotion of that little song half wistful half gay, to the lilt of which the heart of young Italy would beat in time with the future.

"It's extraordinary how interesting politics can be," Prudence declared, and then for the third time she blushed.

"What's your name?" Arthur asked.

"Mario Aprili," the young Fascist replied. "Pardon, signorina," he added, as he offered Prudence his card.

"I'm afraid I haven't got a card," she said. "But my name is Prudence Ogilvie and this is . . . oh, Arthur, what relation are you to me?"

"Well, I suppose I'm your step-nephew, if there is such a thing," Arthur replied rather grudgingly.

"Oh, I never realized that before," she cried, clapping her hands. "Of course, I'm your aunt. Oh, you little brute, I will jolly well make you behave in future."

"Shucks!" the newly apprehended nephew retorted.

Mario Aprili wrote down Prudence's name on the back of one of his own cards.

"*Prudenza*," he commented. "*Bel nome! Mi piace assai!* I have not met an English miss with such a name."

The journey to Rome passed quickly, and when this new friend invited Prudence and Arthur to dine with him before the Paris train left it was a disappointment for both of them when Prudence had to reveal that Mrs Hallam, the wife of one of the Secretaries of the American Embassy, was meeting them.

"And you will stay long in Rome when my friend Arthur goes to Paris?" Mario Aprili asked.

"I'm staying until my brother arrives in about a week, and then I'm going back with him to Citrano."

"Oh, you will go back in a week? It is very probable that I will come to Citrano for party business, *signorina*."

"I'll be going back to England about the third week of March," and in the tone of her voice there was perhaps the slightest, the very slightest suggestion of anxiety.

"It can be the beginning of March when I shall come. And where will you stay now, please?"

"Piazza Trinità de' Monti. I forget the number, but I'm staying with Mr and Mrs Hallam."

Soon after this the train ran into the station of Rome, and there on the platform was Mrs Hallam, dark petite, and chic, a friend of Athene's whom Prudence had met when she and her husband had been in Citrano a fortnight ago.

"Well, good-bye, Signor Aprili," said Prudence. "I hope we'll meet again sometime."

"I am very sure we will meet again, *signorina*. *Allora a riveder La presto. E grazie infinite per la Sua gentilezza.*"

Prudence was wondering if he would kiss her hand, but he was a strictly correct young man and did not kiss the hands of *signorine*.

"So long, Arthur," he said. "I hope we will meet again, and that you will have a fine journey to Paris."

"So long," Arthur replied. "I say, can anybody get a shirt like yours?"

"You like I send you one? I shall send you one to your school."

"I say, thanks awfully," Arthur gulped, hiding his excitement in a muted whistle. Where was Oliphant and his locomotive now?

"And who's the handsome *camicia nera*?" Mildred Hallam asked when they were following the porter with the luggage.

"His name's Mario Aprili," Prudence told her. "We met him in the train."

Mildred Hallam's delicate eyebrows were arched.

"You seem to have made a conquest, Prudence."

"Oh, Mrs Hallam, why do you say that?"

"Because I happened to turn around and see the way he was gazing after you."

"We were just talking politics. I'm not usually interested in politics. But he explained about Italian politics very well."

"I'll say he did," Mrs Hallam twinkled.

Arthur was dispatched to Paris that evening, and three days later when Prudence was sitting at the window of the Hallams' flat looking down at the most magical urban view in Europe Olga the maid brought in a large bunch of malmaison carnations to which was attached a note.

"*Questi garofani per Lei, signorina.*"

"For me, oh, grazie, Olga."

"*Prego, signorina.*"

Olga laid the flowers on a table and retired.

"Olga!"

She turned.

"*Commandi!*"

"No, niente, grazie," said Prudence on second thoughts, and when Olga had left the room she ran to the window and eyed the steps down into the Piazza di Spagna. A tall slim young Blackshirt came round the corner, paused a moment by the lift, and then looked round and up at the houses on Trinità de' Monti.

"I suppose I oughtn't to have done that," Prudence said aloud to herself when she had waved from the window and he had saluted and twice looked round on his way down the steps, and when he had reached the bright baskets of the flower-sellers in the Piazza di Spagna and waved to her before being lost in the throng. "Oh, well, I'm very glad I did, after his taking the trouble to bring me these carnations," she decided.

She opened the note:

Via Boncompagni 248
li 24 gennaio

Gentile Signorina,
    How are you? Will you please come to take lunch with me to-morrow at Castello dei Cesari which is a very nice restaurant on Monte Aventino. I think you will like very much the beautiful view of Rome. It will be for me a very great pleasure.

Your sincere
Mario Aprili

"Oh, I don't think you ought to go and have lunch with a strange young man, Prudence," Mrs Hallam ruled. "I really don't, my dear. What do you say, Herbert?"

"Well, it's a bit of a responsibility for us, Prudence. After all, you don't know a great deal about this young Fascist beau of yours," said Herbert Hallam, diplomatic caution exuding from his pudgy face. "And the way things are just now there's always a chance of a row if these Blackshirts come up against the other side. And that would be pretty disagreeable."

"I wouldn't like your brother to think we'd been careless about you," Mrs Hallam added.

"Oh, I know John wouldn't mind," Prudence averred. "He's tremendously sensible."

"I'm sure he is," said Mrs Hallam, "but honestly, dear child, it is too much of a responsibility for us. I'd ask him here, but Herbert has to think about the Embassy. It wouldn't do for one of the Secretaries to be inviting unknown young Fascisti to dinner. I'm terribly sorry, my dear, if you feel disappointed, but I think you'll just have to write your dashing beau and tell him you're sorry but Momma won't let you go. Pile it all on to me. I can stand it."

So Prudence wrote:

> TRINITÀ DE' MONTI 80
> *January 24.*
>
> *Dear Signor Aprili,*
>   *I'm afraid Mrs Hallam won't let me go to lunch with you to-morrow. Thank you tremendously for the lovely carnations. I wish I could come. My brother arrives here on the 27th from London and I expect we'll go on by the morning train to Naples. I hope we'll meet fairly soon at Citrano. I do wish I could come to lunch to-morrow, but I'm staying with people I don't know very well, and I can't argue with them.*
>   *I've begun to take a great interest in politics and I am reading what Signor Mussolini writes, though I have to use the dictionary rather a lot.*
>
>   *Yours sincerely,*
>   *Prudence Ogilvie*

When John reached Paris the evening before Arthur's arrival he found that Gabrielle Derozier was acting in a play by Camille

Varenne. The theme was crude enough, set in the years of war. A father and son were both serving with the army. The father was a widower with an attractive mistress who started an affair with the son. Finally both father and son arrived on leave simultaneously and there was a clash between youth and age. In the end the son was killed in action, but when the father returned safe to his mistress she refused to have anything more to do with him.

Varenne's masterly treatment of this crude theme gave it a tragic dignity, and with that tragic dignity a general significance for the time which moved John profoundly. It was the kind of play he would have liked to write himself. Not that this particular theme would have been possible in English. The only relations between a father and son that the English would tolerate in books or plays were either a brutal antipathy or a sentimental partnership, both equally false to nature. In England a father could not introduce his son to his mistress without shocking the audience's sense of probability. Fathers just didn't do that kind of thing in England. The reflection on the impossibility of Varenne's theme for an English audience led John on to the reflection that this English inability to appreciate the French attitude toward women was another facet of the English inability to appreciate the political point of view of France during this period of trying to piece Europe together again after the war. Tangled up in an affair which the English believed they had outlived and as a tribute to which the French wanted to see the settlements. It had been so jolly and romantic, the liaison, while it lasted. They had been all in all to one another. What was the use of spoiling a fragrant memory with these sordid arguments about money? Yes, the alliance between England and France had resembled uncomfortably a liaison between a rich middle-aged shopkeeper and a woman of the world. Sir Thomas Trollope and Lady Vawdry? Well, perhaps not so bad as that.

And now this demand of youth that what they had endured during the war should not be repeated. Varenne had shirked, inexplicably shirked the solution of his particular problem by killing off the son. Surely a better last act would have been the rejection of the father in favour of the son. And then of course the father would have retorted by closing down on the financial side.

John's thoughts were thus occupied while he was wiating for Gabrielle to dress. He had sent a note round to the theatre as soon as he reached Paris and he had found waiting for him in the

front of the house a note from her telling him that she and Camille
Varenne were now married and inviting him to sup with them
after the performance.

"My dear John, how glad I am to see you!"

It was Gabrielle herself. Thinking that he would be forty in
October John had recalled that Gabrielle was already forty-two
and admitting to thirty-seven. It was a triumph to be able to feel
as secure as she must that most people would be surprised to learn
that she was even thirty-seven. To-night in that coat of grey
squirrel, her red-gold hair still as lustrous, her generous mouth
still as sharply defined in a graceful bow, her large prominent
grey-green eyes still as luminous and eager for life as ten years
ago, she was externally what she was when she had met him in
Naples coming from New York and they had driven together in
her light-green Panhard to the villa she had found in Sorrento.
Yet as he bent over to kiss her hand ceremoniously he was aware
of some indefinable change even since he had met her last almost
three years ago when she had invited Prudence and David to tea
on their way down to Italy. It was like the sense of autumn that
suddenly makes itself felt amid the full green of summer on a fine
day at July's end. Perhaps it was marriage which had brought
this indefinable added maturity.

"And so you are married, Gabrielle."

"Yes, for more than a year and a half now," she told him.

He was on the point of asking her why she had not written to
let him know, when he reflected that he had not yet told her he
was married himself.

"We have both taken the plunge, Gabrielle."

"*Pas vrai!* You are married also, John?"

"Yes, and I have the daughter you prophesied."

"How glad I am! And how is she called?"

"Corinna."

"*Votre femme?*"

Ah, that subtle change back to the second person plural. In
two words an utterly new relationship was created, for although,
except for a brief interlude in mid-war, they had ceased to be lovers
nearly nine years ago, they had preserved the intimate manner of
address whenever they had met. It would take half a page of
dialogue in English to convey what in French or Italian could be
conveyed by a simple shift from the singular to the plural.

"No, my wife is called Athene."

"English?"

"American."

A light came into Gabrielle's eyes.

"*Je me rappelle!   Alors j'avais raison autrefois*," she murmured, nodding to herself.

They had reached her car by now.   Aristide was standing by the door.   He grinned at John.

"I'm glad to find you back with Madame."

Aristide grinned more broadly.

When Gabrielle and John were seated in the car on the way to her apartment in the Boulevard des Invalides he said he felt quite sad to think they were not driving to her apartment near the Parc Monceau.

"Ah no, my friend John, I have kept Aristide, I have kept Victorine, I have kept my emeralds.   But there are some things I could not ask Camille to accept from the past.   *Du reste*, he has made so many scenes of jealousy with me in my old apartment that it was *plus sage* for both of us to forget it.   But, my dear John, you are not going to change the conversation so easily, I can assure you.   We were talking of Madame Ogilvie."

"Yes, you're quite right.   You did meet her in Citrano."

"Oh, I remember very well indeed.   She was beautiful.   And I remember too very well that you were already a little interested in her during the voyage from New York."

"I knew you'd enjoy this triumph of feminine perceptiveness," John laughed.   "But honestly, Gabrielle, I did not think of being in love with her until the September of 1918.   And we were not married until the October of the following year."

"And her husband?"

"Her husband died."

"*Ah, ça c'était gentil*," she murmured.   "*Une complaisance peu commune*.   But I must not tease you, John.   I am truly so happy that you are happy.   And you have a daughter.   How old is she?"

"She was a year old last Saturday week—the fourteenth."

"*Un petit bouton de rose à présent*," she sighed.   "It was always a grief to my father and mother that I did not marry and give them grandchildren.   And now they are both dead.   *Oui, tous les deux*. So I think it is too late for me to have a child.   Besides, Camille is quite a child enough.   He will be very happy to hear that you are married, I assure you."

"Such a good play!" John exclaimed.   "Oh dear, how I envy French as a language—for a dramatist, anyway.   And how I envy even more French dramatists their actresses."

"But you have a good actress in your last plays."

"May Lavender? Yes, she has given me two good runs of over a year. I must not complain. But when I see French acting I fall into a gloom about English acting. That deadly monotony of the female English voice, except for two or three actresses in every generation. They're as frightened of the letter 'r' as if it inevitably preceded rape or rudeness. They have more difficulty in aspirating 'w' than a Frenchman in aspirating a vowel. And the young men! Why must Englishmen make love on the stage as if the threat of impotence cast a shadow on the time and the place and the loved one?"

"You are so ridiculous, John."

"Well, my dear, you remember the trouble we used to have with young Markham in *Annette*. Why, I used to spend hours trying to show him how I wanted him to play his scenes with you."

"Oh yes, you were very conscientious with poor Markham, John. I used to admire your patience so much. It was certainly not for want of a good example that he never played our scenes exactly as you wanted to play them. *Enfin*, we made quite a little play together of our own at the end. *Mais chut! Apropos*, I sent Victorine home in a taxi."

"Victorine has been married?"

"No, it is strange. Camille always says that she is *goosse*."

"*Goosse?*"

"Ah, you who once upon a time knew your *argot* so well. It is now the word for Lesbian."

"I remember your reading me a lecture once because I told you apropos of Varenne's play *Les Vierges Sages* that nobody would suspect you of being *gougnotte*. You told me it was not at all a polite word to use. And now it is *démodé* as a piece of *argot*. But is Victorine *goosse?*"

"Not at all," she replied. "But Camille suspects every woman of being Lesbian. You know, that was a brilliant play of his. I believe it could be—how do you say—revived with great success now. Ten years ago it was too soon even for Paris, but now it would seem quite *dernier cri*. And I would play the part so much better now."

"Is that what marriage has done for you?"

"No, no, John, but since the war I have had much better opportunity to watch *les malheurs—pas de Sophie, mais de Sappho*. I shall talk to Camille to-night about this project. It will put him in a very good humour."

And for the rest of the drive from the theatre Gabrielle talked about *Les Vierges Sages* which had been such a failure in Paris when it was produced in the late autumn of 1912. She would change the way she had played this scene. She would alter the tempo of that one. It would be so much easier to dress the play nowadays, the way fashion was going. And Camille could add many a satirical line at the expense of the contemporary Parisian world which would be much more quickly understood now than his satire in the days before the war.

Camille Varenne greeted John with outward cordiality, but the visitor fancied that his host's eyes were bilious in the corners and that his lips were ready at any moment to curl up in a sneer. He reminded him of those little furry animals that eye one suspiciously from the dim background of their cages in a Zoo, little animals with unfamiliar names and habits which therefore never became used to the interest of crowds.

However, when Varenne heard that John was in Paris to meet a stepson travelling from Rome and that he was himself immediately afterwards going to join his wife in Italy the wryness vanished from his lips and his eyes cleared, and when Gabrielle began to talk enthusiastically about a revival of *Les Vierges Sages* the last traces of watchful ill-humour vanished.

The conversation was in French as Varenne did not speak English, and John was soon having to apologize for the corruption of his French by Italian.

"We are such bad linguists," he sighed. "It's really absurd not to be able to speak two Latin languages without confusing the two."

"You still speak French very well, John," Gabrielle assured him.

"For an Englishman extremely well," Varenne added.

John shook his head.

"That qualification, *cher confrère*, is damning. But in my Italiante French I must try to tell you how much I admired your play to-night. All the while I was revelling in your exquisite technique I was asking myself how I should have handled such a theme if it had occurred to me. Of course it never would have occurred to me, because it is peculiarly a French theme. But I did try to forecast in my own feeble way what you would do next, and never once succeeded because, master of your art as you are, you always made your people do or say something that could not be guessed and yet when done or said seemed completely obvious."

John raised the glass of Chablis which was the accompaniment of a plateful of delicious *belons* (cunning housewife that Gabrielle was to remember these were his favourite oysters) and drank homage to Camille Varenne and his art.

"I am honoured, monsieur," replied the dramatist who, whatever he may have suffered from John's Italiante French, discovered in him an easy grace of manner which he did not associate with the barbarians across the Manche, and was touched and flattered by the tribute.

"John, John, you take as much pleasure in the power of your charm as a woman," Gabrielle said to him in English.

"*Tu as dit?*" asked her husband quickly, the trace of a yellow gleam in the corner of his eyes.

"I was teasing your friend, *chéri*, as I often tease you. I was asking him where he learned to pay compliments so prettily. But it is not fair to tease him, because he has already spoken to me of his admiration for your work, Camille."

"It was only in the last act," John went on, "that I preserved a tenderness for my own development of the theme."

"And that was?" Varenne asked.

"Why, I did not want the son killed off. I wanted him to come back and take Marguerite from his father, and for the father to squeeze him out by financial pressure. That seemed to me symbolical of what is happening in Europe to-day. This horror and jealousy of youth which is everywhere apparent, this slavery to an outworn financial system, this unhealthy belief in an imperialism now exclusively commercial. No doubt imperialism always was inspired by commerce, from Athens until to-day; but the degradation of commerce itself by international finance makes modern imperialism more poisonous. What is the fundamental disagreement between France and Britain at this moment? Our desire to help Germany back to her feet and the natural dread of France that a restored Germany will threaten her with a war of revenge."

"But you are so credulous in England," said Varenne. "You believe that there has been a genuine change of heart in Germany. There is one way and one way only to preserve ourselves in western Europe and that is to keep Germany impotent. For me *delenda est Germania.*"

"I don't think it's possible to delete Germany as Rome succeeded in deleting Carthage," John argued. "But what I was going to add was that France justly suspects our motives in what looks like a half-hearted attempt at German restoration. They are not altruistic. They are purely selfish. We do not want a predominant power on the continent whether it be France or Germany or any other. My own prejudice is in favour of French predominance. I should have been with the minority who thought that true progress would have been better served by not overthrowing Napoleon. I think that the tragedy of the war is that Britain and France have already broken the links which held them together against a common danger. I believe that between us we might have produced a genuinely more civilized Old World, because we supplemented each other's qualities. If, however, we were incapable of such a marriage, why then I think it would have been better to disintegrate Germany into small states, but at the same time to disintegrate ourselves. To my mind material growth has already advanced beyond mankind's ability to assimilate it, and I think the Old World requires the inconvenience of small states to give its inhabitants a rest. Loose federations should replace imperialisms."

"I'm afraid you wish to fight against a natural law, my friend," Varenne observed. "Deny to man the impulse of aggrandisement and he must decay. I have no criticism to offer against the German lust for aggrandisement. I merely say that we cannot afford it and that we must keep Germany paralysed. We did not create Czechoslovakia and recreate Poland for aesthetic or sentimental reasons."

"Well, I was launched on this political discussion by your play, *cher confrère*. It set me thinking about the future of a youth tied hand and foot by age far more securely than we have tied Germany. And, what is after all the best tribute one writer can pay to another writer's work, it set me off thinking about a future play of my own, inspired by the present unhappy divergence now growing between your country and mine. Lloyd George's game of golf at Cannes finished off your Briand."

"And rightly," Varenne interposed. "We do not expect our statesmen to play the clown at a moment of crisis by being photographed at a lesson of golf. But, pardon, I interrupted you."

"Well, I was wondering if Madame would act in a play of mine of which the theme was a liaison between an Englishman and a Frenchwoman and in the course of developing which dramatically one would symbolize the relationship between England and France."

"It is a good idea, John," Gabrielle said. "I can see a very good part."

"You know that Madame's performance in London in a play of mine ten years ago gave me my first success. I am wondering if she will consider playing in London again should I succeed in writing a play that took her fancy."

John looked at the husband, not the wife.

"It is for Gabrielle to say," Varenne answered. "She will not spend the rest of her life in acting in plays of mine. I am very sure of that."

"I won't promise, John, because I would have to see the part—the play that is, first. But I would very much like to act again in London. First of all, though, Camille must make *Les Vierges Sages* a success in Paris. Once you were going to write me a play about Marie Stuart, John, but nothing came of it. And so I shall not count upon your inspiration of to-night. Now that I have married Camille I am so very independent of other authors."

"There's no doubt of that," John agreed.

He stayed talking for an hour after supper and then asked if they would phone for a taxi. Gabrielle rang the bell.

"*Victorine! Un taxi pour Monsieur.*"

"*Bien, Madame.*"

Presently it was at the door.

"Good-bye, John. Write a play for me. And if Camille thinks it is good I will act in it."

Varenne smiled cynically. Nevertheless John felt no ill-will when he shook his hand in farewell.

Out in the hall Victorine was waiting to help him into his coat. Her eyes were dancing with merriment.

"*Au revoir, Victorine.*" He slipped a fifty-franc note into her hand.

"*Merci, Monsieur.*" She looked back over her shoulder. "*Bonne nuit, et dormez bien,*" she murmured with the faintest echo of a chuckle.

"Well, travelling alone's pretty easy," Arthur declared when John met him as he alighted from the Rome Express at the Gare de Lyon. "But I don't think the other chaps will know that," he added hopefully. "All the same it's a pity you met me here. It wasn't your fault. It was mother's, I know."

"How was she when you left Citrano?"

"All right."

"And Corinna?"

"All right. Everybody's all right. I met a *Fascista* in the train from Naples, and he's going to send me a black shirt."

When Arthur had been dispatched to Hampden House John hurried back across the Channel and on to Rome. He had telegraphed to Prudence to meet him at the station so that they could go to Naples together by the first train.

Mr and Mrs Hallam brought her to the station, and when they had gone she and John took their seats in the Naples train.

"You've become very absent-minded since we last met," he said presently when two of his questions had been answered without regard to what he had asked and another had not been answered at all because she was gazing out of the carriage window along the platform.

"John, I am so sorry. I was just thinking it would be jolly to walk up and down a bit before the train started. There's another half-hour yet at least."

"By all means," her brother agreed. "But you're not usually so fidgety."

They left the carriage and walked up and down the platform.

"Well, I don't know," said John at last, "but your visit to Rome seems to have extinguished what glimmerings of intelligence you had. Have you been seeing the ghosts of dead Caesars?"

"I am sorry, John. Truly I am. I think it must be this sudden change to cold weather."

"Oh, it's not that your teeth are chattering. In fact I should have said to look at you, that the weather was tropical. Your cheeks are flaming."

"John, they're not, are they? They do burn sometimes in the cold."

He intended to eye her critically, but instead he was caught by the beauty of her and found himself staring in admiration.

"Perhaps that's it," he murmured to himself.

"Perhaps what's it?"

"Yes, you would press for a reply to the first remark I've made more to myself than to you," he said. "But I suppose as I've at last succeeded in attracting your attention I ought to inform you that I've just realized you are a grown-up young woman."

"Oh, John, how extraordinary!" she exclaimed.

"That I should just realize. . . ."

"No, no, but I saw somebody I met on the way from Naples at the beginning of the week."

A moment later a tall slim young Fascist was saluting Prudence, and she was presenting him to her brother.

"Is it you who's going to send my stepson a *camicia nera?*" John asked.

"I have sent it yesterday," Mario Aprili replied.

"That was very prompt of you. I heard from Arthur that you'd helped to pass away the journey from Naples to Rome very agreeably."

"Yes, sir, we have had a very good journey. And now you will return to Citrano?"

"Yes, we're going back now."

There was a brief silence.

"It is possible that I will come to Citrano at the end of next month," Aprili announced.

"If you do, come and look us up."

"It will be for me a very great pleasure. *A riveder La, signore. A riveder La, signorina.* I wish you a very comfortable journey."

John and Prudence made their way back to the compartment.

"Don't feel discouraged," said John, as they got in. "He's waiting by the entrance to the buffet to see the last of you. That's always an excellent sign."

"You weren't frightfully cordial, John, were you?" Prudence asked reproachfully when they were sitting back among the dusty plush upholstery.

"Wasn't I? I didn't mean to be discouraging. You should have told me you were hoping to see him and given me some pointers."

"Well, you see, John, there wasn't anything to tell you. It was through Arthur that we started talking. It started about spitting in the train."

"A fine romantic opening," John observed. "I must remember that for a play."

"And then he explained what the Fascisti want to do, and really I couldn't help feeling impressed. I never took any interest in politics, because English politics are so dull. And then he sent me some carnations."

"They've lasted splendidly," said John, looking at Prudence's coat to which she had pinned half a dozen malmaisons. "That young man knows how to choose the freshest flowers."

"Yes, these are some of them," she admitted. "And he asked me to lunch with him at the Castello dei Cesari."

"On the Aventine?"

"Yes, but Mr and Mrs Hallam thought I oughtn't to lunch with a young man I'd only met in the train. I said I was sure you

wouldn't mind my going, but it was no good.   You would have
let me go, wouldn't you?"

"Yes, thanks to a combination of weakness and broadmindedness
I probably should, but the Hallams were right not to let you go."

"I think they would if they'd met him, but Mrs Hallam was
nervous about having a *camicia nera* to their flat because the
Embassy mightn't have approved."

"Well, if he comes to Citrano we shall know more about
him."

"He was attached to one of our battalions on the Italian front
as an interpreter," Prudence said.

"Why, he only looks about your own age."

"I know, he does look awfully young, doesn't he?   But he'll
be twenty-three in May.   So you see he's exactly four years older
than me."

"You managed to work a strong personal element into your
political discussion," John said.   "Did you find out if he had any
money?"

"Of course I didn't!   But his father is a well-known engineer.
Don't you think he speaks English very well?"

"Excellently."

"I liked him, you know."

"*Did* you?" John exclaimed in affected astonishment.

"And Arthur liked him awfully."

"Yes, but Arthur wanted to get a black shirt out of him.   And
anyway I'm not sure that Arthur's impressions matter much in
this case."

"You didn't dislike him, did you, John?" she asked anxiously.

"Not at all.   And listen, sweetheart," he went on gravely.   "If
I think he loves you and you love him I'll fight for you both with
Sir Alexander and Lady Ogilvie till I'm as slim as he is."

"John, you are a darling.   And you know, I think I may have
fallen in love.   But I'm not encouraging myself, you don't think
that, do you?   After all just because you ask a girl to lunch it
doesn't mean you are in love with her, does it?"

"It's not conclusive evidence.   The carnations aren't conclusive
evidence either.   Personally I was most impressed by his standing
in that vile draught by the door of the buffet and gazing at the
Naples train as if it was the Parthenon.   He may still be there;
wouldn't you like to go out into the corridor and peep?"

"Oh, but, John . . ."

"You think that would be unmaidenly.   I'll go and take a look."

John came back from the corridor.

"Yes, he's still there."

She blushed.

"There are still two or three minutes before we leave him desolate," John said. "We'll just step out on the platform, and I'll wave him a farewell."

"John, you are angelic. I do think that would cheer him up. I waved to him from the window of the Hallams' flat as he was going down the steps from Trinità de' Monti to the Piazza di Spagna."

"Westward-ho to Trinidad and Eastward-ho to Spain," John hummed. "Well, you'd better join with me in a friendly wave, as you're already on waving terms. That ought to bring him to Citrano by St Valentine's Day," John added with a laugh, as he and Prudence went back to their compartment, and the train started on the way to Naples.

Athene was on the platform when John and Prudence reached Naples about five o'clock.

"After your gay week in Rome," she said to Prudence, "I don't suppose you'll be terribly thrilled to hear that I've taken a box for *Traviata* at the San Carlo to-night, but I know John loves that opera, and I thought it would be jollier to arrive back in Citrano in daylight."

"Athene darling, I didn't see any opera in Rome. I shall love it," Prudence cried.

John guessed immediately that the real reason for Athene's wanting to reach home to-morrow instead of this evening was that the last time she had met him in Naples was on that October afternoon in 1917 when they had driven back together and she had found that unpaid bill of Wacey's. She had fancied the memory of that evening might cast a shadow. He held her arm close as they walked along the platform.

"Much better to arrive back in Citrano by daylight," he murmured gently.

"And I've booked rooms at Bertolini's," she added.

"So it is to be I who am to see the ghosts of the past," he laughed. "That's where Gabrielle Derozier met me in that March of 1913 and was furious, poor darling, because Claudia Sharpe and

I seemed on such good terms. By the way, what has happened
to Claudia Sharpe?"

"How strange you should ask that. She proposes to visit
Citrano some time this spring."

"What fun! And I had supper with Gabrielle in Paris the night
before I met Arthur."

"You did, did you?"

"She's married now to Camille Varenne who was her lover more
than ten years ago. We talked of her perhaps acting again in a
play of mine in London. I'll tell you more about it some time.
She had a grand feminine triumph over my marriage, and vowed
she had known I fell in love with you on the voyage from New
York in that spring of 1913. I wonder if after all she was right."

"No, honey, I don't think she was right," Athene said softly.

La Traviata!

"Imagine," said John to his sister, "me about a year younger
than you are now, sitting in this box with Mrs Stern and Emil."
He stopped for a moment for the pang of Emil now at the mercy
of the fatuous English prison system to pass. "Down there in
the middle of the *poltroni* was Sir Alexander and the attractive young
woman of twenty-seven with a high pompadour of light brown
hair he hoped to marry. It was June in 1900. Our box was a
small one on the top tier, not nearly such a luxurious box as Athene
has found for us to-night, and though Sir Alexander saw me I
did not see him or her. When I got back to Church Row, he
offered me for the first time a whisky and soda, which I refused,
and a cigar, which I accepted. I count it the first evening on
which he recognized I was more or less grown up. I think he
had intended to tell me of the second marriage he had in view, but
he gave me instead the grand news that I could leave school almost
at once. Oh, it was a very important evening in my life. Among
other things, moved by the tale of Alfredo and Violetta, I decided
to be a writer, and I was just recovering from my first love affair
in the course of which I felt I had been hardly less magnanimous
than the *dame aux camélias* herself. But hush, the prelude is
beginning and I must surrender to thoughts of tears and roses, of
sweet champagne and young love."

Later on when John and Athene came into their room at
Bertolini's Hotel he said to her:

"You don't realize that since Prudence left you with Arthur a
week ago she has fallen in love and that by taking that box at the
San Carlo to-night you finished off effectively any chance she

might have had of waking up from love's young dream."

"John!"

He told her about the handsome Fascist.

"I thought it was something really serious," she expostulated.

"It may yet be," he replied. "We shall see what happens when he comes to Citrano. I hope you noticed how much attention I paid to old Germont to-night. I was studying the technique of breaking in on love's young dream if it became necessary. I think I'll have to buy myself a top hat and frock coat. Don't forget I shall be up against a picturesque young Blackshirt."

"Do you think perhaps it would be wiser to send Prudence back to England?"

"Certainly not. I wouldn't deprive her of this experience for anything. She has to go home, anyway, at the end of March to prepare for her second season. That will give her plenty of time to sound the depths of her emotion. Don't forget that in May 1901 being then still a few months younger than Prudence is now I took Rose Medlicott to see *Tristan* from a box at Covent Garden. And a nice ado there was about it afterwards."

"But I wouldn't like Elise to think I'd been careless over Prudence," Athene insisted.

"I'll tackle Elise, if there's any need to tackle her, but the best thing now is to treat it as the most natural thing in the world that two attractive young people should fall in love with one another. After all, it is the most natural thing in the world, isn't it? Oh, treasure, what would not you and I give to have met years before we did, met and loved and married long ago?"

"Anyhow, I'm glad Leonora is coming out soon, because Prudence can stay with her. I don't like the idea of her being alone at Mrs Barrow's Pension with this devastating young Adonis around."

"But Leonora isn't coming till Julius comes in April. Prudence will be gone."

"She's coming next week. I'm so thankful I held on to the Allegra. Here's her letter:"

88 WELL WALK, HAMPSTEAD, N.W.
January 24. 22.

Athene dear,

After all, I am coming out with the children next week. I'm writing to you direct and not bothering John. Julius is going to Poland with his mother, but he wouldn't hear of my staying on in London. One of the performances of his symphony has

*fallen through, and he says that it's absurd for me to hang on in
London just to hear perhaps two performances in Birmingham
and Manchester. He thinks it would be good for Sebastian to
have a long enough stay in Citrano to pick up some Italian.
I'll telegraph what day we arrive. I do hope the Allegra will
still be vacant. We'll have to go back to America in the middle
of June. All news when we meet.*

Your affectionate
Leonora

"I've telegraphed to ask her if she'll bring out Mairi Macdonald
with her," Athene said. "Nanna wants to go back to England as
soon as possible. So it all works out beautifully."

"I hope you're going to like Mairi Macdonald," John said.
"Everybody teased me about your blind faith in allowing me to
pick a nurse for Corinna. Corinna! Is she very sweet now?"

"Oh, John!"

"Almost three months since I saw her. That's a deuce of a
lump in a baby's life."

"And there's another plan I've been making, dearest one. I
had a letter from Mrs Langridge at Christmas. She sent two
cunning little frocks for Corinna. She hoped we wouldn't be too
long before we crossed to the other side. Now I wouldn't want
to travel with Corinna this year, but I thought it would be a nice
surprise for all the grandparents if Arthur went over. Tell me,
do you think it would matter a lot if Arthur missed the summer
term at school? If he comes out for the Easter holidays he could
study French and Italian with somebody here, and then I thought
he might go to America in June with the Sterns. I'm sure they
wouldn't mind taking him. That would give him a full three
months on the other side and he might travel back by the Mediterranean route and he could go home with us to England at the
end of September."

"I think it's a capital plan. I'll get Madison to equip him with
a certain amount of work, so that he need not be too far behind
the other boys. Not that he'll do it. But schoolmasters like to
feel we appreciate their efforts at education. I think he's happy at
Hampden House."

"He certainly is. He was terribly disappointed you weren't
here for the Christmas holidays."

"Was he? He greeted me in Paris by saying that he thought it
was a pity I'd met him because by doing so I had spoilt the record

at Hampden House for travelling alone under eleven. However, he blamed your maternal fussiness and recognized that I was not intruding upon his independence. He's a grand kid."

Next day when they looked out of the window of their room at Bertolini's the classic bay was a glittering dark-blue picked out with white by a brisk *tramontana*. The sky was cloudless, and out of the north wind the sun was as warm as spring. By noon the big Lancia in which they were driving had reached Piano di Sorrento, where the almond-blossom was already prodigal by the edge of the sheltered orange-groves and lemon-groves.

It was just half-past one when they walked down the winding path through the rosemary below the Villa Allegra and reached the Torre Saracena.

Caterina and Concetta came running out with their fingers to their lips.

"*Corinna addormentata*," they whispered.

Here on the Salernian Gulf the north wind was disarmed by the heights of Monte Sant'Angelo, and in the sunshine streaming across the Tyrrhenian, Corinna lay asleep in her perambulator set against the south wall of the tower. Her nurse who was knitting on a chair beside her rose to greet them.

"She's been sleeping outside for an hour. The sun's warm to-day," she announced.

John looked down at his year-old daughter.

"Full of sweet days and roses; a box where sweets compacted lie," he quoted.

She opened her speedwell-blue eyes and looked at him gravely.

"Neither mine nor yours, Athene, but without a doubt Prudence's eyes," the father declared. "She used to look at me like that."

"Did I, John? What a delicious child I must have been!"

And then Corinna surrounded by five women admiring her emergence from sleep smiled at John, divining not the father of her being but eternal man.

•

"Monica is going to be the most complete little brunette that was ever seen. And I didn't intend that at all," Leonora was saying to Athene in the *salone* of the Villa Allegra on a rain-washed blue day in mid-February. "Just a proper little piccaninny, that's what my daughter is."

"Why is she a piccaninny, Mother?" Sebastian asked, scowling critically at his sister, who promptly scowled back at him and waved a menacing arm from the chair in which she was sitting with a large doll whose blonde vapidity made its owner appear more dark and determined in consequence.

"She just is, Sebastian."

"Why don't you paint her, Mother? You paint yourself in the morning when you get dressed."

"John, did you say you were going to take my odious son down to the tower?" Leonora appealed.

"Do you want to come, Sebastian?"

"Sure, I'll come with you, Uncle John."

"Ask Nanna to put on your rubbers," Leonora said. "It's pretty wet underfoot."

"Oh, gee," Sebastian sighed. "That's the worst of a walk. So much to do before you start off. Where's Prudence?"

"She went to have tea with Mrs Heighington," Athene told him.

"I know she did."

"Then why ask Aunt Athene such an unnecessary question, Sebastian?" his mother exclaimed sharply.

He grinned and followed up the grin with a scowl.

"Because she didn't wanta dress up either. She said it was rancid. Rancid, she said it was," he repeated, rolling the word with relish in the hope that it came within the category of words forbidden to small boys. Perceiving that the word with which he had aspired to shock the company had somehow missed fire, he thrust his hands into the pockets of his corduroy knickerbockers and strode toward the door of the *salone*. In the entrance he turned. "She said it was hell going to tea with that old dame. Hell, she said it was."

"I thought I forbade you to use that word," his mother scolded.

"Well, I didn't. It was Prudence who said it was hell. Hell, she said it was," he repeated emphatically.

"Sebastian!"

"Yes, Mother?"

"Do you want to go and get dressed for your walk with Uncle John, or do you want me to tell Nanna to undress you and put you to bed?"

"I wanta go with Uncle John."

"Then go at once without any more anecdotes, or there'll be trouble," said his mother severely.

Monica made the noise which nurses teach their smallest charges represents scolding inspired by moral indignation.

"That boy is bad," she informed Corinna who was seated opposite her on another chair.   Corinna had been trying to discover how to open a china ball.   In the enthusiasm of being addressed by Monica she flung it from her in an ecstasy and knocked over a glass of freesias on a table close by.   This excited Monica so much that having nothing else to fling from her she flung her blonde and vapid doll, which crashed on the porcelain tiles between two rugs.

"So much for the practical expression of female indignation," John laughed as he followed Sebastian from the *salone*.

Out in the vestibule Bridget O'Brien, an Irish-American girl was dealing with Sebastian's rubbers.   Mairi Macdonald, tall and fair with high cheek-bones, was standing by.

"Well, Mairi, have you learnt any Italian yet?"

"No, sir," she answered in that voice quiet as the lapping of water on the sandy margin of a lochan.

"You ought to learn it easily," he told her.   "You with the Gaelic!"

"It's very difficult, sir," she said.

"Difficult?" echoed Bridget O'Brien, looking up.   "It's worse than difficult.   It's unnatural."

"I will talk in Italian," Sebastian announced.

"Sure, you'll talk in Italian," said his nurse.   "And when you get home you can start selling peanuts."

"All the same I will talk in Italian," Sebastian repeated firmly, when he and John were making their way down through the rosemary.

In the room at the top of the tower they chatted away to one another.   John had had the Bechstein tuned when he heard that Leonora and her children were coming, but he knew it would be useless to ask Sebastian to play, and waited in the hope of his trying the piano.

At last the boy opened the lid and struck a few notes.

"It isn't sticky like that bum piano we had in London, but it's . . . oh gee," he ejaculated with a wry grimace, picking out a few notes, "it's out of tune."

"Is it?   I had it tuned only ten days ago.   A tuner came over from Naples," John said ruefully.

"Well, it's not so very bad.   But hark!"

He struck C—D—E.

John said they sounded all right to him.

"Can't you hear that D is wrong?"

John shook his head, and Sebastian shook his head. "You ought to be able to hear that D is wrong, Uncle John," he said compassionately. "It isn't terribly wrong, but it is wrong."

"I'll get the tuner over again, and you shall keep him up to the mark."

"What's sharp in Italian?"

"In music?"

"Yep."

"I don't know, I'm afraid."

"But you talk in Italian?"

"Yes."

"Perhaps you don't know what flat is in Italian?"

"I don't."

"That's a funny kind of Italian you talk."

"Well, you see, I'm not a musician. I just like listening," John explained apologetically.

Sebastian grunted.

"Who's that?" he asked, pointing to the woman in a coloured reproduction of Giorgione's *Figures in a Landscape*.

"I don't think she's anybody in particular. The fellow on the left is a soldier."

"I guess Mother 'ud look pretty funny if she sat down like that with Monica. Has she been swimming in the ocean?"

"I don't think so."

"Well, why's she sitting there, with nothing but a lil towel round her?"

"I suppose the man who painted the picture saw somebody like that."

"I think she's nuts to sit around like that. And that fellow looking at her. I guess he thinks she's nuts to sit around like that with nothing on except a lil towel."

He passed on to another picture. This was Carpaccio's *Dream of St Ursula*.

"Who's that?" he asked, pointing to the figure of the Archangel Michael, standing opposite the sleeping virgin's bed in the cool clear light of a Venetian dawn. "That's St Michael, is it?" Sebastian commented. "I guess it's a good thing she's asleep. I guess she'd holler if she woke up and saw him standing there. You got a picture of St Sebastian?"

"I'm afraid I haven't."

"Poor St Sebastian! But he didn't holler when they plugged him full of arrows. And when I stuck a knife in my leg I didn't holler. I just said 'Darn you, you old knife.' "

He wandered over to the Bechstein and finally after piling some books on the piano stool clambered up. He threw a quick glance at John who seemed deeply preoccupied with a volume on his knee. Then he started playing the nursery rhyme melody of *Dames, get up and Bake your Pies*, in which he set out to improvise apparently a series of variations. John kept his eyes fixed on the volume, for he felt that from time to time the boy was turning round to look at him suspiciously. Presently Sebastian started off on a Mozart sonata which set him dreaming about these children growing up around him. The picture of the *salone* at the Villa Allegra came back to him like some picture of intimate life hanging upon the wall of an unfrequented old continental gallery. Corinna and Monica eyeing one another from their respective chairs, and the two mothers talking about them. And outside in the vestibule the two nurses talking. Mairi Macdonald was the very girl Athene and he had imagined they would find to be Corinna's nurse. Her voice was gentle as the lapping of water, and the aspirates of her Gaelic accent were sighing through her speech as a faint wind among the lochside reeds. These children growing up to enter a changing world, this new frightening world. Was Emil right in his expectancy of such violent change? Emil in prison on this rain-washed February day! Would Emil equip his small son more usefully than Julius and himself were equipping their children? Was there indeed something much more profound than this unrest that was the aftermath of an insane war which was stirring in the heart of man? Would Sebastian in another twenty years spin life as easily as now his small fingers were spinning that Allegretto of Mozart? And Padraig, what would happen to him if in a desperate struggle for freedom his father fell? The news from Ireland was menacing again. Might it not be wise to give up living in Europe and settle in America? Bob Redroad was coming over this summer to make two or three films with Janet Meriday. He must discuss with him life in California. As far west as one could go. In any case it would be best to give up the tower. It had played its part. The future of Europe was too uncertain. Better to let it go now. Citrano was changing. In another year or two little enough would be left of its peculiar quality. It would have become just one more holiday resort to be exploited by capital. The tower should be easy to sell, and it was really too small for family life. Athene had been doubtful about the wisdom of settling in America, but that was because she had fancied he was making the suggestion to please her. They could cross every two or three years and spend a summer at Nanphant. He would be forty in October. That used to count as middle age. He had enjoyed a much fuller and more varied experience of the world than was granted to most men. For him the west wind of love had been a fruitful and balmy wind, a prospering wind. He lay back in a daydream under the impression that he was listening to Sebastian's music, until suddenly he did begin to listen. It was an Adagio the sweet simplicity of which played thus by a small boy was cold as the afterglow of a sunset in the front of spring, clear cut as the black bough beheld against it, and because it was untouched by conscious sentiment, impersonal and poignant as the song of a bird. Perhaps it was the simile which recalled the dark swan of Tuonela he had listened to at Queen's Hall more than twenty years ago. It could not be this Adagio of Mozart which had brought back to him the music of Sibelius. Yet once again his ears were opened as by enchantment to the song. 'You shall go back ultimately', sang the dark swan of Tuonela, sang that dark swan while the waters of the mere swept by the north wind nagged at the shore. 'There lies the fulfilment of your weird. To my calling you shall come at last. You went southward away from me. Go westward now away from me, if you will, but my calling shall bring you back, however many more heedless years may surge between. Mine, mine is the voice you shall one day hear above all those surging years', sang the dark swan of Tuonela, and dabbling its beak among the sparse rushes of that northern mere the sombre bird was silent.

Sebastian had clambered down from the stool and gone to the window looking northward.

"Prudence is coming, Uncle John," he announced. "I guess she's glad her tea-party is finished."

Presently the rose-flushed face of Prudence appeared at the head of the spiral staircase leading up to the library.

"Was it hell?" Sebastian asked.

"Absolute hell," she cried, flinging herself down on the sofa.

"Didn't I tell mother Prudence said it was hell?" Sebastian demanded triumphantly. "Gee, Prudence, you pretty near got me put to bed because you used that word."

"But as it was, we managed to escape," said John.

"Yep," Sebastian agreed, with what sounded like the plucked string of a violoncello, so absurdly deep was his voice for his age.

"And how was my dear friend Mrs Heighington?" John enquired
"She was simply bl . . . blithering."

"I know the word you wanted to say, Prudence," Sebastian
assured her.

"Yes, all right, but keep it to yourself," John interposed, "or
your mother will be sending Prudence and me to bed."

"She wouldn't do that," said Sebastian, but his smoky eyes
under their dark heavy brows were touched with a faint anxiety.
"Did that old dame give you nice cookies for tea, Prudence?"

"Not too bad. But, John, you know the painting of her that
stands on a gilded easel under a silk veil?"

"Do I not?"

"Well, she told me that Matrassic ought to paint me because
our colouring was almost identical! John, is my face like a pink
cornflour pudding?"

"Under stress of emotion extremely like one," her brother
replied. "But seriously I think it would be a good notion if
Matrassic did paint you. Ostápov told me he's rather hard up at
the moment. I wanted Athene to sit for him, but she won't. I'll
give it to the Judge. He'd love a portrait of you."

"But that picture of Mrs Heighington is so frightfully Royal
Academy."

"All right. I'll tell Matrassic to paint you in what he believes
to be the true style of portraiture. But don't blame me if he
makes you look like a cracked Easter egg. He's an Ovist. I
think the Judge would prefer Matrassic's Royal Academy style.
Still, it's never too late to start on the artistic education even of
a Judge. And your mother can always raffle the picture for one
of her charities."

A day or two after this John went round to see the little Russian
painter who was married now to Eva Zvonskaya. They lived at
the top of a house in one of the steep narrow streets behind the
Piazza. At this season of the year, untouched by the sun, the
cobbles were greasy with damp, and John was glad when he reached
his destination. He had been thinking that it was hardly the best
place for somebody so obviously consumptive as Eva, but he found
that the top floor gave them a terrace at the back in the sun's eye
with a view over the domed roofs of Citrano and the Tyrrhenian.

The little painter's shock of hair fuzzed with excitement at the prospect of a commission. Yes, he had already noticed the signorina. It would be a pleasure and an honour to paint her portrait.

"Now, I'm not going to pretend that I shall like a picture in your most advanced style," John said in Italian, "but on the other hand neither I nor my sister want you to paint her in the style of Mrs Heighington's portrait."

Matrassic made a gesture of disgust.

"What I want really is a picture that will remind me of what she was like at the end of her nineteenth year."

As he was talking his eyes were looking round the untidy room, and in a corner he caught sight of a small canvas.

"I never knew you painted trees. That almond-tree in blossom is exquisite. I wish you'd paint my sister beside a bough of almond-blossom. You'll have to be quick, for the almond-blossom will soon be over," he added, more to himself than to Matrassic.

"It pleases you, yes? I am very glad," said the little painter.

"I should like to buy that picture. How much do you want for it?"

Matrassic shrugged his shoulders.

"I will give it to you, please. It is only a rough sketch."

"Well, you shall give it to me," said John, "but if you can paint my sister as you have painted that almond-tree you can charge me twice what you charged Mrs Heighington."

Matrassic said something in rapid Russian to his wife, who clapped her hands.

"And if you make a success with my sister I think I shall have some more pictures for you to paint," John continued. "Now where would you like my sister to sit for you? Isn't this rather too sunny?"

"It is not good as a studio," Matrassic agreed, "but I can rent now a good studio in Via Umberto Primo. That will be very good business for me, but the winter has been a little difficult, and I could not make an offer for it."

"That's splendid. Then as soon as you're fixed up let me know, and don't forget that in another ten days the almond-blossom will be fading."

John had turned to take his leave, when Eva Matrassic begged him to let her make him a cup of tea. Thinking it would give pleasure if he stayed to drink a cup of tea he sat down again, and his hostess hurried across the room to the samovar. The painter brought him a portfolio of sketches to look at.

"It's no use expecting me to make intelligent remarks," John said. "I can't make intelligent remarks about excessively modern work."

He was contemplating what might have been a giant squid lurking in a sea-cave, but the very fact that it might have been this warned him that it was almost certainly nothing of the kind, and he had learnt by now that modern painters were frequently huffed by being suspected of even as much representationalism as allowed the onlooker to guess wrong.

"What do you call that?" John enquired cautiously.

"Scherzo in B flat."

John wondered what Chopin would have said to such a title, and hurriedly turned over to the next sketch in the portfolio.

"Is this another aspect of music?" he asked, examining what seemed to be a realistic evocation of the large spongy fungus the Italians call a *boleto*.

"No, no," said Matrassic impatiently. "It suggests nothing to you?"

John pondered going nap on the fungus, but he had been caught too often. He hesitated.

"Delphi," said the little painter.

"Delphi?" echoed John, unable to hide his surprise.

"You don't perceive the umbilical suggestion?"

"Oh yes, of course, how dull of me! The navel of the earth. Yes, yes, of course."

Luckily for John the strain upon his mind was relieved at this moment by a knock at the door, which Matrassic opened to admit a woman. At the sight of a stranger she drew back and refusing to listen to Matrassic or his wife hastily retired, leaving with John a brief glance of a pale thin woman in black.

"She was ashamed when she saw you," Eva Matrassic explained.

"But who is she?" John asked.

"It is a terrible story."

"A very terrible story," Matrassic added, frowning.

"That is the Baroness Kleinborch."

"A German?"

"No, no, a Russian, the wife of one of the generals who was defeated by Hindenburg at the battle of the Masurian Lakes."

"At the very beginning of the war?"

"Afterwards he was killed by the Bolsheviks in front of her, with outrages upon his body. Tatiana Glebovna was thirty years younger than her husband, and there were two little boys. She

was afraid that her children would also be killed, and she managed
to escape with them from Russia into Roumania.   In Bucharest
the elder boy died of typhus and to find food for the younger boy
who was only two years old she had to become a *cocotte*, and
year by year she sank lower until in 1920 in Trieste she went to
live with an Italian waiter.   He treated her very badly, though
she has had a child by him, and now a week ago he has left her
stranded here without money and without clothes, because he has
taken all her clothes with him."

"What a ghastly story!" John exclaimed.   "And she is here
destitute with the two children?"

"No, she has only the child of Gino Lupi the waiter.   The
other boy was killed last year by a motor-lorry in Turin."

John asked if he could go and visit her.

The husband and wife looked at one another.

"She has only a wretched bedroom in the house next door.   It
is a very poor place," said Matrassic.

"She would be ashamed," his wife added.   "It was for food
she came this afternoon.   One can imagine what she is feeling.
To have been the wife of a Russian general . . . you do not know
Russia, signore.   They were proud before the October Revolution, and she is still a young woman—perhaps not more than
thirty-two or three.   But now she is like a woman of fifty who
has had a life of perpetual hardship."

"Better you do not go to see her," the painter advised.   *"Wenn
die Sorge schläft, wecke sie nicht."*

"But I should not be waking a sorrow that sleeps," John argued.
"Her sorrow cannot sleep."

"Excuse me, signore," the little painter replied, "but a visit
from you would waken the past, and that is her sorrow.   In the
present she has not sorrow.   She has only anxiety how she will
live and feed the child she has left."

"Leo is right," said the painter's wife.

"But something must be done for her.   My wife will collect
clothes, and I can get up a subscription among the foreigners here."

But as he made these suggestions John was reflecting that though
they might lull his own distress at the tale he had heard they were
for the unfortunate widow of a Russian general a useless alleviation.

"She has no friends or relations?" he asked.   "But if she had,
what chance would there be of getting her back to Russia now?
And that Italian waiter who has deserted her?   I suppose that was
really a good riddance."

"She is better without him," Eva Matrassic agreed. "He was brutal to her."

"Oh, well," said John, "we must do what we can to relieve her present condition. Could she earn her living in any way if her immediate necessities were met?"

Matrassic shrugged his shoulders.

"The widow of a Russian general who has been a prostitute in Bucharest and Constantinople, in Salonica and Belgrade and Trieste and had a waiter as *ruffiano* will not find it easy to earn a living."

"She can embroider," the painter's wife suggested.

"Why, then we'll take a small shop for her," cried John, "and stock it with embroidery, and she can add to her stock. She ought to be able to support herself in Citrano. You must arrange it, signora. You need not say who sent the clothes, because that's a private matter. I would find the money for the shop myself, but it will be better to persuade some of the foreigners to subscribe because they will become customers. I will send you at once what is required to get her into a decent lodging, and when she has the clothes my wife and Signora Stern and my sister will be able to call upon her and she will feel independence coming back."

"She has a baby six months old," Matrassic observed. "If you mean to bring her back into the world out of which she has fallen you will find that baby a problem."

"I'm not proposing to launch her upon a social career," John insisted. He was thinking that he would touch Mrs Heighington for at least five hundred liras, and he was saying to himself that he knew just how to do it.

"I shall tell Signora Heighington that the lifelike picture you made of her inspired me with the idea of having my sister painted by you," he told Matrassic, with a chuckle.

"*Ah no, prego, prego, signore,*" the painter protested. "I have made that painting as Tatiana Glebovna has sold herself in Bucharest."

That evening John told Athene the story of the Russian general's widow, and his plans for her future.

"Why, of course, honey sweet, Leonora and I will do all we can."

"And if Matrassic makes a success of his portrait of Prudence you'll let him paint you?"

"I won't promise that."

"Not with Corinna?" he pressed. "You'd be thinking all the while about her. You'd forget you were being painted yourself.

If we sell the tower and give up Citrano I want a memory of it and of you and of our happiness here."

"We must see what he makes of Prudence.   Has she said when she expects this Fascist beau of hers to present himself in Citrano?"

"No, why?"

"I noticed a letter for the Gentilissima Signorina Ogilvie from Rome in yesterday's mail."

"Oh, they're corresponding, are they? That's why she was chattering so much at dinner yesterday.   The news was evidently good."

"John, I do feel just a little worried.   We know nothing at all about him."

"Don't feel worried.   I'll take all the blame."

"John, John darling, you're growing middle-aged."

"What?"

"Well, isn't it a sign of middle-age when one begins to make matches for the young?"

"I'm not making a match.   I merely want Prudence to know what falling in love means.   Let it end happily or unhappily, she will be the gainer.   Would you have married Wacey if you'd ever fallen in love?"

"No, perhaps I wouldn't."

"Well, I don't want Prudence to go back to England for her second season and let herself be persuaded by Elise into accepting some eligible young man.   But we're counting our chickens . . . the handsome and dashing young Blackshirt may discover that he isn't nearly as attractive as he fancied.   I suppose by this time next year Corinna will be talking quite a lot?"

"Surely she will, but she won't be old enough to fall in love with handsome and dashing Blackshirts and when she is old enough what a dragon she and Poppa are going to find Momma!"

"I wonder."

"I'm just positive."

He kissed her.

Julius and his mother had reached Cracow on February 1st, when the city was covered with snow.   They stayed in the same quiet hotel overlooking the gardens outside the Florian gate in which they had stayed over twenty years ago with John and Emil. For a moment Miriam had demurred, wondering whether an hotel nearer the centre of the city would not be a wiser choice; but as they drove away from the railway station in a sleigh the snowy scene so completely obliterated the aspect of the Cracow in that hot dusty August of long ago that the choice of the hotel became symbolic of the change twenty years had brought in herself, and she welcomed the notion of returning to a place touched by winter as herself by age.

"A pity that motor-cars have found a way of getting about in the snow," she said to Julius. "That lovely wintry silence broken only by the sound of sleigh-bells is gone—that silence to which one morning children used to wake and know that winter was come. We used to love winter then."

The next day being Candlemas, Julius walked across the white empty market-place to the glowing twilight of St Mary's Church. He went early and found a place in one of the carved Renaissance pews where he could pore for a while before High Mass began upon that sublime triptych of the Assumption by Veit Stoss, whose live gold and azure was carved with such boldness of relief that the angels bearing the body of the Virgin aloft seemed to float away with the Queen of Heaven and hang suspended between earth and sky above the altar. Gradually the church filled with worshippers. The celebrant in purple cope and stole blessed and sprinkled and incensed the candles, and while they were being distributed to the clergy and the laity the choir sang Simeon's canticle *Nunc Dimittis*. After every verse the antiphon was repeated. *Lumen ad revelationem gentium: et gloriam plebis tuae Israel. To be a light to lighten the Gentiles: and to be the glory of Thy people Israel.* This festival of the Purification always had for Julius a peculiar solemnity, for more poignantly than any in the Christian calendar did it speak to him as a converted Jew. And now as the gleaming procession moved round the church symbolizing the entry of the Light of the World into the Temple of Jerusalem he gave thanks again that he like Simeon waiting for the consolation of Israel had not seen death before he had seen the Lord's Christ. *To be a light to lighten the Gentiles: and to be the glory of Thy people Israel.* This was the first opportunity he had had of keeping Candlemas in the land which had bred and sheltered and persecuted his forerunners for hundreds of years. To-morrow was Friday. There at dusk in the Casimierz ghetto the doors of the synagogues would be open and the candles in the seven-branched candlesticks would be lighted. The old men in gaberdines with fur-trimmed hats upon head after head that Rembrandt might have painted would be hurrying through the snow to their ancestral worship. And married women with their monstrous wigs, and fluffy-faced young men with oily corkscrew curls smarmed down over the ears. They would all be hurrying through the snow in the hush of the oncoming Sabbath to the candlelit synagogue. *Lumen ad revelationem gentium et gloriam plebis tuae Israel.* But never a Simeon to sing *Lord, now lettest Thou Thy servant depart in peace: according to Thy word. For mine eyes have seen Thy salvation.* All of them blind to the Light of the World which had entered the Temple of Jerusalem.

Julius made his intention at Mass on that second of February in Cracow the opening of the eyes of the children of Israel dispersed across the face of the globe. And as he walked back through falling snowflakes to the hotel beyond the Florian gate he thought with a sardonic smile what a disgrace he himself would be to his kinsfolk in the Casimierz ghetto. In other circumstances his mother would certainly have suggested that they should visit these kinsfolk, but now she, who was either by Christian or Jewish standards an unbeliever, would be ashamed of her son's apostasy from the faith of his race. He was minded to wring from her this admission by proposing a visit to the ghetto to-morrow; but when he reached the hotel she looked so weary and sad that he had no heart to vex her.

"The journey has tired you," he exclaimed, putting his arm clumsily round her in an access of affection.

"No, no, Julius dear, but I cannot get Emil out of my head. I think of him and you and John arguing away together in this hotel twenty years ago, and I think of him now in prison. It haunts me all the time."

"Really, Mother, you torment yourself needlessly. In the first place it is not for as long as all that. He will be free before the year is finished. And in the second place he desired the experience. What do you imagine will be the first comment he makes when he comes out? Do you suppose he will toss his head and drink in the air of freedom again like somebody in a romantic German drama of the early nineteenth century? Do you suppose he will face the world coldly and proudly with the expression of a martyr in a pious picture? Not at all. He will say: 'I had long been convinced that the English penal system was the stupidest in the world, and I'm very glad to have had an opportunity of proving it by personal experience. It is even stupider than I had expected.' Then the Liberty Press will publish a shilling pamphlet in which

Emil will enlarge upon his experience and put forward a few immediately necessary and obvious reforms, after which he will return to uniting the world's workers and devote himself more ardently than ever to the cause of the Revolution."

She smiled less wanly than of late.

"Yes, I believe I have let myself be more upset than I should," she admitted.

"And now I'll put you a question," Julius went on. "Suppose we visited the ghetto this afternoon . . ."

"But we won't, Julius," his mother interrupted quickly. "We have entirely lost touch with everybody in Poland. Twenty years ago there were friends of my father still alive. There will be nobody now who remembers him."

"You're not going to avoid the question. Suppose we did visit the ghetto this afternoon and you met people you had known once upon a time, which would embarrass you more to admit—that you had a son serving a term of imprisonment at the moment or that you had a son who had become not merely a Christian but a Catholic Christian at that? You needn't answer, for I know the answer, and that being so I'm afraid I'll have to be brutal and say that any more lamentations over Emil will rather irritate me, because if you believed in the faith of your forefathers you would be eating your heart out on my account, not Emil's. I am the lost sheep of the House of Israel, not Emil. As a matter of fact you are happier that I am a Catholic than that Emil is a Communist; but back in the ghetto racial snobbery would be too strong even for you."

"Julius, you're right. You make me feel as sometimes you used to make me feel when you were a little boy and giving us so much by your genius. I'll brood no more over Emil. I'm glad you made me come with you to Poland."

A few days after this they set out to revisit the house which at the age of fifteen Julius had insisted on taking for himself in order to recover musically from appearances on so many concert platforms as a boy prodigy.

"I often wonder," he said, "if you would have surrendered to my whim unless John had supported me so strongly. He had a great influence over you, hadn't he?"

"He had an influence over all of us," she said, evading the direct reply.

"You know, I used to fancy you were rather in love with him," Julius continued. "How ridiculous one is at fifteen—so full of intuitive wisdom and so lacking in worldly experience to check it. The notion of supposing one's mother to be in love with a boy twenty years younger than herself!"

Miriam forced herself to laugh at such an absurdity.

"Yes, I actually set out to compose a rhapsody for strings on the theme of you and John, but I didn't finish it, and when I picked it up a year later I thought it abominably sentimental and tore it up."

"Strange child that you were," she murmured.

"Oh, just the usual mixture that any precocity in the arts supplies. Still, I did know my own mind; on that I must congratulate my earlier self."

The problem of finding the sky-blue house in the midst of that immense white plain looked like proving insoluble. And when they found it at last, it was no more than a mound in the snow surrounded by the stumps of plum-trees and cherry-trees. In the hamlet near by they made enquiries for the peasant woman who had looked after Julius during the eighteen months he had stayed here communing for the sake of music the heart of Central Europe. She had died soon after the Russian soldiers had destroyed the house in the second year of the war. Then they asked for the priest with whom Julius had studied Latin and German and Polish. He had been dead ten years.

"So that was why he never answered my letter telling him I had been received into the Church," Julius said. "I wonder if the schoolmaster is still alive."

They went on to the village twelve miles away where the schoolmaster had lived. He had retired from teaching, but he was alive and well.

"That I should have gone to bed last night without the slightest premonition of what to-day would bring," the old man exclaimed. "Death comes like that sometimes. It is a warning. But how sad that Father Rucinski is not here."

"He died before the war, did he not?" Julius asked.

"It was better so," the schoolmaster replied. "We suffered much here during the war. But I did not lose my piano."

He pointed to the Blüthner which Julius had left behind when he gave up his sky-blue house among the cherry-trees and plum-trees in the corn.

"Father Rucinski presented it to me," the schoolmaster went on. "He was crippled with rheumatism for two years before he died and could no longer play his violin. What evenings we used to have in those winters of—how long ago? Twenty years? Yes, yes, twenty years it is. Yesterday to a man of my age. What evenings, what evenings!"

"Do you remember when we used to play trios, Pan Adamski," Julius asked.

The old schoolmaster chuckled.

"Yes, yes, and when poor Father Rucinski had to turn his violin into a violoncello."

"Schubert in B flat, and the lovely long one in E flat, and the Brahms in B flat," Julius continued. "And that evening when we wrestled with the Tchaikovsky in A minor—the one he wrote in memory of Rubinstein?"

"Yes, yes," the schoolmaster cried. "And I remember you said Rubinstein must be turning in his grave to hear us. You haven't changed a great deal in twenty years, Pan Stern. I knew you at once. And I've read about you in the papers. We often get papers from America here. Many of our people are over in America. You haven't brought your violin with you."

"No, I left it in Cracow. I was afraid of damaging it on this journey to revisit the place where I learnt so much. I am playing in Warsaw at the end of the month."

"What will you be playing?"

"The Tchaikovsky Concerto, and I shall conduct my Second Symphony."

"Your symphony, eh? Isn't that wonderful! That would be something to hear."

"You must hear it," Julius told him.

The old man made a gesture to imply the hopelessness of such a suggestion.

"I'm serious," Julius insisted. "You are coming to Warsaw as my guest, Pan Adamski."

"Too far, too far for me to venture," the schoolmaster sighed.

"We'll talk about that later. Meanwhile can you find lodgings for my mother and myself for a week or so in the village?"

"But it wouldn't be comfortable."

"We don't want to be comfortable, Pan Adamski," Miriam Stern put in. "We only want to stay here."

So lodgings were found, and Julius produced wine and various tinned delicacies for their meals in the schoolmaster's house.

"I had hoped to stay in my own house," Julius said. "But nothing remains of it except a mound in the snow and the stumps of the trees."

"Nothing, nothing," the schoolmaster sighed. "It was one of
the casualties of the war, that old house.   Ah, those evenings with
Beethoven and Brahms.   Yesterday!   Only yesterday to an old
man.   I seem to fancy the overtones are still sounding in my ears."

That evening after supper the schoolmaster reproached Julius
for not having brought his violin.

"I might have heard again the great Chaconne from the Partita
in D minor," he sighed.   "Can you play Bach now as you played
him when you were a boy?   Ah, madame, did ever any boy play
Bach like your son?"

"Yes, it was a piece of selfish caution not to bring my fiddle,"
Julius muttered.   "Inexcusable caution."

"I have Father Rucinski's violin too," said the schoolmaster.
"It's not the best of instruments, but perhaps . . ."

"Of course," Julius exclaimed.   "Where is it?"

The schoolmaster went to a cupboard and took out the battered
case.

"It has not been played since the good priest died," he muttered
as he took out the violin.   "You see two of the strings are
cracked."

"I have strings with me," Julius said.   And presently the
instrument was restored to life.

"The Partita in D minor," the schoolmaster begged.

And while Julius played it to him one might have fancied that a
man was drinking pure spring water after long thirst.

"And now while we are in the key of D minor, let us play the
Brahms Sonata, Pan Adamski," Julius suggested.   "That was the
last sonata we studied together.   Do you remember?"

The old man shook his head.

"I would not venture to play that with you now.   We must
go back to something simpler."

And he found in a dusty heap of music the early Mozart violin
sonata in C major which has the poignantly sweet *adagio sostenuto*.

"It is not for you in the full vigour of your genius, that *adagio*,"
said the schoolmaster.   "It is music for the very young, in playing
which the old can live again in their second childhood."

"I'll make Sebastian play that with me, *ma mère*," Julius said,
using the form of address that Emil and he had always used to her
in childhood.

"You have a son who plays the piano?" the schoolmaster asked.

"Yes.   He's just seven now.   He may be a great pianist.   I
do not know yet.   But I think myself he is more likely to be a

composer. I do not want to exploit his playing," Julius added half to himself.

"As you were exploited," his mother commented, a little wistfully.

"There's no comparison between myself as a child and Sebastian," he replied. "None whatever. We had to escape from an inheritance. My chief grievance against Emil is that he wants to inflict our inheritance on the western world."

"I don't think that's a fair way of putting it," his mother protested.

"If we were living in the fifth century instead of in the twentieth, should we not see Emil as one prepared to let the eastern hordes stream through against the Roman Empire? It was I with my fiddle helped him to escape from his inheritance and now he wants to return to it and, what is more, submerge Europe beneath it."

The old schoolmaster looked up nervously at the vehemence with which Julius spoke.

"You are embarrassing Pan Adamski," said Miriam. "I want to try the Blüthner. May I?"

She seated herself at the piano and began to play nocturnes and ballades and valses of Chopin.

"You melt the snow, madame," said the schoolmaster when she left the instrument.

"Julius has not yet told you that he is a Catholic," she said.

"Indeed?" the old man exclaimed. "That will rejoice the soul of our dear friend. He was always so anxious not to try to influence you, Pan Stern, but he often used to say to me how hard it was to resist the temptation because he felt your heart was turning toward our holy Faith. And you are a Catholic. *Nunc dimittis servum tuum, Domine, secundum verbum tuum in pace . . . lumen ad revelationem gentium, et gloriam plebis tuae Israel.* And how long since you found the Light of the World?"

"I was received into the Church in Italy in the early summer before the war. I wrote to tell Father Rucinski, but he was already dead."

"He died two years earlier. He used to talk about you to the end of his life. He too loved so much the great Chaconne from the D minor Partita."

"It was with that Chaconne that two nights before my baptism I played myself out of nineteen centuries of obstinate Jewry, out of the fleas and grease and lees and the swarming myriads of Central Europe, out of nineteen centuries of grubdom."

"I think perhaps those winters of music with our dear dead friend and myself . . ." The schoolmaster broke off abruptly. "But who am I to claim a part in this conversion? Forgive my presumption."

"Those winters of music were precious, Pan Adamski. They will be precious to the end of my life," Julius declared. He put out a hand and touched his mother's arm. "It was you, *ma mère*, who told Father Rucinski that if my life here should incline me to be a Christian you would not oppose it. How furious our Emil was!"

"And Father Rucinski said that, though he should make no effort to influence you, he should treat you as one searching for the truth," Miriam recalled.

The three of them sat silent for a while in the snowy hush.

"Listen, Pan Adamski," said Julius at last. "I must be selfish and insist that you come to Warsaw as my guest. I want you to hear my symphony."

When Julius and his mother returned to Cracow he bought a fur coat for the schoolmaster so that he could travel warmly, and at the end of the month the old man made the journey to Warsaw.

"Well?" Julius asked when the concert was over.

"Wonderful, wonderful," the old man said. "I wish our dear friend could have been beside me. And the seat next mine was empty. The only empty seat I saw."

"I know," said Julius. "I reserved it for him."

"There was an instant in the last movement, very near the end of the symphony," said the schoolmaster, "when I could imagine that I heard the Soviet armies turning back on that Assumption morning in 1920. And it was then most of all I wished that Father Rucinski were beside me that we might look at one another and smile and say, 'The Queen of Heaven's prayers have prevailed. Poland lives again!' Forgive me, if I intrude upon your music with my dreaming, but that was what I heard in that moment just before the symphony came to an end."

"Then you heard what was in my mind when I wrote those bars on the other side of the Atlantic," Julius cried in exultation.

He turned to his mother:

"Now do you understand why I *know* that Emil is wrong?" he demanded.

"The better I understood the sorrier I should be for him," she replied. "But you cannot accuse him, Julius, of lacking faith in his own ideals."

After the old schoolmaster had gone back to his village, while Julius and his mother were still moving from place to place in Poland, the battle between them over Emil continued. The effect on Miriam of such a battle was tonic. By the time it was necessary for Julius to return to England to keep his concert engagements she had no other thought than to be as stoical as she knew he himself would be.

"What an argumentative month," she said, when they went on board the steamer at the Hook of Holland.

"You're looking very much better than when we left England at the beginning of it," her son observed, with a smile of satisfaction.

The picture Matrassic painted of Prudence was a success. The fuzzy-haired little man himself was really proud of it, although he was inclined in public to deprecate the amount he had sacrificed to conventional portraiture when he found that everybody at once recognized the original of his exquisite arrangement of almond-blossom and girlhood.

Nevertheless John could not persuade Athene to sit.

"But it can always be destroyed if you don't like it," he argued.

"It isn't that, John. It's the process which I dislike. Even if I'm being photographed I become self-conscious, and I get so mad with myself for being self-conscious that I look a harridan. You never wanted any photograph of me."

John agreed that every photograph of her he had seen had not spoilt the picture in his mind's eye.

"Let him paint Corinna, who has inherited her father's lack of self-consciousness. But really, John, I won't let him paint me."

So when the peach-blossom was full-rosed Corinna was painted by Matrassic, and a charming picture he made of childhood gazing in faint perplexity at the great world that began to stretch before it. In point of fact what was really perplexing Corinna was not the world but Matrassic's fuzzy hair.

Whether she did finally decide that the painter was a cat and salute him by the Italian equivalent of 'puss, puss' might be doubted; but at that date when every hint of a new word was disputed by four languages—English, American, Italian, and Gaelic—Italy was not going to relinquish the triumph.

"*Si, si, a detto 'mish, mish'. L' ho sentito,*" Caterina shrilled.

"*Anch' io ho sentito, 'mish, mish'*," Concetta avowed, adding that the word had been so clearly heard that she had looked round to see where the cat was.

John declared that it was Matrassic's turpentine which had made Corinna sneeze; but that the rival languages were disturbed by this alleged Italian victory was evident when he heard on one day Corinna's Gaelic nurse trying to elicit 'piseag' and on another day Sebastian urging her to say 'puss, puss'.

"She's pretty stupid," he told Corinna's father when the attempt failed.

After Corinna Matrassic painted Monica sitting among purple anemones, but Sebastian declared Giorgione's *Figures in a Landscape* had implanted in him a suspicion of painters.

John himself while all this painting was going on worked at the play he designed for Gabrielle Derozier's reappearance in London after ten years. The theme of a broken liaison was to symbolize the present relations of England and France, and the writing of it gave him a good deal of pleasure.

"Which is a bad sign for its merit," he said to Athene.

"Why, John?"

"Because exhilaration acts on the pen like alcohol. It lulls self-criticism. Don't you remember at school when you thought you'd done well in an examination paper you usually found you'd done badly? And *vice versa*. Unless you feel discouraged at the end of a morning's work it means you haven't tired your brain. Rejoice therefore when I'm gloomy at lunch."

However, in this case John misjudged his pen, for the exhilaration of writing *How It Was Sweet* was the exhilaration of breathing in the strong prevailing air of the moment, and in this play he managed to express the spirit of that year 1922 which history would recognize as the first of the three fatal years during that uneasy repose between disaster and catastrophe.

John had just finished his second act on a March morning of windy sunlight and sudden black showers, and had gone to judge the weather from the east window of his room to decide on the appropriate moment to dodge the next shower in order to reach Fofo's for the agreeable half-hour of gossip and vermouth before lunch, when he saw his sister walking across the sand with Mario Aprili.

A minute or two later the face of a slightly apprehensive Prudence was seen at the head of the spiral staircase.

"Are you hideously busy, John?"

"No, I've finished for to-day. I was just considering the weather with a view to going out."

"Athene and Leonora are at Fofo's now. And Mr Noel. And Mrs Heighington, and lots of people."

"And you've kindly come all the way down to fetch me? What an amiable girl you are!"

"Well, as a matter of fact . . . Oh, John, he's arrived!"

"Who?"

"Aprili."

"*Evvero Marzo è pazzo* when April arrives in the first week of it."

"Oh, John, please don't talk Italian to me. I'm much too nervous to understand."

"I was quoting the Italian proverb that March is mad, and saying how true it was."

"John, do help me. You are brutal."

"Help you?"

"Yes. He's here. He's waiting outside the tower."

"Who is?"

"Mario Aprili!"

"That comes of not distinguishing between a final 'e' and 'i' in Italian. I thought you said Aprile—the month of April, which I thought was a bit mad even for March. But who's Mario Aprili?"

"John, you know, you really can be fetid when you like. It's my young man in Rome."

"Your Blackshirt beau?"

"Yes, of course. I met him in the Piazza—luckily just in time before I went into Fofo's. I'd been to Madame Kleinborch's shop to buy a handkerchief. I don't know what I'd have done if he'd come into Fofo's when everybody was there."

"So you've brought him down and deposited him on my doorstep like a foundling."

"Well, you see, I thought you'd come up with us to Fofo's, and then you'd introduce him to people. I mean it'll be so awkward for him only to know me in Citrano."

"And a bit awkward for you. All right, Cressida, bring in Troilus. Or perhaps I'd better act up to my part and fetch him myself."

As John went along to the door of the tower he noticed that the faces of Caterina and Concetta were pressed against the kitchen window in as awkward an adoring rapture as two of Benozzo Gozzoli's angels.

"So you've managed to get down to Citrano," said John. "*Ben arrivato!*"

The slim and handsome young Fascist clicked his heels, and shook John's proffered hand with a light bow.

"My sister and I were going up to the Piazza.   You'll come with us, won't you?"

"It is very kind of you, sir.   I am very pleased to come."

John went in and shouted for Prudence.

"Hurry, we'll just make Fofo's before the next shower."

As the three of them set out across the beach for the flight of steps leading to the Piazza John threw a glance over his shoulder. The rapt countenances of Caterina and Concetta were still pressed against the kitchen window.

Their progress across the Piazza gave a greal deal of aesthetic pleasure to the inhabitants of Citrano.   Two or three *Fascisti* had been seen there, but *Na{ionalisti* had been observed more frequently; and certainly no Blackshirt or Blueshirt comparable to Mario Aprili had gratified their swift Italian response to beauty.   Moreover, the rose-flushed beauty of Prudence, herself so slim and graceful, provided the perfect feminine complement.

The wrinkled old woman who sat with her tray of coral charms outside a diminutive shop when the sun shone beamed at John as if to congratulate him on the pleasure he had given to the Piazza by showing off such a handsome couple.

"*Buon giorno, Rosina.*"

"*Buon giorno, signore.   Quant' è bella la primavera!   Adesso viene la stagione!*"

Her weather-beaten face was furrowed by the benevolent grin of age admiring youth and spring and rejoicing that it lived yet to see come once again the sweet o' the year.   And as she spoke the silver rain of the next shower streamed down and drove her to the shelter of her diminutive shop.

"We timed that well," said John as they entered Fofo's.

The dark eyes of Fofo sank a little deeper into the circumfluent fat at sight of the *camicia nera*, for as a Giolitti man he did not approve of this new and disturbing thing called *Fascismo*.   Then thinking to himself that after this year he would be quit of business he shrugged his shoulders.   Politics would not concern him when he was at peace among his vines and olives.   With whatever shirts men covered their bellies they must always line them with oil and wine.

"What shattering people you do produce, Ogilvie," Geoffrey Noel gulped in John's ear when they were all seated round the big table in the middle of the café.

"This is what Prudence discovered in Rome," John murmured back.

"Really? Well, I must say—m-m—she has extremely good taste. And with the right figure these black shirts are very becoming. Who was it said 'black is a pearl in a woman's eye'?"

"I don't know," John replied, looking round the café. "But it would seem that in this case there are enough eyes to make a necklace."

When the time came for the gathering at Fofo's to disperse Aprili had been invited by Athene to lunch at the Torre Saracena, and Leonora had suggested Prudence should bring him back to tea at the Villa Allegra. Noel had named the following day for dinner, and Mrs Heighington had proclaimed a *festa* at Mon Repos early in the following week, qualified by the reminder that it would be a quiet *festa* on account of Lent.

"But no doubt it will make up in gossip what it lacks in gaiety," Geoffrey Noel observed to John.

The sun had asserted himself over the showers by three o'clock, and John suggested that Prudence and their visitor might like a walk before they were due at the Allegra.

"Well, what do you think of him?" he asked his wife when they were left together.

"My dear, he's ravishing! I just forgot every duty I owed Elise as Prudence's chaperon."

John laughed.

"So I shall be exonerated," he said. "Well, she's certainly in love with him. Did you think he is in love with her?"

"I think he's very attracted."

"And you agree with me now that it's much wiser to let them find out for themselves what they feel about one another by giving them the reasonable opportunity to do so?"

"Yes, in the circumstances. But I'm glad Prudence is going back to England at the end of this month and that she won't be our responsibility during a Citrano summer."

The weather by the middle of the month was so fine and warm that John suggested a visit to Minerva's cape. Bearing in mind, however, the reputation of March for madness they did not go by boat or plan to stay the night at the Marina di Cantone. It was to be a drive by car as far as Nerano, whence they would walk the three miles along the cliff path to the Punta, picnic among the debris of Minerva's temple, and drive back to Citrano at dusk. The party consisted of Athene, Leonora, Prudence, Geoffrey Noel, John, and Mario—he had become Mario in the course of a fortnight.

At this time of year the site of the great temple was covered with crimson peaseblossom which crept everywhere, hooking itself by minute green tendrils to the rest of the vegetation, and filling the air with fragrance. This tiny wildflower was indeed the parent of all the sweet-peas in English gardens, the scent of which by now was gradually being lost in the effort to produce flowers of greater size, pretentious frills, and more variety of colour.

"There is a moral for the world in this small wild sweet-pea," John observed. "Strange that it blossoms here so prodigally among the relics of a dead imperialism, which died because it sacrificed native fragrance to size and colour and frills."

He was sitting with Mario looking across the dark blue water of the *bocca* to the ruined Roman lighthouse on Capri three miles away. The rest of the party were searching for the little terra-cotta heads of Minerva that were still to be found among the debris, souvenirs of the goddess that used to be sold to trippers nearly two thousand years ago. It was one of these which John had found and presented to Athene when they picnicked here with Wacey and Leonora and Julius and Geoffrey Noel that June day on which the Archduke Francis Ferdinand was assassinated at Sarajevo. It was then that looking at Athene John had suddenly realized for the first time how much she resembled an Hellenic convention. Comparable high cheek-bones had their goddesses on painted vases, and comparable dark slanting eyes, and comparable long-legged grace of form.

"Is this for me?" she had asked, taking the little head whose nose had vanished, whose cheeks were pocked by weather, but the curve of whose helmet was still visible. And for a second he had seemed to be alone with her on that headland, and the trivial words she uttered had seemed fraught with profound significance. But the impression had passed as rapidly as a bird across the vision at dusk . . . and four years were to pass before the significance was revealed to him in all its fullness.

"You think that the imperialism of Rome is for ever dead, Mr Ogilvie?" Mario asked, and John came back to the present with a start.

"I cannot see what can revive it."

"Pardon me if I disagree with you," said the young man. "I believe it is the destiny of *Fascismo* to bring that empire to life."

"You think what Venice failed to achieve modern Italy may achieve?" John asked.

"If modern Italy were truly united," said Mario gravely.

And as John eyed his profile and his dark grace against the glittering Tyrrhenian outspread between this headland and Africa he was suddenly captivated by the notion that Italy might indeed repair the havoc of fifteen centuries and restore to the Mediterranean its spiritual and material pre-eminence.

"To restore to the world what Britain and America have absorbed between them and save it from the barbarism now threatening it from the East," he muttered to himself.

The fancy offered such a completely fresh vision of the future that it struck him with the miraculous force of a conversion.

"But it will need a very different Italy from the Italy of to-day," he insisted, fighting with himself to retain his own prejudice.

"Of course," Mario agreed. "But when *Fascismo* conquers Italy the *rinascimento*—how do you say it?"

"The rebirth."

"The rebirth will be made," Mario declared, with the assurance of faith.

John pondered in silence the new idea. The March sky burned with May's azure. The sweetness of the wild peas was heady as wine. A rock-thrush, fluting his snatch of mellow song, flashed in a dark sheen of blue from boulder to boulder of the limestone. The voices of the others searching for the terra-cotta heads of Minerva or iridescent fragments of mosaic were like echoes in this sepulchre of dead Imperial Rome the ghost of which had been summoned back to earth by this handsome boy to enter again a living body.

"It had never envisaged such an Italy," John said at last. "During the war I spent much of my time in the Aegean and I must confess that at any rate so far as the Eastern Mediterranean was concerned I built my hopes entirely on a great Greece. I thought of Italy in terms of Genoese castles and Venetian forts, in other words as a commercial enterprise which had failed because it could not maintain itself against the Turk. Even now in spite of the rejection of Venizelos I still hope for a great Greece and believe that it is the duty of my country to help keep the Turk back from the seacoast of Anatolia. But I begin for the first time to doubt whether after all it is not better that Italy should hold Rhodes. Spain? Spain turned her back on the Mediterranean for the gold of the Americas. France? France used the Mediterranean to further her ambitions in the East. Britain did the same. Germany has eyed it covetously with the same object in

view. So too Russia, and emphatically I agree that the whole
Dalmatian coast should have been secured to Italy. Moreover,
I have always believed that Tunis was Italy's due. Likewise Italy
should have as much liberty in Ethiopia as the French in Morocco
or ourselves in Egypt. But you'll admit that since the *risorgimento*
Italy has given up to party what was meant for mankind?"

"Pardon?"

"Has been the prey of corrupt domestic politics?"

"Indeed yes, but *Fascismo* will make clean that corruption,"
Mario announced fervidly. "We cannot allow any more of those
Orlandos and Nittis and Giolittis and now this Facta! *È una
vergogna, una vergogna!* We are shamed before all the world.
Excuse me, you have read perhaps *Il Popolo d'Italia?*"

"Oh yes, I read it."

"And so you have read what Benito Mussolini writes?"

"Oh yes."

"And do you not think he writes well what he writes?"

"I think that if I were an Italian I should be a *Fascista*, though I
have a respect for Don Sturzo and the *partito popolare*."

Mario shook his head.

"We are not against religion, but it is bad when the clericals
interfere in politics. And the *partito popolare* is clerical. It can
go so far, but in the end it will lead us back to corrupt politics.
For these we must finish. We cannot tolerate no more to be ruled
by old men who have spent their lives to seek power and money
for themselves. But that is not all. We must drive out Communism. We must destroy such a pest, because if Communism
can win Italy it can win all Europe. Do not think that we are
the enemy of the people. We *Fascisti* desire that the people shall
have justice. We do not desire to exploitate them like Liberal politicians. We desire that the people shall take a part in the rebirth
of our united Italy. But they must learn discipline. How is it now?
At any moment a strike of trains, a strike of electrics, a strike of
trams, and now a day for a general strike. *È schifoso!* It is quite
abominable the impotency of those politicians to maintain public
order and decency. The world laughs at us. You know how we
were treated at Versailles. It is enough. There must be an end.
And when we have made an end of this confusion we shall show the
world an Italy able to prove to the world that Rome is indeed eternal."

"And the desert shall rejoice and blossom as the rose, and the
corn-ships from Africa shall once more pass through this *bocca*
as they passed through it two thousand years ago. Well, Mario,

I won't say you have yet convinced me of Italy's truly imperial mission. I shall wait to see whether you *Fascisti* achieve power and what you will do with it if you do achieve it. Meanwhile, perhaps it is a good omen for you that Cardinal Ratti was elected Pope last month. I think of him staying on at his post in Warsaw confident that the miracle would happen and that the Soviet hordes would be turned back. The only foreign diplomat who had the courage and the faith to hold fast."

"Pardon me, you are not a Catholic?"

"No, the only Catholic member of my family is my daughter. She is to hear her first Mass at Easter when she will be fifteen months old. However, perhaps I shall follow her example."

The young man's eyes brightened.

"Then you are not against Catholics, Mr Ogilvie?"

"Certainly not."

John wondered if the obvious pleasure this admission gave him had anything to do with a future he was considering for Prudence. He fancied that it had.

"I know that at present you are very much occupied with political activities, Mario," he went on. "But I suppose you are planning a career for yourself?"

"Oh yes, I study now to be an engineer and when I am complete I will work with my father. I am not at all inclined for idleness. In the new Italy there cannot be idleness for anybody. That is where the socialists do not understand us. We are not for the privilege of money. We are for a State in which everybody will give the best work he can make for the State. And we are determined that Italy will have respect from other nations. Italy cannot live on *tourismo*. To live so is to live like a *cocotte*. We cannot tolerate that. We have the greatest past of all nations in the world, but we must not allow ourselves to be crushed by such a past. We must have a mission in the world to-day. We cannot tolerate to be a museum for tourists. *Fascismo* is youth. We can respect age, but we must not be ruled by age. Not by the age of our history, not by the age of our politicians. The whole world suffers to-day from age. After the war it must be youth which makes its own future."

"*Se il giovane sapesse, se il vecchio potesse, e non c' è cosa che son si facesse.* If age but could, if youth but knew, there's nothing this world might not do. You don't agree with that ancient proverb?"

"But excuse me, Mr Ogilvie, if youth makes a mistake for want of experience youth will have the energy to mend the mistake, but age cannot mend the mistakes it makes. It is too tired."

"I think you're right," John agreed. "The vigour of a nation may probably be judged by the youth of its statesmen. How old is Benito Mussolini?"

"He is now thirty-eight."

"Well, we'll see what he does before he reaches forty. I envy you rather, Mario."

"Why, please?"

"Because something tells me that Fascism will succeed."

The young man smiled like a boy.

"You think so. I am so very glad."

"And I see no prospect of any such movement of revivification in my own country. We are like the sweet-peas that came from this crimson wildling. We have size and colour and form, but we have lost the vital fragrance. Remember when you rebuild your Roman Empire, Mario, that there is a nobler end for imperialism than shop-keeping on a grandiose scale. I've enjoyed our talk. When do you leave Citrano?"

"I must go now very soon, alas."

And as he made this announcement he threw a quick glance in the direction of Prudence. John caught in his eye the look of urgency.

Later when dusk was falling over the olive-groves of Nerano John sent Prudence and Mario ahead in the Fiat.

"Why, John, I thought you were going with them," Athene said.

"The Lancia is more comfortable," he replied. "Besides, I like being with you. We four are the veterans of Minerva's cape."

"*Dulce sodalitium*," sighed Geoffrey Noel. "Incredible to think that we were all four of us there on that fatal June day in 1914."

"We must go again when Julius comes," Leonora said eagerly.

"And we three regarded Noel in 1914 as those two ahead of us in the Fiat regard us in 1922," John said. "Now the three of us have become Noel's contemporaries, merged for youth in the dark backward and abysm of time known as pre-war."

He chuckled to himself as he leant back comfortably in the Lancia between Athene and Leonora.

About two miles beyond Citrano a great bastion of limestone thrust itself into the Tyrrhenian down the north-easterly slope of which a path ran in a long gradual diagonal toward the sea. This path was easily reached from the corniche road hewn from the heights that sometimes fell a thousand feet sheer to the indigo water below. The Citrano side of the bastion was precipitous and barren; but that path down the gentler slope of the Salerno side, sheltered as it was from the sun and from the fierce salty winds of the south-west, descended at first through a thicket of lustrous green arbutus and ran on through miniature groves of tree-heather, the ground beneath stippled in March with the crimson of a myriad cyclamens.

On the morning after the picnic Mario and Prudence turned aside from the corniche road and took that path out of the world. They walked in single file, for the way was narrow. They walked in silence too, and their footsteps were muffled by the dead leaves which had drifted into the path and lain there year after year in the shade and dampness. At last they reached a small grassy plateau some fifty feet above the sea and stood listening to the music of it playing through the innumerable caves and fissures of the land's end.

"Oh, look, Mario, there's a land cave. Shall we explore it?"

They scrambled up to a great gash in the limestone and found themselves on a level green terrace in front of a high shallow grotto in the middle of which stood a great mushroom-shaped stalagmite. From the arched roof pale greenish-blue and tawny stalactites dripped at long intervals.

They emerged on the fine young grass before the grotto, and exploring to the left they came upon the inspiration of the scented air. A diminutive glade in the brushwood hidden from the casual glance by a clump of arbutus was completely white with violets. Heedless of the damp, Prudence threw herself down at full length and drank in the fragrance of them as if indeed she were drinking from a spring of crystal water.

Then she picked a bunch of these white violets and gave them to Mario, who had sat down beside her. He murmured his thanks in a low husky voice, and pinned them on his black shirt just below the blue ribbon of the war cross.

"I go back to Rome after to-morrow," he said.

"And I go home to England next week," she said.

They sat in silence among the white violets, gazing at the sea through the trunks of the tree-heather and at the limestone pre-cipices towering to the melting azure of the March sky.

Presently he leaned across and took her hand. A fleck of crimson burned upon the cheek that was nearer to him, and as she looked into his eyes this fleck seemed to burn more fiercely against the paling rose of maidenhood that flamed and fainted in that moment of its full awakening.

"Ah, Prudence, you know I love you."

"And I love you."

He drew with a kiss the sweet bow of her mouth, with a long kiss from which she sank back pale as the white violets to recover from their fragrance the breath stolen by love.

"I was too rough?" he asked anxiously.

"No, no, but it is the first time I have kissed anybody like that. It's frightening and wonderful and . . . oh well, it's just that."

"It was not my resolve to tell you that I love you," he said gravely. "Because I must always remember that until Italy is born again I have much to do. And it was not right to make love when we cannot be married yet. But when it came over me that I go away after to-morrow and you go back to England I was not able to hide no more that I love you."

"When did you love me first, Mario?"

"When I see you first," he replied simply. "And when you loved me first?"

"Well, I think it must have been at the same moment. You see, I never could manage to dream about you, and I think that's always a sign of being in love with somebody."

"*È vero*. I never can dream you. You will tell your brother that we love?"

"Not if you'd rather I didn't."

"Yes, please, I wish you to tell him. He is very *simpatico*. He understands very well about *Fascismo*."

"And he understands a good deal about love," Prudence added. "But I won't tell anybody else because I couldn't argue about this with anybody. I know John will advise what is best. And if you're going back to Rome the day after to-morrow"—she blinked away a tear from those speedwell-blue eyes—"there won't be much time for anybody to criticize. We've danced a lot together all this lovely fortnight, but oh, Mario darling, won't it be wonderful when we dance together to-night? You must make the band play *Evergreen Eve* twice." She began to hum the tune of the foxtrot to which she had danced so often with him, wondering what would be the end of this delicious uncertainty.

"Mario darling," he repeated. "Please to say that again. *Mi piace tanto tanto.*"

"Mario darling."

"*Ah, come mi piace!*" he cried, and he gathered her to him for that second kiss of young lovers to which something is added of sweet security that almost compensates for what must be for ever lost of that first wild rapture.

And then for an hour they sat among the violets, regardless of the damp, for lovers seem to escape rheumatism as drunken men escape injury. And they talked as lovers do about the minute circumstances associated with the growth of their love, as whether he was sitting in that chair when she said that, minutiae of absorbing interest to themselves but not to be set down in words for other people. At last they had to forsake that small violet-strewn glade in order to reach Fofo's in time for the gathering before lunch, in order to listen to the tales of others, they who could have told the history of the world in two monosyllables.

They lingered for a silent minute in that air which held the fugitive present in its fragrance.

"*Dimmi, dimmi, Prudence, mi vuoi bene?*"

"*Ti voglio bene assai,*" she responded in the words he had used so often to her during that sacred hour of youth.

"*Com' è carino il tuo accento inglese!*"

"John says my English accent is frightful."

"*Non è vero.* I love your English accent."

"*Ti voglio bene assai.*"

They stood locked in a last kiss before tearing themselves from that carpet of white violets, and too soon that narrow path up into the world was somehow widened to hold them alongside one another all the way.

The ballroom of the Hotel Excelsior was unusually full that Saturday night, for during Lent the management paid a tribute to old-fashioned opinion by closing it on Wednesdays and Fridays. After Easter the french-windows would be opened and the company would dance alfresco on the great terrace that looked across the roofs of Citrano to the outspread sea.

It was a cosmopolitan gathering. There were the *pesce cani* of many a nation, the sharks who had grown rich out of the world's agony; and although these, either by a longer familiarity with money or by a general coarsening of social standards, were less obviously what they were than the monsters who had appeared in the months that immediately succeeded the armistice, they were still an affront to the civilization which the war was claimed to have secured for humanity.

There were Americans used to travel in Europe and there were Americans unused to travel in Europe, for whom the former were inclined to be apologetic. These untravelled Americans were becoming rarer as the spirit of curiosity to inspect the democracy for whose safety their sons and brothers and husbands had been fighting grew less with the recession of the war. Within a year or two they would be seen no more on this side of the Atlantic, and would relapse into as profound an ignorance of Europe as Europe's ignorance of America.

There were English people who had come to spend a cheap holiday in Italy thanks to the fall of the lira and who were depressed about the unpunctuality of the trains and the loss of the leather straps from their trunks. These would admire *Fascismo* so long as *Fascismo* was content to cure such obvious abuses as the unpunctuality of trains and the theft of leather straps, but when its influence extended beyond that they would suspect a plot between the Pope and the Duce to run Europe in the interests of Roman Catholicism and feel that Italy needed a lesson. There were plenty of Germans too who to the amazement of such English people had money to spend in travelling about Italy when all the while they were pretending they could not pay the reparations exacted by Versailles.

"Artful dodgers, these German fellahs," a lanky Englishman observed to John, who had brought Prudence to the Excelsior this evening. "Moaning and groaning about their poverty, and look at that party drinking champagne in the corner. I mean to say, what? I hope Lloyd George takes a strong line at Genoa when this conference starts next month."

"You surely don't expect them to forgo travel until the last mark has been taken away from them?" John asked.

"They started the war. Let 'em pay for it. Why should they travel? Listen to the noise they're making. Beastly language! Can't stand it. Fat as porkers too. And yet these sentimentalists tell you they're starving. And these organ-grinders! As soon as they see an Englishman they think he's made of money. Always believed it was a mistake letting them come in on our side."

"We should have lost the war if they had held fast to the Triple Alliance," John said coldly.

The lanky Englishman turned round and stared at him in amazement.

"You don't really think that?"

"I don't think. I know. I was at Gallipoli."

"But I mean to say, what about Caporetto?"

"What about the Twenty-first of March, 1918? These things happen, don't they, in war?"

"Well, you're the first person I ever heard make such a comparison. You've staggered me. You have, upon my word. Bustable is my name."

"Ogilvie is mine."

"Oh, really? You're the playwright, of course. I saw a very amusing piece of yours called *The Balloon* last year. Are you writing anything now?"

"Yes."

"I always envy you writing fellahs, you know. Jolly easy life of it, what? I mean to say you can do your work where you like and when you like."

"Yes, it's a lazy nomadic existence," John agreed. "And of course we don't even have to write it out again in a fair hand now that we have typewriters."

"I never thought of that. Yes, of course that must save you a lot of extra trouble. I wish you'd tell me something. How do you think of a play? I mean to say, I've never met one of you literary fellahs before, and I've always wanted to find that out. I do wish my wife hadn't gone off to bed early. She caught a bit of a headache in the sun. She botanizes. Came home to-day with a bunch of fly-orchises. And by Jove, it's a good name for them. They are exactly like flies. But you were going to tell me how you thought of your plays."

"Was I?" said John. "I'm afraid I don't really know."

"Just comes like that, eh? Extraordinary! But when you start a play do you know how it's going to end, or do you just let your characters sort of carry you along?"

"I try to control them."

"Quite. Quite. I say, that's a good-looking girl dancing with one of those theatrical Blackshirt fellahs. English, I should say.'

"It's my sister."

"Really? And you let her dance with these Italians? But expect you keep a pretty sharp look-out, what?"

"Why?"

"I've always heard one wants to be rather careful of them with one's womenfolk."

"I wonder you ventured to bring your wife to Italy, Mr Bustable."

"Well, we took advantage of the exchange. But I don't really enjoy travelling on the Continent. All this cooking in oil. But my wife likes it. Not the oil of course, but the churches, and as I told you she botanizes a lot. We lost our two boys in France. And our only girl got married last year. Well, I think I'll be off. I like to be in bed by eleven. I'm awfully glad to have met you. Quite an excitement in my uneventful life."

The lanky Englishman stalked off along the side of the ballroom. His place was taken by Geoffrey Noel who had tripped into the Excelsior for a moment to survey the scene. He asked John who his friend was.

"A Mr Bustable, an Englishman," John parodied. "He thinks I'm rash to let Prudence dance with one of these theatrical Blackshirts."

Noel mumbled indignantly.

"Preposterous! I wish such duffers would stick to golf instead of blundering round Italy like bluebottles."

"Yes, they are exasperating, and yet they're so good within the narrow confines of their education and experience. That fellow, for instance, lost both his sons in the war. Obviously for him it was the end of any real interest he took in life. Yet there wasn't a word of complaint. If only fellows like him were educated when young what a Europe we might help to build! It's this prolongation of adolescence. No boy should be allowed to remain a day longer at a public-school than he would be allowed to remain at a council-school. If he has the brains let him go to a university at sixteen and get out into the world by nineteen. If he has no brains let him work with his hands as a boy from a council-school is expected to work. And let the council-schoolboy *with* brains take his place at the university. Democracy! What is our democracy, Noel? A lazy mule by the worn-out stallion Privilege out of the spavined mare Trade Unionism. And the breeding of the other democracies is if anything even worse. No wonder these young men in Italy are sick of it, for here the lazy mule has that foul and contagious discharge of mucus from the jaw known as glanders."

"And what would you substitute?"

"A true aristocracy of mind, and if a nation would spend upon its education half of what it will spend even now after a world war upon its armaments such an aristocracy might be attained within the years of a generation."

"And you think that young Aprili and his friends will achieve such an aristocracy?" Noel mumbled.

"I think this fellow Mussolini has grasped one essential of

government, which is that you cannot create a vital State out of a class. He used to be a socialist, and in turning against his old comrades he has turned against their exclusiveness. That's why he hates the Muscovite variety of communism. He wants to bind the axe with a *fascia* of rods cut from every class of the community. I imagine that if this Fascism is to succeed it will have to be what we should call socialistic in most of its administration. I suppose too that for a while the power of Fascism will require a dictatorship. I see no other way of using the lictor's axe to cut away rapidly enough the jungle which the *laissez-faire* of the nineteenth-century liberalism has allowed to choke the avenues of true progress."

"Our young friend has certainly been a most successful missionary," Noel declared.

"Not by his arguments," John answered. "A flame is burning, and I have been kindled by it."

"I should feel inclined to say—m-m-m—that somebody else has been kindled by it."

He nodded in the direction of Prudence and Mario who were dancing now to the strains of their favourite foxtrot *Evergreen Eve.*

"Yes, I was noticing," said John.

On their way back to the Villa Allegra after the dancing John and Prudence took the path down the steps and across the beach which he and Athene had taken that night after the party at Ostápov's. Then it had been starshine. To-night the moon was brilliant and still high over the sea, not having yet abandoned all her wintry silver and remoteness.

"It's more than two years since we walked together on the sands that day at Nanphant," she said at last. "Do you remember, John?"

"Very well. It was in the January after Athene and I were married."

"I was going to be seventeen that May, and this May I'm going to be nineteen," she continued. "If I were married when I was twenty you'd call that fairly soon, wouldn't you?"

"I waited a good deal longer than that."

"John, let me take your arm." She put her arm through his and he clasped her hand. "John, this morning Mario told me he loved me."

"And what did you say?"

"I told him that I loved him. And, John, I do, I do. John, you do like him, don't you?"

"I like him extremely."

"And he adores you. He really can't believe you are an English-

her for more than a year, in a state of even greater uncertainty about the future than you."

He waved to his sister and hurried off through the rosemary to the tower.

Athene was still up when he arrived home.

"Well, I suppose Elise will have a right to call me down as the very worst chaperon in the world," she said when the tale had been related. "Still, it's up to some young Englishman to cut out this young Italian, and if no young Englishman can do it, there's no more to be said. And Mario goes to-morrow . . . well, there's a responsibility off our shoulders."

"And who are we to question love in Citrano?" John asked.

"Indeed no, dearest one, we can't say anything. No, no, we surely can't."

John and Athene had agreed it would be best for him to escort Prudence as far as Rome.

"I know the Hallams would meet her and see her off by the Paris train, but I expect she'll want to meet Mario," Athene suggested.

"Of course she will," John agreed. "We can stay a couple of nights in Rome, and that'll get her home in good time for the grave task of preparing her trousseau for the season." He chuckled. "Elise is dreaming now of a marriage in June to the heir of some mushroom peerage spawned from the blood and tears of war. I fancy my stepmother is going to be disappointed."

On the day before she left Capri, Prudence went along to Madame Kleinborch's tiny shop in one of the narrow streets leading into the Piazza. She wanted to take back presents to England, and Leonora was with her. The widow of the Russian general had recovered wonderfully in a few weeks from the destitution, squalor, and misery by which she had seemed on the point of being finally overwhelmed so short a time ago. Indeed, nobody who saw the thin little woman in black stitching away at her embroidery at the back of the shop would have believed the tale that the Matrassics had told John at the beginning of February. Her hands were still rough with work, and her complexion was sallow with the sallowness that comes from poor food and perpetual anxiety. That she was not yet much over thirty would have been astonishing news, for she looked at least ten years older. Still, her dark eyes were clear again, and confidence in herself was growing daily so that she was no longer afraid of the polite manners of her former life which in the abyss she had tried to forget.

When Prudence had made her purchases and she and Leonora were walking back to the Allegra Leonora said:

"Well, I guess I'd feel pretty pleased with myself over the Baroness Kleinborch if I was John. That certainly was a grim story."

"I know he helped her, but I only heard that she was the widow of one of the Russian generals defeated by Hindenburg and was starving on account of the Bolsheviks. And of course I know she has a baby."

"Yes, that was some of the story, but there was more than that . . . well, well, he pulled off something pretty difficult when he established her as a feature of Citrano life within two months."

"He's awfully good at understanding," Prudence said.

"Don't I know it, angel child? Nobody knows it better than Leonora. Well, you're leaving us, and we'll be back in America by the time you come back in the summer. It's too bad."

"It has been sweet of you to have me all this time at the Allegra."

"My dear, I loved having you. You've got to come over and stay with us in New York next year. You tell your mother I'll find you the perfect American husband."

Prudence laughed at such a plan, but it was a slightly embarrassed laugh.

"Yes, I know," Leonora went on. "But perhaps you'll see him in Rome."

"You mean Mario?"

"Sure I mean Mario. I liked that boy quite a lot. I think that boy has a good deal in him."

"I'm glad you do, Leonora."

"You're telling grandma!" Leonora put her arm in Prudence's. "It's a shame to tease you, darling," she said softly. "I'm not trying to coax a secret out of you. I'm just wanting you to be happy one day with your Mario. Oh, I know, I know," she went on as Prudence opened her big blue eyes. "I know it's nothing at all but a little Citrano moonlight . . . for the rest of the world."

"Well, as a matter of fact, Leonora, we are in love with one another," Prudence admitted. "But you see, there can't be anything like an engagement yet awhile. So the only person I told was John, and he told Athene."

"And it was too bad to make you tell me," Leonora said. "But I won't tell anybody else. That's a promise. Only when somebody's as happy as I am in her marriage she wants to think of other people being happy when they get married. And I'd an idea perhaps you'd like to know that I thought you would be happy . . . with your Mario."

"Dear Leonora, you are so sweet to me. But nobody else is going to know anything about it except you and John and Athene."

Nevertheless when she was saying good-bye to Caterina and Concetta next day, Prudence was left under no illusion about their attitude.

"*A riveder La, signorina. Buon viaggio e presto ritorno. Evviva i Fascisti!*" cried Caterina.

"*Si, si, evviva i Fascisti!*" Concetta echoed. "*Sono molto bravi, i Fascisti.*"

"The Torre Saracena is becoming quite a political centre," John said as the Fiat in which Prudence and Mario had driven back from Nerano started for Naples. "If the Blackshirts have plenty of Marios Mussolini need not worry about the women of Italy."

"You don't really think Caterina and Concetta guessed anything about me and him?" Prudence asked.

"Good gracious, no," he ejaculated. "How could they?"

It was in Mario's little apartment in the Via Boncompagni that he and Prudence said good-bye. She and John had gone there to have tea with him, and John had left them together until it was time to start for the station. The two days in Rome had passed as rapidly as all days pass for lovers on the edge of parting.

"And you will come back to Italy in the summer?" Mario had asked for the hundredth time.

"By the end of July, I hope," she told him once more.

"Four months," he commented gloomily. "It's a very, very long time."

"But you'll be so busy, Mario darling."

"Yes, I shall be very busy. There will be trouble, I think, on the first of May."

"Not fighting?" she asked in alarm.

"A little fighting, perhaps. The *arditi del popolo* will make trouble on that day, and there will be strikes. And when there are strikes there is always fighting."

"But you don't think anything could happen to you?" she gasped, turning pale.

"No, no, darling." He sighed. "I cannot say it so sweetly as you say it for me. Say to me 'darling'."

"Darling, I love you," she murmured more softly than her heart was beating.

The windows of the room were sapphires in the dusk of March when they kissed their last farewell. Then Mario switched on the light, and John came in to say it was time to go and eat at the station. A chill wind from the east was raising the dust at the top of the Viminale when they drove past the fountain in the Piazza delle Terme. The baths of Diocletian loomed forbiddingly beyond. The meal in the station buffet was draughty and restless. The train of *wagons-lits* looked funereal with its drawn shutters.

John tipped the attendant of the coach in which Prudence was to travel, and before he left her compartment flung down upon the seat a small volume.

"It's a selection of Browning's poems," he told her. "There's nothing like Browning for young women who have loved and been loved in Italy."

Presently she was in the prison that a *wagon-lit* becomes when it is carrying a heart further away every moment from where it longs to be.

John and Mario left the station together. As they passed a group of workmen standing at the corner of the Piazza del Cinquecento, one of them noticing the *camicia nera* spat and growled an obscene epithet. Mario's lips tightened.

"This cannot continue much longer," he muttered. "It must finish."

"You won't do much reading of engineering books to-night," John told him. "I think we'll go to a cinema."

In the train northward bound Prudence sat alone in her compartment, thinking of the Roman fountains . . . of the pines in the Borghese Gardens . . . of the view from the Pincio . . . of that lunch at the Castello dei Cesari on the Aventine and of the big window by which she had sat looking now at Mario, now at Rome outspread below, and the hazy blue Campagna beyond . . . of *Rigoletto* at the Opera House . . . and of the copper coin she had dropped in the fountain of Trevi that so in honouring an old votive superstition she might be sure of coming back to Rome . . . to Rome . . . Rome . . . Rome . . . Rome . . . the wheels of the train rumbled kilometre after kilometre northward bound.

At the end of the first week in April Julius Stern reached Citrano after a very successful concert at Queen's Hall when his Second

Symphony had been performed again and he himself had played
with a distinguished English violoncellist in the Brahms Double
Concerto.

Julius had brought out Arthur, who was depressed by everybody's assumption that Sebastian would be a good companion for
him. He took an early opportunity of protesting to John against
such an assumption.

"I can't lug him about with me everywhere," he complained.
"You might ask Mother not always to say when I'm going out
that Sebastian can come. He's only just seven, and I'm eleven
now. Besides, he will hum to himself all the time. And in the
Piazza yesterday he started to imitate conducting an orchestra and
everybody turned round and grinned."

"I'll see what can be done about it," John promised. "But you
might remember that Sebastian's father lugged you out here all
the way from England, and what is more important in June he
and your Aunt Leonora are going to lug you all the way out to
America."

"I don't want never to take him out with me, John, but I don't
want always to take him out," Arthur explained. "Only you'd
better not say anything to Mother, because she'll make me go out
with Sebastian all the more if you do. She always makes me do
what I don't want to do."

Indeed, the prospect of Arthur's being spoilt by a quartet of
grandparents on a visit of three months had made his mother more
than usually strict with him, and there was some justification for
his suspecting her of mere contrariety. John decided that the
most tactful way to smooth matters out was to invite both boys
to accompany him on marine excursions, the excitement of which
served as a bridge over the vast chasm that separated seven from
eleven.

"He's not a bad kid, but I think he's going to be rather
conceited," Arthur observed to John when after a day
among the Siren Isles they had deposited Sebastian at the Villa
Allegra and were walking back through the rosemary to the
tower. "We haven't got any kids as young as him at Hampden
House, but if he talked there like he does here he'd get jolly well
ragged."

"Did you get much ragged when you first went there?" John
asked.

"A bit," Arthur admitted. "But not much after my first term.
And not at all after I made that record for Hampden House by

travelling back alone from Rome to Paris when I was ten. And when Mario sent me that black shirt I was almost the most popular boy of my age in the school because I let every chap wear it, and if the Fascists win in Italy I shall present it to the school museum. And missing next term ought to make me pretty popular."

"On the principle that absence makes the heart grow fonder?"

"You're ragging me now, aren't you?" Arthur asked, with a quick flash in his dark eyes.

"No, no. I'm curious to know why missing a term should put your number up."

"Well, it'll be another record when I come back alone from America before I'm twelve. And I might be in the second eleven at soccer next autumn. I've got a good chance. I shall run four times round the ship every day on the voyage back to get into training."

"Strong stuff," John commented. "You'll be very popular too with all the slightly seasick ladies in deck-chairs."

"Oh, hurrah!" Arthur suddenly ejaculated.

"Hurrah for what?"

"I've just remembered to-morrow's Good Friday as well as Mother's birthday, and we'll be able to see the procession. I should think it would be too late for Sebastian, wouldn't you?"

"I wouldn't count on that," John warned him. "I'm pretty sure he will be allowed to sit up for the procession."

So indeed he was.

It was such another nocturne of black and silver as that which John had watched with Gabrielle in Sorrento nine years ago; here in Citrano where the procession moved slowly through the narrow cobbled alleys it was even more impressive.

Sebastian gazed with an entranced scowl at the twelve small boys representing the twelve disciples, at the hooded *frati di misericordia* with their unbleached candles, at the bloodstained figure of the dead Christ upon the bier, and at the life-sized waxen-faced image of His Mother dressed in the heavy black weeds of a Neapolitan widow.

"Well, honeybunch," said Leonora, when the lanterns and candles and shadowy forms had passed out of sight, "wasn't that beautiful? Which of the disciples would you have liked to be?"

"Judas," Sebastian declared firmly.

"Darling! Judas Iscariot? What makes you say that?"

"Because the people laughed at him, and the boy was crying."

"But you wouldn't like to be laughed at, would you?"

H

"If the people laughed at me I wouldn't cry," Sebastian affirmed. "I'd kick them. Or hit them with my rope."

This arrogance was too much for Arthur.

"Then they'd hit you back," he said.

"Then I'd hit them back again with my bag of silver," Sebastian declared.

"Then they'd hit you back again," said Arthur, resorting to the schoolboy's verbal war of attrition.

"No, they wouldn't."

"They would."

"They wouldn't."

"They would."

"That's enough, Arthur," said his mother. "It's not a very interesting argument for other people."

Simultaneously Sebastian was discouraged by *his* mother from further discussion, and the families walked back through the moonlight, the chanting of the *Stabat Mater* dying away behind them upon the stilly April night.

At the tower a telegram was waiting for Athene.

"Oh, my dear," she cried in dismay. "We forgot Jennifer's birthday. Isn't that too bad! And no excuse at all," Athene went on, "for not to remember somebody else's birthday on the same day as your own is just the muddy depth of egotism. We'll telegraph her to-morrow."

On Easter morning Corinna heard her first Mass. She had been fifteen months old on Good Friday. It was not to the crowded Duomo she was taken but to a minute church beside the road that wound up into the hills behind Citrano. The edifice of limestone and weather-stained stucco was dedicated to the Holy Child and was the favourite place to hear the midnight Mass of Christmas, when far more worshippers than the little church could hold thronged the wooded garden in which it was set and all the length of the winding paved road that led up to it. For the rest of the year it was used only for early Masses on the great festivals. On this April morning at seven o'clock the shallow domed roof was half covered with a radiance of the convolvulus called Morning Glory in the full perfection of that deep lucid blue which by noon would be a mat of withered flowers like shrivelled toy balloons.

When Corinna was carried in by Mairi and saw the fountain of blossoms pouring in a blue cascade over the porch of the church she stretched out her hands in delight to greet such beauty. She was still laughing at the thought of it when she and her nurse passed through the door, and at the sound of her clear laughter the bright silk handkerchiefs on the heads of the women and girls bowed in prayer stirred like butterflies and settled again as their wearers smiled a welcome and bent again over their tinkling rosaries. Monica not a month away from her second birthday and therefore already aware of the hushed attention that church demands gazed at Corinna severely from dark solemn eyes.   However, after this single breach of decorum Corinna's behaviour during Mass was beyond criticism.

Not so the behaviour of the German delegation at the World Economic Congress in Genoa on that Easter morning, for it was then that they went over to Rapallo and signed with Chichérin, the Soviet Foreign Minister, a political and economic agreement which alarmed the rest of Europe by the prospect it offered of an extremely unpleasant alliance.   The German delegation assured the other delegates that by establishing a joint peace with Russia no disloyalty was intended to the Congress, and that in recognizing the Soviet Government by restoring to it the palace of the former Russian Ambassadors to Berlin it was reacting to reliable information that the other Powers were on the verge of concluding agreements with the Soviets.   Mr Lloyd George, as President of the Congress, delivered a stiff jobation to the Germans on the enormity of their trying to make friends with the Bolsheviks behind the backs of the other Powers, and the German delegation was punished by being debarred from participation in the commission for Russian affairs.

"It seems to me inevitable that unless the problem of German reparations can be solved Germany and Russia must get together, and when they really do it's going to be a bad look-out for the rest of Europe," John observed to Julius.   "I can't imagine more fertile soil for Bolshevism."

"I think the French are being rather hysterical," Julius said. "If the whole future of Europe is to depend on the French being paid the uttermost farthing of their indemnity before anybody else there's not much prospect of picking up the broken pieces."

"I blame America for the French attitude," said John.   "If America hadn't refused to France the joint guarantee with us against being attacked by Germany everything might have been easier.   As it is the French are convinced that if they don't help themselves nobody else is going to help them.   I'm beginning to turn against democracy, or rather the three-legged monster bred from the English, French, and American revolutions which we call democracy. Wilson had his faults, but he had a much better opportunity of judging the wisest policy for the future peace of Europe than Congress."

"Beginning to turn?" Julius repeated. "It had not occurred to me that you ever had the least belief in democracy."

"Oh yes, I believe in genuine democracy, but I've no great belief in the expression of it through parliamentary institutions. *Vox populi vox Dei?* Not when the voice of the people we hear is the ventriloquism of the Press and of party politicians. The more I study the aims of these Blackshirts the more they appeal to me. I wish you'd met young Aprili. I think you'd have been impressed. A breath of new life is blowing through this country. Where else in the world is it blowing in Europe except perhaps in Russia, and that now seems a wind in the wrong direction?"

"You'd better tell Vecchione how much you admire the Blackshirts," Julius said. They were on their way to visit Ernesto Vecchione, one of the Ministers in the Facta Government, which was trying with no more success than the Governments before it to gain the confidence of the Italian people and win from her late Allies a just recognition of the part played by Italy in the common victory. His wife was a Russian woman who had been arrested in the abortive 1905 revolution and nearly been sent to Siberia. John and Julius had met her at Ostápov's villa, and it was on her invitation that they were calling upon her husband to-day. He spent most of the time in Rome, but had allowed himself a few days' *villegiatura* for Easter. She intended to pass the rest of the season in Citrano in what the Contessa del Bufalo called "that poky little Villa Marigold" which for fifteen years now had seldom been unlet for more than a week at a time. On the rare occasions when it was empty the Marigold resembled a house in a stage set which was merely waiting for its tenants to add a last dab of dry rouge with the hare's-foot before they took possession of it and the curtain went up. And when it was occupied its occupants never seemed to be living in it but to be playing a scene for the passers-by. It looked over the wide terrace beyond the Piazza and so had a continuous audience from those who strolled up and down enjoying the view of the Marina.

"Do you remember that preposterous Georgian prince and his American wife who were in the Marigold in the spring before the war?" John asked.

"Yes, yes, a dreadful creature," Julius replied. "The rutting elk you called him."

They had reached the little villa covered now with creamy banksia roses coming into full bloom, and were presently sitting in the *salone* overcrowded with hideous mock Moorish furniture, that *salone* in which how many honeymoon couples had had to make up their minds whether marriage was likely to prove a success or a failure.

The Honourable Ernesto Vecchione was young for the post in the Cabinet he filled. He could not have been much over forty-five, and that was young indeed for one of these Governments of political dotards which the Fascists accused of imperilling the future of Italy. He was a clean-shaven man, the pallor of whose face had degenerated into pastiness; but a pair of luminous and acute grey eyes kept his features alive. For many years he had been the London correspondent of one of the great Italian Liberal papers and spoke English perfectly. Before that he had been a newspaper correspondent in Russia, which explained Signora Vecchione, who was the last woman one would have expected to hear was the wife of an Italian Deputy. She looked some years older than he— farouche and sloppily-dressed and weather-beaten, and with a glitter in her eye that suggested madness. Ostápov declared she was mad, but thought that no good reason for declining the invitation to meet her husband.

"You never know in this country when it may not be very useful to have a friend in Government circles," he had bellowed.

The genial vinous Russian was at the Villa Marigold this afternoon, and the slightly chill formality of their host put no damper on the boisterousness of his greetings.

"I am so sorry I did not ask Madame Ogilvie and Madame Stern to come to tea," Signora Vecchione said. "But I did not know you were married. It is only now that Monsieur Ostápov tells me. I am so sorry. So rude . . . I am quite ashamed. . . ."

"Yes, my wife is most upset," Vecchione himself added.

"Well, to be candid, Excellency," said John, "we hoped to talk politics and were quite glad to come by ourselves."

"Politics, eh?" the Minister echoed, with a smile that vanished on a sigh. "I thought I was having a week's holiday. I would rather talk about London where I liked living so much. I was there ten years."

But John was not anxious to talk about London. He was indeed determined to talk about Fascism.

"I suppose I oughtn't to say this to a member of the present Government, but I've been asking myself lately whether this new movement may not be the forerunner of a really profound change in our political point of view."

"Not at all, not at all," Ostápov put in. "Just Catiline stuff. Nothing more."

"Not even as much," Vecchione added. "This noisy renegade Socialist can criticize, but nothing is easier than criticism of the Government in power. What evidence is there that these Fascists can match destructive words with constructive actions. They are not likely to achieve political power—they have hardly twenty deputies in the present chamber—but if by some mad whim of he electorate they should be entrusted with the formation of a Government it would be a mere burlesque which would not last two months."

"But, Excellency, if instead of regarding them as a new political combination," John argued, "you regarded them as a new political idea. . . ."

"New?" Vecchione snapped. "Did you say 'new'? What novelty do you find in a collection of political adventurers banding themselves together to prey upon public opinion?"

"If you put it that way . . ."

"I could not put it any other way. What do these *condottieri* want?"

"Another parallel with the fifteenth century," Ostápov shouted. "The fifteenth century was the century of the *condottieri*."

Vecchione looked round in astonishment at the interruption and Ostápov waved the cup of tea with which he had been served by his hostess as if it were the bottle of red wine that usually supported his arguments. "Signor Ogilvie and I once fancied we had discovered a rhythmic ebb and flow of five centuries in history . . . hence we are searching for parallels to the present century in the fifteenth, in the tenth, and in the fifth . . . but please excuse the interruption. You were asking what these *condottieri* of the twentieth century wanted."

"It is not difficult to answer. They want office," Vecchione declared.

"I wonder if you're justified in treating them as merely another political party," said John. "It seems to me that they're aiming at the destruction of political parties."

"So they claim," Vecchione scoffed. "But let them obtain office and you will see that *plus ça change plus c'est la même chose*."

John shook his head.

"It's something more radical. Suppose parliamentary institutions have, for the time at any rate, outlived their utility. Lots of us in England think that, but we are handicapped by a filial piety for the mother of Parliaments. In Italy parliamentary institutions have always been excrescences on the body politic."

Signora Vecchione swooped, her eyes bright as a goshawk's.

"You have not lived in Russia, monsieur, or you would not talk so. It is for lack of a Parliament that we have the present horror of the Bolsheviks. If the Italian Parliament is destroyed we will see such a horror here in Italy."

"But the Fascists offer the strongest guarantee against Bolshevism," John argued.

"Yes, if words could guarantee," Vecchione laughed harshly. "Oh, I'll admit to you that this cry of youth to be heard makes a strong appeal to the emotion. Youth was sacrificed in the war by older men. Youth is unwilling to trust its future to the men who made such a mess of the world. It is all very plausible, but why should we suppose that youth can do any better? No, no, *Fascismo* is purely destructive, and if it were victorious it would mean the end of Italy. We have not fought this war to establish a tyranny."

"He is frightened," said Ostápov, when the three guests were walking back from their tea-party.

"I'm not surprised," said Julius. "If I were a forty-five-year-old Liberal politician and found myself living among that mock Moorish furniture with that weather-beaten dame and her glittering eye I should feel frightened. I should be wondering all the while if I were something which had been left behind by a previous tenant."

"But as a matter of fact," Ostápov chuckled, "I think his fright gave him a sort of life. The average politician in office is not usually so definite as that. I was quite impressed, I assure you. They tell me he was a very good journalist and that he has a brain. We could not judge his brain this afternoon because he is frightened. He can see no future for himself almost at the very moment when to his great surprise his ambition has been realized before he hoped it would be. I do not suppose he ever dreamed of cabinet rank so soon, and now he fears it will be snatched from him by the Blackshirts."

"There *was* a sense of death about him," Julius said, half to himself. "I'm not surprised, John, that you're putting your money on these Blackshirts. I don't know much about them. They may be a very low form of life, but however low they must be better than what our friend Vecchione stands for. And Vecchione is many times better than the average politician. At least he gave us his straightforward opinion, and had the guts to say how much he hated the *Fascisti*. A pity a man like that should be tied to the corpse of nineteenth-century Liberalism. I suppose he's an anti-clerical too?"

"Yes, yes," Ostápov said. "But what I find so strange is how an ambitious young political journalist could risk his career by marrying that fantastic woman."

"She may have grown fantastic," John suggested.

"No, no. She must always have been fantastic," Ostápov insisted. "I expect it appealed to the romantic side of his Liberalism that she should be arrested for a political offence. I should fancy that poor Vecchione was once excessively romantic."

"If he expects to revive nineteenth-century Liberalism, he must still be excessively romantic," said John. "Yes, it was a queer afternoon. That ridiculous little Villa Marigold designed for honeymoon couples and containing instead that pasty-faced Italian politician with the entrée to Bloomsbury and the freedom of the office of the *Manchester Guardian*, and that weather-beaten Muscovite woman with a glittering mad eye."

John began to him:

> *"Giovinezza, giovinezza,*
> *Primavera di bellezza,*
> *Nel Fascismo è la salvezza*
> *Della nostra libertà."*

"Is that the anthem of your Blackshirts?" Julius asked.

"That's the anthem."

"It would make a good marching song for boy scoutlets—I forget what they are called."

"Wolf Cubs."

"Appropriate indeed for the children of Romulus," Julius observed.

"You've given me an idea—a rather terrifying idea," John exclaimed. "Blackshirts are grown-up boy scouts. Yes, that's just what they are. They've brought our football to the Continent, and at the rate they're playing they'll be better than we at it presently. And now, my god, they're going to bag the monitorial system and the public-school ethos. If they get better at that than we are . . . no, it doesn't bear contemplation. Tell me, Ostápov, are there Bolshevik boy scouts?"

"The equivalent, yes."

"We're heading away from individualism all right," said John. "There's no doubt about that."

That night a letter reached the Torre Saracena from Jennifer Pendarves:

PENDARVES HOUSE,
ST PEDROC R.S.O.
SOUTH CORNWALL
April 19th, 1922.

Dearest Athene and dearest John,

Thank you a thousand times for remembering my eighteenth birthday, and for sending me that lovely tortoiseshell box. We're all frightfully gloomish to think you won't be back at Nanphant before the autumn. Christabel and I biked over a week ago to see how it was getting on. Loveday Williams thought we were coming to announce your return and almost cried with disappointment. She said when she saw us coming through the gate she was 'so happy as a piece of gold' because she was sure we had good news. Harry Dunstan said it was enough to break the flowers' hearts to be opening so handsome and not a soul to see them. Father is frightfully proud. He got two A.M.'s at the Truro show, and Geoffrey Vivian got nothing this year. Hugh and Richard went to France this vac. instead of coming home, which was rather bestial of them. I'm going to stay with the Constantines in Penzance for Will Constantine's twenty-first birthday dance, which makes Christabel somewhat jealous. (It doesn't at all! [signed] Christabel) I had to let the poor creature write that. Small things please small minds!

You will come back in the autumn, won't you? We're longing to see Corinna. She ought to be pretty hot at talking by then.

I'm afraid this is a very dull letter, but nothing happens here except such ordinary things. Tell Arthur a badger chased Jimmy Bray down the lane by Church Cove, but they dug it out and brought it round in a bag for subscriptions. Father was rather sick and wouldn't give a penny. He said if the badger did chase Jimmie Bray it was a pity it didn't catch him. Much love from us all, and do be sure to come back in the autumn. Thanks again most awfully for the tortoiseshell box.

Your loving
Jennifer

P.S. Miss Christabel Pendarves presents her compliments to her cousins and begs to inform them that her sister who is

*now suffering from the dillusion that she is grown up keeps her
lipstick in the tortoiseshell box from which it is easily bagged by
her charming younger sister.*

   P.P.S.   Ha-ha!   Sixteen, and can't spell dellusion!
                                                    Jennifer

"Oh dear," Athene said with a laugh and a sigh. "Two such
lovely places with such lovely memories! How difficult it is to
be fair to them both!"

"Make the most of the tower this summer," John warned her.
"I think next time we come to Citrano we shall be renting a villa
for the season. Only yesterday Fofo had an offer within ten
thousand liras of what we're asking."

Athene shivered.

"When you talk like that I can hear the swish of Time's scythe."

Claudia Sharpe reached Citrano not long after this.

"I know, I know. It's nine years. Don't look at me so hard,
John," she said, averting with a wave of the hand his glance.

"So far as you're concerned it might be a year," he told her.

"These kind contributions to homes for the aged poor," she
murmured.

Nevertheless John was not conscious of flattery. A fine classic
profile like Claudia Sharpe's, a little heavy though it may seem in
the thirties, will carry a woman comfortably into the fifties without
administering shocks to friends who meet her again after long
intervals. And Claudia Sharpe was still ten years from the mid-
fifties.

"I am so glad to see you again," he assured her, when keeping
the custom of the country they were sitting over their vermouth
outside Fofo's before lunch upon a velvet morning in early May.

"And don't I know just why you're glad to see me?" she twinkled
at him.

"Well, you *are* linked up with an important date in my life."

"Yes, yes, I was at Bertolini's wasn't I, when you kept your
date with Gabrielle Derozier?"

John grinned.

"But before that you were a fellow voyager on board the *Princess
Sophia*. And you were the first person to whom I ever talked about

Athene. It was the day after we had passed the Azores. I asked you to enlighten me a little about the Langridge *ménage*. And I think you suspected me of falling in love with Athene then."

"Which you denied most positively."

"But you said you wouldn't blame me if I did. You said Athene was a lovely woman, and I said she might be twenty-three but that she was still a lovely girl."

There was a silence.

"What a long time I took to find out you were right," John said at last. "She was thirty-three in April."

Claudia Sharpe lifted her glass.

"Let's drink to all of us," she twinkled. "And here come Athene and Arthur."

Arthur was full of news. The *camicie nere* were going to hold a big meeting in Citrano at Pentecost.

"Say, Arthur, your friends are just stirring up trouble. In Rome on the first of May there were quite a few people killed. We don't want them killing people here in Citrano."

But Arthur's Fascist enthusiasm was not to be disposed of so easily.

"They wouldn't kill Socialists if the Socialists didn't kill them first."

"Why, aren't they wonderful then!" Claudia Sharpe teased. "Some fighters, eh? After they've been killed they just jump right up and kill the other side. My, isn't that fine?"

"I didn't mean the dead ones killed the others. I mean the Blackshirts who aren't dead. And I'm jolly glad."

"Just a perfectly good young reactionary. I guess you'd have killed John Brown if you could."

"Yes, I would. I'd have killed every Yankee I could," Arthur affirmed.

"It's not all quiet yet on the Potomac for Arthur. He and Grandpa Gilmer will have a bully time next month listening in a rage to the tramp of Yankee feet through Georgia."

Julius and Leonora arrived at Fofo's. Mrs Heighington came in wearing a new hat. Geoffrey Noel tripped across the Piazza.

"Well, I don't know," said Claudia Sharpe. "They all told me Europe was so much changed since the war, but it seems to me just the same little old Europe I've always loved. Oh, John, I haven't told you yet I met a friend of yours on the voyage over. And a friend of yours, Mr Stern. Yes, a Mr Redroad who directs films in Hollywood. He's coming down to Citrano presently.

And I met my first movie star.　Miss Janet Meriday."

"He's a capable fellow, Redroad," Julius said.

"I should say he was.　He took me out to a place near Rome where they were shooting a scene.　They'd built up a kind of skeleton theatre and set it alight, and what that man could make an Italian crowd do with about three words of Italian nearly made me sing 'Hail, Columbia'.　I don't know whether it was Redroad's magnetism or the crowd's intelligence, but the combination certainly was effective.　And they were all feeling a bit on edge because the day before the same crowd had been taking part in a scene of Christians being thrown to the lions for a film about Nero."

"That must have been jolly exciting," Arthur observed.

"It was just a little bit too jolly exciting, old son, because one of the actors got in wrong with one of the lions and was carried out of the arena."

"Not by the lion?" Arthur exclaimed.

"By the lion, and he was very nearly dead before they rescued him."

"Good lord!　I say, I wish I could have seen that."

In justice to Arthur it was not so much his own blood lust which inspired this ejaculation as the disappointment of not being able to offer his schoolfellows the authentic narrative of an eye-witness. It would be a good story, but not so good as it might have been.

"I think it's a horrible story," Athene said.　"I hope they won't bring any lions along to Citrano."

"Mother!" Arthur protested.

"And tell us something about Janet Meriday," Athene went on. "Is she very alluring, Claudia?"

"Why, yes, I suppose she'd be considered alluring.　I don't think she'd lure me very far, but that hardly counts.　She's just a beautiful doll, and makes up for any deficiency in conversation by looking at one with concentrated intelligence when one is chattering nonsense, and the more nonsense one talks the more fiercely intelligent her gaze."

Julius groaned.

"I hope we'll be on the way back before she arrives here."

"I believe they're coming fairly soon," said Claudia Sharpe. "They're going to shoot some scenes for a film called—oh dear, I'm afraid I've forgotten what it is called, but it's all beautiful lowbrow adventure.　Then they're going on down to Sicily to shoot some scenes there."

Bob Redroad and Janet Meriday arrived a few days later, and

provided Arthur and Sebastian with three blissful weeks watching
a persecuted heroine carried off by brigands to sea-caves, dragged
through the undergrowth, and even flung into the water to be
rescued by a dashing hero.

"I think I'll be a film actor," Arthur announced.

"I'll be a film actor too," said Sebastian.

"You can't be everything I'm going to be and do everything
I'm going to do," Arthur retorted irritably.

"Why can't I, Arthur?"

"Because you can't."

"That's the kind of stupid answer Nanna says," Sebastian
pointed out. "That isn't an answer at all. You don't want me
to be a film actor, Arthur. That's why."

"Well, if you know the reason, why ask?"

"Because you don't like to be asked questions."

"Sebastian!"

"Arthur!"

Both mothers had intervened, and the two film stars of the future
sat apart brooding upon their ambition. General opinion supported Claudia Sharpe in considering Janet Meriday better to look
at than to converse with.

"Still, she must be pretty tired by evening," John urged in her
defence. "I don't think I'd be a social success at dinner if I'd been
dragged about all day in this heat by four bandits. Bob Redroad
says she's a swell worker, and after all that's what he wants."

"My, my, what a queer kind of a life," Claudia Sharpe exclaimed.
"Just make-believe all the time."

"I wonder if it's any more make-believe than the lives of most
people," John speculated.

"I don't suppose it is," Julius agreed. "The politician has to
build an effigy of himself which he presents to the world. So
does many a priest and many a schoolmaster."

"And many authors, and for that matter many a shopkeeper and
many a jobbing gardener," John went on.

"And many a wife," Athene put in.

"Well, yes, that's true enough," said Claudia Sharpe. "And
even spinsters on the edge of middle-age still work hard at make-
believe. At least a Janet Meriday doesn't pretend not to pretend.
I take back what I said."

At the end of the month Bob Redroad and Janet Meriday departed to Sicily, whence they were going at the end of July back
to complete some work in Rome.

"But we'll put in a quiet month in Citrano before we sail.
Janet wants to get some bathing."

"I should have thought she'd had enough bathing to last for a
long time," said John. "Arthur swears that you had her flung
into the sea six times one morning before she was flung in to your
satisfaction."

"She's a swell girl," Redroad grinned. "But I want to talk
over films with you, John. I can't talk when I'm working on
location. But I want a story from you."

"About bandits?"

"All right, laugh away, John. But you can't laugh the films off.
Well, I'll be seeing you, I hope, in July."

The Fascist demonstration held on Sunday, June 4th, was not
a tremendous display of potential force, but it was sufficiently
impressive to persuade many of the prosperous inhabitants of
Citrano to climb up and take their seats on the fence of undeter-
mined opinion. If they were not prepared to give their open
support to the new movement they thought it a judicious act to
send privately a subscription to the Party funds. It had been
rumoured that Benito Mussolini himself would address the *cittadini*.
Citrano was never slow to believe in its own importance to the
political future of Italy and perceived nothing out of the way in
the leader of the *camicie nere* coming all the way down from Milan
to address from the steps of the *municipio* the populace of Citrano
gathered in the Piazza at least a thousand strong. However, if
Mussolini failed to put in an appearance, Mario Aprili, to the
delight of Arthur, did. He had never enjoyed anything in his
life so much as walking about the Piazza and promenading up and
down the terrace beside Mario Aprili on that blue June day. His
brain reeled at the thought of what he should have to tell Hampden
House when he returned there next September. His absorption
in the making of the film had all too frequently been interrupted
by the fiction that he was technically back at school. Lessons had
been seeming an intolerable affront to the joy of life. Now after
listening to the speeches on the Piazza by the Fascist leaders of
this demonstration and observing Mario standing rigidly at attention all the time Arthur felt that life was real and earnest. He was
filled with resolution to work hard until he sailed for America.
Moreover, he made up his mind that when he went back to
Hampden House he would set an example of virtue, courage, endur-
ance, and high-mindedness which would influence the whole school
to follow his example. The facile Italian oratory intoxicated him.

He thought with disquietude of the years of his life he had already wasted.

And Arthur was not the only one in Citrano that June day to be fired by the speeches calling upon youth to rouse itself and lead the new world which had emerged from the war forward to the perfection of itself. Two elderly town counsellors were not content to subscribe secretly to the funds of the Fascist party but were moved by the breath of this political *primavera* to slide down from the fence and mount the steps of the *municipio* to harangue their fellow citizens with the fervour of converts. Don Rocco Picarelli and Don Augusto Di Fiori looked apprehensively at Don Alfonso Massa. There was a kind of menacing ground-swell in Don Augusto's fat, herald of storm. Fofo's eyes bobbed like floats. He made a gesture which signified to the other members of the triumvirate which had for so long controlled the life of Citrano that those two buffoons spouting on the steps of the *municipio* were finished.

"But perhaps," Don Rocco whispered hoarsely in Don Alfonso's ear, "perhaps these Blackshirts will gain power."

"*Sacramento di California!*" Don Augusto gurgled. "It's not possible."

Fofo shrugged his shoulders.

"For me it is the same because I sell my business and retire, but those two . . ." he did not finish the sentence. There was no need. Don Augusto and Don Rocco knew that Don Alfonso's gesture had slain the rash enthusiasts already, and they nodded grimly over their commercial corpses. The *Camorra* would hold out for a long time even against *Fascismo*.

And then suddenly from the balcony of the Villa Marigold a voice screamed in rage. It was Signora Vecchione, her hair in wisps round her weather-beaten countenance like Medusa's snakes, her knotted forefinger levelled in denunciation of the orator.

Her maid Mariuccia forced her way through the gaping crowd on the terrace.

"*Mamma mai!* She'll throw herself over the balcony before I can get to her," she was muttering to herself.

At last Mariuccia reached the Villa Marigold, and presently her mistress was persuaded to go back indoors. The french-windows were closed.

After the demonstration was over Mario introduced John to several of the leaders. He found them all as much elated by the consciousness of a regenerative mission as Mario himself. It was difficult to believe they were discussing politics. The atmosphere was that of a religious crusade.

"I grow more and more deeply impressed by the potentiality for good of your movement," John told the young Fascist as they walked on the terrace in the dusk of that Whit Sunday, the golden sea outspread below, the upper limestone precipices of Monte Sant' Angelo still rosy from the setting sun which the dark gorges below had already lost.

"That dreadful woman, the wife of Vecchione," the young Blackshirt exclaimed, turning a resentful eye upon the closed windows of the Villa Marigold.

"Ah, well, she's not quite responsible for her actions."

"Vecchione is one of our very bitter opponents. He tries all he can to persuade the Government to suppress us. Let them try. They will not find it very easy."

"I don't think I should worry about Vecchione," John said. "I talked to him the other day about Fascism, and he is frightened of it. A Liberal politician must be frightened of such a challenge to his sacred beliefs. You must remember that if you were twenty years older you would probably have been a Liberal yourself. All young men of imagination were Liberals at the beginning of this century. What a man like Vecchione fails to understand is that reactionary methods, or what seem like reactionary methods, are necessary from time to time because Liberalism has outrun the capacity of the majority to be liberalized. Do I make myself clear?" he asked, noticing a puzzled expression in the eyes of his young companion.

"Perhaps not. I am perhaps a little stupid for my English," Mario replied.

"Well, the fundamental creed of Liberalism is that the majority will respond mentally to Liberal legislation. More and more power is given to the people in the expectation that the popular mind is all the time steadily developing. The growth of enlightenment is assumed as a law of nature. Perhaps it is a natural law, but Liberals make the mistake of thinking that it is a law which works much more quickly than it does. As I see the world to-day, it is suffering from an excess of material advancement which the mind of man has not yet had time to digest. What I perceive in *Fascismo* is an effort to restore discipline and to regulate the mind of man to esteem and make full use of the wealth at his disposal. That must involve a certain amount of interference with the freedom of the individual, and the Liberal who has effected so much for man during the nineteenth century by his insistence upon freedom is naturally dubious about a political theory which apparently scoffs at freedom."

"But the Liberal is quite willing to encourage the Socialists who have no respect for the freedom of anybody except themselves. Look now—Giolitti has handed over the factories to the workers and nearly brought the country to ruin. *Fascismo* believes that every class has its rights, but no rights without duties at the same time."

"Oh, I know, I know. But you must allow for this exaggeration of rights at the expense of duty. It has been preached and practised since Luther. I fancy humanity is beginning to swing slowly in the other direction, and I am fascinated by the experiment which is now being developed in Italy. But be tolerant of your Liberals, Mario. There was a *risorgimento* once upon a time, remember."

"We do not wish for violence. We must defend ourselves against violence, that is all, and we must teach to politicians like Vecchione that the time has passed for the game of politics. Excuse me, what is your opinion of this League of Nations?"

"I'm afraid I'm prejudiced. I've never believed that anything good came out of Geneva. From a practical point of view I think the League of Nations died on the day the United States refused to come into it. I think too that it was ridiculous to exclude Germany. And as long as there are Great Powers the effectiveness of a body like the League of Nations must remain problematical. In fact, I feel about the League of Nations much as I feel about Liberalism. I think both are too credulous about human nature and too sceptical about God. But what of yourself, Mario? How goes the engineering?"

"I work hard."

"And Prudence?"

"I think perhaps we may be married after this winter. I have talked about our marriage with my father, and he has been very kind. I thought that this summer when Prudence comes to Citrano you will perhaps let her stay with my father in Verona. You know my mother is dead, but as I told you my father's sister makes his household."

"I think that's an excellent notion. And then Prudence will have to tell her own father and mother. Once you have met again and decided that you know your own minds it will not be fair to keep them in ignorance."

"Indeed, no, please.   I would not like that at all."

The heights westward were dark by now against a crimson sky.

"It's time for vermouth," John said.

They turned toward the Piazza.   As they passed the unlighted Villa Marigold a dark form leaned over the parapet of the balcony, muttering.

"*Quella pazza!*" Mario exclaimed.   "She has cursed me when we pass."

"No, no, she was just muttering away to herself, poor mad soul."

"She has cursed me," the young Blackshirt repeated gravely. It was evident that the incident had made an unpleasant impression upon him.   He was pensive in Fofo's.

June was always the quietest month in Citrano.   The northern visitors, Claudia Sharpe among them, had mostly departed and the Neapolitians had not yet arrived.   Arthur, under the spell of the Fascist demonstration and an ascent of Vesuvius to which John treated him after they had driven Mario into Naples next morning, worked with intense concentration for the remaining ten days before he was to sail with the Stern family from Genoa to New York.   The spurges were dying in sunset hues, and the big campanulas spread their pale-blue cushions in northerly crevices of the limestone, the last flowers to bloom before the rains of autumn's approach should again kindle a flicker of green from the drouthy soil.

Julius suggested to John a visit to his friend the Bishop, but failed to persuade him and went off in the end by himself for the week-end after Pentecost.

"Well," said Julius, when he got back to Citrano, "I asked his Lordship to remember if ever you turned up in San Gennaro seeking the truth, that you had been seeking the truth for quite a long time and that your final decision was not likely to be an emotional whim."

"Oh, you told him that, did you?"

"I also told him that you had had your daughter baptized into the Catholic Church.   His Lordship sent you his parental greetings and will give you hospitality at any time, corporeal as well as spiritual.   Well, John, we shall be off on Wednesday.   I hate just missing Corpus Domini here, but it can't be helped, we shall get it in Rome. Try to make some satisfactory arrangement with Bob Redroad and come to America next year. Athene's people will be wanting to see Corinna and we shall be wanting to see you both. As soon as we've packed Arthur off to Atlanta we shall all go up to Vermont, and I'm going to get down to a violin concerto which has been haunting my mind for some time now."

There was a letter from Prudence waiting for John when he and Athene got back from Naples on that Wednesday evening after seeing off the Sterns:

57 CHURCH ROW,
HAMPSTEAD, N.W.
June 11th.

My dearest John,

    I was thrilled to death to hear about Mario's visit to Citrano. He told me you were awfully sweet to him, and that you'd agreed to back me up in a visit to his father and aunt in Verona. And then I'll have to break it to Mother. At present she's fearfully pleased because Mr Rigden has invited David and me to come out with him in his new yacht to Citrano at the end of July, and Noll Erpingham too. That's what pleases Mamma. She didn't say so, of course, but I know she thinks that the Mediterranean moonlight shimmering on the pearls of a coronet will be irresistible to me, though why I should be supposed with all the moonlight in the universe to be irresistible to the Lord Erpingham I don't know, the said Lord Erpingham having come of age only last month. Still the yacht project knocks all other projects on the head and makes Citrano a certainty. I had been dreading plans by Mother for a round of country house parties during August, and that wouldn't have been at all funny.

    Next month! Oh, John, I'm so excited. Give my love to darling Athene and to Arthur if he hasn't already sailed, and kiss Corinna for me. I keep going to dances, but I dream all the time I'm dancing that I'm in Italy. Mr Rigden asked me a lot of questions about the harbour at Citrano. I told him I was sure it was a splendid harbour. I hope it is, because I wouldn't like his nice new yacht to be wrecked on my account, and he himself is rather a pet.

Your loving
Prudence

"I knew Turner wouldn't be able to resist buying a yacht," John laughed.

"I'm thankful this news didn't arrive before Arthur went away," said Athene. "It would have spoilt his visit to America. Well, dearest, I tell you right now that if Turner proposes all sorts of adventures round these coasts Mrs Ogilvie remains where she is. Because if there's one pastime I loathe it's staying with people in their yachts. So don't you dare encourage him to suppose I'll sail one sea mile with him."

"Not even as far as Capri?"

"Oh, well, perhaps as far as Capri if the weather is very calm."

Next day Corinna was wheeled in her perambulator to see the Corpus Domini procession. She came back under a coverlet of red rose petals which had rained down upon her from pious balconies.

"Oh, it was beautiful," Mairi breathed in awe, "we could never have such a beautiful Corpus Christi procession in Moidart. And Corinna laughed and waved to the little boy in front of the procession."

"He was supposed to be St John the Baptist."

"St John the Baptist?" she echoed in amazement, for never had Mairi Macdonald pictured St John the Baptist as a little boy of five with nothing on except a wreath of light blue tulle round his middle. "Saint John the Baptist," she repeated. "Fancy that now. Well, indeed, I would never have thought it was Saint John the Baptist. But it was very beautiful."

That night came a letter from Ireland:

Dublin
June 12, '22.

My dear John,

　　　We stand on the edge of events now. Will it be civil war? The Republicans are in the Four Courts, and that's where I am. I have been up in the North-East working in the hope that the condition of the Nationalist minority there may bring the pro-Treatyites and the anti-Treatyites together. Well, we've heard enough about Red Terrors, but an Orange Terror isn't to be sneezed at. In Belfast they specialize in murdering and maiming children. In the Mater Misericordiae (the Catholic hospital) are fifty children under sixteen who have been treated for bullet and bomb-splinter wounds during the last three or four months. On the night of Pentecost the hospital was surrounded by a howling mob who started to fire through the windows with rifles and revolvers. The doctors and the nurses had to run from ward to ward and lift the patients who couldn't get out of their beds and deposit the poor creatures on the floor under the windows out of gunfire. And the next day you might see men and women on crutches and stretchers escaping south with the other fugitives, preferring the open road to the hospital. The Dublin workhouses are full of refugees, and a thousand have reached Glasgow, which has seriously worried the British Government because there's an unemployment problem in Glasgow, and that's a much more serious thing than the murder or mutilation of a thousand Catholics. Do you realize that in the last two years nearly 25,000 Catholics have been driven out of the Six Counties by the Ulster Special Constabulary working in alliance with the mob? The damage done to Catholic property exceeds two million pounds, but as the Northern Ireland Government are drawing a subsidy of six and a half million a year from the British Government, my bold Orangemen can show a handsome profit. But I didn't set out to give you a catalogue of horrors and terrors. I just felt an overpowering desire to write to you in case I might not be writing to you again. We stand on the edge of events. The mine may go off at any moment. And if there's civil war I may be far from posting letters, may even never post another letter at all.

I'm not worried about myself, for if I'm killed I'll be with my Nora. But I am worried about my mother and Padraig. It goes against the grain to say this, but perhaps my mother might be happier to come to England till the troubles are over. And that will mean she'll want to have Padraig with her. Well, that's all right, but I charge you, John, to see that he keeps up with his Irish and that you'll stand out against Ellen's trying to send him to an English public-school or any such idea. I've left a letter to be opened in case I'm killed, and in that I've left it as my last request that your advice is always to be heeded. I didn't want to make you his formal guardian for your own sake. I wouldn't like to think the boy might count as a nuisance in your life. I'm not worrying about the religious side. I seem to be seeing very clearly as I write this and I'm as sure as I am of eternal life that you'll make your submission.

I don't have to tell you what you've meant to me for twenty-five years. God bless you, my dear John.

Yours always

Fitz

Don't write to me. There's no address will find me until these troubles are over. God bless you once again.

That for the first time in writing to him Fitz should address him as 'John' instead of 'Judge' filled John with a premonition of ill, ridiculous though, he kept telling himself, such a reason was.   His first impulse was to pay no attention to his friend's injunction, and to write at once to Tinoran on the chance of his receiving the letter. On second thoughts he decided to obey.   It would be impossible not to write an intimate letter, and Fitz would resent such a letter falling into the hands of his enemies, as well he might.   He compromised by writing to Mrs Fitzgerald and asking her if she had opportunity to tell Edward that he had received his letter and that all he asked in it should be carried out.

On June 22nd Sir Henry Wilson was shot on the steps of his house in Eaton Place by two Irish patriots who had both served in the British Army during the war, and one of whom had lost a leg at Ypres.   Obviously they could not hope to escape capture. There was no evidence to show that these men—Reginald Dunne and Joseph O'Sullivan—acted except of their own initiative. Indeed in a speech which Dunne prepared for his trial, but was not allowed to deliver, he wrote:

"We took our part in supporting the aspirations of our fellow countrymen in the same way as we took our part in supporting the nations of the world who fought for the rights of small nationalities."

It was not to be expected that the British Government would refuse the opportunity which the assassination of Sir Henry Wilson offered to threaten Ireland again.   An ultimatum was sent by the Prime Minister demanding that the Free State Forces should expel the Republicans from the Four Courts.   On June 28th the bombardment began with arms and ammunition supplied by the British Government.   It was the prelude to a year of civil war.

Yet, two days after Sir Henry Wilson was assassinated, a man of much greater value to the future of Europe was assassinated in Germany without touching the imagination of a single British statesman.   Walther Rathenau, too, was shot dead in front of his house by what were called Nationalists.   The thought of a Jewish Minister of Foreign Affairs for the Reich maddened them.   It was Rathenau who had been chiefly responsible for the agreement with Chichérin signed at Rapallo on Easter Sunday.   Probably if any British statesman tried to consider the consequences of Rathenau's assassination he decided that a fellow who tried making agreements with the Bolsheviks was better out of the way.

The immediate result of the German statesman's death was a cata-

strophic acceleration of the fall of the mark, and the first prominent appearance upon the political stage of a man called Adolf Hitler.

The destruction of the Four Courts by the end of the first week
of July afforded a popular gratification in England which was
voiced most loudly by those members of the Government whose
behaviour had been devoted to exacerbating the relations between
Great Britain and Ireland.

"But I do think the Irish are an impossible people," Geoffrey
Noel said to John, who had been railing at these speeches. "No
sooner does one give them what they want than they start quarrelling
among themselves."

"But we don't give them what they want," John contradicted.
"That's the whole point. And not being adepts at compromise
half the country is prepared to fight for a logical conclusion. I'm
sure that I myself would have done what Griffiths and Collins did,
but there's no getting away from the fact that they agreed to sign
the treaty under duresse. It is arguable that the British Government would never have dared to start the war again under the
frowns of the whole civilized world, but the moral decay of the
British Government has been so complete that one must sympathize
with the doubts of Griffiths and Collins. They saw the men they
were up against, came to the conclusion that they were a set of
murderous gangsters with better arms and more ammunition, and
decided to take no risks."

"Really—really—my dear man, you do use the most extravagant
—m-m—language," Noel protested.

"It's the only way I seem able to make any impression on British
complacency. Thank goodness, I'm not in London at the present
moment. I should quarrel with most of my friends on this
question. Whatever facts I produced, whatever arguments I
brought forward to support my conviction that the British treatment of Ireland is an unbroken record of crime inspired by a
mixture of greed and fear, at the end of it that conviction would be
treated as a piece of perverse eccentricity. There is no dum-dum
bullet of logic which will pierce the mental hide of an Englishman,
and damn it, he doesn't even roll up like an armadillo, he doesn't
even charge like a rhinoceros, he just grins."

John was silent, and presently leaned across the table to refill
Geoffrey Noel's glass. They were sitting at a round table beneath
a locust-tree on the terrace of a small wine-shop famous for its red
Citrano. From where they sat the dusty corniche road below the
terrace was invisible and they looked across to where the limestone

heights swept down to the sea a mile or so east of the little town, to that long diagonal path, indeed, down which Prudence and Mario had walked on that March day to tell their love among the white violets.

"Ostápov is right," John said at last. "White wine, not red, should accompany political discussion. Or better still, not wine at all but spirits. Wine is dishonoured by politics. Which reminds me, did you read in *The Times* the discussion in Parliament about the Honours list? It would seem that the Honours handed out by the Coalition Government have become more than even this Parliament can stomach. I was particularly amused by the case of a new peer whose hundred million company went bankrupt before the war, but who with great acumen made a large personal fortune by equipping aeroplanes on Government contracts and instead of attempting to pay the shareholders or even recoup the debenture holders evidently sank a handsome sum in the party funds, for which he was rewarded with a peerage. I was enchanted too by the Prime Minister's defence of party honours as a bulwark of the country because a nation politically organized was twice as safe as one which was not. In the eighteenth century you only bought individual members of Parliament. In the glorious present you buy the whole Government."

"Come, come, my dear man!"

"Well, you buy the party machine, which is practically the same thing. In other words our great democracy is so well organized by plutocracy that the slave believes it employs its master. What puzzles me is why no really rich man ever starts doing something with his money. True the Press magnates exercise some influence. But imagine somebody like Rockefeller determined not to play the game with his fellow plutocrats. What a grand time he could have!"

"He'd probably lose all his money."

"Yes, but it would be worth while. He could put aside enough to keep him in comfort for the remainder of his days, and blow the rest. Think of spending a couple of hundred million with no other object than to upset complacency. Minor plutocrats sometimes beget spendthrift sons, but the major plutocrat seems to guard himself against that by marrying the right kind of cheese-paring woman."

John had risen from the table under the locust-tree while he was talking and had moved across to the parapet of the terrace whence he could watch the dusty road running east and west. Noel followed him.

"Rich people are always on guard," said the latter. "Even my wife who once upon a time when she hadn't a cent was completely frank and carefree became guarded when she inherited that money. Astonishing creature! She talks now of buying a ranch in New Mexico. I hope she won't. It's difficult enough to get my money when she's in Europe, but if she goes off to America I don't know what will happen. And now that slut of a wife of Francesco is swelling up again. My house will be littered with babies presently."

"My poor Noel! Hullo, here comes La Vecchione."

"Where? Good gracious! Come away from this parapet at once."

As he spoke Noel hurried back to the shade of the locust-tree and waved urgently for John to join him in his retreat.

"Why so flustered because the weather-beaten draggle-tailed Russian wife of an Italian Minister is walking about in the sun like a mad Englishman?"

Geoffrey Noel blew furiously through his empty pipe as he always did when he was excited or embarrassed.

"A most extraordinary thing happened—m-m-m—last week. Really the most extraordinary thing that ever occurred to me. I hadn't meant to say anything about it to anybody, but in case there's any unpleasantness perhaps it's as well that you should— m-m—know about it."

John supposed that poor Noel had been threatened by one of those skeletons which come dancing out of the dark cupboards at the back of an epicene's mind. He was wrong.

"That woman's mad. She's mad, Ogilvie. Last week Francesco brought me a letter which he said she'd given him in the Piazza. 'A letter for me?' I said. 'But I don't know the woman.' And I don't. Ostápov asked me to come and meet her at the Dioniso, but I flatly declined. You know I make it a rule never to go out of my way to meet a strange woman deliberately. However, Francesco insisted that Signora Vecchione intended the letter for me. And how do you think it was addressed? *À Monsieur Noel, grand poète, grand esprit, et grand amoureux.*"

John nearly tilted over backwards in a volley of laughter.

"My dear man, it's nothing to laugh at," Noel mumbled indignantly. "Of course I sent back the ridiculous missive unanswered, and forbade Francesco ever to accept another letter like that. And then what do you think happened?" he gulped.

"You came back from a party at Mon Repos and found her waiting for you in your bed?" John suggested.

"No, nothing quite so bad as that, though that idiotic slut Francesco married had let her in while I was out and she had left a sheet of paper pinned to my piano with a drawing-pin—a sheet of foolscap scribbled all over in red ink. I've kept it of course as evidence in case of any more unpleasantness. Look at that!"

Noel drew from the pocket of his white drill coat the damning communication and handed it to his friend.

"Did you pin this red rosette to the corner?" John asked, grinning.

"Of course not, of course not," Noel puffed through his pipe.

"*Grand poète, grand esprit, grand amoureux,*" John read out. "That's what she wrote on the envelope."

"Appalling creature!" the victim exhaled. "Read on."

"*Les verges sont prêtes. Viens! Viens! Je suis le sacrifice. Je m'immole sur l'autel de l'amour douloureux. Viens! Viens! Les verges sont prêtes. La baguette t'attend. Elle est liée des ficelles cramoisies. Ton esclave s'incline devant l'amour éternellement cruel. Viens, grand poète! Viens, grand esprit!! Viens, viens, grand amoureux!!!*"

John finished with another volley of laughter.

"She wants you to go and beat her."

"I've never had such a preposterous request in my life," Noel gasped. "What am I to do? She's capable of saying I have beaten her. It's like a chapter in some disgusting book about flagellation."

"She doesn't want to beat you, that's one good point," John laughed. "After all she can't compel you to beat her, whereas the other way round she might chase you all over the Piazza with a rod."

"Do you think I ought to show this letter to the *maresciallo*? It's always best in Italy to get in one's own story first with the police."

"Oh, I think that's an excess of caution in this case. I wonder why she fixed on you," John murmured pensively.

"I really can't imagine," Noel spluttered. "Until she gave that letter to Francesco I wasn't aware the wretched woman had noticed my existence."

"Because you're not at all my idea of a flagellant," John added.

In the end it was decided, in the favourite phrase of middle-aged officers and bureaucrats, to take no action, but to wait and see what the enemy did first.

"You're not the only person La Vecchione has disturbed," John told Noel. "Poor Mario vowed she cursed him from the balcony that Sunday when the Blackshirts held their demonstration. He was quite worried by her ill-wishing."

"Now if she had chased *him*," Noel mumbled enthusiastically, "it would have been intelligible."

Signora Vecchione did not pester Geoffrey Noel with any more communications, but he never left his *villino* without locking the door of his study and his bedroom.

For the rest of that blazing July John worked hard to finish the play he was writing for Gabrielle Derozier. He sent it off to her on the last day of the month.

"I've a feeling it's the best play I've written," he told Athene.

"I think it's wonderful."

"But you're always too kind a critic," he said, with a smile.

The post that evening was full of news. Arthur was having a grand time in America. Leonora wrote to say that Julius was making splendid progress with his violin concerto and hinted at another baby on the way. Ellen Fitzgerald wrote that her mother had seen Edward and had given him John's message, and that now Edward had vanished into the country held by the Irregulars. She was longing to see Corinna again, and was there any prospect of another play from John soon? Miriam Stern wrote that she and Astrid with Yan were spending August in a village near Cromer, and that Emil was apparently in good spirits and likely to be back in the world by the middle of November. A postcard from Rome told of Bob Redroad and Janet Meriday arriving in two or three days. Finally there was a telegram from Lisbon to say that the *Queen of Devon* was sailing from there next day and might be expected at Citrano any time after a week hence.

"Now that's what I call a post," John declared. After its richness had been suitably enjoyed he turned to *The Times*, and frowned.

"It looks as if we're going to fall in with French and Italian ideas and refuse to allow the Greeks to occupy Constantinople," he muttered. "But one might have known that the pro-Turkish party in England would be too strong for Lloyd George. I hope the Greeks will be able to hold out in Asia Minor, but now's the time they need Venizelos. Still, we encouraged them to go for the Turkish Nationalists and we ought to see them through."

"I wonder if Prudence has let Mario know she will be here any time after a week," Athene said.

"Sure to have," John replied, and fell back again into an exasperated contemplation of the Mediterranean. "Upon my soul," he ejaculated at last, "if we lack the imagination and the vigour to rule the Mediterranean the sooner the Blackshirts take control in Italy and restore the Imperium Romanum the better."

Early on the morning of the first of August Mario Aprili sat by the open window of his little flat in Via Boncompagni sipping a cup of coffee, and between every sip reading over again a telegram from Lisbon:

> *We expect to arrive in Citrano about a week from now it would be so lovely darling if you were there when I arrive I am sailing to you in a dream all my love*
>
> *Prudence*

The spidery post-office writing in thin Italian ink sprawled across the flimsy buff paper, but to him it was brighter than the brightest lettering of a missal.

"*Quant' è carina,*" he sighed to himself.

A big-wheeled cart from the Campagna rumbled past. It was heaped with yellow gourds, and the driver with his wife and three or four children sat under a large scarlet parasol hung with orange tassels. This picture of fecundity was suddenly pleasing to the ascetic young man. He was on the verge of forgetting his dignity as a *Fascista* and waving down from the wondow to the occupants of the cart. He played with the notion of hiring a *carrozza* and driving out along the Appian Way in order to lean back and dream of Prudence in the sunlight of this golden morning. He defeated the temptation, put the telegram out of reach, and settled down to study a work on the construction of bridges. It was hard going. At least, the constructive part of it was. It was only too easy to cross bridge after bridge and find Prudence waiting for him beyond the last arch of every one of them. She would have sent that telegram from Lisbon just before the yacht left. At this moment she would be sailing out of the Tagus. He put aside the book on bridge-building to consult Larousse and see if it afforded him an illustration of the mouth of the Tagus. Yes, there was the usual inky little illustration, but he preferred the picture of her departure from Lisbon that filled his mind's eye. The yacht would probably call next at Gibraltar. And then? It might go to

Tangier or to Algiers, or to Cagliari or to Palermo. Still, she must have felt secure of its reaching Citrano not much more than a week hence. It would be as well to leave Rome on Saturday . . . and make up his mind to spend a fortnight in Citrano. They had not swum together yet. To swim beside her into a sea-cave . . . but if he was to take a holiday on Saturday he must work all the harder for the rest of this week. He turned resolutely to study the construction of bridges. In order that a girder may become straight under its working load it should be constructed with a camber or upward convexity equal to the calculated deflection . . . calculated deflection . . . deflection . . . she might have left Lisbon last night . . . she might be here even sooner. . . .

He rose from the table on which lay the book he was studying and studied for a while the date and time of the telegram instead. It was not perfectly clear whether it was sent yesterday morning or yesterday evening . . . but what did it matter? She was to be in Citrano about a week after it was sent . . . owing to the yielding of joints when a beam is first loaded a smaller modulus of elasticity should be taken than for a solid bar. . . .

He read for an hour, and then decided he was entitled to the reward of reading through once again her last letter:

STANACRE HOUSE,
STANACRE,
WORCESTERSHIRE
Sunday, July 23.

My darling,
> *This is the last letter I shall write to you before I sail from England. I am staying here with my grandmother over the week-end. She's not really very old, not quite eighty yet, but she seems tremendously old and made rather a point of my coming to see her before I left. I know she's left me some money, and I very nearly plucked up courage to suggest that it would be useful to have it now. However, I don't think I will in case she thinks I want her to die, which would be rather frightful.*
> *The 'Queen of Devon' sails from Plymouth early on Wednesday morning. I leave here to-morrow to collect my luggage in London and pick up the rest of the party. I'll telegraph you from Lisbon which is to be our first stop. I do hope the Bay of Biscay won't be too ghastly. Not that I'd mind being seasick if it wouldn't interfere with lovely thoughts of you.*
> *Mario, we shall be seeing one another perhaps in a fortnight.*

*I can hardly believe it. But perhaps you won't be able to get
down to Citrano for a bit after I arrive. Still, you're bound to
be able to get away for a bit in August, aren't you?*

*If we can be 'fidanzato', or ought it to be 'fidanzati', perhaps
I'd better write engaged—I was going to say if we can be engaged
before I go back to England I'll be able to write home about it
and get John's support. Do you really think there's a chance
we may be married early next spring? I can hardly write the
question. It makes my hand tremble so. People who laugh at
love, how contemptible they are! Of course it simply means that
they don't know what love is. I used to think it must all be
rather exaggerated. And now if I read all the poetry in the
world about love I would still be wanting to read more—and more
—and more! I wish I could write a poem of love to you, but
women don't seem very good at writing love poems. There's
rather a lovely poem by Christina Rossetti which begins:*

> *I wish I could remember that first day,*
> *First hour, first moment of your meeting me.*

*Luckily I can remember the first moment perfectly well, but I
can't write a poem about a railway carriage. Oh, and I can see
you now, Mario darling, walking down the steps into the Piazza
di Spagna. If I live to be a hundred I shall still see you and the
way you turned back and waved before you vanished in the crowd.*

*Of course it's lovely to be sailing out to you, but in some ways
I wish I were coming by train because then I'd be sure of meeting
you in Rome, and it would have been rather delicious to lie awake
in the sleeper and listen to the train rumbling along through the
night to bring me nearer and nearer to you. I must stop maunder-
ing on. I'll telegraph to you from Lisbon when I can find out
more or less when we're likely to reach Citrano.*

I adore you. Ti voglio bene assai. Ti bacio in bocca.

                              Tua

                                   Prudence

"*Ti bacio in bocca*," he murmured to himself, and the sweet bow
of those red lips formed upon the empty air for her kiss and then
dissolved again. He turned back to bridges . . . in dealing with
the action of travelling loads much assistance may be obtained by
using a line termed an influence line. Such a line has for abscissa
the distance of a load from one end of a girder, and for ordinate
the bending moment . . . and her chestnut brown hair, and her

blue eyes and sudden blushes, and the warmth and frankness of her so unlike the fair English girls he had met who seemed like flowers which had been pressed between blotting-paper . . . the bending moment or shear at any given section, or on any member, due to that load. Generally the influence line is drawn for unit load . . . his father had been wonderfully sympathetic when he had told him about Prudence . . . no doubt it made a man sympathetic to lose a much-loved young wife . . . and Aunt Giulia too had been sympathetic . . . but how much more sympathetic would they be when they saw Prudence . . . in September when his father always took his holiday beside Lago Maggiore. . . . Prudence could stay with them . . . John would arrange that . . . if the load is carried by a rail girder with cross girders, at the intersection of bracing and boom . . . he forced himself to read on.

At half-past eleven Mario walked to a small restaurant in the garden of which dappled by sunlight at the back through vines he ate his lunch . . . an omelette and some cream cheese followed by a cup of coffee. He was on the point of returning to his flat when another young Fascist came into the garden and, pulling a chair up to Mario's table, addressed him urgently:

"Listen, Mario. I cannot go to the meeting at . . ." he named a small town near Rome where the Socialists were very strong. ". . . My mother is ill and has telegraphed for me to go to her at once and I can catch a train at two o'clock. If I wait to go to the meeting at five o'clock I cannot get to my mother to-night. If you will speak for me, *caro*, I shall be infinitely grateful."

"Of course I will go."

"*Grazie, grazie infinite, Mario. Sei gentile assai. Mi dispiace.* . . ."

But Mario cut in upon his friend's thanks by rapping on the table for another cup of coffee, and the two of them sat for a quarter of an hour talking eagerly of the prospects of *Il Fascismo* and of the necessity of dealing ruthlessly with the opposition.

"I must go now, Mario. How is the Commendatore?"

"My father is very well."

"Please remember me to him respectfully when you write."

The two young Blackshirts passed out of the restaurant into the glare of midday on the hot street. They saluted one another formally with arms out-thrust in the old Roman fashion and went their different ways. The driver of a *carrozza* crawling by looked at them and spat into the gutter.

Back in his flat Mario took a siesta on the bed under the impression that he was composing an oration on the glory of an Italy revivified by the united effort of a nation in which every class would play its part; but the image of Prudence haunted his fancy and presently he slept for an hour or so. He woke, murmuring her name as her dewy lips faded from his, back into the dream he had quitted.

A high white wall hid the courtyard of a factory from the road which turned sharply into the town at the end of it. The angle of the wall knife-sharp in the sunlight cut in half a line of newly built workmen's tenements. Beyond them stretched a dusty waste-ground littered with rubbish. Upon this high white wall the diminished shadow of a tall slim young Fascist kept pace with its owner as he pressed on in the stale sunshine of the afternoon toward the meeting-place. He had come by train from Rome, and the ten minutes' walk from the railway station in such heat had bedabbled his brow with sweat. Round the angle of the wall four figures appeared. Two were in shirt-sleeves, their clothes stained by toil: two were in dark clothes with slouch hats and crimson neckerchiefs. The newcomers perceiving the approach of the Fascist stopped. Their diminished shadows were drawn upon the wall like four black dwarfs.

"*Andate via!*" cried one.

"*Vatene!*" cried another.

"*Cacca di fascista!*" cried a third.

The fourth spat in the dust and passed a hand quickly under his coat, seeming to scratch his armpit.

But the tall slim young Fascist held on his path.

"*Canaglia,*" he muttered to himself.

"*Dietro! dietro! Alla larga! Alla larga!*" the figures shouted.

From round the knife-sharp angle of the wall came the sound of an excited crowd.

The young Fascist held on his path, and his diminished shadow kept pace with him along the high white wall.

The four figures parleyed together for a moment or two. Then they fell back behind the wall, and the young Fascist came on.

"*Questi vigliacchi,*" he commented aloud contemptuously.

The dust on the path was so thick that he moved as silently as his own shadow on the wall.

The young Fascist turned the corner.   There was a crowd a couple of hundred strong, men and women, filling the road between him and his destination.   The sight of him roused shouts and screams of threats and foul epithets.   He looked ahead for signs of his comrades.   There was no sign of them.   For an instant he hesitated, and a stone crashed against the wall in front of him, and another behind, and two or three more fell quietly in the dust at his feet.

"*Dietro! Dietro!*" the crowd yelled in rage. "Back! Back!"

But he kept on, and the crowd baffled by his contempt began to retire.

It was then that a man in a crimson neckerchief broke from the edge of the crowd and slipped round behind the young Fascist without his perceiving what had happened, so firmly fixed were his eyes upon the crowd before him, so intent was he upon quelling them and forcing his way through to the meeting-place.

A woman shrieked.   A shadow leapt upon a shadow, and the young Fascist fell forward upon his face, the blood that was pouring from his back swallowed by the parched dust.

The crowd dispersed.   The murmurs died away.   The young Fascist alone now in the stale sunshine clawed at the dust in an effort to raise himself, but collapsed at last.   When his eyes were glazing in death he heard faintly behind the high wall along which he and his shadow had passed:

Giovinezza, giovinezza,
Primavera di bellezza. . . .

"*Viva l' Italia!*" he raised himself to gasp in a voice that was like the voice of a shadow, and then 'Prudence' he breathed as breath left him.

The Rome papers did not reach Citrano until the evening. John was sitting in Fofo's when Geoffrey Noel came in with the *Messagero* and the *Popolo d' Italia*.   He passed the latter to John.

"The whole Italian Press is making a fearful clamour about this Greek landing in Eastern Thrace," Noel said.   "It looks as if they would have to withdraw at once."

"Good God!" John exclaimed, turning pale.

I

"What's the matter?"

John pointed to a headline in the paper he was reading. He could not speak.

"The son of Commendatore Enzio Aprili murdered by Socialists," Noel read aloud. "Yesterday, Mario Aprili of the Fascio Romano di Combattimento . . ." he mumbled on through the details of the outrage.

John could not stay any longer in the café listening to poor Geoffrey Noel's shocked exclamations. Only from Athene could he endure comment upon this ghastly news.

"And our beloved Prudence is at sea, wondering if he will be in Citrano to greet her," she said. "And you will have to tell her what has happened, John dear! That poor child, that poor beloved child. You must write a letter to his father in Verona."

"In Verona," John echoed. "A fit address indeed."

But he was grateful to Athene for providing him with a task, and spent the rest of the evening writing and tearing up draft after draft.

"Oh, I'd better write in English," he exclaimed at last. "My Italian has gone to pieces."

On the same evening as a telegram arrived from Naples to say that the *Queen of Devon* might be expected to drop anchor off Citrano about lunch-time to-morrow there came from Verona heavily bordered with black a memorial card of Mario Aprili, born on May 22nd, 1899, who died on August 1st, 1922. This was accompanied by a letter from the Commendatore Ingeniere Enzio Aprili to thank John for his words and to express a hope that he might have the privilege one day of meeting the *gentile signorina* whom his son had hoped to marry. He would not venture now to intrude upon her grief with his own, but he begged Signor Ogilvie to say whatever word he thought was fittest to say. He was sending back a packet of letters which perhaps Signor Ogilvie would give to the *gentile signorina* at a suitable opportunity. The numbers 1 to 20 had been written on the envelopes by his son. Naturally the letters had not been taken from their envelopes, and he was glad to say he had been able to prevent the police from reading them. There was also an envelope which contained a few white violets on which was written '*25 marzo 1922*'. And there was a telegram from Lisbon sent on July 31st.

"I must wait till I get her alone," John said to Athene miserably. "I can't tell her the moment the yacht arrives. She'll just think at first he hasn't been able to get away from Rome. God, it's a horrible business!"

It was eight days after that August morning when Mario had found it so hard to concentrate upon the theory of bridge-building because Prudence was sailing to him in a dream with all her love that the *Queen of Devon*, flying the blue ensign with the badge of the Royal Western Yacht Club, dropped anchor in the small harbour of Citrano, which she seemed completely to fill, though her tonnage was not much more than three times that of the *Argo* of five years ago in the Aegean.

John and Athene stood on the mole, waving away at intervals to Turner Rigden and Prudence and David and Erpingham and . . .

"Why, I believe that's Torbock," John said. "Yes, it is. And Mrs Torbock."

"Fine-looking craft," commented Bob Redroad, who with Janet Meriday had by now reached Citrano for a rest after their work on location.

"And where's Dorothy?" John asked when the party from the yacht had landed.

"Gee, she wouldn't come," Rigden replied indignantly. "Neither she nor Madge nor Dollie. Went up to Sutherland instead. Said they'd be seasick all the time. And we had a glorious voyage, didn't we, Prudence?"

"Glorious," she agreed, and her eyes were wandering along the mole. "Mario didn't manage to get here, John?"

"No, no . . . he couldn't manage it."

"I expect he has some political business."

Mercifully for John the Torbocks came up to shake hands with him at that moment.

"I'm sure you didn't expect to see us," Mrs Torbock said.

"I didn't, but that makes it all the more of a pleasure."

"Walter's acting as a kind of secretary to Mr Rigden, and I'm just being given a wonderful holiday."

"By Jove, Ogilvie, it's grand to see you," the Major exclaimed. In his yachting cap he was more genuinely the Major than at any time since he had been demobilized.

"Indeed yes," said his wife.

In the emotional condition that John was in, the hint of emotion in the voice of Mrs Torbock and the contrast between the Torbocks now and two years ago made the desire for tears pluck at his eyes.

"Well, David," he asked quickly, "how goes it?"

"Oh, absolutely grand. Noll and I have a scheme to persuade Mr Rigden to do an Aegean cruise."

"We're rather keen to get a wild goat which is only found on a desert island in the Cyclades," Erpingham explained.

"Antimilos," John said.

The two young men looked at him with an expression of surprised admiration for a sporting intelligence of which they had not suspected him.

"They're almost extinct," said Erpingham.

"And frightfully hard to get," David added.

"I must talk to Turner about the scheme," John murmured. It was presenting itself as something for Prudence. "I'll come along too and show you some scenes of war."

"That would be marvellous," said Erpingham politely.

"Yes, marvellous," David agreed.

But John was not misled by the adjective into fancying an enthusiasm which did not exist. What interested David and Noll were the wild goats of Antimilos. To stalk them up and down precipices would be pretty good sport. To visit the scene of wars ancient and modern or pore upon the broken monuments of the classic world would be merely 'marvellous', which was only a trifle more complimentary than 'amazing'.

Rigden was sending the yacht back to Naples for some minor repairs which might take two or three days. The Torbocks were going with her. He and the rest of the party would stay at the Excelsior.

"Prudence will come down to us," said Athene quickly.

"But you haven't room, she says," Turner Rigden expostulated.

"Yes, yes, we'll fix her up all right," John assured him.

"You always have your own way, John. Anyhow, you're all coming back to lunch with me in the yacht. How can we get hold of Miss Meriday, Mr Redroad?"

"I'll go right up to the hotel, Mr Rigden, and fetch her along."

"Say, I like that fellow, John," Rigden said when Bob Redroad, with David and Noll Erpingham for company, had started off to the Excelsior. "You know, I'm getting very interested in films."

"Don't get too interested in them till I hear if Gabrielle Derozier likes my play, because I don't want you to desert the theatre till you've put on *How It Was Sweet*."

"If Gabrielle Derozier says 'yes', *How Sweet It Was* goes on at the Sheridan. Don't you worry about that."

"Yes, Turner, but the title is *How It Was Sweet* not *How Sweet It Was*."

"Well, I'm not an expert on English grammar, but what's the

idea of turning the language upside down?"

"It's a quotation from Browning:

> *How sad and bad and mad it was—*
> *But then, how it was sweet!*"

"Well, why couldn't this bloke Browning, whoever he may be, have said 'how sweet it was!'"

"It wouldn't have scanned!"

Turner Rigden shook his head.

"Anyway, we'll get a bit of publicity out of explaining why the language had to be turned upside down," he said hopefully.

It was about four o'clock when they got back to the Torre Saracena, so much had Rigden enjoyed showing the glories of the *Queen of Devon* to his guests with prodigal hospitality, and they only got away then by promising to dine with him at the Excelsior that evening.

The dread moment was postponed for a while by the meeting between Prudence and her nineteen-month-old niece full of energy during tea after her siesta; but when tea was over John braced himself to suggest going up to the roof of the tower which was sheltered from the sun by a great orange and white awning.

"I'll stay down with Corinna," said Athene.

"How lovely to be back here," Prudence sighed, as she and John sat back in chairs, and listened for a while to the cicalas ratcheting from an olive-grove half a mile away like a distant saw-mill. To her the ratcheting kept repeating, 'Why isn't he here? Why isn't he here?' To him it said, 'You must tell her quickly, you must tell her quickly.'

"You're . . . you're very disappointed that Mario hasn't been able to meet you," John began.

"I thought there might be a letter. I telegraphed to him from Lisbon."

"It's not Mario's fault," John said painfully.

"No, I'm sure it isn't. He probably meant to come and was prevented at the last minute. I expect there'll be a letter to-morrow, or perhaps he'll be here himself. Perhaps he'll be here to-night."

"No, he won't be here to-night, Prudence."

She looked round startled by the sharpness of his voice, her speedwell-blue eyes wide with a question. He jumped up from his chair and sat beside her on the flat red tiles of the roof and caught hold of her hand.

"My precious little sister, I have something terrible to tell you . . ." He stopped.

Her hand slipped from his and clutched it again.

"Not about Mario?"

"About Mario."

"He's been hurt?"

"Badly hurt . . . very very badly hurt."

"John, he's not dead . . . oh no, he's not dead! No, John, no, no!"

Her voice was like a child's voice trying to propitiate the hand that strikes it.

"Darling, you must try to be brave, because . . ."

"He *is* dead. He's dead, he's dead," she repeated, staring into the distance of sea and sky between the awning and the parapet.

"He was killed in a fight with Socialists . . . some of what they call the *arditi del popolo*. He was alone. He was stabbed from behind."

"*Arditi!* They call it bold to stab in the back a man who is alone. But, John, he can't really be dead," she cried. "Oh, when was it?"

"On Monday last week."

"And I've been sailing to meet him and thinking of him all the time, and he was dead . . . but John, if there's a life hereafter, wouldn't he have appeared to me and warned me not to expect to see him at Citrano? I wonder if he had my telegram from Lisbon?"

"Yes, he had your telegram. I wrote to his father who sent it to me to give to you, and the twenty letters you wrote him from England. He hopes that he will be able to meet you one day, but now he does not want to intrude upon your grief with his."

"Mario was his only child, and his wife is dead. I can't cry, John. Why can't I cry?"

"One can't sometimes, sweetheart. When Miss Harford, my secretary, brought in the telegram to say that the *Whinchat* had been torpedoed and that heavy loss of life was feared she burst easily into tears because of Zoe, but I could not cry. So I know what you feel like now. And I know there's nothing I can say to help. I can only just love you more than ever."

"Hold my hand, John dear, I like you to hold my hand."

They stayed thus for a long time silent, the cicalas ratcheting from the olive-grove, until the distance of sea and sky between the awning and the parapet was washed with the gold of the fast westering sun.

"I can't go to dinner at the Excelsior to-night," she said at last.

"Of course not. I'll stay here with you. I know Athene will be kind and go alone."

"No, no, don't stay here with me, John. I'd like to be quite alone."

"He looked round at her for the first time since he had told her that Mario was dead, and was shocked by the pallor of her cheeks and the faded blue of her eyes.

"Would it bother you very much if I stayed?" he asked tenderly.

"Could you ever bother me?"

And the kind tears came, and he could hold her in his arms.

"Once long long ago you were upset by some nursery misadventure and you came to me for consolation and sat on my knee and cried, and I told you some story and you grew happy."

"I remember," she murmured, her face buried in his arms. "You were always such a darling to me."

"I can't tell you a story now that will make you happy, precious little sister. All I can tell you is how dear you are to me, and always growing dearer, and that I thank God it was I who had to tell about Mario because you must feel how utterly I understand what you are suffering. But if you'd rather be alone I'll leave you much against my will and go to the Excelsior."

"Well, you see, John, nobody knows about Mario, and if you stay with me because I'm supposed to have a headache they'll all be disappointed and think me so selfish. I don't want to spoil Mr Rigden's pleasure, because you've no idea how kind he has been to me, or David's or anybody's by letting them know what has happened to me."

It was at this moment that Athene came up on the roof.

"I wanted to come long ago, honey sweet, but I thought you'd rather stay quietly with John for a while. Dearest dearest child, what can I say? What can anybody say?"

The problem of the dinner was put to Athene.

"Why, I don't like the idea of your being here alone, but I do understand what you feel about upsetting other people. Still . . ."

"I'd like to sit by myself with Corinna," Prudence said.

John and Athene glanced at one another. They had divined why, and so they both went up to the Excelsior.

Before they started John went into the kitchen and asked Caterina
and Concetta not to say a word to the Signorina about the death
of the Signorino. And Athene told Mairi to let Prudence stay
with Corinna until they came back.

"If Corinna wakes will I not sing to her?"

"Oh yes, sing to her as you always do."

It happened that Corinna did wake, and by those Gaelic lullabies
the grief of Prudence was hushed for sleep to come to her as well
as to the child.

When next morning John and Athene were sitting up on the
roof over coffee Concetta told them that she and Caterina had
met the Signorina in the Piazza when they were on the way down
to the tower. She had said she was going for a walk. John asked
which way she was going from the Piazza and he was told she took
the road toward Amalfi.

"I think I know where she's gone," he said to Athene. "And
when I'm dressed I'll go along and meet her."

"John, you don't think . . ."

"No, no," he broke in. "I'm not worried in that way. And
don't you be anxious. But it will be a hot dusty walk back from
the cliffs and she may be glad of my company by then."

"The cliffs?" Athene echoed apprehensively.

"Dearest, don't worry. There's really nothing to worry about."

Nevertheless, John walked more quickly than he was wont on
such a summer morning. On the road a mile or so east of Citrano
below the terrace of the wine-shop where Geoffrey Noel had
confided to him his embarrassing adventure with Signora Vecchione
he saw Signora Vecchione herself walking towards him, the morning sun behind her. He hurried past her, with a formal salute, a
sudden rage springing in him against all that such a woman stood
for. No doubt it was unreasonable to feel resentment against
somebody whom the world counted mad, and no doubt it was
superstitious to a contemptible degree to link Mario's death with
the curse she had put upon him that Sunday evening when they
were walking up and down past the Villa Marigold. Yet in that
she was an expression of the decay from which youth was struggling
to escape he could not but hate her. Was all advance to be denied
to mankind except at the cost of blood and tears? Communists

might ask the same question. Emil attributed all the horrors of the October Revolution to the active opposition of reactionaries. Liberals like Ernesto Vecchione esteemed themselves the true progressives and considered the doctrines of Fascism retrograde and noxious. To him the Blackshirts were apostles of violence and as such subversive of the Liberal policy of *laissez-faire*. What men like Vecchione failed to take into account was the catastrophic quickening the war had set in motion. There was no longer time for *laissez-faire* to work its slow cure. He was left stranded with the outmoded remedies and worn-out theories, the sour ideals and faded illusions of which his wife seemed the symbol. Men like Vecchione demanded that youth, which had sacrificed so much of itself in war for what, no matter how it started, had developed into a purely material struggle of rival greed, should continue in peace to sacrifice itself to the same greed.

John turned to look back along the corniche road at the gaunt figure of Signora Vecchione stirring up the white dust with her slipshod gait. She appeared insignificant enough on that road hewn from precipices, a solitary mad-woman whom one should pity, not hate. He felt a little ashamed of the repulsion she had roused in him. Yet he waited until she had disappeared round a bend of the road before he turned aside and took that long diagonal path toward the sea, down which Mario and Prudence had walked not much more than four months since. His action was such a one as a man makes who seeks to avert the evil eye.

Even at this season of the year, after three months without rain, the north-easterly slope of that high promontory kept its odour of damp earth, the thickets of arbutus and tree-heather their woodland freshness. The path was packed with leaf-mould which gave a resilience to the step. A heavy-winged hoopoe skimmed the *macchia* and sank lazily into a spinney of Aleppo pines.

At last John reached the grassy plateau some fifty feet above the sea where he had expected to discover Prudence, by the account she had given him of her walk with Mario that morning in March. To find it empty cast a chill upon his heart. He lay down and peered over the edge at the indigo-dark water which slowly rubbed itself against the fissured cliffs and gurgled in holes that peered above the insignificant tide.

"No, no, it's a monstrous fancy," John said aloud to challenge the silence. And he thought that the monstrous fancy must have been inspired by memories of Zoe last night.

"Prudence," he stood up and shouted.

Her name was echoed by a face of limestone where the cliff towered sheer above the plateau, a great rocky tapestry of mingled orange and madder and mauve. He scrambled up to the high shallow grotto beyond and stood listening to the water drip at solemn intervals from the arched roof. He touched the top of the stalagmite in the middle of the grotto and drew back his hand with a shudder, so wet and cold was the great mushroom of stone.

There was no flowery scent to guide him on this August morning, but presently he found Prudence lying face downwards in that diminutive glade which in March had been white with violets.

He called her sharply by name.

She turned and sat up.

John managed to check any exclamation of the relief he felt. He did not want her to think that such a dreadful fancy could have had even a momentary sway over his mind.

"I'm not going to bother you," he said. "But I thought you might like my company on the way back to the Piazza."

"How did you guess I was here, John?"

"You forget you told me about this place. Let's go and sit for a while by the edge of the cliff."

She got up.

"It was here we first told each other we were in love," she said, looking down sadly at the ground where not so much as the leaf of a violet remained among the short withered grass.

"But some of the flowers will have dropped their seeds, and flowers will bloom again from those among which you sat."

"Oh, John, please don't tell me now that time will heal everything. Perhaps it will. But I don't want to be told that now."

"Darling, I wasn't dreaming of telling you that. Time may never heal this, even if it deaden it. What I meant was that you could always come here on a March day and know that some of the violets grew from flowers you saw together. That was what I meant."

She took his arm.

"Forgive me, John, for suspecting you of conventional consolation."

He was startled by the sudden maturity of her phraseology. So much older then had she grown since yesterday!

They scrambled down to the level by the cliff's edge.

"This was so green when Mario stood here that day and we listened to the singing of the sea. The sea is not singing to-day and the grass is brown. John, it was very short our time together, wasn't it?"

"Very short."

They sat down, and she had leaned her head upon his shoulder.
"I love you more than ever, John. You're so much a part of that
short time. You don't mind my loving you more because of that?"

"Precious child, why should I?"

"I don't know. It sounds as if I was making an emotional
convenience of my love for you."

Oh yes, oh yes, ages older than yesterday!

"Well, that's what your love for me ought to be. And
that's what I hope it will be until I drift ashore in the eighties
and you breast the sixties like a full-rigged ship. And now do
you think you could bear to hear about a plan for the immediate
future?"

"Yes, of course, John dear. I don't want you to think I'm
going to indulge my own sorrow at the expense of everybody else.
You'll know and Athene will know that I must have moments of
utter desolation, but you'll both of you know also that I don't
want mine to be a selfish sorrow, and that I should hate to be pitied
by people who can't possibly understand what I have lost. What
is the plan, John? Tell me."

"Well, we talked it over last night at dinner. David and Noll
are anxious to shoot one of the few remaining wild goats left in
Europe on a small desert island in the Aegean called Antimilos.
Turner who longs to give pleasure, particularly expensive pleasure,
was quite willing to take them to the island in the yacht. So I
suggested that if the yacht was going as far as Antimilos it might
go on and visit islands of greater interest to most people than
Antimilos. I said I should like to come and show them Lipsia
and Icaros not to mention Delos. I said we might even go as
far as Mileto where I had a strange adventure in 1917. And there
is Athens to see. In fact I was so eloquent on the subject of the
Aegean that Bob Redroad began to see it as a location for future
films. Nothing will satisfy Turner but that Bob Redroad and
Janet Meriday should come too, and so there it is. The only
disappointment is that Athene flatly refuses to come. She says
it's because she doesn't like small boats, which shook Turner's
pride in the *Queen of Devon*; but I know the real reason is that she
doesn't want to leave Corinna. We plan to sail on Monday. Now
you'd rather come too, wouldn't you? I thought you and I might
stay in Lipsia with some old friends of mine while the others go
chasing goats. But, listen, if you'd rather stay here, you must
tell me frankly."

"Wouldn't Athene like me to stay?"

"Athene would like you to do what you would like, though I know she thinks it would probably be better if you went to Greece."

"You *are* going yourself, aren't you, John?"

"Oh yes, I'm certainly going."

"Well, I should like to be with you."

"That's splendid. We'll be able to talk a lot together when you're in the mood. Tell me, did you sleep last night?"

"I slept for a bit, and then I lay awake a long time."

"And were out of the house before seven o'clock. Look here, I'm going to roll up my coat for a pillow. Lie down now and sleep for a while if you can. Then we will go up to Fofo's before lunch. It has to be done some time."

It was noon when Prudence woke.

On the vigil of the Assumption the *Queen of Devon* weighed anchor for the Aegean. In every window of Citrano candles were burning, and many sailors were home from the sea to keep with their families the little town's patronal festival. For them it was the Assumption of that black-faced Madonna whose miraculous picture behind the high altar of the church was unveiled for veneration. This was Our Lady of Citrano on whom how many of her children had not called in vain when they were in peril on the sea. It was a breathless evening of stars when the yacht sailed; but the stars seemed dim and remote compared with the candleshine in the windows, as if Our Lady of Citrano had descended from that Heaven to which she had been assumed and had brought the brightness of the constellations to earth.

There was yet another addition to the party bound for Greece. This was Geoffrey Noel, who was still bewildered by the way his host had swept him aboard.

"Almost—m-m—like the press gang," he said to John. "But really I'm quite overcome.

> *I have put my days and dreams out of mind,*
> *Days that are over, dreams that are done,*"

he quoted. "I just happened to say at Fofo's that I should never see Greece again, and Rigden practically deposited me in the yacht.

I've not been further than Naples for sixteen years. But you might assure young Erpingham that I'm not quite as old as all that. . . ."

"As all what?"

"Well, I happened to say something about Swinburne apropos of Balliol, and he asked me if I was up at Oxford with him. 'No', I said, 'nor was I at Cambridge with Milton.' Extraordinary notions of age these young creatures have."

"Never mind, Noel, you're bound for Greece again."

"I know. It's really a miracle. I only hope Francesco won't get into trouble while I'm away. Suppose that ghastly Vecchione woman casts an eye on him!"

"Well, that illumination's great," Bob Redroad came along the deck at this moment to exclaim. "I wish we could get that effect on to the screen. Say, Janet, aren't those candles great?"

"Perfectly divine."

"Here's your cloak, Miss Meriday," an eager voice broke in.

"Oh, David, isn't that sweet of you? And must you call me Miss Meriday? It makes me feel kind of frumpish."

"Strange thing the way women must have admiration," Noel observed to John when David and Janet Meriday had wandered aft, and Bob Redroad had gone upon the bridge to note anything from there that might come in useful one day for a picture.

"Come on now, Prudence," the voice of the owner was heard from the head of the companion to the saloon, "I want my evening constitutional."

The candle-shine of Citrano vanished behind the eastward outthrust of the cliffs. The *Queen of Devon* was faring upon that immemorial Odyssean course.

On the same August evening in the heart of the Slieve Mish mountains half a dozen men were sitting outside a stone dug-out that, even in the glow of the sunset, was hardly distinguishable from the wild crags among which it was set. None of the men was talking. Each was preoccupied with thoughts of the news which had reached them of Tralee's having been occupied by Free State forces. At this rate there soon would not be a town left in the hands of the Republicans. The sun went down into the Atlantic behind Mount Brandon. Northward the wings of night were already brooding over the grey waters of Tralee Bay, but southward the waters of Dingle Bay were sheened by the after-glow against which in the western sky two of the islands of the Blasket group stood black. Still the men sat silent. Presently, however, one of them with his eye to the north picked up a rifle.

"What's that?"

The others turned to look where far down the mountain slope a small figure was making its way up, the twilight on its heels.

"It's a boy," said one.

"He'll be bringing a message," another guessed.

"There's too many messages being sent," grumbled a third. "The Staters will trail us, the way these messages do be coming."

"Keep an eye behind him, Hegarty," said Edward Fitzgerald. "The boy may be showing the way to a Stater patrol."

"It's Larry Keenan's young brother Joe," one of the men announced with relief as a bare-legged boy of fourteen, breathing hard from the haste he had made up the rough mountain slope, drew near.

"Why, Joe, what brings you here?" Fitz asked.

"It's my brother Larry, Doctor," the boy panted. "He's been hit bad, but he came home last night and my mother says for the love of Jesus would you come down with me and take a look at him. Larry would not let me come till now because he said it would be dark."

"I'll come back with you right away," said Fitz. "Is Larry very bad?"

"My mother thinks he's very bad, Doctor."

"If I have to stay down in Derrybeg for the night, Hegarty, I'll get communion to-morrow morning and find my way back by the Dingle side after dark. I'll give five whistles—two, one, and two. So long, boys."

"I was afraid you mightn't be after coming back with me, Doctor," said Joe Keenan when he and Fitz dropped out of sight from the dug-out down the rough mountainside.

"I wouldn't let Larry want for my help. Didn't you know that?"

"It wasn't Larry I was thinking about. I was thinking . . ."

The boy broke off, and Fitz divining that it was of ghosts and fairies he was thinking did not embarrass him by pressing for an explanation.

It was a long walk to where the cottage of the Keenans stood at the head of a small glen filled with birches and hollies, a couple of miles inland from the dunes and wind-swept sandy levels by the shore of the bay.

"Glory be to God, Joe found you, Doctor," cried the widow Keenan, a woman not more than forty, but from the hardness of life seeming much older. It was from her that Larry took his pale-blue eyes and sandy hair.

"How is he?"

"I sent Tom for Father O'Connor an hour ago. God forgive me if I've fetched him without cause, but I fear for Larry, Doctor. Will you take a look at him?"

Fitz walked across the floor of beaten earth strewn with sand to the inner room where Larry was lying.

"He's after bleeding very fast, Doctor, and can't speak, only in a whisper. He got away from the Staters and was shot in the chest and they never knowing they'd shot him. Oh, Doctor, if there's any life in the dead, Ireland will be saved from murder, for there's dead enough to save the country."

Fitz passed through the door and came to the side of the wooden bed on which Larry was lying. The patchwork coverlet was drenched with blood.

"Larry! Larry!"

The twenty-year-old boy opened his eyes, and tried to breathe out a greeting to the man with whom he had fought, with whom he had been hunted, with whom he had hidden, and with whom he had once taken a hostage's life in the darkness of a November dawn.

"Don't try to talk, Larry."

Fitz bent over to examine the boy, but no doctor could do anything for him now. It was a miracle that with such a wound he had managed to make his way to the cottage in which he had been born and in which until the last two cruel years he had lived his short life.

"Your mother has sent for Father O'Connor, Larry."

The boy closed and opened his eyes to show he understood.

"I'll come back in a minute."

Fitz went into the living-room where Mrs Keenan was on her knees before a picture of the Sacred Heart. She rose to her feet.

"Doctor, is there any hope?"

He shook his head.

"Oh, for the pity of Mary will Father O'Connor come in time?" she moaned to herself.

"You must pray, Mrs Keenan."

Fitz returned to the inner room and sat on a stool beside the bed, watching life ebb from the boy, moment by moment.

The living-room was furnished scantily with a rough table, two or three stools, and a cupboard with doors, the unexpected mahogany of which came from the harvest of some wreck of long ago. In the open fireplace turfs were smouldering beneath an iron pot hung from a bracket. On the unpapered walls were a chromo-lithograph of the Pope Pius XI tricked out with tinsel and coloured glass, another picture of the Sacred Heart of Mary, and a third of the Sacred Heart of Jesus before which the mother was kneeling.

Joe Keenan was sitting on a bench at right angles to the fireplace, chewing away at a hunk of bread thinly smeared with raspberry jam.

On an impulse Fitz went back into this room and looked at the door.

"I'll put the bar down," he said.

As he spoke there came a sharp knocking. Mrs Keenan scrambled to her feet.

"Glory be to God, Father O'Connor is after coming."

Fitz held up his hand.

"Ask who it is," he whispered.

The knocking was sharper.

"Ask if it's Tom," Fitz whispered.

"Is that you, Tom?"

"Open the door," a voice called roughly. "Open at once or the door will be broken in."

"Put out the light, Joe," Fitz whispered. The boy blew out the small paraffin-lamp.

"Ask what they want," Fitz whispered to Mrs Keenan.

"What would you be wanting?" she quavered.

"We want Larry Keenan," the voice outside shouted back. "Will you be opening the door, or will we be breaking it in?"

"Those that come through that door looking for Larry Keenan go where they deserve to go," Fitz shouted back.

The new voice surprised the party outside. The murmur of discussion was audible.

"Who's that yapping about going where they deserve to go?" the first voice shouted again. "These are Government troops. Open the door, and put up your hands."

"Those that come through that door looking for Larry Keenan go where they deserve to go," Fitz shouted back again.

"It's yourself, Edward Fitzgerald. No true Irishman speaks like a bloody Cockney," a new voice yelled from the other side of the door.

A moment later there was a crash of glass. The beam of an electric torch flashed upon Fitz. As he turned to fire at the window he was shot through the heart and fell forward dead.

"Now, Mrs Keenan, perhaps you'll be opening the door and saving yourself the expense of mending it," said a voice through the window. "And light the lamp again first."

"Light the lamp, Joe," his mother quavered. "Oh, Jesus, Mary, Joseph," she wailed, "if there's any life in the dead Ireland will be saved."

As she passed the body of Fitz on her way to lift the bolt of the door she bent and made the sign of the Cross upon his forehead.

The room was filled at once with Free State troops. A big lieutenant looked down at the dead man.

"I knew I was right. Well, if these Cockney Irishmen come to Ireland looking for trouble we can give it to them. Now, where's your son, Mrs Keenan?"

She pointed to the inner room, but when they entered to fetch him they found that Larry Keenan was dead.

By the side of the bohereen that led up from the road between Dingle and Tralee to Mrs Keenan's cottage at the head of the glen Tom and Joe raised two small heaps of stones and stuck two white crosses on the top of them. On these they painted in red lead:

Pray for the soul of LARRY KEENAN, I.R.A.
who died in defence of Ireland August 14th 1922
R.I.P.

Pray for the soul of EDWARD FITZGERALD, I.R.A.
who died in defence of Ireland August 14th 1922
R.I.P.

It was Pat Hegarty who told them what to paint when they brought to the five men in the dug-out on the Slieve Mish mountains the tale of that night in Derrybeg.

"And it was the Lieutenant who called him a Cockney," Pat Hegarty muttered to himself.

Three months later from an ambush Pat Hegarty shot that lieutenant.

It was not until August 30th that the *Queen of Devon* dropped anchor in the harbour of Lipsia and John saw again almost exactly five years later the two conical hills scaled with houses to their summits. The voyage had been a rich one. Syracuse and

Olympia, Sparta and Epidaurus and Mycenae—these had all been explored at leisure. It had been decided to return by way of the Gulf of Corinth. So Athens was held in reserve. John had warned Theodore Ladas of his proposed visit and had received a telegram in Calamata urging the whole party on board to enjoy the hospitality of Grazia di Dio; but he was anxious to spend a few days alone with Prudence, and the yacht went back to Milos so that the hunt for the wild goats could be carried out. Geoffrey Noel was particularly excited at the prospect of a brief stay in Milos, not for the sake of the wild goats of Antimilos but because once upon a time he had done some digging there with members of the British Archaeological School.

"And there was really the most beautiful young man I have ever met," he hummed and mumbled to John. "Of course he'll be married now, with a large family, but I hope I'll be able to dig him out. I remember his name."

"Well, I mustn't say you've already had experience in digging out the antiquities of Milos," John laughed, "or I shall be as tactless as Noll. But you surprise me by your tribute. I should have preferred to leave him on his Grecian urn with brede of marble men and maidens overwrought."

Bob Redroad and the owner of the *Queen of Devon* had no intention of scrambling up precipices and tramping over a stony wilderness in the head of August; but they were quite happy discussing the future of films and did not mind what their fellow voyagers did, provided that they were left to lie stretched out in comfortable deckchairs. Not that Redroad lacked energy, but he had spent it all for the nonce in three months of arduous work drilling Italian crowds with at most a lingual equipment of a dozen infinitives.

However, to David's delight, Janet Meriday put on breeches and declared herself prepared to accompany the hunters.

"I think she's a wonderful girl," he confided to John.

"Yes, I thought you did."

"Well, I mean it's a pretty sporting effort. And she looks awfully well in breeches. Most girls look rather grim in breeches, I always think."

"But Janet has a film figure," John reminded his brother. "In due course she will be teaching thousands of young women to don breeches with an air."

"Yes, it's extraordinary to think of people seeing her on the films all over the world," David reflected. "I was talking to Major

Torbock about her last night, and he told me Mrs Torbock considered her one of the greatest actresses anywhere. She's an
awfully nice woman, Mrs Torbock."

The motor-boat was grumbling alongside at being kept waiting.
Prudence and John went down the ladder on the port side. In a
few minutes they were on the quay at Lipsia and Theodore Ladas
was greeting them:

"My dear friend," he cried, holding John with a hand on each
shoulder and gazing at him affectionately. "This is more than a
pleasure. And your sister! But what a pity you didn't bring
Mrs Ogilvie as well. What a disappointment for us! Now, we'll
drive right out to Grazia. You sit in front with Costa. You
remember Costa?"

John shook hands with the chauffeur and asked him in Greek
how he was, thereby gaining a warm smile of welcome.

"Euphrosyne would have driven down with me," Theodore
Ladas went on. "But we no longer have the Daimler, and this
Ford is a bit of a squash for more than four. I'm going to sit
next Miss Ogilvie. That's it. Now we're off. Damn that dog!
They will lie about in the middle of the road. Not too fast, Costa.
That's our square, Miss Ogilvie. We're rather proud of it. Ah,
you ought to have seen your brother stalking up and down it five
years ago. He ruled Lipsia for nearly a year, you know. You
wouldn't think so, to look at him now, eh? Still, you don't show
any signs of the years, my friend. Not like me."

"I hope I'll have such a head of hair when I'm your age, Ladas.
It can be as white as it likes."

"I'm sixty-seven now," the older man announced, tugging at his
pointed white Vandyke beard as if he could pluck from it a few
years and fling them from him. "Ah, I've never got over the loss
of my boy. My boy was killed at Dorian," he said, turning to
Prudence. "A splendid lad, wasn't he, Ogilvie?"

"Splendid."

"Ah, if he'd been alive now I should have tried to make a match
between him and this lovely young lady at my side."

"And how are Euphrosyne and Aglaia?" John asked quickly.

"Aglaia's married. Yes, married to another soldier. Ion
Stathatos. In the cavalry. She's in Cephalonia now with the
children—a boy and girl. He's in Asia Minor. The news does
not sound too good from the front. Ever since our troops were
prevented from marching on Constantinople at the end of July
the Turks have become more and more insolent and confident.

And now they seem to have attacked our lines on both sides of Afium-Karahissar. Lloyd George's speech at the beginning of the month encouraged us, but I don't like the tone of the British press generally, and as for the French and Italians! Well, I suppose the country deserves it for turning on Venizelos as it did."

"There doesn't seem to have been a serious break through."

"Not yet. Not yet," said Theodore Ladas. "But I don't feel easy. Yes, Aglaia will be worried. I wanted her to come here with the children, but they have a lovely place in Cephalonia and it's no fun travelling with two small children from the Ionian Islands to the Cyclades. But I still have Euphrosyne."

"She has not married?"

"No, nor shows any sign of wanting to, and she'll be thirty soon."

The car reached the top of the island's northerly slope, and their host suggested that Prudence should alight and look at the view.

"You know it too well, Ogilvie."

"Never too well," said John. "There goes the *Queen of Devon*."

A light breeze was blowing from the north-west. The white yacht was steaming through a dark blue sea on which a myriad wavelets danced like lighting butterflies.

"Andros, Tenos, Myconos, Delos, Naxos, Paros," Theodore Ladas told Prudence, pointing to a wreath of islands that rose paler than the dark blue sea.

They got back into the car, and as it descended the south-westerly slope another wreath of islands appeared, darker they against the sun than the sea they adorned.

"Cythnos, Seriphos, Siphnos, Antiparos, and Paros again," said Ladas.

Presently the car turned off from the main road into that avenue of gnarled holm-oaks, passed through those gates of wrought iron between the two marble Doric columns, and reached the house of Grazia di Dio which some Venetian noble had built three centuries ago.

John beheld with emotion the well-remembered wide roof of shallow cupolas; and there coming down the steps to greet them was Euphrosyne, with her black cloud of hair and ivory complexion, and profile that Praxiteles need not have idealized, Euphrosyne tall and slim as ever but, though indefinably so far as outward features went, a more mature Euphrosyne now.

"So after all, we do meet again," John said. "And how glad I am to see you!"

"I can't tell you what a pleasure it is for us," she replied. "And this is Prudence—you will let me call you Prudence just like that? Because John used to tell me about you when you were a little girl."

"Did he?" Prudence exclaimed, blushing. "I wish I'd known he ever mentioned me. I should have been so excited."

They passed through the great vaulted hall and out to the loggia, over the parapet of which one looked down two hundred feet of cliff to the orange-grove, and the yellow crescent of sandy beach, and the islanded sea beyond.

"I'm going to take Miss Ogilvie down to see where she can swim whenever she wants to, like Aphrodite herself," their host proclaimed.

"I'd love to come. But I'd rather you didn't call me Miss Ogilvie," said Prudence.

"Father, you are the most energetic person. Prudence may want to rest after the drive," his daughter protested.

"No, no, really, I'd love to go down to the sea," Prudence insisted.

"Of course she would. We'll leave you two elderly people together," the host said enthusiastically. "I'll just go and get a couple of walking-sticks."

John followed him out to the hall, and told him quickly about Prudence's tragedy.

"I tell you so that you don't say anything too severe about Italians."

"My dear friend, thank you, thank you. I appreciate your confidence. That poor girl. Why couldn't Leo have come through, and met and fallen in love with your sister? But, oh, good lord, why do I talk like this? It's an old man's babbling."

When Euphrosyne and John were sitting out in the loggia he told her about Prudence.

"Five years ago when I was mourning for Zoe and you were mourning for your brother you spoke to me in words I shall never forget. I wish Prudence knew you so that you might console her as you once consoled me. She has been wonderfully brave. But I wanted you to understand her sudden long silences."

"Πάθη μάθος," Euphrosyne murmured.

"Yes, but alas, the wisdom of Aeschylus doesn't help a girl of nineteen. She is aware of the suffering, but she is not aware that it is teaching her anything except to conceal it out of consideration for other people. However, it was lucky I was able to get away from Italy for a while."

"It's a disappointment not to meet your wife, John. Tell me about her . . . but what a stupid request . . . what is her name?"

"Athene."

Euphrosyne's eyes lightened.

"And that was your mother's name you told me once. You are faithful to our Hellas! I have a foreboding of disaster over there in Ionia. Hellas too must learn by suffering. Is your Athene like her name?"

So John told the story of Athene and himself.

"I should like her, John."

"I'm sure you would."

"And your daughter is Corinna. That too is a lovely name to a Hellene. I shall write a song about her."

"You are still writing poetry?"

"I published a book last year."

"And you never sent it to me."

"But, John, you cut yourself off so completely from Hellas. It is only now you have remembered your old friends."

"You can't suppose that my heart ever forgot them? But letters are hopeless when two people are writing about people and places the other has neither met nor seen. Then the letters grow less frequent and at last they stop. And that gives a sense of final severance, whereas now we meet again without either of us feeling that it was the other who failed to sustain a friendship. I have cherished the thought of you all these five years for what you said to me about Zoe, not merely after she was lost, but that day in Delos when your poet's eye pierced the essential quality of my love for her."

"Yes, I think you are right, John. A long exchange of letters over a period of years almost always does mean the disillusionment of friendship. And you yourself coming back here now, does it reopen the old wound?"

John shook his head.

"No. The shock at the time was so tremendous that my senses were obliterated. I come back to Lipsia as if to a place in which Zoe had already died when I first visited it, or as if I had loved her in another place altogether. It was here in Grazia that I sat with her, down in the orange-grove which your father is showing to Prudence at this moment, the night before she sailed away. You gave me the key of the gate at the bottom of the cliff-path."

"I remember."

"I said good-bye to her for ever at the top of the path before we came back to join the dancers. She broke off some leaves of rosemary and gave them to me, and I put them in the pocket of my white tunic, and when I was ill the tunic was washed and the leaves were lost. But what are dead leaves of rosemary? Your words were not lost. I was fretting that her body had never been found, and you said to me that here earth and sea were equal and that she lay with coral as peacefully as beneath the cold earth, and you asked me when the time came for me to leave this island of the south wind not to hate it because the south wind had turned to rain."

"I remember, and you told me that if you could have foreseen what would happen to you here you would have chosen to suffer it, and that though you had lost her she would live with you for ever young and always fair."

"That is what I should like Prudence to realize, but of course she is too young to appreciate yet the treasure of perpetual youth in memory. I shall talk to her a lot about Zoe; a tale of star-crossed love is healing to sorrow."

And with this intention in view John took Prudence to place after place in Lipsia which gave him an occasion to speak of Zoe.

On the third day of their stay at Grazia there came a letter for John from Athene:

> TORRE SARACENA,
> CITRANO.
> *August 24th, 22.*

My dearest,

I am taking the chance of catching you with this at Lipsia after your telegram, but I thought it wiser to send other letters Poste Restante, Athens, as we arranged. One from Gabrielle Derozier I opened because I was so anxious to know what she thought of the play. She writes with the greatest enthusiasm, and I hope Turner will be equally enthusiastic. I'm so sure she and you will both have a great success. I wrote to her (saying who I was!) and explained why you couldn't answer her immediately yourself.

I'm wondering what the effect on you of revisiting Lipsia has been. I mean whether it has been very poignant for you. I understand so well why you wanted to take Prudence there. I felt a little worried after you left lest you should fancy all sorts of reasons for my not coming which didn't exist. There was only one reason and that was Corinna, who has been talking incessantly in three languages ever since you went away. I should have been tormented by worry all the time, cruising around without feeling I was in direct communication with Citrano. By the way,

Bodisko and Olensky arrived last week, and Fofo tells me that B. was enquiring anxiously about the possibility of our selling the Torre Saracena. I know you'll hate to get rid of it and so shall I, but if it lies between Citrano and Nanphant, you know which I would choose.

Arthur writes boisterously, but I'm glad to say does not suggest avoiding next term! All my love.

Athene

Prudence too received a letter from Athene which she gave John to read:

My dearest Prudence,

I hope this letter will reach you. I just wanted to tell you how deeply I was moved by your courage throughout what I know was so much the most terrible week you have ever lived through. I did appreciate how hard you were trying all the while not to let your grief disturb others, and I do want you to know that I was aware of the effort you were making. I have loved you ever since I saw you first, but now I admire you as much as I love you.

I'm hoping that John's companionship has been a great help. My dear love to you.

Athene

To Athene John wrote:

Grazia di Dio,
Isle of Lipsia,
Sept. 1, 22.

My dearest,

It was a joy to get your letter. I have often told you of this lovely house, and it has been a delightful experience to revisit it. I found Euphrosyne Ladas the same as she was five years ago, and the quality of her latest verse is really good. Now, I fear, her passionate love for her country may have to suffer another torment. The news of what is happening in Asia Minor is of course severely censored in the press, but rumour flies swiftly in this part of the world, and it is impossible not to expect the worst. I won't bother you with a string of unfamiliar names, but the Greek Army is apparently already in full retreat with the Turks sweeping them on toward the sea. We lack the moral courage to take a firm stand against the French and Italians,

who have helped the Turks by supplying them with munitions
and armaments and are encouraging them to drive the Greeks
into the sea. In justice to Lloyd George I believe he was anxious
to help, but the rest of this detestable Coalition Government will
not support him, and the British Press as a whole is screaming
that we will not go to war again on behalf of Greece. I'm longing
for Turner to get back from the wild goat expedition so that I
can try to make him ginger up his own 'Sunday Journal' to speak
out plainly on the issues at stake.

The argument that because the Greeks turned down Venizelos
and brought back Constantine we are no longer under any obliga-
tion towards them is utterly at variance with the promises we
made from 1915 onwards. I feel a sense of personal mortification, because by seizing the Cyclades in December 1916 I forced
the hands of the Government at home and made the recognition
of the Venizelist Government unavoidable. I worked passionately for a strong Greece because I believed that a strong Greece
was the greatest guarantee of our naval security in the Eastern
Mediterranean, but if I had thought that we should be afraid to
make Italy keep her word by restoring Rhodes and the Dodecanese
I would never have worked for anything except an Anglo-Italian
entente in the Mediterranean. I pointed out over and over again
that if we were not prepared to create a strong naval Greece
dependent upon us we must help to create a strong Italy tied to
us by material interest. I sent note after note to warn the
authorities at home that if we left Italy unsatisfied in the Mediterranean she must in time turn to Germany and that we should
find such an alliance a deadly menace to our naval security. Such
a measure could be counterbalanced only by a strong Greece and
a strong Serbia. Now we shall let Greece be smashed and at
the same time we shall have antagonized the Italians and the
Turks, not to mention the French.

If Italy is difficult now, what will Italy be like if the dreams
of Fascism are realized? It is true that when I was writing of
the danger of an alliance between Italy and Germany I had not
foreseen that Germany would be so completely defeated. There
certainly does not seem any danger now from Germany in our
lifetime. Nevertheless, the heart of the British Empire is the
Suez Canal, and can we afford to improvise our policy in the
Mediterranean from week-end to week-end?

Forgive this tirade, but it is a bitter thought for a man to discover that the whole of his energy during the war was a waste

of his own time and of his country's money. And that's what my years in Greece will be seeming to me if we allow the Greeks to be thrown out of Asia Minor and Eastern Thrace, though we shall have to act at once if that is not to happen, and I understand from Turner that the most important matter on the tapis at present is whether the Unionists will succeed in turning out the Coalition. The plotting is fast and furious. They have a fellow called Baldwin, the President of the Board of Trade, who is being approached to light the fuse and blow Lloyd George sky-high. Bonar Law, of course, is to become Prime Minister. There's no doubt that if the Greeks really are knocked out the Unionists will undermine Lloyd George's position by persuading the country through their Press that he is a warmonger. The Liberals of course have never forgiven him for destroying their confounded party. They prefer the Turks to L. G. If there were any men with brains or guts or imagination on the Labour benches what a chance they would have, but they're a feeble crew, voices and nothing besides. It's a degrading form of government, modern democracy. I am beginning to realize the amount of harm Abraham Lincoln did, tell your father when next you write home.

I'm writing under the nervous irritation of waiting for news of what really is happening in Asia Minor. Euphrosyne who has a Pythian soul expects the worst. Her only brother was killed in the last war, and now they have her brother-in-law to worry about. Our host himself, who was for a long time completely broken up by his boy's death, has recovered his gallant enjoyment of life, and has been devoting himself to Prudence without letting on to her that he knows what happened just a month ago. I had to tell him and Euphrosyne because I feared outbursts against the Italians, who naturally are not much loved in Greece at this moment.

Of Prudence herself it's difficult to write. That Mario's death has profoundly affected her goes without saying, but I have tried to let her see by example not by precept that it does not mean she will never be happy again. I have told her a great deal about Zoe and tried to suggest how much my memories of Zoe help me to understand what she is suffering now. But that is all. She has not got a sentimental mind and she has a frankness and honesty which prevent her falsifying emotion. She has seen with her own eyes what I must boast is a perfect marriage, and she must recognize that what was not debarred to me by an experience at thirty-four is not debarred to her at nineteen.

I am going to suggest to Turner when they get back from their wild goats to-morrow or the day after that we shall go to Mileto. If the Greeks are retreating as fast as rumour declares, the situation there may be very dramatic, and it was to Mileto I went with the Turkish prisoners immediately after Zoe was drowned.

David is in the process of falling in love with Janet who, in a pair of ravishing breeches, is to be initiated into the joys of wild goat stalking. She and the wild goats between them are compensating for missing the stalking at Achnalochlannach. I try to fire Noll Erpingham with ambitions as a hereditary legislator, but he seems to think that taking his seat in the House of Lords next session for one day by permission of the College is as much as he can be expected to grapple with at present.

So Bodisko is still nosing about after the tower. Well, if he pays our price let him have it. We owed him a lot four years ago when he got between you and Olensky and pushed you closer to me. I shall be celebrating the anniversary of that party at Mileto. Little did I dream of such a party when we sailed in over the mines and under the Turkish guns to rescue Peterman.

It's grand news about Gabrielle. I'm sure Turner will be delighted when I tell him. We'll go and see her on our way back through Paris when we meet Arthur at Southampton toward the end of the month. By Jove, he's due back on the 25th. Kiss Corinna for me. I will teach her some Greek endearments soon. All my love.

John

Two days later the *Queen of Devon* returned to Lipsia, and Theodore Ladas was much depressed because the new arrivals would not accept his invitation to spend a week with him at Grazia. However, Euphrosyne supported John, reminding her father that the moment when the Greek army was in such peril was no moment for the ball he had set his heart on giving. So he had to be content with giving a lunch instead.

"Well," Bob Redroad declared, "the location of your house, Mr Ladas, has got every set I ever saw beat. Say, Janet, couldn't you play a big romantic part in a setting like this better than ever you played one in your young life?"

"It certainly is a wonderful location," Janet agreed.

"Look down at that grove of orange-trees beside the water. Doesn't that make you think of Venus rising from the sea and all the rest of this classical stuff John's been cramming into us? You know, John, you'll send me back to America an honest-to-god highbrow."

"I wish I could," John exclaimed. "I wish I could persuade you to let me write you a scenario for a film of the Odyssey. Damn it, the Odyssey has everything you want. Two vamps—Circe and Calypso. Charming *ingénue*—Nausicaa. Faithful wife—Penelope. Faithful servant—Eumaeus, with dog complete. Bathing beauties—the Sirens. Fat comedian—Polyphemus. And a fine Wild West finale when Odysseus shoots up the suitors. What more do you want?"

"It's too fanciful for the public, John. It might go in England where they're used to pantomimes, but we've got to think of America first. The great American public doesn't want fairy tales. It wants real life. Only, speeded up of course. I don't suppose this trip of Janet's and mine to make pictures on location in Italy will be a success. When we get back they'll say it could all have been done better and quicker and cheaper in Hollywood."

"But wouldn't the idea of seeing a film of the Odyssey made in the islands—m-m—among which Odysseus had his adventures have an educational appeal?" Geoffrey Noel asked.

Bob Redroad looked at him compassionately.

"Educational?" he ejaculated. "Say, Janet, did you hear that?"

Janet smiled at Noel as one might smile at the sweet innocence of a child.

"If everybody had your ideals," she gently sighed. "You know the way I feel, Mr Noel? I feel this cruise is just a lovely lovely dream. Do you ever feel that kind of dreamy feeling in a beautiful place, Mr Noel?"

And as Janet floated away to keep a swimming engagement with David, Geoffrey Noel mumbled to John:

"Oh dear, how extremely stupid! Just a pretty platitudinarian —m-m—not so much brains as an egg-shell."

David and Janet went off to bathe together from the crescent of sand beyond the grove of oranges. When Theodore Ladas had shouted to know who was for a swim Noll Erpingham had jumped up at the same time as David; but he must have received some discouragement from his friend's eye, for he threw himself back in his chair in the loggia, murmuring that on second thoughts he would rather stay where he was. Prudence had gone for a last stroll with Euphrosyne. Turner Rigden was at the beginning

of a very long cigar, talking to John and Redroad about his
ambitions for putting British films back on the map; Major Torbock
was nodding approval of every word his employer uttered.
Geoffrey Noel was in a philhellenic trance, composing a sonnet
to a shepherd boy in Milos who had shepherded him about the
island when the others were trying to diminish by a head or two
the wild goats on Antimilos. Noll Erpingham was apparently
reading a fortnight-old copy of the *Weekly Times*. Actually he
was wondering if he should assert his rights of majority on his
return to Norfolk by cutting down an avenue for which the
Dowager Lady Erpingham had an affection but which, if he meant
to make a good landing-place for the aeroplane he intended to
acquire, must be abolished. The host had taken Mrs Torbock
to give her an even better view of the islands than was obtainable
from the loggia.

"It was awfully sporting of you, Janet, to come and bathe,"
David observed as they made their way down the zigzag path wide
enough for two to walk abreast.

"But I shall love it, David."

"I say, let me carry your bathing-dress."

"No, it's not a bit in my way." This was strictly true. "You
shall carry it back for me."

Down they went, resting at each pine-shaded gazebo to look
over its parapet at the green waters of the cove and the sea beyond
shimmering in the hot September sun, or to look back at the old
white house of Grazia di Dio above the sheer cliff where nothing
grew except rosemary spreading its fans upon the face for protection
against the wind.

"I think this place is pretty good, don't you?"

"I think it's absolutely divine."

They had reached the iron gate at the foot of the cliff-path, and
passing through it they entered the verdurous twilight of the
orange-grove where the dry leaves fallen on the green-stained
ground not yet plumed by autumn's pale young grass exhaled a
delicate fragrance when crushed by their footsteps. The glossy
foliage of the trees was hung with unripe fruits, and through the
colonnade of slim smooth trunks appeared the crescent of sand
lapped by the bright Aegean, each horn of which was crowned by
a miniature marble temple that served as a dressing-place.

"I think this is almost the best beach we've struck yet," David
observed, treading water.

"I think this is the best, too," Janet agreed.

They swam for a while, and then sat in the burnt herbage at the edge of the orange-grove with their feet on the sand.

"I suppose you know that I'm in love with you?" David blurted out after a long silence during which both of them had been drawing pictures in the sand with their big toes.

She looked round with eyes like pansies.

"I knew you liked me, David."

"But you're not in love with me," he challenged.

"Why, David, I like you terribly, but you're so much younger than me, aren't you?"

"I'm a year or two younger."

"You're only twenty."

"I'll be twenty-one in a few days," he exclaimed indignantly. "And you're twenty-three."

"Ye-es, I'll be twenty-four next year." And so she had been now for two or three years. She could not be perfectly sure, so quickly time passed.

"Two years older! What's that?"

"It's a terribly long time, David dear, when it's the woman who's two years older."

"If you were in love with me, it would be nothing."

"You know how fond I am of you. Well, we've been such friends, haven't we, all this long cruise?"

"But you're not in love with me?" he pressed.

"Why, David, I don't believe I am. I just hate hurting you by saying that, but I couldn't bear not to be perfectly frank with you, because I am so very very fond of you."

"Fond perhaps," he muttered gloomily. "But not in love." His fair curly hair drying all ruffled in the sunlight made him look more boyish than ever.

"I don't believe I ever have been in love, David. Perhaps I'm too much wrapped up in my art. I often sit around for hours doing nothing when I'm not making a picture, and I suppose most people think I'm just doing nothing. But my friends know I'm thinking about my art. And you're one of my friends, aren't you, David dear?"

"Of course I am."

"You know, I think friendship is such a wonderful thing. I just can't tell you how wonderful I think friendship is."

"It isn't so wonderful as love."

"Oh yes, it is, David. It's much more wonderful than love."

"Do you mean to say my friendship for Noll Erpingham is more wonderful than my love for you. I never heard such rot."

"Well, you needn't be rude about my opinions," she sighed reproachfully.

David looked aghast at such a suggestion.

"Janet, I wasn't being rude. I was just speaking emphatically."

"Very emphatically."

"Well, our cruise will soon be over," he said. "And you're going back to America and I'll be going up to Oxford again."

"There you are, you see. You're still a student. You don't want to be falling in love when you're a student."

"Why not?"

"Why, because it interrupts your work. You've got to make good at college, David. I wouldn't want to hear you'd messed up your college career, would I?"

"I don't see what difference it would make to you. As far as I can make out you consider me an infant-in-arms."

"David, I don't," she protested. "I think you're one of the sweetest boys I ever met."

"And now, I suppose, that I've told you I'm in love with you, you'll be bored by me."

"David, I won't be. How can you say such unkind things?"

Again those eyes like pansies were regarding him, and this time a dewdrop, a large dewdrop, rolled off each one. Bewitched by this capacity to move an audience which he had never suspected in himself David suddenly made up his mind to seek a wider public than a barrister and become a film actor.

"This is my last year at Oxford," he began, "and I've started eating my dinners at the Temple."

"Is that some restaurant which freshmen and sophomores can't go to?" she asked.

David postponed conducting Janet round the vision of his future to explain the system by which a law student of the Inner Temple kept his terms by eating three dinners a term until he had eaten thirty-six.

"Oh my, David, I do think these old British customs are so cute. When I was in London I went and ate a dinner at the old Cheshire Cheese, and I remember now somebody pointed out the Temple about two blocks up on the other side of the street."

"I never went to the Cheshire Cheese."

"You didn't? Oh, David, you ought to go. It's the cunningest old place with sawdust on the floor and you sit on a wooden bench which is as uncomfortable as death but you don't mind

because you eat this wonderful pudding full of oysters and beefsteak and little birdies and I don't know what not and there's a
waiter who talks like somebody in a Dickens novel, and Bob was
tickled to death when the waiter thought he was an American
because we always think Bob's so terribly British. Oh, you ought
to go to the Cheshire Cheese, David."

"Well, I will," he promised as fervidly as if in obedience to his
lady he were undertaking some tremendous quest. "But what I
was going to tell you was that I thought of giving up the Bar
and going in for films. Do you think I'd have any chance of
making a success as a film actor?"

Janet stiffened slightly as every professional does when asked
by an amateur what chances he stands as a competitor.

"That's a pretty difficult question to answer," she replied.

"Well, of course I know I'd have to begin at the bottom and
work jolly hard, but do you think I'd stand a chance of getting
anywhere after a time?"

"Why, David, I can't really tell you. I'd want to see you act,
wouldn't I? I don't think it's something you can decide all at
once. I mean I wouldn't like John to think I'd been putting
all sorts of queer ideas into your head. And I don't feel Lady
Ogilvie would like you to quit studying the law to go in for films.
Anyway, you've got another year at college, and that'll be time
enough to discuss the matter seriously. You'll still only be
twenty-one."

"You needn't keep rubbing it in about my age," he grumbled.

"Now don't be foolish, David. We're talking about your choice
of a profession. We're not talking any longer about love. If a
year from now you still have a passion to go on the films I promise
you that Bob and I will do all we can to help. But you've got to
promise me that meantime you'll work hard at what you are doing.
Is that a bargain?"

"All right," David agreed. He was a little relieved that he
would not be called upon to announce immediately a projected
change in his career to John. He had a notion that his elder
brother might laugh at him . . . or at any rate might want to laugh,
which would be just as bad.

"And now, David dear, don't you think we ought to be getting
dressed and going back to the house? I wouldn't like to keep
everybody waiting. And we're just as good friends as ever we
were?" she added.

"Of course, Janet, you can't love anybody as much as I apparently love you without being good friends. At least I shouldn't think you could."

She rose, slim herself as the smooth trunk of an orange-tree in her white and emerald bathing-dress, and kissed David on the forehead maternally. Then she ran splashing by the edge of the water to put on her clothes in her miniature temple. David sloshed his way through the sea a little dejectedly toward the other temple.

Turner Rigden tried hard to persuade Theodore Ladas and Euphrosyne to make the voyage to Mileto. Ladas himself was tempted to accept the invitation, but his daughter was firm. They would dine on board, but that was all.

"I could not bear to see the evidence of our defeat, John," she told him when they were promenading the deck after dinner under the stars. "And my spirit warns me not to go."

"I shan't try to make you change your decision," he said. "I have too great a regard for your foresight. I only hope you're wrong for once."

"I don't hope, John. I know I'm right. Well, if I ever write enough poetry worth printing to make another volume I will send it to you this time. A pity nothing remains of the Bœotian poetess Corinna who defeated Pindar once at the Theban games and whom indeed she is said to have taught. Perhaps your Corinna will write poetry. One day you will bring her to Lipsia, will you? I shall never marry, and in another ten years I expect I shall long always for the company of children as one begins to long for the flowers now in this month of September so weary of summer."

"To meet you again has been an enchanting experience. I wish Athene had been with me."

"Indeed I wish she had. But you will bring her some day, I hope. And now, good-bye, John. Your theory about letter-writing between friends is very plausible, but now that we have met again and have picked up the threads I think we must write to one another sometimes."

"Oh yes, now that we are up to date again my theory can be discarded."

"I find that sister of yours so delightful. I shall come some time to England and carry her back with me to Lipsia for our sweet spring and you shall come and fetch her away. But why do

K

was on the mainland with Joe Hoggart?"

"How's Joe?"

"Gone back to England. He hadn't the heart to start in growing licorice again after the mess the Turks made of his place."

"Yes, I remember Spiridon Xyndas. He'd made his way from beyond Angora, and Stern came back about three in the morning soaked through with sea-water, and I sat and listened to him *really* examining Spiridon till the sun was streaming into this very room. I can see Stern now pale with exhausted vitality, and you coming in about eight o'clock and being told you'd have a six-thousand-word telegram to encode that afternoon which would keep you up most of the night. And I remember as I went off to bed I heard you whistling between your teeth:

> *I do like to be beside the seaside,*
> *I do like to be beside the sea.*"

Withers showed his yellowish teeth in a grin.

"Well, I'm still beside the seaside. I am, and that's a fact. But it's a bit of a coincidence you should turn up in Icaros again now, because the Greeks are on the run again. We'll be packed out presently with starving refugees from Anatolia. If there isn't a bloody massacre across the Gulf I'll be very surprised. Defeat? It's been a complete rout. Well, Mustapha Kemal has thrown the Greek army into the sea, that's putting it terse. Of course as soon as the Greeks were stopped by the Powers from marching on Constantinople at the end of July I knew this was bound to happen. Well, I've warned them at home what's likely to happen in Smyrna and Mileto and all along the coast, but of course as usual they'll wait and see. Here, who would you say was the ruler the English looked up to most?"

"Queen Elizabeth."

"Go on, don't be silly. That's a woman. You know my opinion of women. Women don't come into this. Guess again."

"Alfred the Great, perhaps."

"That's right, but who ought it to be? I'll tell you. Ethelred the Unready. Ah, you didn't know I was so well up in history, did you?"

The Vice-Consul chuckled to himself.

"You think the situation in Mileto is serious?" John asked.

"It's more than serious. It's chronic."

"Because we were thinking of going there in the yacht."

"Nice-looking craft that. I never thought when I was shaving this morning and saw her coming into the harbour that you were on board. Well, at present there's a British destroyer and an American destroyer and an Italian destroyer in Mileto supposed, mark you, supposed to be able to deal with any situation that may arise when the Turkish army marches in. The *Iron Duke* is at Smyrna where of course there's a much bigger Giaour population, and I hear Marines have been landed. But take it from me, Commander, once the Turks overrun Smyrna—Giaour Izmir—a few Marines won't be able to do much. . . . Still, you'll see how things look when you reach the harbour and decide what to do then."

John was up early next morning when the yacht sailed from Icaros to Mileto. It was Saturday, September 8th.

"The last time I sailed over this water it was mined," he told the Captain by whom he was standing on the bridge.

"That was in that little craft you had in 1917, eh?" the Captain asked.

"Yes, we were a good two feet above them. From the bows we could see the brutes gently swaying in the tide below. The water's very clear."

"Very clear. Sandy bottom."

The neck of the Gulf was narrowing all the time. Presently they passed the fortified islet to port just before the entrance to the harbour. The Greek flag was fluttering in the light northwest breeze, but there was no sign of any troops.

"Deserted already," John muttered.

"Looks like it, Mr Ogilvie. Still, the Turks can't have arrived yet, or the flag wouldn't be flying."

The forts on the headland to starboard appeared equally empty, but here too the light-blue and white flag was flying.

"I reckon the Turks must be pretty near, though," said the Captain. "But how was it you weren't fired on from those forts if you got as far as this?"

"Curiosity."

By the time John had briefly told the tale of the *Argo's* arrival in Mileto in 1917, the *Queen of Devon* was entering the harbour.

"One British destroyer and one American," the Captain commented.

"I expect the Italian moved to Smyrna," said John.

"We'll anchor in mid-harbour," said the Captain.

"Yes, indeed, look at the quays!"

They, and the road round the harbour, were thronged with people, the sound of whom travelling across the water was like a continuous wail. Besides the two destroyers, there were merchant ships of various nationalities all anchored in mid-harbour.

"Hullo, they're signalling from that destroyer."

"Telling us not to land," said the Captain.

"Can I have the motor-boat?" John asked. "I'll go across and speak to the commanding officer.

The latter turned out to be an officer whom John had often met in Lipsia five years previously when he was First Lieutenant in the *Weasel*.

"Good lord, what brings you here, Ogilvie?" exclaimed Lieutenant-Commander Latham. "Well, I don't see why you shouldn't go ashore, but you certainly oughtn't to risk taking any ladies who are on board. We're standing by to take off any of our nationals, if necessary, but I understood from Smyrna that not much trouble was expected."

"The people on the quays sound nervous."

"Yes, but you know what these birds are like. The slightest thing starts them panicking. You might look in at the Consulate and find out about matters."

"Who is the Consul?"

"Fellow called Drayton. Rather a pompous sort of bloke."

"I think I remember him in Athens in 1915."

"Apparently they don't give him a Vice-Consul, which worries him a lot because before the war it was a Consulate-General and his predecessors all had Vice-Consuls to come it over."

"I know; a friend of mine was Vice-Consul here. Well, so long, Latham. I'll let you know if there's anything of interest to report."

"Yes, will you? And I'd tell your lads to stand away from the quayside with your boat while they're waiting for you. If those poor devils of refugees started to rush it they might sink it. Is it too early to offer you a drink?"

"A bit too early," John smiled. "It's only just after nine."

The motor-boat returned to the yacht where John announced he was going ashore. The owner, in pyjamas and a blue and silver dressing-gown, thought it was too early in the day.

"I'm coming," cried Redroad, who had been fascinated by the appearance of the white town with its cupolas and minarets and cypresses, but even more fascinated by the crowd along the quays.

"This is a great chance to get some ideas for grouping."

With Redroad and John went David and Noll Erpingham. The motor-boat had orders to come back at half-past twelve and the coxswain was warned to stand off from the quay until he was hailed.

The road round the harbour was packed with refugees from the interior who had fled before the Turkish advance, bringing with them what they could carry of their possessions, bedding mostly and bundles of clothes. As they made their way through the unhappy swarm to reach the Consulate they passed a woman lying on the ground screaming in the pangs of childbirth.

"My god, it's frightful," David muttered, turning as white as his suit.

"I wish Turner had been dressed," John said. "This is the sort of thing he should see with his own eyes instead of reading about it in his paper."

At the Consulate the Greek and the Armenian Bishops had been trying to persuade Drayton to send a telegram to the Archbishop of Canterbury imploring his Grace to persuade the British Cabinet to demand that Turkish troops should not be allowed to enter the city but treat for its surrender outside. It was understood that the Metropolitan Chrysostomos of Smyrna and the Armenian Archbishop had sent a similar appeal.

"These ecclesiastics here have odd ideas about the British Cabinet," said Drayton when the two Bishops had departed. "All the same," he went on, breathing on his pince-nez and rubbing the lenses, "they have some reason to feel apprehensive, for if the Kemalist army enters Mileto the worst may happen. I don't know why you chose this particular moment to revisit the place, Ogilvie. However, it must be a great deal worse in Smyrna."

Presently Drayton asked John if he would come into his private office for a moment. John supposed he was intending to make some criticisms of the political bickering at home which had ended in leaving the Greeks to the mercy of their ancient enemies; but it was to ask about Emil that Drayton had taken him aside.

"Of course we always did think he was a misfit in the Service."

"Because he made the rest of you feel uncomfortable?" John asked, with a hint of contempt in his tone.

"He was so arrogant mentally," Drayton insisted. "And he rubbed up people at home the wrong way. Oh, I'm not denying his brains, and with brains a good deal of practical ability at his job. I was really sorry when he was sent to prison. We all were. Of course, he was here as Vice-Consul in Blakeley's time. It was a Consulate-General before the war."

"I know. I stayed with him here in the spring of 1914. You say you're worried about what may happen, Drayton. I think Stern was pretty worried that summer and autumn, but he managed to persuade practically the whole of the British colony to leave before the Turks went to war. You haven't thought it necessary to urge a clearance?"

Drayton's lean face flushed.

"There was no reason to fear anything until that break through at Afium-Karahissar a fortnight ago. You forget how rapid and unexpected the Kemalist advance has been. There are several warships in Smyrna, and we have two destroyers here. I don't expect any danger to our nationals."

"Well, you know best, Drayton. I thought I'd take my party for a walk towards Calamana, and give them a view of Mileto. Well, I hope you won't have too difficult a time presently."

"By the way, Ogilvie, if you find people telling you that British transports with soldiers from Gibraltar are on their way to Smyrna, discourage the rumour. It appeared in the London Press, and a lot of the Greeks here are talking of barricades and trying to stop the Turks on the outskirts of the city."

"Why was such a paragraph allowed to appear?"

Drayton shrugged his shoulders.

"I suppose the authorities at home thought it might encourage the Greeks to resist."

"That seems to me a more criminal act than anything Emil Stern ever did," said John. "Well, I mustn't be taking up any more of your time. You can rely on me to discourage anybody who suggests that British politicians care a damn about anything except the next election and retaining office."

John and the others were strolling up a street behind the Consulate toward Calamana when they heard a sound of screaming ahead, and a woman suddenly plunged down on her knees in the road before them, begging to be saved. Almost at the same moment Turkish cavalry came cantering round the corner with rifles held across their saddles. They swerved to avoid riding down the woman still kneeling in the road and passed on their way.

"God, that was dramatic!" Bob Redroad exclaimed.

By noon Mileto was completely occupied by Turkish troops, and that first morning it looked as if order would be kept, though some of the native Turks were emerging from their squalid quarter in the south of the city to rob the refugees.

John felt uneasy, however, and when they returned to the yacht he asked Turner to let her stand by in the harbour in case of an emergency.

"You owe any help you can give," he told him. "You're a member of the Coalition which is responsible for letting down the Greeks."

"Gee, old man, don't look at me so fiercely. The *Sunday Journal* backed up Lloyd George as long as it could. It's Bonar Law and his lot who are taking the line that what the Turks do to the Greeks is no concern of ours. And of course it is a point of view we have to consider since they threw out Venizelos."

All that night rifle shots were heard intermittently, and shrieks.

In the morning John persuaded Turner Rigden to accompany him ashore. The little man did not like it, but his guest was ruthless. He had a member of Parliament with him and he intended to shock him if it was possible. A mob was yelling in the Square outside the Orthodox Cathedral as they passed along a side street to the Consulate.

They found Drayton much shaken.

"A ghastly thing is happening," he stammered. "They've nailed the Orthodox Bishop to the door of his cathedral and are pulling out his beard. The old man was in here only yesterday trying to telegraph an appeal to the Archbishop of Canterbury. My God, my God! They've landed bluejackets from the destroyers, but they can do nothing. Commander Latham is sending me a guard from the Consulate. There was a lot of murdering and rape last night, especially in the Armenian quarter. I've been trying to get into communication with the Consulate-General in Smyrna, but the line is cut."

"We'd better go back to the yacht, John," said Rigden nervously. "Look here, Mr Drayton, if you want to send any British subjects aboard I'll take as many as I can and land them at the Piraeus."

"Thanks, I may want to take advantage of your kind offer," said the Consul. "Thank you very much."

"Is there anything we can do in the city?" John asked.

"Of course there isn't, John. What can we do?" Rigden protested.

"No, no, I think you'd both better get back. The Turks will respect the Union Jack. At least I hope they will. And if the situation grows worse the British and American bluejackets will evacuate their nationals. I wish I could communicate with Smyrna. I wonder if things are as bad there."

They were to hear later that they were much worse than in Mileto.

"Gee, old man, I don't know why we came ashore this morning," Rigden moaned, when they met a cart with eight bodies accompanied by a priest who had volunteered to bury them.

Further along a Greek at the door of a house beckoned to them to come inside.

"Here, look out, John, he may be up to some mischief."

But John insisted on following the man through a passage to a garden at the back. There they saw half a dozen half-naked girls lying dead. They had been shot through the breast and their thighs were clotted with blood. Besides the girls there were three or four dead women with dead babies. Apparently they had been flung over the wall to prevent their being eaten by the dogs and in the hope of getting burial for them.

"You give me British flag to bury them," said the Greek. "I take cart with British flag and goddam Turk let me pass."

"Haven't you your camera, Turner?"

"No, I didn't bring it."

"A pity you didn't. You might have taken a photograph of that group and shown it to some of your fellow M.P.'s."

"Come on, John, we can't give this poor devil a Union Jack. I'll be sick in a minute."

John told the man he should go to the Consulate and ask there for a Union Jack, but he knew how fatuous his advice was and left the garden, raging against the lack of imagination and courage and the moral laziness which had allowed such a state of affairs to develop as had developed in Mileto.

"Don't you feel a personal shame over this?" he asked Rigden as they walked back toward the quay.

But before the question could be answered an Armenian with his face smashed in came running towards them pursued by Turkish soldiers. John managed to get tangled up with the pursuers and perhaps the fugitive escaped, but if he did he would only be for a short respite, because there was no mercy for any Armenians. They were being slaughtered at sight.

Rigden was so much upset by that morning in Mileto that when he got back to the yacht he gave orders that none of the boats was to be launched without leave from himself.

"I'm sorry, John, but there's no sense in letting you wander about Mileto. You can't get between a prisoner and the soldiers chasing them without ending up badly sooner or later. If I hadn't told that blasted Consul I'd stand by we'd be out of this bloody harbour in an hour."

John found that everybody was against him and he had to remain on board.

During the next three days several British refugees were brought to the yacht, among them the wife of Colonel Turquand, who had been killed in trying to defend his maid-servants against ravishment. The Colonel, a retired Indian Army officer over eighty years of age, had been struck on the head by one of his own vases. Then he had been shot, stripped, and mutilated. Mrs Turquand's mind had broken under the horror of the scenes of murder and rape she had witnessed.

On the third day the wind which had been blowing from the north-west shifted to the south. That night the Armenian quarter was fired, and the conflagration spread to the European quarter. Soon nothing was left of Mileto except the Turkish and Jewish quarters lying close together on the south side of the city and therefore protected by the direction of the wind from the flames which consumed all the rest.

The harbour seemed to be the centre of a volcanic eruption, and when one of the merchant craft caught fire Latham sent a signal from the destroyer that the *Queen of Devon* was to remain at anchor no longer. The final horror of many horrors was when Mrs Turquand, who had eluded the observation of her attendant, flung herself overboard just as the yacht reached the narrow entrance of the harbour. It was impossible to put about or even to slow down, for the *Queen of Devon* was being followed closely toward the open sea by a Greek merchant-ship crowded with fugitives.

"I'm glad you brought me to Mileto, John," Prudence said to him when the reek of the burning city and the shrieks of fugitive women and the rattle of the fusilades were behind them and the yacht was steaming toward the Piraeus through the Aegean dusk, a gentle breeze on the starboard quarter blowing from the north again now that Smyrna and Mileto were destroyed.

"Why?"

"Because it strengthened me. One reads about human misery . . . or at least one doesn't very often because one doesn't want to feel depressed . . . oh, John, but to see and hear it as we did in Mileto . . . I couldn't be too much taken up with my own grief ever again."

Later when the rest of the party had gone to their cabins John talked to Turner Rigden.

"Whom do you consider primarily responsible for that destruction and mutilation and rape and pillage?" he asked.

"Well, as far as I can make out Johnny Turk was too good a man for Johnny Greek, and there you are!"

"I consider we are primarily responsible," John declared.

"Now, don't talk in that exaggerated way. Why are we responsible?"

"Through laziness chiefly. We will not make the effort to think out cause and effect. It was wrong to let the Greeks go into Asia Minor unless we were prepared to stand firmly behind them."

"I don't see how we can afford to quarrel with the Turks. We've got to think of India, John."

"All right. All right. Then we should have thought of India before we encouraged the Greeks to land at Smyrna."

"Public opinion . . ."

"Exactly," John broke in. "It would have meant losing votes if the Government had come to terms with Turkey at the expense of the Greeks while Venizelos was in power. Venizelos was a popular hero. And rightly. Then his own countrymen rejected him, and ever since you and your fellow newspaper proprietors have yapped at his heels with the common cry of curs. You may be right in thinking Turkey a better investment for the future than Greece. It's a pity though that that wasn't discovered before the war . . . before we led Greece on to suppose her help was so valuable that after the war we should express our gratitude practically, regardless of the embarrassment such an expression of gratitude might be to the restoration of old friendships."

"We've got to make friends with Turkey again," Rigden affirmed. "How can we guard our oil interests in the Middle East without being friends with Turkey? The idea of going to war again with Turkey to protect the Greeks is just madness, and by jiggs, what madness!"

John sighed wearily.

"If you'd given as much of yourself, Turner, as I gave of myself to Greece you'd understand what I'm feeling at this moment. But mind you, it's not the mortification that comes from the feeling that one has wasted so much of one's prime on a job which wasn't worth doing; it is the deeper mortification of knowing that the best one gave of oneself was the worst one could have given to a friend."

"You know, John, I don't like turning round on Lloyd George, but I'm beginning to think he's got to go. He's becoming dangerous. As soon as we reach the Piraeus I'm going to cable the *Journal* that our line in future is to be 'No War'. I think Bonar Law is the man we want as Prime Minister."

John looked at his host in disgusted amazement.

"Turner, if you and I are to keep friends we'll have to avoid politics and stick to plays or films."

A few minutes later they went up on deck for a last stroll before turning in. The moon had not yet risen. Eastward aft the sky above Asia was stained as by the reflection of the lights of a great city. Smyrna and Mileto were still burning.

By the time the *Queen of Devon* reached the Piraeus, Rigden was feeling that he must get back to England as soon as possible. His guests were to have a morning in which to explore Athens, and then the yacht was to sail to Brindisi, where the owner planned to disembark and return home by train. Bob Redroad and Janet Meriday who were sailing from Genoa were accompanying him. From Brindisi the yacht was to go to Citrano, and thence proceed home with those of the guests who wished to make the leisurely journey by sea.

"I'm not going to try to show you all Athens in a few hours," John told Prudence. "We'll take our letters and go and sit on the Acropolis."

The atmosphere in the streets was tense. Those who in groups at the street corners gesticulated at one another seemed to be arguing with weapons in their hands.

"Six years ago I drove from the Piraeus to Athens through a surging mob," John told his sister. "I think it won't be long before such a mob is surging again. I smell revolution."

It was peaceful enough on the Acropolis once the guides had been convinced that their services would not be called upon. John and Prudence sat leaning against one of the columns of the Parthenon, earth and sea and sky before them.

"It is offensive to break this peace even by tearing open envelopes," he decided as he laid down upon the warm marble the packet of letters he had collected from the *poste restante*. Then he noticed one in the handwriting of Ellen Fitzgerald. Dread caught at him.

"I'll just open this one," he murmured. He read it through

and sat back, pale and silent. "My friend Edward Fitzgerald has been killed," he told Prudence. "I don't think you ever saw him. On the night we sailed from Citrano," he went on. "On the date he foresaw twenty years ago. His vision came to him on the night of the Assumption, but he was killed on the vigil. He did not foresee the year. That was a blank. He saw his death on the night of August 15th, 1901, but before that in the March of 1900. . . ." John was silent. He was standing again with Fitz by the lamp-post at the corner of Trelawny Road. The grey brick houses, losing perfect definition in the acrid foggy air, ran like a line of cliffs on either side of the road, their lighted windows seeming remote as the windows on shore beheld from the sea. He saw himself and Fitz standing minute in a chasm of those nightmare houses which unfettered sleep builds as fast as thought. He saw the face of his friend greenish-white in the sad glow of the incandescent gas-light. And in memory the face grew larger, the glittering pale-blue eyes more light, the wide eloquent mouth more red, the thin fanatic nose more peaked, the cheek-bones more gaunt, until in fancy that face was suspended like a decapitated head.

> *"I mean the cold death of the man who dies to prove himself right. I don't yet know how I shall gain such a death, but I do know that somehow I shall gain it."*

And then on the feast of the Assumption the following year just before he himself had had that strange experience in St Mary's Church, Cracow, Fitz had beheld the wall of the little hotel bedroom in Tralee turn to a kind of mist in which appeared by the side of a bohereen a heap of stones with a white cross stuck on the top of them, and this picture had melted and in its place written in blood-red letters was *Pray for the soul of Edward Fitzgerald I.R.A., who died in defence of Ireland*, but the date was blurred.

And now twenty-one years afterwards this letter from Ellen Fitzgerald told him of her brother's grave beside a bohereen— of a heap of stones and a white cross and of that very inscription printed above it in red lead.

"Surely this is a proof of personal immortality," he muttered to himself.

"What did you say, John?"

He told Prudence about the promise he had given to Fitz if his vision of the future should be fulfilled.

"I've been thinking, John, that I should feel nearer to Mario if I became a Catholic. If I'd married him I should have become a

Catholic. Anyway, I've made up my mind to learn something about Catholicism when I go back to England. I feel so much further away from him as I am. You see I don't really know what I do believe. I think they teach us religion in a very muddled way in the Church of England. I always used to feel at school that the Chaplain was embarrassed by it. And that embarrassed us."

"I think everything in England is in a gentlemanly muddle at the moment," John said. "I don't think we realized that we set out into a new world when we decided to go to war eight years ago. Of course there's a lot of talk about pre-war and post-war, but so far it's only a sort of sentimental division of time. War only accelerates change which is already in the mind of man. I get depressed sometimes by the failure of older people to understand that. Unless they can face up to the necessity of moving with the times we shall require another war and perhaps after that even yet another war before the world settles down to make the most of its opportunities and the best of its resources. Communism or Fascism—they may be mutually destructive, but they are both expressions of distrust in the individualism which has made such a mess of the world. We are watching now, I fancy, the beginning of the end of an epoch which started with the Renaissance and the Protestant Reformation and the discovery of America and the conception of England as an extra-European state. Obviously the only system that can preserve Christianity as something more alive than a nebulous code of ethics bearing very little relation to the teaching of Christ Himself is the Catholic Church. I hope you will learn something about it. I've already set you an example by having Corinna baptized into the Catholic Church. She might easily live right through this century, and I don't feel it's going to be a very easy century to live through without a fortress of the mind to which one can retire and from which one can re-enter the fight invigorated."

"You've talked to me quite differently, John, since I lost Mario."

"Well, you see, you've lived a few years in these few weeks."

"Yet during the war thousands and thousands of women had to face up to the deaths of those they loved, didn't they? I've no right to consider myself an exceptionally tragic figure. I don't, John, I don't really."

"I've never thought you did. I think you've preserved your sense of proportion most admirably. Indeed I'm beginning to believe you're a very remarkable girl."

"Well, I'm not really in the least remarkable. But I can't help liking you to think so because it is so encouraging, and I feel I want to live up to your idea of me, and I will too if you'll go on being encouraging. You won't ever hint to Mother, will you, about Mario?"

"Certainly not if you don't want me to."

"I shall have a battle with her if I want to become a Catholic and I should hate her to accuse me of being sentimental. However, if you become a Catholic now, you'll get the blame."

"I expect I shall. But I'm not going to become a Catholic immediately. I've waited so long that I shall wait a little longer. You may have to wait too. I doubt if either Sir Alexander or your mother will agree to any sudden step."

"I'll be twenty next May."

"But not twenty-one."

"Yes, I suppose I'll have to wait. Oh, John, forgive me for going on about myself when you've your own sorrow to think of. I wish I'd known your friend Fitz."

John passed across to her the letter he had received from Ellen:

TINORAN,
CARAGH LAKE

My dear John,

Edward was shot by Free State troops on the night of August 14th. He had gone down from the mountains to attend to a wounded Irregular who died the same night. They are buried together beside a bohereen that runs up to a little glen called Derrybeg not far from the road from Tralee to Dingle. The two Keenan boys, brothers of Larry who died with Edward, have put up white crosses on two heaps of stones above their graves, and on the cross above all that is left in this world of Edward they have painted in red lead 'Pray for the soul of Edward Fitzgerald, I.R.A., who died in defence of Ireland. August 14th, 1922. R.I.P.' Mrs Keenan says the graves shall never go untended while she lives.

I know how dear Edward was to you, and I know that you sympathized with his political views. I wish I had the satisfaction of believing that that he died for was worth the sacrifice. I don't mean Ireland but the kind of Ireland he and his associates hoped to create. And the bitterness of it is that those with whom he had fought against the British from the Easter Rising onwards called him a Cockney Irishman. They thought because he had been to an English public-school that he was less of an Irishman

*than they.   Oh, I know he used to be so very anxious to assert
himself over his London surroundings that sometimes he would
be seeming like a character in a Boucicault melodrama.   But it
is a bitter thought that they should sneer at him for a Cockney.
Ah well, he's passed beyond sneering now and is with his Nora
again.   God be good to them both!*

*I do not think that my mother will last much longer.   When
she heard of the death of Edward she just sighed and said she
would be seeing him very soon.   I feel a little worried what is
best to do.   It might be better to bring my mother over to London
so that I can look after her.   Meanwhile, I'll stay here with her,
but the house is very melancholy.   It's a terrible thing to say,
but in some ways I'm glad that Edward's life is done.   This
civil war is so ghastly.   And I don't think he would have been
happy at the end whichever side won.*

*Perhaps you'll write and give me your advice.   I don't think
I could live in Ireland.   But what would Edward say if I took
Padraig to live in England?   Do write to me.*

> *Your affectionate*
> *Ellen Fitzgerald*

*I open this letter to add a postscript.   A letter of Edward's
has been found in which he charges my mother and myself to take
your advice about the future.*

"And what will you advise, John?" his sister asked.

"Oh, to come to England.   It's obvious that things are going
to be much worse in Ireland.   I only hope that all this sacrifice
of life will not be wasted by leaving a discontented and thwarted
nation when exhaustion brings the struggle to an end.   The folly,
the folly of partition!"

"I don't really understand about Irish politics, I'm afraid."

"Like the great majority of English people.   And they're so
simple really.   Ireland wants to live her own life.   That's the
alpha and omega of Irish politics."

The *Queen of Devon* passed through the canal before dusk, and
the sublime voyage westward through the Gulf of Corinth was on
a moonless night.   By morning the yacht was leaving Greece astern.

"You rather rushed us at the end," John told his host reproachfully.

"I want to get back, old man. I didn't bargain to spend so many days in Mileto. Gee, I was afraid the yacht would catch fire. Besides, the political situation at home is getting tricky. L. G. may be able to hold on, but he may not, and I've got to watch the line we take in the *Journal*. No damned editor can be trusted in times like these. I'm clear after what we saw in Asia Minor that we can't afford to quarrel with the Turks. You saw for yourself, John, the Greeks are no damned good. Where should we be in another war if we had to rely on the Greeks?"

"So in spite of our promises and encouragement you intend to abandon the Greeks?" John asked.

"Any promises made were made to Venizelos. And when the Greeks put him out we had no further responsibility."

"I don't accept that."

"Come down to earth, John. It's what the British public accept, not you. You're only a single voter."

"Votes, votes, votes. All permanent values, all long-sighted policy, all enthusiasm and endeavour to be sacrificed to the vote-catching slogan of the moment. That's really what's taking you home in such a hurry, Turner. You can scent a General Election on the autumn air, and you think your constituency requires attention."

Turner Rigden grinned. It was impossible to be angry with him.

"And listen, John," he continued, "I'm counting on putting up that play of yours with Gabrielle Derozier either this autumn if she's free or early in the New Year."

"Acquiescence," John said to himself when, after Turner had left the yacht at Brindisi and gone northward with Bob Redroad and Janet Meriday, he was pacing the deck. "I've been inclined to despise Torbock for his subserviency to his employer, but is my own attitude any more dignified? Acquiescence! Acquiescence! Life is so easy when people like Turner Rigden are friendly. I write a play and that's the end of my troubles, and then I expect other people to be independent. We all bow down in our different ways. Hullo, Noll, what do you bow down to?" he asked.

The young peer looked puzzled.

"I mean what do you respect in this world?" John pressed.

"That's rather a searching question, isn't it?"

"The *status quo*, I suppose, when it comes to it," John suggested.

"After all, your future depends upon its preservation. We'll ask David. David, what do you respect most in this world?"

But David was thinking about Janet Meriday and said he did not know.

" And you, Prudence?"

But by this time the rest of the party had rallied and opposed a solid front to John's questions. In any case David and Noll Erpingham were too much preoccupied with reaching a decision whether they should carry on in the yacht to Southampton or get off at Citrano with John, Geoffrey Noel, and Prudence. In the end they decided to stick to the yacht, and do a spot of reading on the voyage home. Both were taking their final schools next June.

John volunteered to escort Prudence to Verona, but she thought when it came to it that she would rather not go.

"You see Mario's father doesn't speak English very fluently and his aunt doesn't speak it at all, and I speak Italian so wretchedly . . . no, I think I'd rather not go."

So in the third week of September the Torre Saracena was left empty. A night was to be spent in Paris on the way so that Athene could meet Gabrielle and John could talk to her about the play. They were to cross the Channel by Havre because Arthur was arriving back from America at Southampton.

"I've a feeling we're leaving it for good, you know," Athene said to John.

The others had already gone up the path through the rosemary to the waiting cars.

"Well, if we get our price we've made up our minds to sell, haven't we? But we haven't got our price yet."

"We shall, I think."

She sighed.

"Oh dear, these moments in life when one deliberately chooses change. What lies ahead? We've been so happy here, haven't we, John?"

She cast a lingering look upon the pictures and the books and the chairs in the library and then turned quickly away to descend the spiral staircase.

"At last we meet again, and it will soon be ten years since we met."

It was Gabrielle welcoming Athene to her apartment in the Boulevard des Invalides.

"Well, you certainly don't look a day older, madame," said Athene.

"Ah, no, madame, one can be kind but one must not be too kind. And I must say the same to you."

"Then now it's you who is being too kind," Athene laughed.

There was not a trace of yellow in Varenne's eye to-day. He was reassured by the evidence of Athene's attraction.

"I have read the play to Camille, John, translating so well as I could while I was reading, and he finds it very good, though of course it is impossible to give him the shades of the English lover. But you are very cruel, John, I think."

"Cruel?"

"Yes, I think so. I think it is cruel both to the English lover and to his French mistress."

"I wasn't intending to be cruel," John said, "I was trying to present two points of view."

"I think it's rather cruel, madame," Athene agreed. "But I do think it's the best play he has written."

John was surprised to find that his play produced this effect; Athene had never suggested as much when he had read it to her.

"I protest I wasn't aware of trying to be cruel," he declared again.

"Never mind," said Gabrielle, "what is of importance is that it is a good play, and for me a really splendid part. But when I remember Annette and compare Annette with Marguerite how far away seems Annette and how young seems the man who made her and the woman who played her."

"*Qu'est-ce que tu as dit?*" Varenne asked.

"*Je parlais d'autrefois,*" his wife replied. "But we must now talk in French please because Camille cannot understand a word of English."

So for the rest of lunch the conversation was in French, and at the end of it Gabrielle had definitely promised to play in *How It Was Sweet* sometime early in the spring of 1923.

"We won't talk business now," John said, "but as soon as I get back to London I'll ask Turner Rigden to send over his representative to discuss all that side of it with you." He raised his glass:

"To Marguerite."

After lunch Gabrielle insisted upon paying a visit to the hotel to see Corinna and present her with a doll nearly as big as herself.

"She is like you, madame . . . or may I say, please, Athene?"

"Why, please, I wish you would."

"And you will call me Gabrielle? Yes, she is like you, Athene, the way her eyes are set; and she is like John, too, but perhaps more like that charming young sister of his. How is she, John?"

"She's with us now."

"She is with you—and you did not bring her to lunch! But you are really odious."

John saw that Gabrielle was hurt by their not having brought Prudence, and taking her aside he explained that it had been Prudence herself who had been shy of coming. Then he told Gabrielle the reason.

"Ah, I understand. I understand. She feared I would ask her about her young men. And indeed of course I would have asked her. Let me, please, see her though."

So John went in search of his sister.

"Ah, my dear, I am not at all disappointed," Gabrielle exclaimed. "But it was bad of you to hide yourself. Athene, your train does not depart until about seven, I think. Let me take Prudence for a drive if she will come with me. Will you come, Prudence?"

They drove to a restaurant in the Bois and sat down under the trees for an hour in the spun gold of the tranquil September afternoon.

"Already see—a few leaves are turning yellow. It is truly autumn already," Gabrielle sighed. "It is selfish of me to carry you away from the shops, but I am *émotionnée* this afternoon. And you bring back to me so much the John of eleven years ago when I was Annette in his first play. Ah, he was already much older than you, I can assure you; but he was still in his twenties . . . and so was I!"

"You were in love with each other, weren't you?"

"Yes, we were in love. But it is very natural for a young writer of plays to fall in love with his first heroine."

"When I first met you that April in 1919 . . ."

"Yes, it was in April," the older woman murmured.

"I asked John if he had ever been in love with you and he said he would tell me when I was older."

"And now you are older, and it is I who tell you."

"You are going to act again in a play of John's, aren't you, madame?"

"Please call me Gabrielle. So it will be for me not quite so much September and more April. Pardon me that I am so

émotionnée this afternoon, but I am so happy to think that again
I shall be acting in a play of John's. You know my mother was
English?"

"Yes, John told me."

"It is very beautiful, you know, to love and to finish with love
and then to be friends. It is beautiful, and a little rare. And you
are so like John. We were at Sorrento together in the April of
1913 and I met Athene then and perhaps I guessed already that
she was to be John's wife one day. Anyway somehow I knew
our love must come to an end, and so it happened without bitterness. Oh, you are so like John as he was then. It was sweet
of you to drive with me this afternoon, because for me it is a
memorable day. We are all so settled. I am married. John is
married. I meet his wife. I see his lovely little daughter. And
then just when I have made myself happy by acting again in
London and in another play of John's I see in his sister so much
of the John of eleven years ago. I tell you, my sweet Prudence,
it is excessively emotional for me. But this must be great nonsense for you. Talk to me about yourself. Have you loved
yet?"

"I was in love, yes," Prudence said slowly.

Gabrielle waited for her to go on.

"And he was killed last month."

"So, like John you have suffered for a love that was suddenly
torn away from you. I am so sorry. Please to pardon my sentimental dreaming. You were patient to listen so kindly. I will
not be so foolish as to try to say consoling words, for I think
consolation is a great impertinence. But you will be my friend,
yes? You see, I will be in London very soon now, and I will not
know where I am. I will be just a ghost."

A yellow leaf came spinning down through the fine golden air
and lighted upon the table at which they sat.

"A ghost," Gabrielle repeated, picking up the leaf. "A ghost
of April like this poor leaf. So you will be my friend, yes?"

"I'd love to be your friend."

"How warmly you have said that! But I will make you shy
if I comment so soon upon you. Please not to think I will embarrass you. And now let us go before the afternoon begins to
turn chill."

Gabrielle drove Prudence back to the hotel, but she would not
come in again. When the omnibus was waiting to take the
Ogilvies to the station the porter gave Prudence a small packet.

"Madame Varenne has left it here to be given to you, mademoiselle."

In the train to Havre Prudence opened the packet. It contained a heart-shaped sapphire on a fine platinum chain, and on a card was written:

Souvenir of a happy autumn afternoon
Gabrielle

Arthur arrived back from America, richly bronzed and loaded with a variety of expensive mechanical toys on which heavy duty had to be paid at Southampton. His speech was now a curious mixture of American phrases uttered in an English accent and English phrases delivered in an American accent. He was full of plans for introducing American notions at Hampden House when he arrived; but within a couple of days the conservative atmosphere of England had put a brake upon his aspirations, and he became doubtful whether his status in the school would allow him to put them into practice. In the end he went back to Hampden House with a mind concentrated upon the ambition of getting his Second Eleven colours for soccer.

"And of working pretty hard too at your Latin to make up for this very long holiday," his mother had suggested.

"Of course," Arthur had promised, and in the same breath had added that left half-back was the position in the team at which he aimed.

When Arthur had gone back to school John went down to Nanphant with Athene and Corinna. He was glad to be away from London and the expression of so much uncomprehending opinion about the state of affairs in Ireland and the Near East. The revolution had progressed apace in Greece since he and Prudence had sat on the Acropolis above a disillusioned Athens. The Salonica troops mutinied. From Mytilene a revolutionary committee sent an aeroplane to Athens, demanding the dismissal of the Government, the dissolution of the Chamber, the holding of a General Election, and the abdication of King Constantine in favour of the Crown Prince. On September 27th King Constantine abdicated and was succeeded by King George II. The next day revolutionary troops entered Athens, where, what seemed to British opinion, the fickle mob welcomed them with acclamation. Numbers of prominent politicians and military and naval leaders and even the ex-King's brothers were arrested. Venizelos was invited to collaborate with the new Government in an effort to save Hellas from the catastrophe in which she had been involved.

Meanwhile, the tension between Turkey and Great Britain continued acute, but at last on October 10th an armistice was signed and Greece was sacrificed. The Italian Government took advantage of a shattered country to tear up the agreement of 1920, by which the differences between Greece and Italy over the Dodecanese Islands were to have been settled. The British Government protested, but the protest was ignored, and Italy annexed the twelve islands with the deliberate intention of challenging one day Great Britain's position in the Mediterranean.

A gale was blowing with fury from the west when John kept his fortieth birthday, but that did not deter Jennifer and Christabel from bicycling over from Pendarves House to assist at the celebration.

"I wish both of you didn't look so much older," John complained. "What's the use of coaxing the glass to be kind and assure me that when one reaches forty there's nothing to it, if two massive young women come over and remind me of my age? And yesterday you were a pair of freckled kids!"

"Not yesterday," Christabel contradicted loftily. "Ages ago— over four years ago. Don't forget I'm seventeen now."

"I don't forget. I suppose you'll be getting married next year."

"I might," said Christabel.

"I don't know who to," her elder sister scoffed.

"Nor do I, which increases the probability," Christabel retorted.

The day after John's birthday a letter came from Ellen Fitzgerald to say that she and her mother with Padraig were installed in a new block of flats which had been built at the end of Trelawny Road.

By the same post there was a letter to ask John to come up to town and discuss the question of putting on *How It Was Sweet*.

Two days later when John left for London the gale was over and it was the perfection of Cornish October weather.

"Which means, in my opinion, the most lovely weather the world holds," John said. "Don't you think so? I say, look at Corinna."

By the edge of the lily-pool Corinna was gazing down at her reflection in the greenish water.

Athene took an apprehensive step forward.

"It's all right. Mairi is holding an alert hand within reach."

"What are you looking at, sweetness?" her mother asked.

"Corinna," came the answer. "Corinna sitting in a cloud."

"What a lovely place to sit, darling."

Corinna nodded a grave assent.

"I don't think that's bad judgment for a year and nine months," said John. "She'll know her own mind one day even if she should always prefer to sit among the clouds."

"Come down out of the clouds yourself," Athene warned him. "You'll miss the train if you don't get off at once."

The block of new red flats at the corner of Trelawny Road made the grey houses look shrivelled and shabby, and John could not suppose that Mrs Fitzgerald would be lamenting the house at the corner in which her husband the Doctor had started his practice at the beginning of the 'eighties. However, when John called at Trelawny Mansions he found that Mrs Fitzgerald was little likely to see again that grey house at the corner, or indeed ever to rise from her bed. The old lady was not yet seventy-seven, but she looked much older, and frail as a wind-dried shell.

"No more violence," she murmured to John when he sat beside the bed in her room the windows of which looked across the expanse of St James's School playing-fields golden-green in the mellow light of the October noon. "It leads to nothing but evil," she went on. "Violence makes violence. Evil makes evil. Don't teach Padraig violence. Six years old last July. A splendid little boy."

"He's very like his mother."

"Yes, poor Nora. She was lost to her boy through violence. Violence . . . och, it's a terrible thing is violence, John. When the Doctor was alive he was a great Nationalist, but he would never hear a word for violence. He hated it. He did not think Home Rule for Ireland was worth winning if it had to be won with violence. No, no, not worth the winning. But Edward thought otherwise, poor boy, and now he's gone. I'll be seeing him very soon, and he'll be understanding now that violence is evil. So promise me, John, promise me that you will not teach Padraig to believe in violence."

"I can promise you that sincerely," John replied.

She felt on the coverlet for her rosary, and presently the room was silent except for the dry tinkle of the beads.

"She won't last very long, I'm afraid," Ellen said to him when he came out of her mother's room.

"But with that secure faith in immortal life, with that certainty of seeing others who have gone before, what joy death must be! Just now your mother was talking about dear Fitz as if death was just a matter of knocking into his head a little common sense. Well, I have to go and see Turner Rigden now.   By the way, I have a good part for you in my new play, but I don't think it's likely to be produced before next February.   So don't turn down any offer that comes along meanwhile.   Tell me, what about finances?"

"I've saved a bit, and mother has about a hundred and fifty a year of her own.   We'll try to let Tinoran later when these troubles are over.   It's useless at present."

Turner Rigden had just come away from the fateful meeting of the Unionist Party at the Carlton Club on October 19th at which, by an overwhelming majority, it had decided to withdraw from the Coalition.   The R.A.C. was in a buzz of excitement, many of the Coalition Unionists having returned there to talk over their disruption.

"Bring me a bottle of the Bollinger I like," Rigden told his particular smoking-room waiter.   "And ice it well.   Damn it, John, I feel kind of feverish."

"How did you vote, Turner, if I may ask an indiscreet question?"

"God damn it, when it came to it I followed Austen and Balfour, and stuck to L. G.   I switched the *Sunday Journal* hard against him a fortnight ago, but when it came to the point I couldn't vote with Bonar Law.   The speech that turned the scale against L. G. came from Stanley Baldwin."

"He seems rather a sound fellow, so far as one can apply such an epithet to any politician."

"Sound?   A foxy double-crossing . . ."

"But Turner, Turner," John interrupted, "those are epithets you can apply to most politicians.   And the Coalition *had* begun to stink, you know.   You can't expect the English to stand for a Welshman as dictator, and Lloyd George was well on the way to that status.   He was useful during the war, but for his handling of Ireland alone he deserves to go.   If he'd even had the guts to resign over that miserable Greek business . . . and you yourself have been criticizing him in your comic paper."

"I know.   I know.   All the same when I heard that fellow Baldwin get up on his legs and stick him in the back I felt sort of sick.   Well, by this evening Bonar Law will be at work forming a Government. You'll soon hear what the rewards are to be. You see if Baldwin doesn't get one of the plums. Hell, I wouldn't put it past Bonar Law to give him the Exchequer. I wish they'd hurry with that champagne."

"It's no use, Turner. I can't feel hot and bothered over the rending of the Coalition. I've no admiration for Bonar Law and I know nothing about this fellow Baldwin, but it seems to me that any Government is better than the Coalition. And I think you'll find that's the prevailing opinion in the country. What a pity the Labour Party have such a set of duds running them! A really capable Labour Government is what the country needs now."

"A Labour Government?" Rigden gasped. "By god, John, you may be one hell. of a dramatist, but you're not practical. You're a dreamer. A Labour Government? Why not invite Lenin to come over and take charge right away?"

"This bogey of a Labour Government! All you fellows have against a Labour Government is your dread that you won't be able to make so much money."

"A Labour Government always does unsettle the City."

.."The City! You know, Turner, I've a horrid fear that one day this great country will come to grief for fear of upsetting the City. And the Stock Exchange!"

"Well, the Stock Exchange is the barometer of the country's prosperity."

"I don't believe it. I think this country has a fundamental prosperity far beyond the ability of the Stock Exchange to judge or ruin. You can caricature the country with your Press. You can exploit it with your financiers. You can humbug it with your politicians. But only up to a point, Turner. We reached that point once or twice during the war, and I don't think it was the Press or the financiers or the politicians that saved the country. I think the country saved itself."

At this moment the Bollinger arrived.

"That's better," Rigden sighed after drinking deep. "I wanted that. I tell you, John, that meeting at the Carlton upset me."

John laughed.

"I suppose you'll hold your seat in South-East Kensington quite easily?"

"Oh, I think so. Say, John, have you heard of the British Broadcasting Company?"

"No, what's that?"

"Well, the idea is to have a monopoly of broadcasting in this country. I was invited to take up shares and I refused. I wonder if I was right."

"But what is broadcasting?"

"Why, it's entertainment by way of wireless telephones. They're going to start this autumn. I'm afraid it may affect the Press. There's a proposal to give out news. That's what worries me. If it was just entertainment I wouldn't give a damn, but I don't like this idea of news by telephone. The Newspaper Proprietors intend to take a strong line. You start a thing like this, and before you know where you are it's got beyond you. Yes, we may have to fight it. . . ." Rigden drank another glass of champagne.

"Anyway, with all your worries, Turner, you haven't got to worry about Gabrielle Derozier. I'm glad that's fixed."

"Yes, Beaton came back from Paris with the contract. We're paying her a hundred a week and a handsome percentage above a gross of twelve hundred. If the show goes she'll do well. It's a bit of a risk, though, bringing a French actress over to England. They're very conservative in this country."

"That's what you learnt at the Carlton to-day, didn't you?"

When John left the R.A.C. he went back to Church Row where he was staying while he was in London.

The paper-boys were shouting the news of Mr Lloyd George's resignation.

"It was high time," said the Judge. "He did a wonderful job during the war, but Europe must settle down, and we have to set an example."

"Well, not even my contrariness will prompt me to defend the Coalition," John replied, "though I can't pretend to enjoy the prospect of a Unionist Government. Still, I must say this man Baldwin attracts me as a potential statesman. Do you know him?"

"I've never met him, but I hear him very well spoken of by friends of mine whose opinion I regard."

"My friend and patron Turner Rigden believes him to be foxy, but the losing side in a game of political intrigue always believes in the foxiness of its opponents."

"I've certainly not heard any tributes to his—er—foxiness. On the contrary I hear he is a very simple man, who has taken up politics from a sense of duty. An old-fashioned type altogether, and that undoubtedly is what this hectic post-war world needs. However, Bonar Law will certainly be Prime Minister, and I'm not so sure of him."

"Nor I," said John. "I distrust the lad of pairts in politics, and I regard him as one of the men most guilty over Gallipoli, while his Irish record is deplorable."

"Well, well, but you have to admit that the Irish problem is baffling. When you think what we have agreed to surrender, and still they're not satisfied."

John shook his head.

"I'm not going to argue about that. I'm in a state of depression about small nations at the moment. This Greek debacle has dealt me a terrific blow."

"But surely it would have been madness for us to go to war with the Turks?" I'm convinced that our future in the East depends on the restoration of the old friendship with Turkey. Another war might have exacerbated matters beyond the hope of an ultimate reconciliation. I can understand what you feel after that experience in Mileto, which by the way seems to have had a tremendous effect on Prudence's imagination. Still, as I told her, what she saw in Mileto was only what thousands and thousands of girls like her had been seeing all over Europe during the war. I should suppose that the Greeks would have learnt their lesson and be willing now to confide their case to Venizelos to extricate them from the mess."

"You thought Prudence had been influenced by the experience of this Aegean cruise?"

"Most decidedly."

John debated with himself whether he should tell his father about Mario Aprili; but he abstained, for he did not think the secret would be kept from Elise, and the only person to tell her mother was Prudence herself at her own discretion. Presently the debate with himself was closured by the sound of the telephone. It was James Yarrow ringing him. He had just returned to London from Tahiti.

"I thought you were in the Far East, James."

"So I was, but I wanted to see Ponape before the Japanese sealed it up, and from there I wandered across the Pacific."

"Are you glad to be back in Europe?"

"Not overjoyed."

"Let's dine together at Bélanger's."

It was not until James Yarrow was talking to him again across a table that John realized how much he had missed him during the last three years.

"Well, they've got rid of Lloyd George, James."

"Sez you. The Unionist Party thought he was going to turn into another Henry VIII. One Welsh dictator was enough to teach the English a lesson."

Next morning there was a letter from Fofo to say that Signor Bodisko was prepared to pay Signor Ogilvie's price for the Torre Saracena if he could have possession immediately. It was advisable that Signor Ogilvie should come out and conclude the business before the political situation in Italy made business impossible.

"James, will you come out with me to Citrano to-morrow?" John asked over the telephone.

"Yes, if you'll travel second-class," was the reply.

"This is my treat," said John. "I'm selling my tower at a handsome profit. We'll catch the nine o'clock train at Victoria."

"If the passport mandarins will disgorge visas."

"Oh, yes, we've all to-day. Meet me at my club to-night and I'll give you your tickets."

They reached Citrano on Monday, October 23rd. It was full of Fascists gathered for the Congress at Naples next day.

"Curious cockroach effect," Yarrow observed.

There was indeed some justification for James Yarrow's remark. John had grown so accustomed to embody the idea of *Fascismo* in the face and figure of Mario that it came as a surprise to find how few of the Blackshirts reached, at any rate outwardly, so high a standard.

"It's a kind of nightmare of boy scouts," Yarrow said. "Look at them now. They can't even march up that slope."

The slope in question was one of the steep narrow alleys leading up to the Piazza, the cobbles of which were so greasy from the autumn damp that the troop, trying to advance with the quick step of marching *bersaglieri*, slid back as fast as they advanced so that they appeared to be moving against an escalator.

"And look at that conspiratorial clown," Yarrow went on, pointing to a gawky Blackshirt who, in the middle of the Piazza, was receiving folded notes from various messengers and perusing them with an expression of ferocious secrecy. He had the long chin and narrow head that in combination are a certain indication of the most wearisome type of loquacious and pragmatical bore.

"Well, James, I admit I'm a little disappointed by this gathering, but we've struck a poor lot. The ones that demonstrated here at Whitsuntide were a superior collection."

"I think if we've got to be ruled in future by bricklayers or clerks I prefer the sway of the former," Yarrow said.

"Well, let's go to Naples to-morrow and hear what Mussolini has to tell his assembled legionaries. There's more in this than you'll allow, James."

Yarrow grunted.

"I think you're well rid of your tower, charming place though it is. You mark my words, these people will be impossible if they gain power, and Europe is getting in such a mess that people like this are quite capable of gaining power nowadays."

They passed into Fofo's where the proprietor behind the counter was busy with his groceries, his eyes bright as a mouse's darting from one to another of the Blackshirts sitting about the café. John presented James Yarrow.

"You come to see our *rivoluzione, signore*. Very nice. I thinka you have a good affair to sell the Torre Saracena," he added, turning to John. "*L' Italia nostra . . .*" he shrugged his fat shoulders. "Perhaps it is good so. Perhaps it is bad. *Chi lo sa?* Myself I finish Fofo's at *Natale*. For me no politics, no nothings. Only my olive-trees, my wine-trees, and my *caccia cavallo* cheeses."

Next morning James Yarrow and John went into Naples to hear Mussolini address a grand parade of over forty thousand *Fascisti*.

"I challenge the Government either to settle the urgent problems of internal and external policy in accordance with the demands of a renewed Italy or immediately to resign and hand over the administration to the Fascist Party."

Forty thousand enthusiastic arms acclaimed the challenge. Forty thousand throats cheered Mussolini.

"So might cockroaches wave their antennae," Yarrow muttered.

"Careful, James. We don't want to be butchered to make a Roman holiday."

John thought it wise to steer his friend away from the outskirts of that immense gathering.

"Queer little tough," Yarrow observed when they were pacing the tranquil gardens beyond Santa Lucia.

"Something more than that," John murmured. "His vitality is terrific."

"I wasn't impressed."

"I wonder what he'll do?"

"Go on bellowing, I should imagine. It seems to be what his audience demands. It's a form of revivalism of course."

"But he has caught the imagination of young Italy."

"I should prefer to call it the emotion."

"Well, if he can direct such emotion to a practical expression, he may re-create Italy."

"But who wants Italy to be re-created?"

"It might set an example to the rest of Europe."

"A very bad example," Yarrow snapped.

"You prefer Communism?"

"I find black and red ants equally obnoxious in formication."

"But the question is whether, the way man has enslaved himself to his blasted machines, he can avoid formication of one kind or another. The dice are loaded more and more heavily every day against the individual, and at least the Fascist ideal aims at more inclusiveness than the Communist ideal. It doesn't exalt one class at the expense of another. It aims at a more reasonable distribution of wealth. And ethically it rather resembles the English public-school system as perfected by Dr Arnold. From the moment these continental nations took up football we had to face the fact that sooner or later they would copy the public-school system. Headmaster, masters, monitors, fifth-form boys, fags ... the whole hierarchy is to be found in Fascism."

"That doesn't recommend it to me," Yarrow replied. "I consider the English public-school system soul-destroying. But at least if an individual does survive it he can develop a life of his own when he has escaped from school. Those Blackshirt buffoons intend to impose their system from the cradle to the grave."

"I wish you'd met a young friend of mine who was killed this summer by the Socialists. I think you'd have recognized the potentialities of Fascism."

"My dear John, obviously you could find for me plenty of good-looking school-heroes, but they don't justify the public-school system. The mere fact that Fascism is built up on a military basis is enough to condemn it, because it must end in expressing itself by military action. You remember that among other things the war was a war to end war. What a damned silly piece of politicians' rhetoric! Every war must be a war to make the world safe for war. Diana of the Ephesians had a hundred breasts. Bellona has a hundred wombs. Why, even in Greece you and I can find a lesson. From the moment Venizelos fired the Greeks with his Big Idea, war with Italy or Turkey was inevitable. Now if he's wise he'll make friends with Turkey and keep his weather eye on Italy."

"It's a mortification to look back now to our time on Lipsia."

"Why?"

"Such an expense of spirit in a waste of shame."

"Don't start dramatizing yourself, John."

"I'm not."

"You're on the way to it when you begin to fancy that anything we did had any profound bearing on what has just happened in Greece. What we did in the Aegean was to work very hard and enjoy ourselves in between."

"I worked very hard. I couldn't say you worked very hard, James."

"Yes, I supposed you would try to get back at me for accusing you of dramatizing yourself. But never mind about that. What I'm beginning to ask myself is whether the English *laissez-faire* may not after all really be the most profound political wisdom and the chief cause of the predominant position we occupy. Other nations always accuse us of perfidy and cunning, but in point of fact both are nothing but laziness. I do think that must be why we've lasted so long. We tire everybody else out. We don't burn up our own energy by the kind of absurdity we've just been watching."

"Your astringency is grateful, James."

Two days later a Manifesto was published, announcing that the *Fascisti* intended to march at once on Rome in order to cut the Gordian knot and hand over to the King and Army a renewed Italy. The Government at once resigned and the King, who was enjoying a holiday, hurried back to Rome to see about the business of forming a new Government—the third in nine months. Meanwhile, the old Government had to remain in power and, alarmed by the Fascist mobilization, it proclaimed martial law. The King, however, refused to sign the proclamation and thus averted civil war. Some of the Conservatives suggested to him that he should invite Mussolini to form a Government. So Mussolini took the train to Rome and by the last day of October the new Cabinet was sworn in. The mobilized *Fascisti*, who had been cheated of their march on Rome to cut the Gordian knot by their Leader's preceding them in a train, were granted a triumphal march through the capital.

"And that's that," said James Yarrow.

The legal business of carrying through the sale of the Torre

Saracena to Bodisko, who was not in Citrano himself, lasted as long as all such transactions in Italy in spite of the Fascist Government, which within a few days of assuming office had sacked a number of railway officials, achieved punctuality for the trains, and secured travellers against having the leather straps stolen from their luggage.

Geoffrey Noel was much worried by a report that a purge was under consideration which was designed to expel all foreigners suspected of abusing Italian hospitality by offences against pudor.

"Really, Ogilvie, I don't know what to do," he hummed and mumbled, dancing about John's library in his agitation. "What between your leaving Citrano and this preposterous perquisition of one's—m-m—temperamental—m-m-m—and this slut Francesco has married, I do not know what to do. If I leave Italy and go to live in France I feel it may annoy Vanessa, and that will mean all sorts of difficulties over my money. Really, I've hardly slept a wink since I heard of this intolerable interference with one's private affairs."

"Oh, I don't believe you'll be interfered with," John told him. "You've been living in Citrano for more than twenty years, and surely Francesco's marriage ought to be an unassailable alibi in the matter of pudor. I shouldn't take any steps until you hear something more definite than rumour."

"I was quite impressed by *Fascismo* at first," Noel continued. "I had some charming talks about it with Mario. But all this interference with private lives is very objectionable. I suppose a dose of castor oil is better than being shot, but I do think it's inexcusably vulgar."

"Certainly so far it has been a singularly unbloody revolution," said John. "And when you think what Latin nations are capable of in the way of revolutionary savagery it is remarkable."

But he spoke a little too soon. That very night a party of *Fascisti* visited the Villa Marigold where, when the Cabinet resigned, Ernesto Vecchione had retired to join his wife. The ex-Minister was dragged out of bed and beaten up so severely that he died two days later. His widow later was driven out of the country.

"Why, why, why, must there always be violence?" John cried. "Now I suppose the Socialists will take their revenge by shooting or stabbing a Fascist, and then the whole miserable competition of revenge will start off."

"That was evident from a first glance at those thugs," James Yarrow said.

John's mind went back to that March day on Minerva's Cape when the air was odorous with the scent of the wild crimson pease-blossom and he had listened to the dreams of a handsome slim young *Fascista* for a new Imperium Romanum.   He would surely have disdained to help drag a man from his bed and beat him into insensibility.   Was it a law of nature that no reform could be achieved without blood and tears?

Certainly Vecchione was likely to be an uncompromising and able opponent of the new régime, but why was brutality necessary? Why could he not have been banished?   Well, the treatment of Ernesto Vecchione had taken away some of the pain of leaving Italy.   Athene had felt sure when they left the tower last month that they would not come back to it, and at the moment he had been stabbed by a pang for the ruthless insistency of change.   Now already the Torre Saracena was as much in the past as his rooms at Oxford or his bedroom in the first house in Church Row or the little house in Millbank whose furniture had been brought out here and was now going back to England.

Anyway, Citrano itself was gone.   With Fofo no longer at Fofo's, with new hotels and new residents, with the inevitable tightening up that the new régime would cause . . . *l' Italia nostra* had vanished in the shrug of Fofo's fat shoulders.   The new Italy might be more efficient, but our Italy was gone, and with it that 'seaside house by the farthest south where the baked cicala dies of drouth'. . . .

"*A rivederLa, signore, buon viaggio e presto ritorno,*" Caterina and Concetta were calling where they stood waist-deep in rosemary.

The voyage might be good, but the return would not be quick. John turned his back resolutely and did not look round again.

In Rome on the way back to England John wrote to Athene:

GRAND HOTEL
ROMA
November 11, 22.

My dearest,

    James and I could not resist dallying here for a few days in the lovely little summer of St Martin.   The sun looks into my window in the morning like a great topaz.   The sky washed by rain is of a blue that in a letter to you I don't mind calling a

*'yearning' blue, though it's an epithet I would not dare to use out-
side a letter!   In spite of the Fascist Revolution the City itself
lies in a trance of beauty.   I have a conviction that it will be a
long time before I see Italy again, and though I have drunk of the
water of the Fontagna di Trevi and dropped into it a coin I have
an uneasy emotion that perhaps I shall never see Rome again.   It
may be the breathless magic of the air which gives me a sense of
being suspended for an interval of time in which I wait for external
circumstance to decide my course.   I hang like a spider from its
strand of gossamer (and like a spider upside down!) at the mercy
of whatever wind shall take me.*

*Of course it has been 'commovente' to abandon the Torre
Saracena, and the excitement of the Revolution was not enough
to distract my mind from questioning the finality of the step I
have taken in selling the tower to Bodisko.   I go back to that
May of 1914 when I bought it and remember that it was intended
to be an abode for such a different world.   Yet imagine what
would have happened if I had not bought it.   I certainly should
not have spent that last year of the war in Citrano, and you and
I would not now be man and wife and there would be no Corinna.
It is the thought of the profound influence the buying of the tower
cast upon my future which agitates me now in reflecting upon
what may be the result of selling it.   Have we done wisely or
unwisely?*

*I seem to discern an answer in the political upheaval which
within hardly more than a fortnight has transformed Italy.   As
you know I was completely in sympathy with this thing called
Fascism while it was fighting for its future.   It seemed to express
more truly the spirit of youth in this post-war world than any manifestation I had encountered.   All that it aimed to abolish was
what I longed to see abolished, and now already I begin to doubt
its excellence, because already in victory it seems tainted with a
materialism which if less ugly than the materialism of the falsified
democratic ideals against which it set out to fight contains in
itself a dangerous poison for the human mind.   Chiefly owing to
the action of the King the Revolution has been carried through
with a minimum of violence, but the beating up of Vecchione shook
my confidence.   I recognize that he stood pre-eminently for all
that Fascism wanted to destroy, but there was a cowardice in the
way he was attacked which nauseated me.   A Fascist might argue
with me that Mario Aprili was attacked with equal cowardice, but
he lost his life through his own courage and his contempt for his*

adversaries. He was not dragged from his bed and beaten by half a dozen young bullies in whom individual bravery probably did not exist. I was revolted too by the display of herd emotion on which Mussolini played at Naples on October 24th. It seemed to me an expression of exactly the same kind of mass hysteria of which we hear in Russia. I suppose when Peter the Hermit preached the First Crusade he evoked a similar outburst of mass hysteria, but the material circumstances of the Middle Ages did not encourage the dehumanization of mass hysteria in the way that the material circumstances of to-day encourage it. The impulse to take the Cross may have been inspired by herd emotion, but the subsequent action in carrying it worthily depended upon the worthiness of the individual.

The Church has not yet recovered from the policy of trying to burn and torture people out of heresy, and if Fascism intends to repress critical opinion it will so twist and distort its original conception that within a year or two that conception will no longer be recognizable. If the men at the head of it possessed a true spirituality it would still be wrong to force their ideas upon the rest of their fellow countrymen, but when the men at the head preach merely the material guidance of Italy as the object of Fascism the claim to have the right to force their ideas upon the minds of others becomes intolerable. And then there are the nobodies who are brought to the surface by a movement like Fascism. They swarm already. Revolution is as bad as war in that respect. I look back to the war and recall the countless nobodies who mistook their self-importance for patriotism, and confused obstructiveness with duty, and now here they are again as Blackshirts this time. I know that it is too soon to attempt to calculate the end of the Fascist Revolution. If it lasts long enough to catch the children it may last a very long time. It may indeed be the herald of a shift in the attitude toward life, possibly even as portentous for human development as the first Protestants of the fifteenth century. However, I feel sure that a country which is putting into practice revolutionary theory is no country for anybody except its own natives.

I ran into Daniel Rayner three days ago in the English bookshop in the Piazza di Spagna. To my surprise he was enthusiastic about Fascism, discovering in it the expression of some of his own theories of human relationship, which he has developed considerably in the course of his wanderings through Australasia. Yesterday I met him again and he condemned Fascism fiercely. The

*previous day he had been watching from the pavement a procession,
and one of the Blackshirts lining the street had pushed him back,
treading on his toe in doing so. The individual in Rayner
asserted itself. He had no more use for blood and soil and the
mystical strength of the Fascio, and as for the Roman Empire
there were no words to voice his contempt for it and its legacy to
man. I think it was probably Rayner's innate homosexuality
(always debarred from expressing itself practically by an equally
strong respectability) which attracted him to Fascism at first. I
asked him if he was going to stay in Italy and he told me he was.
I suggested that a condition of hate was bad for the inner tranquillity of the artist, but in point of fact I believe that hate is
becoming the driving force of his genius and that without it he
would be lost. His attitude towards his cortège of female disciples
is like a female cat's towards her cortège of Toms. He enjoys
the competition and then spits at the winner.*

*It had been my intention while I was at Citrano to visit the
Bishop of San Gennaro and ask to be received into the Church;
but the Fascist Revolution preoccupied my speculation so much
that I decided it was the wrong moment to take a step which I
have waited to take so long. If I had heard the news of Fitz's
death at Citrano I should not have hesitated, but now I shall wait
until this gossamer from which I hang spiderlike shows me the
direction in which I am to move.*

*To-day is Armistice Day. James and I dined together that
day in 1918 when I was wondering what your future and mine was
going to be. And now we have already celebrated the third anniversary of our wedding day. Blessings on it and you! I always
enjoy James's company enormously. His conversation has for
me the quality of a persimmon, and I am enjoying just now
the eating of as many of them as I can get hold of. We shall
be in London by the 14th and I shall wait there until after the
Election, because I want to be at hand when Emil comes out of
prison.*

*This is a long letter, and I have spent two hours in writing it
because I keep stopping and gazing out at this bemused Roman
air, wondering of what this golden stillness is the prelude.*

*Well, I suppose Olensky will dance for Bodisko on the roof of
our tower next summer. I gave Geoffrey Noel some furniture,
and various souvenirs also to Madame Kleinborch and the
Matrassics and Ostápov and dear Fofo and Margherita, Caterina
and Concetta, and other friends. The rest of the stuff I have had*

put into store at Naples until we decide where it is to be sent.
I feel as I finish this letter as if I had finished a play.   Kiss
Corinna.   My dearest love.

John

On November 15th the General Election was held and resulted
in a majority for the Unionists of nearly a hundred over Labour,
Liberals, National Liberals, and odds and ends. The country
seemed surprised by the masses of female voters who turned out to
poll, but the astuter members of the Unionist Party began to appreciate what an addition of strength had accrued to it from that
enfranchisement of women which it had so much dreaded. The
political influence of women should have been obvious when the
Coalition was returned within a month of the Armistice; but the
full measure of its capacity as a drag upon progressive government
was not apparent until this General Election conducted on Party
lines.

"And I was a supporter of women's enfranchisement," John
lamented. "I believed it would be a progressive vote, misled by
the fact that the women who agitated for it were all progressives.
What a failure of imagination!"

"It was," said James Yarrow drily. "It was like thinking that
a beefsteak and kidney pudding has ever enough kidney in it."

Two or three days after the result of the General Election was
known John took Prudence in response to an invitation from David
and Noll Erpingham to lunch with them in Balliol. They were
in Oxford by eleven o'clock of a November day that was like a
ghost of one of those days in Rome during St Martin's little
summer. The air was not less deeply tranced than there; but here
it was silvern and cold, and the etiolated blue of the zenith faded
into whiteness all around.

"I could not have chosen a more perfect day to revisit Oxford
in my present mood," John told his sister.

"What is your present mood?"

"Why, a mood of realization. I think it is only now that I
know with certainty the death of the world in which I spent my
youth." He did not add that it had been the spectacle of those
forty-thousand Blackshirts bespelled by Mussolini's voice at Naples
which had been the instrument of this realization.

"But don't you think that the young men of to-day are really just the same as they were in your time?"

"Yes, yes, no doubt they still are, but how long will young men be able to hold out against the changes this century must bring?"

"Why do you say 'hold out', John? Why should they hold out against change? Surely change as such isn't necessarily bad?"

They had been walking under the walls of New College and as Prudence spoke they turned the corner into Queen's Lane. A train of women's bicycles were waiting along it for their owners to emerge from the lecture they were attending. The strokes of noon clanged, and a moment later Queen's Lane was in a formication of female undergraduates, short-skirted, gowned as ridiculously as male commoners, wearing upon their bobbed hair floppy mortarboards. They mounted their bicycles in a fever of industrious deediness and went pedalling into the High to disappear round Queen's College like a flock of starlings.

"That I should have lived to behold such a sight," John exclaimed. "Well, that's one change which I denounce as bad."

"Oh, John, don't be so absurdly pre-war! Why shouldn't women go to Oxford?"

"Let me keep a few prejudices. I'm not going to argue the point."

"Because you haven't got a good argument," his sister challenged. He shook his head.

"You're not going to tempt me. And if you admire female undergraduates, why the devil didn't you go to Oxford yourself? Female students at students' universities like the Scottish and Continental universities? Yes. Female undergraduates at masters' universities like Oxford and Cambridge? No. I believe it even violated the true spirit of Oxford when compulsory celibacy for Fellows was abolished."

They wandered along towards Madgalen, arguing lightly, and at last they came to the lawns between New Buildings and Cloisters where the Eighteenth Century eyes the Middle Ages.

"It was unpatriotic of me to bring you here instead of to my own Exeter, but on such a day for ghosts I did not want to see dead men cross the quadrangle or turn in to a staircase. Not that plenty of the dead I knew do not haunt these lawns. I knew so many people all over the University. I doubt if anybody ever did have quite so large and varied a set of acquaintances as I had, and I don't think I should be exaggerating if I said that I was on nodding terms with at least two hundred people up at Oxford during my time

who were killed in the war.   I want to be able to think that it was
worth while.   Oh God, Prudence, how passionately I want to be
able to think that.   And it will only have been worth while if we
do make a better world.   And the miserable programme that this
new Government offers the country is a mockery of the dead.
When you think of those unemployed men marching down to
London from all over the provinces to see the Prime Minister, and
then to hear he hasn't the guts even to see them . . . nearly a million
and a half unemployed in the country which has just won the
greatest war in history, and the newly elected head of the Government will not listen to their case!   Is this an indication that evasion
of responsibility and *laissez-faire* were what the bodies of the ghosts
who haunt this country died for?   Those who died for Ireland will
soon rest in peace, for at least much of what they died for will
have been won.   Those who died for Russia can contemplate what
may be a vast and ruinous experiment but may be an experiment
that will save the future of mankind: they can in fact contemplate in
death life.   Those who died for Italy can contemplate another
experiment which may prove ridiculous but may prove sublime;
but they too in death see life.   And those who died for England
and for Scotland and for Wales, what do their ghosts contemplate
on this already dislustred day that is the ghost of a day?   A few
elderly politicians clinging to office as those few yellow leaves cling
to that oak-tree.   Will posterity believe that the first act of a new
Prime Minister at such a time was to refuse to see a deputation from
men some of whom had marched all the way from his own great
city of Glasgow to lay their case before him?"

"John, do you believe that Mario can see me now?" Prudence
asked, looking round through the creeping mist for the direction
in which the one expected will come.

"I believe he is aware of you, but I don't suppose that
the perceptions of the dead can be expressed in terms of the
living."

"You don't believe in communication between this world and
the spirit world?"

"I have never had an experience which convinced me," said John
cautiously.   "But, as I told you on the Acropolis, the exact vision
my friend Fitzgerald had of his own tomb over twenty years
before he died has satisfied me that personal immortality is true.
I think your aspiration to become a Catholic is the right way to
put yourself into communion with Mario, and I hope you will hold
to that aspiration and fulfil it.   I had intended to be received into

the Church before I left Italy, but some imperative within forbids me to take that step yet, and I am waiting for the explanation of that mental veto. And now we'll walk along to Exeter and embarrass the present owner of my rooms of twenty years ago by asking him if we may take a peep at them. And after that we'll go along to Balliol."

The trees in the deer-park were fading into mist when they turned into the Cloisters.

"You know, John, I think Noll Erpingham's rather a dear," Prudence said to her brother when in the dusk of that November afternoon they were driving to the station. To his satisfaction a few hansoms still survived and it was in one of these that they were driving. They had just crossed St Giles and were in Beaumont Street, the façade of Worcester before them dark against a pale mauve sunset.

> *"The whistle sounds the signal to cease play,*
> *The groaning Half rubs gently a sore knee,*
> *The athlete homeward jogs his cheery way*
> *And leaves the High to darkness and to tea,*

and then all I can remember is:

> *Save where the kettle sings by fireside bright,*
> *And tinkling teacups soothe November colds."*

"All you can remember of what, John?"

"All of a parody I wrote of Gray's *Elegy* for a University magazine exactly twenty years ago this November when I was six months older than you are now. I think David's mulled claret must have gone to my head. In this twilight and in this hansom I am back in my second year at Oxford. Yes, I think Noll's a very agreeable creature."

"You were rather severe on him, John, about his opportunities as an hereditary legislator. He looked quite dejected once or twice."

"Oh, that was the mulled claret too. All the same, I do think a young man like that with a great name should earn his right to bear it. You'll have to take him in hand seriously."

"Me?"

"Why not? He's obviously interested in you."

"John, what a ridiculous thing to say!"

"Oh, I don't mean to suggest he's in love with you. But he's reached the stage of looking round to see if you'd noticed his last remark. Yes, I think you'll have to take him in hand."

Prudence was silent for the rest of the drive to the station.

Emil came out of Wormwood Scrubbs that November, but John did not see him immediately, because he went away with Astrid into the country for a fortnight.

On November 27th the Revolutionary Court-Martial in Athens tried the ex-Ministers, Generals, and Admirals whose incompetence and dishonesty were believed to be responsible for the disaster in Asia Minor. Six of them were condemned to death and shot next morning.

This gesture stunned the new Unionist Government, which ordered the British Minister in Athens to ask for his passports and leave Greece. Diplomatic relations between the two countries were indefinitely broken off.

"The English shot an admiral for cowardice early in the eighteenth century," James Yarrow said to John. "But I don't remember that they ever shot a general, and they certainly never shot a member of the Cabinet."

"Yet incompetence, laziness, and in some cases actual dishonesty could be charged against the majority of the party politicians who have led our country during this century, and though certainly none of our own admirals or generals could be accused of physical cowardice, were moral cowardice a military offence even many of them have deserved a court-martial."

James Yarrow smiled sardonically.

"By the rapidity of their reaction," he said, "the shock must have been severe. I should suppose one would have to go back a long way to find an instance of such promptitude in the action of the British Government."

"A very long way indeed," John agreed. "I remember those three weeks in May and June we waited at Gallipoli for an answer to that cable from Ian Hamilton on the answer to which success or failure at Gallipoli depended, and I remember that no answer was forthcoming because the leaders of the Unionist Party were black-mailing the Liberal leaders into surrendering to them an equal share of the responsibilities and emoluments of office. In the end Gallipoli was lost on account of that delay, but the British people did not demand the impeachment of any politicians when the war was over."

"Criticism is stifled during a war because the interested parties proclaim that it will impede the progress of the war and is therefore unpatriotic, and when the war is over everybody says comfortably that after all everybody did his best and that nothing is to be gained by raking up past mistakes."

"Though occasionally somebody is sacrificed as the scapegoat of incompetence, laziness, dishonesty, and moral cowardice. Hubert Gough, for instance, was sacrificed for the disaster of March 1918 for which he was completely blameless."

"And sometimes but very rarely a politician is thrown overboard by his colleagues," Yarrow went on.

"Yes, but always in shallow water," John pointed out. "Politicians never drown another politician, and the victim always squeezes himself back on board again and finds another cabin."

A few days after this conversation James Yarrow asked John if he had read the Parliamentary Report in that morning's paper.

"Not yet. Why?"

"Well, read it, and then you'll see the depths to which politicians can descend. Apparently the wretched Gounaris wrote to Curzon on February 15th of this year and told him that unless the Greek army in Asia Minor received reinforcements and fresh war material it could not cope with a Turkish offensive. To this Curzon replied with a hope that the military position in Anatolia was less immediately critical than Gounaris suggested. Birkenhead has now declared he never saw these two letters. Lloyd George and Austen Chamberlain vow *they* never saw them. Up gets Lord Salisbury and asserts that the late Cabinet must have seen the letters and that Birkenhead's only object in raising the matter in the House of Lords was to prejudice opinion against Lord Curzon while he was away trying to come to terms with Turkey at Lausanne."

"I wonder what did happen," said John.

"Next day the matter was discussed in the House of Commons, when Mr Lloyd George admitted that the correspondence must have been circulated to him as the head of the Government and that he had to assume he had received it. The ex-Minister for War, Worthington-Evans, insisted he could not possibly have seen the correspondence because if he had he would have brought it to the attention of the Army Council in view of the situation at Chanak. Lord Birkenhead continued to insist the letters had never been shown to the Cabinet. Then Mr Lloyd George remembered that at the time of the circulation of the correspondence he had been ill and was not being shown any papers. He also remembered that he and Lord Curzon interviewed the lately shot Mr Gounaris on January 12th and that he had warned Mr Gounaris that there would be no peace unless the Greek forces retired from Smyrna."

"My god," John exclaimed. "And nobody rose in the House of Commons to ask Lloyd George to explain why then, if he gave such a warning to the wretched Gounaris on January 12th, on August 4th when the military situation was much worse he fervidly supported in the House Greek claims to Asia Minor and Eastern Thrace and paid such a glowing tribute to Greek arms that excerpts from his speech were published in a Greek Army Order of the Day and distributed among the troops in Asia Minor."

"The Greeks themselves have conveniently shot Gounaris," James Yarrow pointed out. "And since the British nation does not demand the death of incompetent, lazy, or dishonest politicians all is well. The throwing of the Greek army into the sea is after all a matter of minor importance compared with the reputation of the political leaders of this country."

"But this is beyond the relief of bitter comment," John exclaimed. "Three months ago I was hearing the roar of a mob which at that moment was plucking out the beard of the Bishop of Mileto who was nailed to the door of his cathedral. I was seeing the bodies of ravished girls and spitted babies. And we consider justice satisfied by breaking off diplomatic relations with a Revolutionary Government which believing it had been betrayed by its politicians and generals exacted from them the penalty of death. The wretched Gounaris himself who was dragged from a sick-bed to be shot had warned British statesmen six months before that disaster was inevitable, and the only indignation such a revelation arouses in Parliament is that it seems an attempt by the Opposition to secure a Party advantage. Suppose that a British army had been driven into the sea, and that it were proved the disaster was due to months of complacency and optimism and the neglect of arms and equipment, should we not exact a reckoning?"

"I doubt it," James Yarrow replied. "Two or three scapegoats might be found, but not among those really responsible. Then we should be urged not to waste precious time in useless recriminations but to set to work to repair the damage. And don't talk about British armies being driven into the sea. The way they're handling this post-war Europe we may get another war sooner than you think."

"Ah, not in our time, James. I don't believe that even another Coalition Government could achieve that."

John was glad that he met Emil again at the house in Claremount Gardens rather than in the flat in Brunswick Square, and that he met him without Astrid. It had not been deliberately planned thus; but Yan had had an attack of croup, and his mother was waiting two or three days in the country before she travelled back with him to London. Emil himself had had to come up on business and was staying in Hampstead until Astrid returned.

John was deeply moved to see his friend again and this emotion must have been evident to Miriam Stern, for she went to the escritoire that stood between the windows and took from it the basket-shaped box of gilded filigree lined with sandal-wood which John and Emil had presented to her at Fontainebleau more than twenty-two years ago. She looked back in memory to the sight of those hundreds of clouded-yellow butterflies in a great field of clover on the outskirts of the forest. She heard herself exclaim again that the golden minutes of that golden summer were staying with them. And now here was the box in which John had thought of putting three of those golden butterflies to commemorate for him and Emil and Julius a golden minute that would stay with her. And to the filigree box was affixed a small golden plate on which was engraved:

The Summer of 1900

"I wondered if you had lost this box," John said. "I never dared to ask you." He opened the lid. Yes, there were the three clouded-yellows still recognizable, though time had indeed clouded the yellow, and the dust upon their wings was almost all gone, leaving them dull and diaphanous. "How well I remember our search in Paris for that box, Emil. We went to a Duval restaurant afterwards for lunch, and argued about *l'affaire Dreyfus*, and my first frogs were bad. You prophesied our friendship would not last because we couldn't agree on the general principles of human conduct."

"And wasn't I right?" Emil asked.

"I might have agreed with you even last January," John replied. "But now I see you after those infernal months of prison I think friendship can survive political differences . . . if indeed we do differ so profoundly over politics."

"I knew I was right," Miriam Stern exclaimed. "I felt the warmth of that dead summer coming back to warm this room to-night."

Emil did not scoff. It was clear that he too was enjoying such warmth after the dehumanization of an English prison.

When an hour or so after dinner he suggested going downstairs with John to the little room at the end of the entrance-hall his mother applauded the suggestion.

"Anna shall put the tray in there, and I'm going off to bed. I find I can go to bed early very easily nowadays, John. It suits my grey hairs."

"Your grey hairs suit you," John told her.

"Sixty in a few weeks," she reminded him. "And I was thirty-seven when those butterflies danced above that clover-field."

She put the filigree box away in the escritoire. Emil had gone downstairs by now.

"John, you don't know what a joy it has been to me to fancy that you and Emil were to each other as you were once upon a time. I have hated to watch you grow apart."

"Yes, we *were* growing apart. And I don't think Astrid encouraged the contrary process."

"She's been wonderful all this year."

"I'm sure she has. But she disapproves of me, Miriam, as a frivolous entertainer. Perhaps a year in Holloway would soften her heart. However, I have hopes with my next play of earning her respect."

"I look forward to that, John. I hope I shall meet Gabrielle Derozier when she comes to London."

"Of course you shall."

"Good night, John dear."

"And we had no music to-night," he said, glancing at the Steinway.

"I had music all the evening to myself in the relief of having Emil back in the world and in the feeling that you and he were nearer to one another than for such a long time. Do go now and join him."

There were the same two chairs on either side of the gas-fire, and Emil was sitting on the one on which he always used to sit facing the door into the little room at the end of the entrance-hall.

"I used to think a lot about this room in Wormwood Scrubbs," he told his friend. "And for some reason or other that absurd picture of my grandfather's used repeatedly to occupy my mind's eye."

John looked up over the mantelpiece at the four men in black cloaks sitting with heads close together at a table, reading some document by the light of a candle, and at the young woman with the tray of food listening anxiously by the door, and at the old woman in the background blowing up the fire with a pair of bellows. *Poland 1863.*

"I remember complaining once apropos of that picture how dull the contemporary world was, and you prophesied that it would not be long before the world blew up. Victoria and Franz Josef would be dying soon, you said, and after them would come the deluge."

"And how right I was! And the deluge won't subside again in our time. I think our children will be old before it does. Perhaps not even they will live to see it subside."

"You think we shall have more war?"

"Any amount of it. Capitalism won't be content to expire quietly."

"Emil, what did you hate most about prison?"

"The humbug of it—the pretentious veneer of efficiency. You can imagine what any bureaucracy would become if it could always successfully hide its incompetency and laziness. Well, for years the Home Office has been very nearly successful in doing that, and our prisons are the perfect expressions of a branch of bureaucracy which is most difficult to strike at. I wish for some reasons I had undergone a sentence of penal servitude. Wormwood Scrubbs is bad enough, but I've no doubt that the convict prisons are an immensely greater disgrace to a State which supposes itself to be civilized."

"Are our prisons and prison system worse than any others?" John asked.

"No, I daresay in some material respects they are better than most, but in one way they are worse than all the others put together. They claim a moral value and a moral intention. New Caledonia and the Devil's Island do not claim that. They are frankly brutal . . . but don't let's talk about prison. Even twelve months in the Second Division at Wormwood Scrubbs is a foul experience. Lots of people think the Second Division is luxury compared with hard labour. Apart from being able to have visits from outside, more often in the Second Division there is no difference whatsoever between that and hard labour. You pick oakum and sew mail-bags in both. I suppose when the treadmill was still in use there was a difference. Oh yes, prison is a foul experience, and I'll admit that at times I was shaken in my hopes for communism."

"You were?" John exclaimed in surprise.

"Yes, I saw what a feeble creature man is when he tries to produce equality, and how equally feeble he can be when he tries to provide a manner of life for his fellows. I'm glad I had this prison experience for that alone. I'll never be cocksure again."

It was true that Emil had lost his serene air of superiority. Those months at Wormwood Scrubbs had struck at his faith in man. Three years' penal servitude might convert him to a belief in God.

"Well, you know, you are much more human," John told him. "What did Astrid think of the transformation?"

Emil smiled.

"She thought the experience had softened me; but she attributes it to the lowering diet. Oh, that food, John! I never detected much of the epicure in myself and thought I had trained myself to be more or less indifferent to what I ate. But the food at Wormwood Scrubbs! It's foul. It's really foul. Of course it's intended to lower the vitality, and it certainly succeeds."

"I always tell my father that every Judge should be compelled to spend a year in getting practical experience of what he's condemning men and women to undergo."

"I was allowed paper and pencil during the last three months of my sentence," Emil went on. "But all I wrote was confiscated before I left prison. These poor little bureaucratic minds with their dread of revelations! These wretched little ostriches!"

"Well, don't let's talk about prison any more. I suppose you'll write something about it?"

"No, I don't think I shall. For the first three months I was fuming to be free and able to criticize; but gradually I realized the futility of persuading others that I could take an objective view of my own experience, and at the same time I discovered a way of turning that experience to my own benefit. Astrid is right. It has softened me, but I don't think it has weakened me, John. I shall be more pliant in future, but I think I shall be just as tough. And so you re-visited Mileto and found that dull fellow Drayton in charge of a difficult situation? Well, I'm not sure that grim disaster may not be for the best. We shall see what Venizelos makes of it. I'm inclined to think he will succeed in doing a deal with Turkey if he has the courage to suggest an exchange of populations. I'm sure that's the only remedy for the problems of the

Balkans, and for that matter the rest of Europe. We don't seem
ripe yet to get rid of nationalism, and that being so we must get
rid of minorities. If the problem of minorities had been boldly
faced at Versailles we might have had a healthier Europe by now."

"You're not abandoning your hope of general communization?"
John asked in surprise.

"Certainly not, but I'm beginning to wonder whether we Communists haven't been putting the cart before the horse."

"In what way?"

"Why, by assuming that because nationalist revivals have so
far been identified with the bourgeois we must achieve our object
through internationalism. Tell me about this Fascist business in
Italy, John. I suppose that is on a par with Mannerheim and his
Finnish Whites? In fact, the bourgeois response to the Red threat."

"Yes, to a great extent it certainly is, but it is also an attempt to
create or, as the Fascists claim, to revive an Imperialism. I was
rather impressed by it at first, but I discover in it now the same
threat to man that I discern in Communism. It portends the
destruction of the individual."

"John, John, you'll have to face up to the facts of human development. Circumstances have already destroyed the individual. He
destroyed himself by the machinery he invented. We are moving
now toward so complete a change of all human values that a century
hence the people of the nineteenth century will seem more remote
than for us seem the Incas. We are on the edge not of a political
change, John, but of an evolutionary change. That's why to me
your excitement over what happens in Ireland seems almost
parochial."

"On the contrary, Emil, the more profound the evolutionary
change with which mankind is threatened the more anxiously do I
turn to find in Ireland a fount of spiritual life from which humanity
will by God's grace be healed again. It happened before in the
Dark Ages, and I see another era of darkness enveloping the soul
of man."

"Yes, well, of course, that sort of apocalyptic talk appears to me
as reason disordered by emotion, but I don't say so offensively.
And I'm not trying to be offensive when I ask why you should
expect a fount of spiritual life to well up from a country which has
exalted violence in the way Ireland has exalted it."

"I shall not be exalting violence myself, Emil, when I say what
I'm going to say, for I hate violence: but it is important to understand that the Irish on account of their invincible belief in the life

to come do not regard the temporal life of a man as all-important. Where I think them open to reproach is the carelessness with which they will accept the responsibility of launching a man into eternity. And though I've not surrendered my opinion that the fundamental blame for what has happened in Ireland rests upon England, I do believe that the spiritual health of Ireland is in danger from this acceptance of violence as natural. It has taught me to beware in the future of supporting any movement that must involve violence if it is to succeed. And Ireland may one day regret the intransigence of these unhappy days."

"I still think that you exaggerate absurdly the importance of Ireland," Emil insisted. "It seems to me to have the same kind of significance in Europe as Albania—and that is purely strategic."

John smiled.

"You've never taken much trouble, Emil, to find out why Ireland might have something more than a strategic significance in modern Europe. And I'm not trying to be offensive when I say that jealousy lies at the root of your scorn for Ireland and Poland. As a Jew you resent their collaring the limelight of oppression. But you must grant to Fitzgerald a life of enviable directness of purpose and the courage to face whatever awaited him at the end of his quest. I look back to that school debate about Home Rule in the spring of 1900. Fitz's threats sounded so melodramatic and improbable then. And the reality was so much more melodramatic than anything he could have imagined. Obviously it can only be a short while now before some agreement is reached in Ireland, and I imagine that in another ten years or so the Tammany clique that runs Northern Ireland will have been exposed and partition will vanish before the demand of public opinion. Even if nothing more be achieved than what has been achieved already, how fruitful Fitzgerald can count the forty years of his life!"

"From his own point of view perhaps. But would they seem fruitful to many others? I suppose that depends whether Ireland was beheld in its true proportions against the rest of the world."

"You are talking, Emil, rather in the way the Great King talked about the Greeks. I believe Atheism will find the Faith of Ireland as tough a proposition as the Persians found the Greeks."

John related to Emil the story of Fitzgerald's vision in the inn at Tralee.

"How do you explain that away?" he asked.

"One must simply call it coincidence," Emil replied.

"Well, I find it much harder to believe in such a coincidence than to believe that it was a true vision of his end.   It impressed me so much that I have decided to take the definite step of becoming a Catholic."

"What an astonishing reason for taking a step like that!" Emil exclaimed.

"Oh, as you know, for years I have accepted the Catholic Church as the only credible guardian of revealed truth.   All that stood in the way of my taking the definite step of joining it has been the lack of conviction in myself of the supernatural.   This the death of Fitzgerald has provided.   I can find no natural explanation . . ."

"Coincidence," Emil interrupted.

"It's a coincidence beyond my imagination."

"No coincidence should be beyond the imagination," Emil affirmed.   "Life itself as we know it depends on a coincidence."

"That's what you are driven to believe when you reject a first cause," John maintained.

"What evidence have you that Fitzgerald did not arrange beforehand that if he were killed his grave was to be as he dreamt it twenty years before?"

"He wasn't that kind of person.   No, you must either call it coincidence or a supernatural warning; and, as I said, I find coincidence less credible.   However, the death of Fitzgerald must count as the occasion but not the cause of my resolve to become a Catholic, and to become a Catholic does not imply a retreat from reality."

"I can hardly accept that," Emil said, with a smile.   He smiled much more often since he had been in Wormwood Scrubbs.   "I think to-day such a step is more than ever a step on the retreat from reality.   It is an admission that the only solution for the problems of this world is an optimistic confidence in an ideal solution hereafter.   I disbelieve in any hereafter, and therefore I regard Catholicism as an evasion of the issue before humanity."

"But even if a life hereafter be an illusion surely you will grant that Catholicism provides the most practical pattern of morality for man?"

Emil looked sharply at John.

"You're going to give Catholicism a merely pragmatic value, are you?"

"No, no, Emil, that's not fair.   I have remained on the threshold all these years just because I was not willing to accord it a merely pragmatic value.   I am trying to counter your argument about evading the issue before humanity.   I will substitute Christianity for Catholicism and ask you what Communism can offer to man which has not already been offered by Christ. I accept Christianity as the most practical rule of life for the attainment in this world of a perfect human society, and I find in Catholicism the most practical system by which that rule of life may be followed. I do not perceive any necessary opposition between Catholicism and Communism unless Communism goes beyond economics and claims to rule ethics and provide a substitute for revealed religion. I recognize that some form of economic communism is inevitable, the way man has chosen to develop. Capitalism was always anti-Christian and could never have established itself without the weakening of the Catholic Church by the Protestant Reformation. I believe that the destruction of Capitalism is a moral necessity for mankind, and I am convinced that the identification of Catholicism with Christianity will achieve this."

"The identification of Catholicism with Christianity? What do you mean by that?"

"I mean that within a comparatively short space of time—at most fifty or sixty years—there will be no effective organization of Christianity outside the Catholic Church. Surely atheistic Communism recognizes that already. The ease with which it has overthrown Russian Orthodoxy has not led it to underrate the strength of Catholicism."

"Oh, no, we don't underrate the forces of reaction."

"But as long as you identify Catholicism with reaction you will be misunderstanding it so completely that in the end you may be led to underrate it. Or rather, I should say, so long as you identify it with the conventional forces of reaction like landed property and privilege and big business. What you will be up against, you atheistic Communists, is the conviction of the Church that the gates of hell cannot prevail against it. You have nothing like that to sustain *your* faith. You may believe—I believe myself—that humanity must adopt your economic theories or come very near to perishing. But your system will last only so long as the belly rules the other members, and I've a notion that, as man develops, the belly will gradually become less and less dominant. I believe it may go the way of the spleen and the little toe and male nipples and other outlived conveniences."

"Well, if the domination of Communism once established lasts as long as the domination of the belly it won't have had a negligible run."

"No, not negligible—until you compared it with the run of Christ's Church. But why do we argue about our fundamental

beliefs? Let us repeat them. You have been so much less arrogant to-night, Emil. What did you learn in prison?"

"I think before I went to the Scrubbs I didn't really feel any
compassion for my fellow men, but I think I have compassion now.
I didn't realize this change in myself when I was still inside. It
was when I saw Astrid again and Yan. And I thought of the
people still inside and realized I had learnt to love mankind. I'm
rather worried about it really, because it might turn me into an
I.L.P. sentimentalist. However, I console myself by saying that
this mood won't last and that it is merely an expression of the relief
of being out of prison."

"You hated prison much more than you expected, didn't you?"

"Yes, I did. For one thing I loathed the masculinity of it.
There is something filthy in a unisexual aggregation. Men in the
mass are repulsive. I'd never realized that. I expect women in
the mass without any males would be equally repulsive."

"I shouldn't have thought you would have suffered so much
from that masculinity. I grew very bored by it at Gallipoli; but
then I never had any illusions about exclusively male companionship
or supposed that life was tolerable without women. On the other
hand, there was a time when you despised female companionship
and shrank from female love."

"That's true, but you must remember I dealt harshly with the
usual homosexual temptations. After I grew out of adolescence I
never allowed my imagination to contemplate physical intimacy
with my own sex. It was the ignominious intimacy of prison life
which revolted me, all the more so because there is a continuous
undercurrent of thwarted and distorted physical desire. It's
ghastly, John. It defiles one, and now when I look back upon
those wretched beings immured in that existence it fills me with a
longing to set free not only them but all the rest of humanity which,
though outwardly at liberty, is in effect as fast in prison as the
dwellers in Wormwood Scrubbs. The compassion I feel is for
humanity in chains."

"Surely that is an essentially Christian emotion? As I understand the Atonement, it was a Divine act of liberation from the
chains with which man had bound himself."

"Dogma! Dogma!" Emil exclaimed.

"Oh, you may rail at dogma, but what are dogmas except the
answers to the riddles which perplex us?"

"Extremely inadequate answers."

"Have you ever studied dogmatic theology?"

"No, because it involves an assumption I am not prepared to grant. I do not believe in a first cause."

"And I do not believe in coincidence. However, this is the first time for many years, Emil, that you and I have been able to discuss such things without mutual exasperation. I thought we had grown irremediably apart from one another. I don't feel that any longer. And I'm particularly glad to feel that to-night, because I have a sensation of having come to the end of a period in my life, and if meeting you again after these months in prison I had found you hardened in the attitude you had reached last January we should have parted presently as strangers. Instead I feel nearer to you than I have felt since we were at school. It is a coincidence that we should be sitting on either side of this gas-fire as we sat so often once upon a time, a coincidence I feel as heartening as a warm drink in cold weather. I wish Astrid didn't disapprove of me so much."

"She doesn't disapprove of you at all. All she thinks is that you are too readily contented and too much spoilt by easy circumstances."

"Well, she has reason," John admitted. "Success, a happy marriage, delightful friends . . . but I am always conscious of fortune's kindness, Emil. And though I may be spoilt by easy circumstances I'm not in fact so readily contented. I shall try to earn her respect during the next ten years."

They sat talking for a while about books and people they had known at school, until John said he must go home. Emil bent over and turned out the gas-fire.

"How that pop brings back old Sunday evenings when I left you with the thought that to-morrow morning was Monday and that I had not yet written my Latin prose for Askew," John sighed.

Next morning John received a letter forwarded to Church Row from Nanphant:

> *Melvaig,*
> *Near Lochinver,*
> *Sutherland*
> *December 11th, 1922.*
>
> *A charaid,*
> *I am writing to you at the advice of our friend Mr MacLean Sanders of Edinburgh to notify you that the Shiel*

*Islands of which we have been talking once are presently for sale,
and that I believe you would buy them for a bargain if you had
a mind to them. If you are favourable to the above idea it will
be best to communicate with Mr Andrew Thomson, S.S.C., of
Thomson, Menzies and Thomson, Elmbank Street, Glasgow, who
has all the details of the property. If I have intruded upon your
privacy with this letter I hope you will understand that it was
done with the best intentions. I will be glad to hear from you
at your convenience. They have arrested some more land raiders
in the Long Island. It boils my blood to read such things.*

Do charaid dhileas

Tormoid MacIomhair

Your faithful friend, Norman MacIver! Faithful friend indeed
to bear in mind that vision of the Shiel Islands two and a half years
ago, that vision of them floating between sea and sky in a clouded
blue tralucency before they dissolved in the southerly haze.

That night John took the train from Euston and reached Glasgow
in the murk of a foggy wet December morning. The electric light
was irradiating the musty interior of the lawyer's office when he
reached it at eleven o'clock.

Mr Andrew Thomson was a little man with a long obstinate
upper lip, the irises of whose pale-blue eyes gave him a look of
bardic remoteness which was not at all in keeping with his dry
voice and precise manner.

"I understand that the Shiel Islands are for sale and that you are
in charge of the business," John began right away.

"The Shiel Islands—imphm—yes—imphm—the Shiel Islands,"
said Mr Thomson, crossing his thumbs and clapping his out-thrust
fingers together. "Yes, we have been entrusted with the disposal
of that property." He looked critically at his visitor. "Am I to
understand, Mr"—he referred to the card on the desk in front of
him—"Mr Ogilvie, that you are interested in the property?"

John felt inclined to ask Mr Thomson what on earth except his
interest in the Shiel Islands would have brought him to his office
on this murky December day, but contented himself with a straightforward reply, adding that he had never visited the islands.

"It's an interesting little property," said Mr Thomson. "The
group consists of three islands, two of which I understand are joined
by a strip of beach, and the total acreage is estimated at about six
hundred acres. You'll please understand, however, that we cannot
guarantee the precise acreage within some ten acres. I hope I've

made that perfectly clear. My client would rightly resent any suggestion that he was trying to make any claim for the property to which it was not entitled. So that if we say the acreage is about six hundred acres we shall say as much as we are prepared to say. Is that perfectly clear, Mr Ogilvie?"

"Perfectly clear. What is the name of the present proprietor?"

"The islands belong to a Mr Roderick Mackenzie of Ullapool who has grazed them now for many years. The grazing is said to be very fine—very fine indeed, Mr Ogilvie. It will maintain easily four hundred sheep, and we are instructed to say that were the cliffs properly fenced at least another hundred sheep would not be excessive. You are interested in sheep, I take it, Mr Ogilvie."

"No, I'm afraid I'm not."

"Oh, you are not interested in sheep. I have no information, I'm afraid, about the islands' capacity or suitability for cattle. I am under the impression that the landing facilities are not particularly up to date, but I can make enquiries of our client and let you know in due course what he considers the prospects for cattle."

"But I'm not interested in cattle either."

"Dear me, that's very unusual. I mean to say, we do not usually get enquiries about islands off the west coast of Scotland from people who are not interested either in sheep or cattle. You are looking for a sporting property perhaps?"

"No, I'm not interested in sport," John said.

"Well, the price my client asks for the Shiel Islands is fifteen hundred pounds," Mr Thomson snapped, "and I'm afraid that as you are neither interested in sheep nor cattle you'll find that a pretty stiff price for a group of three uninhabited islands without a residence. You see, the whole point of the Shiel Islands is the fine grazing."

"I'll make you an offer right away. I'll offer twelve hundred pounds."

"I beg your pardon?"

"I'll offer twelve hundred pounds."

"But I understood you to say you had not visited the islands?"

"No. I've had no more than a distant glimpse of them from the Sutherland coast."

"And you make a firm offer of twelve hundred pounds?"

"I do."

"Well, I haven't the pleasure of acting as your agent, Mr Ogilvie, but if I had that pleasure I should feel called upon to protest very strongly—very strongly indeed—against the rash step—the very

rash step—of offering twelve hundred pounds for a group of uninhabited islands upon which you have never set foot.   However,
it's not my business to give you good advice, and I must warn
you that I'm empowered by Mr Roderick Mackenzie to accept any
reasonable offer for the Shiel Islands, because he is giving up his
business as a grazier and is retiring to live in Milngavie with a
married daughter."

"I'm delighted to hear you can accept my offer, and we can
consider the business settled.   Will you get in touch with my
solicitors—Chipping, Rosebotham, Barlow and Tuke of Lamb's
Conduit Street—and get the necessary deeds out for the convey-
ance.   I'll write you a cheque on account for £120, which I assume
will clinch the bargain."

"Thank you, Mr Ogilvie, that will be quite satisfactory.   I hope
you won't regret so impulsive a decision.   Possibly I should have
referred your offer to Mr Mackenzie, but you rather carried me off
my feet.   Imphm!   However, I believe it is a fair price for both
parties, and that is as it should be.   But I must warn you, Mr
Ogilvie, that the mining of gold and silver is reserved to the Crown."
Mr Thomson emitted a dry little chuckle.   It was evident he did
not think the Crown was likely to derive any benefit from such a
reservation.

"And when will you be visiting your islands, Mr Ogilvie?"

"I'll try to get up next month."

"You may find the weather too tempestuous in January.   You'd
be well advised to wait until the spring.   But if you do decide to
make the attempt you'll be well advised to call upon Mr Roderick
Mackenzie at Ullapool, and I'm sure he'll be delighted to give you
the benefit of his experience.   He's an old man of over eighty now,
but a very remarkable specimen."

John parted with Mr Andrew Thomson on terms of real cordiality.   Perhaps those flecked bardic eyes were unduly belied by
the dry voice and precise manner.

When he left the office of Thomson, Menzies and Thomson,
John sent a telegram to Norman MacIver:

> *Thanks to you dear friend the sluagh have presented me with
> the islands and I shall come next month to persuade you to visit
> them with me*
>
> *John Ogilvie*

Athene was a little apprehensive when she was told about the
Shiel Islands.

"It doesn't mean that I'm proposing we should go and live there," John assured her. "But for years I've longed at the back of my mind to own a little piece of Scottish soil, and I could not have let this opportunity pass without dreading that it would bring me ill-luck."

"And you haven't even seen them!"

"Except that they stole my fancy away on that August day when Poland turned back the Bolshevik armies from the gates of Warsaw, and then I saw them like a celestial vision thirty miles off."

"And there's no house on them?"

"Nothing except a small thatched bothy used by shepherds and fishermen. I'll tell you more when I've been up there next month. If I go immediately after Corinna's birthday I could take Arthur and David. I think they'd enjoy the adventure. They'd both be back in time for the beginning of their respective terms. Of course if it's bad weather we shan't be able to get across."

Corinna's birthday fell on the second Sunday of the new year. She was impressed by the two rose-red candles on the sugared cake, and anxious to eat the melted stumps when they had burnt themselves down to the level of the icing.

"You won't try to reach the islands if the weather is too bad," Athene asked before John and Arthur set out to catch the Cornish Riviera express at Gwinear Road next morning.

"Don't worry. We'll only cross the Minch if the weather is breathless. And I'm convinced it will be."

"You look so elated, darling."

"I feel elated," he told her. "Good-bye, Miss Two Years Old." He bent to kiss Corinna, who presented him with a bunch of Scilly White narcissus picked by herself.

"I'm rather excited, John," Arthur confided when they were settled in the railway carriage. "It is rather exciting to go to a desert island."

"I'm rather excited myself," said John.

They picked up David at Euston, and Inverness was reached on a morning of still frost. They drove by car to Melvaig, and as at the end of the last December of the nineteenth century, John beheld Suilven standing up in the west like a huge grape-dark hand, miles away above the desolate moorland beyond Strath Oykell.

"Marvellous to be here again," said David, who, to Arthur's admiration, was in his kilt. "I loved our cruise in the yacht, but I did miss the stalking."

"More than you would have missed Janet Meriday if you hadn't met her?" John asked.

"That's a bit involved, isn't it?" David countered, but his cheeks, already flushed by the northern air, took on a deeper flush.

"Janet Meriday, the movie star?" Arthur asked quickly. "Good lord, David, did you have a date with a movie star?"

"She was with us in the Aegean," said John.

"Well, I saw Douglas Fairbanks in New York," Arthur proclaimed. "And I was going to ask him for his autograph, but a bell-hop came along and told him he was wanted and I didn't get another chance."

Norman MacIver welcomed them, sitting cross-legged on the platform that resembled a wooden bedstead and surrounded by odd bits of homespun and half-made garments.

"And you'll come with us to the islands?" John asked eagerly.

"No, no, not now. Maybe in the summer I'll come with you, but not now. Och, I'm after having a bad attack of sciatica. Well, well, and so you're a landed proprietor. I hope to goodness you'll set a good example whatever. Yes, yes, I'd like fine to be going with you, and the weather will be beautiful for crossing, but it would never do for the sciatica."

"Well, I shall hold you to that promise for the summer," John warned him. "I shall bring my small daughter for your blessing. She has plenty of Gaelic already."

"Is that so? Isn't that splendid now? And who's teaching it to her? A girl from Moidart, eh? Well, well, they have plenty Gaelic in Moidart. It's not the best Gaelic. The best Gaelic is in Wester Ross. Still, if she shan't have the best Gaelic she shan't have Gaelic that tastes of the English."

John let David and Arthur walk on to the car and turned back into the shop.

"Your letter reached me at the very moment when I was waiting for a signpost to the road I should take," he told the tailor.

"Is that so? I'm very pleased. As soon as I heard that Ruairidh Mor was selling the islands it came to me that you might be glad to buy them. He'll be expecting you."

"Yes, I asked him to arrange for a boat to-morrow if the weather was fine. We're going along to Ullapool now. I do wish we could have had you with us."

"In the month of Chune if God spares us I shall come with you. But don't forget they are fairy islands. They will lead you . . ." the hunchbacked tailor broke off.

t>br />

style="text-align:center">*West to North*m> 343

"Where will they lead me?"

"That's it, who knows? Well, well, *beannachd leibh*."

John shook the tailor's soft dry white hand and hurried after David and Arthur.

When John enquired in Ullapool for the house of Mr Roderick Mackenzie he found that there were half a dozen Roderick Mackenzies in the place. *Ruairidh Mòr agus Ruairidh Beag. Ruairidh Ian agus Ruairidh Sheumais. Ruairidh Chaluim a' bhreabadar agus Ruairidh Eachainn a' bhuachaille.* Big Roderick and Little Roderick. Roderick the son of John and Roderick the son of James. Roderick the son of Malcolm the weaver, and Roderick the son of Hector the herdsman.

John remembered that Norman MacIver had called him Ruairidh Mor.

Big Roderick deserved his name. The old man stood a full six feet two inches, with a big hooked nose and high cheek-bones and a great beard as white as the sea-foam.

"Very pleased to meet you, Mr Ogilvie. What a fine day we have. Beautiful weather for the islands," he said, pumping John's hand up and down as he shouted his welcome. "This is my daughter Mrs Macpherson," he continued, introducing a handsome woman of about forty. "She's after coming to take me away with her to Milngavie, and I don't like the idea at all, at all."

"Indeed, somebody has to look after him, Mr Ogilvie," the daughter explained. "He's eighty-two now and he can't be living all alone. Mother died two years ago."

"Yes, yes, I'm all alone now," the old man shouted. "But I don't like city life at all. Nothing but noise and dirts and crowds."

"Oh, it's not as bad as all that, Father," Mrs Macpherson protested.

"Indeed it is much worse whatever. But now that I have sold the islands I may as well leave Ullapool. Yes, yes, I would all the time be wanting to go out to them. I will come with you to-morrow."

"Indeed you'll do no such thing, Father," said his daughter severely.

"Hark at that now! What a life, not to be able to do what one wants to do."

In the end, however, Ruairidh Mor had his way. At break of the January dawn he was sitting at the tiller of the *Kittiwake* like an old viking, and the silky grey waters of Loch Broom resounded to the chug-chug of the fishing-boat's motor. Ullapool receded.

The little white town built to the design of a single architect a century ago to serve some commercial enterprise had a curiously foreign look, and viewed an hour later against the great yellow orb of the rising sun it rose out of the glittering sea-loch like the beginning of the harbour of Cadiz.

"Quite unlike any place I've seen in Scotland or England," John remarked.

When the *Kittiwake* had rounded the northerly slopes of Loch Broom and left the Summer Isles astern, the Shiel Islands came into view some twenty miles to the west, backed a further twenty miles beyond by the snow-crowned hills of Harris. The vast sky was serene, the sea motionless.

"What's that?" Arthur cried, pointing to a dark shape to port which appeared and disappeared from the water in lazy curves.

"That's a whale," said Ruairidh Mor.

"A whale?" the boy echoed in amazement. "Did you say a whale? Good lord! I never knew there were whales round about Britain."

It was obvious that his opinion of Britain had gone up.

By two o'clock the *Kittiwake* was passing the outlying basaltic rocks and islets of the group—bizarre black shapes that teased the fancy to find comparisons. Suddenly above the islands there was seen a huge pine-shaped cloud of barnacle geese, and the air was full of their piping.

"I didn't know you had geese, John," his young brother exclaimed. "Why, there are hundreds! I should like to have a shot at them."

"Very difficult to shoot," said the late owner of the islands. "They make a terrible mess of the grass on Castle Island. The only way I could find to shoot them was to soak corn in whisky and scatter it about and then the geese would be eating it and making themselves so drunk that we could come near enough to shoot them."

"Rather complicated," David observed.

"Yes, it is very complicated," the old man agreed. "But geese are very complicated birds."

And now the *Kittiwake* was passing as noble a stretch of cliff as John had ever seen. For half a mile a black face of mighty hexagonal columns set close as organ-pipes rose five hundred feet from the bottle-green water upon which it cast a shadow. Neither the Giant's Causeway nor Staffa could produce a basaltic effect of comparable grandeur. Beyond this sheer black face the cliffs ran down to the sea in steep grassy braes scattered with fragments of columns which the lichen had wrapped with grey and orange tapestry. The grass itself, disdainful of January, preserved some of the lustre of its summery green.

"That's what we call Garbh Eilean—Rough Island. Very good winter feeding, but one loses too many sheep over the cliffs. I was always saying I would fence the islands away round. I was saying so ever since I bought the islands twenty years ago, and I rented them for thirty years before that."

"Fifty years!" John exclaimed.

"Yes, and this will be my last visit to them," said the old man. "But I know every rock of them, and if I shut my eyes there is not a little bit of the islands I cannot see."

The *Kittiwake* had dropped anchor in a roadstead sheltered from the north by Castle Island, a level grassy plateau of some seventy-five acres above two-hundred feet cliffs. Southward the two larger islands were joined by a beach of rounded grey stones, about a hundred yards in length and fifty yards wide, at either end of which the cliffs rose sheer for several hundred feet.

"It looks very peaceful to-day," said Ruairidh Mor. "But I've been on that beach in a gale when the waves were breaking high on both sides and the noise of the rolling stones was like cannons."

When they landed on that grey beach and stood there between sea and sea and cliff and cliff Arthur declared that usually places were not as good as books but that this place was better than any book.

John climbed by himself to the top of Rough Island by a narrow track which wound up the face of the cliff at the end of the beach and in the course of the ascent brought the climber now to a grassy ledge from which he looked sheer down into the silver-grey water south, now to one from which he seemed suspended over the bottle-green water north. At the top he sat down to recover his breath. David and Arthur were wandering about the low-lying land of Church Island, so called from the remains of some holy man's cell. He shouted to them, and they must have heard his voice, for the small figures stopped to look for the sound; but they could not trace whence it came and presently continued upon their way.

The view from the summit of Rough Island upon this crystalline January day was a sublime harmony of earth and sea and sky. Eastward the embattled line of Ross and Sutherland became at either end a fleet of snowy mountains which rose from the horizon like isolated frigates.   Westward the Long Island lay like a clay-more, its hilt the Harris hills, its damascened blade the Lewis coast piercing the north.   Southward the clustered pinnacles of Skye towered in a fume of gold against the low wintry sun, and beyond that gothic mass to west the dim hills of Uist floated like shapes of smoke across a limbo that was neither land nor water nor air. Northward between Lewis and Cape Wrath the dark verge of the sea ran sharp as a knife's edge against the greenish Arctic heavens.

And if the natural scene was outside the experience and even the imagination of all except a handful or so of the dwellers in Britain, the wild life was hardly more familiar.   A skua was ranging the air in dark zigzags searching for some gull he could compel to dis-gorge and whose disgorged catch he would seize with lightning dive before it dropped into the sea.   The whale they had sighted earlier was swimming round the islands in a slow switchback of lazy plunges.   Grey Atlantic seals had entered the roadstead to gaze curiously at the *Kittiwake*, their heads bobbing above the bottle-green water like footballs.   An eider-duck skimmed the surface of the water; and in a fold of the land that ran down in fold upon fold to the sea on the south-westerly side of Rough Island two ravens flirted clumsily in the thin sunshine.   The barnacle geese had lighted on the sea beyond Castle Island, waiting for the human intruders to depart before they resumed their grazing.

John felt as if he were being granted a vision of the hidden Scotland.

"You have come back," sang the dark swan of Tuonela.   "Here lies the fulfilment of your weird.   To my calling you have come at last.   You have heard my voice above the surging of the heedless years."

Printed in Great Britain by R. & R. CLARK, LIMITED, *Edinburgh.*